No Gods of Conscience

Unlife Legend
Book One

Jason J. Bilicic

LAST LAMP PUBLISHING, INC.

323 PARK
PRESCOTT, AZ 86303
UNITED STATES OF AMERICA

Published by Last Lamp Publishing, Inc-09/15/2004

ISBN: 0-9761227-1-5

Printed in the United States of America
Los Angeles, CA - Los Angeles Printing

This book is printed on acid-free paper

Cover art by Steve Roberts

To Monika Ragland
You put the first fantasy novel in my hands when I was ten.
Whether you felt it was what I had deep inside of me, or
just wanted to shut me up…
Thank you.

PROLOGUE

Cora was mundane by all accounts, and through the eons, there had been several. Sandy rock stretched endlessly in every direction, unadorned and uninterrupted, save for the cracks that constant heat and dryness had caused over the years. No trees could be seen, no water found. Nothing lived anywhere on all of Cora. Threuen created the desert plane by accident centuries before, and had since only employed it for magical experimentation and as a meeting place for the gods. It was the latter of these uses that brought the many gods of Reman to Cora today.

As he hurtled through the stifling air that hung above the arid plain, he reached out with his essence and scoured the rocky surface, searching for any early arrivals. There was always someone. He would be able to feel them at any distance. It was his plane, and though he called and directed the meetings, he was seldom the first to arrive.

God of magic, Threuen created Cora while attempting to reshape the Grayhost deserts of Reman. Uninhabitable, he generated a dimensional parallel to the lifeless dunes in order to attempt the magical graduation of the environment into one that could support life so that the magically bred Nemian peoples, a race that he had created in the outskirts of the Grayhost, could have a place to expand their civilization. Unable to successfully alter the sandscape, he was left with Cora. Being chief among the gods, he designated it the meeting place of the gods, should the need arise. It seldom did. The gods, being fairly mindful of each others' efforts, and generally restricted to carrying out the grievances that they might arrive at on Reman through their followers rather than in person, rarely needed to meet as a group. It was far easier to address the struggles of the many races below in their own world, rather than dragging petty disputes out before all of the deities, but of late, the balance of power had begun to shift erratically. Whatever the cause, it had dramatically reduced the power of the god of magic, forcing Threuen to bring all of the gods together again.

Three of his peers had arrived already. He could feel them as he fell through the atmosphere. He would love to have transported himself directly to the meeting place, but he had, himself, made it impossible to directly teleport on Cora, thus negating the possibility of anyone taking the council of gods by surprise, and more importantly, it eliminated the likelihood of having any of the gods become bored at a meeting, and leaving suddenly.

Arsonin, god of merchants, ambition, and now generally considered the god of thieves was already waiting. His sweeping black robes reached all the way to the ground, interrupted only by the scarlet flutes that he'd had sewn in, the satin hem lightly brushing the sandy stone. The number of rings, pendants, and brooches that the god wore could not easily be counted. Vanity was one of his more prevalent pursuits, thus he passed it on to man, whom he had created back when the power existed to perform such feats.

With him stood Gul Thannon. Having been created by Arsonin, Thannon, as he had come to be called, developed a close relationship with the god of ambition, though the two did not often share the same following. Thannon, the god of murder, torture, and domination, believed that all of his aims could only be achieved artfully through subtlety, though his followers were quick to design less than subtle methods for carrying out his desires. The priests of Thannon, and the unnatural messengers that they created, were notoriously feared for their unscrupulous torture and mindless slaughter.

Surprising to Threuen, Talvo, the oldest of the gods, creator of Reman, god of war, and patron to the dwarves, was with Arsonin and Thannon. The sturdy dwarven god appeared to be taking part in their discussion, which was odd. At all previous meetings, the ancient god had kept himself apart, wanting little to do with the younger deities, expressing regularly that they were brash in the ways that they dealt with the happenings on Reman. It had been the followers of Talvo that had crushed nearly every expansion of any god other than the Meriss, but they were the judges of morality, and while Talvo supported war and the glories of combat, he had never failed to express to his followers the need for honor and proper conduct.

"What could possibly have the three of them chatting together," Threuen mused, letting the possibilities run through his mind. "Probably just trading shots before the rest arrive." He smiled as he came within hearing distance of the three gods, but even as he did, they fell silent and rushed to their places, for Threuen controlled the magic of all beings, which had become the only mode of power that any of the deities had, save Halkam, and while Threuen did not have the overall strength that some of the other gods had, he could rend them of their magic with only a thought, leaving them helpless. Thus, he commanded great respect.

"We are honored," announced the three gods in unison as the god of magic touched down on the rock plain. Talvo's face was flushed. He was angry. Threuen felt that it was a healthy sign.

"As am I, to see you, Talvo, Arsonin, and Thannon." The gods of war, ambition, and murder all bowed together, with practiced synchronicity.

Threuen was about to address the three gods, inquiring as to their previous conversation, but he felt several others coming, forcing him to respectfully wait. Kyndron, the champion of Thannon, with his many wicked blades, Halkam, the god of the farmers and laborers, and the Meriss arrived, taking their places. Kyndron was a minor deity and was therefore not allowed to sit in the front circle of the meet, but instead, was able only to sit behind Thannon.

The Meriss, having never felt that the races of Reman were very stout or worthwhile, chose to arrive as a crystalline being, rather than adopting a form common to the world below. They, the Meriss was collective being, seemingly many powerful spirits that had bound themselves eternally together, floated in their place, awaiting the arrival of the other gods. Though they doubted the abilities of the surviving races of the world, the Meriss too depended on magic, and responded to the calls of Threuen. Of all of the deities worshipped on Reman, the Meriss were the most secluded and the least understood. While being the god of judgment and morality, the Meriss had a very close relation to the god of death, which heightened the respect offered by other gods.

Halkam was a simple god, and he looked the part. In his rustic leather clothes, which Arsonin felt were a travesty, having openly mocked them on numerous occasions, the plain looking man took his place amidst the gods. Fairly incapable when it came to wielding magic, Halkam and his followers had the tendency to be consumed by the numerous exchanges designed by the other gods, yet he and he alone had maintained the largest following through the years, never having been anything less than honest and providing for his worshippers. A crooked smile was all he that used to greet the other gods, save the Meriss. Upon seeing the deeply colorful shimmering crystal that hung in the air at his side, he bowed deeply, and tipped his wide-brimmed hat.

"I am honored to see you, Halkam, and you Meriss." Threuen shifted his gaze to the crouched form behind Thannon. "Kyndron." The dark god's champion did little more than peek from behind his master. He was petty and purely evil, often becoming the object of hatred amidst many of the productive gods of Reman.

The god of magic could feel a great number of other deities entering Cora above him. A great many gods existed for Reman, but most were minor, having been generated as the offspring of major gods, or were placed into power by cultists, erratic true believers that funneled their every heartbeat into the deity they sought to empower.

They began to land only a few moments later, taking their places behind the most powerful gods. Irreas, the clever god of riddles and manipulation, who was worshipped by politicians and scammers. Gimeon, the god of nature, followed almost exclusively by reclusive druidic tribes that passed their lives maintaining and protecting Reman's natural wonders. Artrim, the cult god of fire.

Many others dropped from the sky, taking their places in the meet, but once the major gods of the realm arrived, the meeting would begin. Only one was missing, and soon he arrived, just a touch later than all of the others, as he always had.

Vysoric was the keeper of death, and the god of divination. Seers and coroners alike kept worship with him, needing to know the future of the land, and keeping contentment with the death that they often saw there. Vysoric arrived, his pale face a stark contrast to the gray robes he had draped upon his emaciated frame. Never had anyone heard a noise from the god of death, for only in their minds did he communicate, shooting his thoughts to them. Though he was seldom active on Reman, all of the gods feared Vysoric, feared that he may know even their grisly ends, regardless of the time that may lie before it.

"An honor to see you, Vysoric," Threuen announced. The morose looking god bowed his head in response. "Let us begin." The god of magic stepped to the center of the circle of deities, his bright blue robe nearly glowing under the hot sun of Cora. "It has come to my attention that a number of the gods are conspiring amongst themselves to alter the state of affairs on Reman, arranging and predetermining outcomes for the mortals. This is an old rule. It is strictly forbidden."

"It is true," Thannon said. "I have spoken with Arsonin, for we have both discovered that the grandfather dwarf has allowed the mortals, Arsonin's race, to quest for the infernal knowledge again. He cannot do this."

"Men! You speak lies," Talvo erupted from his seat, his stumpy legs carrying him halfway across the circle. The crowd of minor deities clamored as he did. "It is on Reman, and is the affairs of men. I have not manipulated the situation at all. I leave such foolishness to Irreas."

"But," Arsonin interrupted with a flourish of his heavily jeweled hand, "the Meriss do have a part to play in your little crusade, and that does seem to suggest that you have already conspired to join your efforts. Tis' forbidden old father."

"That is centuries old, and precedes the ruling that we are not to do so," Talvo barked. "Not to mention," he pointed to the Meriss, "their part is only to make sure that the participants are pure."

"Do you see," Threuen called out to all of the immortals in the circle, "why we do not meet this way, and why you are forbidden to meet and plan the lives and events of Reman?" He paused while Talvo walked, grumbling, back to his seat. "One angry spat and the whole of the lands could be thrown into turmoil." Murmuring could be heard as the minor gods agreed with the lord of gods.

"But we acted only to protect our interests from those that had already broken the law," Thannon called out. "We demand that we are exempt from the law during this little quest that the old grandfather has his followers tramping all over Reman for. We deserve that right." Most of the gathering applauded, some cheering for the ruling.

"Threuen must be fair to all of us," called out one deity, his hideous black mask almost definitely associating him with Thannon.

"The old knowledge will be sought after," the god of magic boomed. "The law should not be reversed at this time, but it was not designed with the notion that a prophecy had been laid in any of the books given to the humans."

"Was it not said," Arsonin interrupted the chiefest of gods, causing some of the minor deities to gape at his boldness. "Was it not said that my children would not be subject to any predestinations by any god, due to their short lives and the rate at which they multiply. It was deemed dangerous to give such an ambitious and near-sighted people any artifact or knowledge of power, was it not?"

"Indeed it was," answered Thannon, seconding the idea that Talvo had acted outside of the law once already.

"It was said," Threuen acknowledged as he waved the gods of ambition and murder to silence. "And as it was said, all three of you will conspire for a final time. Talvo shall be present to make his intention understood. Thannon and Arsonin will be present to give their input and make sure that they are properly represented, particularly since the humans are Arsonin's people, and they should not be led solely by the old grandfather, though I cannot say that Thannon is the best influence to offer worshippers, so I will ask the Meriss to oversee the conference. Does this meet with all of your needs?" Threuen asked as he held his hands outstretched to the entire meet.

"This is foolish!" Talvo called out, his chain mail clinking as he shifted in his seat. "They will warp and pervert the quest until it no longer earns anyone anything."

"And what is it that they trek for?" Arsonin asked, knowingly, arching an eyebrow. "Is it such a good thing?" The god of ambition laughed mockingly. "I accept this bargain."

"As do I," Thannon said, standing as he did, displaying his black robes, their silver sequins glimmering in the desert sun.

All that were present could feel the Meriss accepting the arrangement.

"I have a need," Halkam called out. "I see what is to come, I think, though I am certainly not so adept as Vysoric. I see my people being destroyed or sucked into the menace that these three represent. Never have such terrible elements been bound into a contract together as are these three now: murder, ambition, and war. My kind will be the ones to pay the price. This journey needs to be limited in scope as to protect the laymen who neither care for nor heed the word of these higher gods." Again the gathering applauded the wisdom of their betters offered by the god of farmers and laborers.

"I agree," stated Threuen. "The journey shall be the only portion discussed in this conference, and the involvement of Halkam's congregation shall be limited as much as possible. Is that heard?" Talvo nodded, having no reason to involve anyone else in this matter. The glory of his church had been battered enough for one day. "Only the journey. Nothing after."

"Indeed," Arsonin scoffed, "the farmer's people shall barely be touched."

"It is agreed," Thannon said.

"Good!" Threuen's voice burst across the desert plain as he spun slowly, taking the whole host in. "From this day forward, there shall be no conspiring by any gods, and there shall be no further prophecy laid upon the shoulders of a race other than those you have yourself created. These four shall stay behind and discuss this situation until the sun of Cora sets, and then they too shall cease ever again speaking with one another outside of this meet. Any who offend this law will lose magic for eternity, never to be reversed." The crowd erupted with excitement and worry. "From this time forward, all conflicts between the gods shall be carried out only through our religions, only by our followers, and only on Reman!"

NO GODS OF CONSCIENCE

Book 1 of The Unlife Legend

Someone was there. The thief tilted his head, concentrating on the silence that filled the room. He heard a soft noise, a subdued scuff that instantly drew all of his attention. He worked his jaw, lightly scraping his teeth together as he waited. He heard it again. It was so soft that he nearly lost the padding sound to the internal thrum of his breathing. *Footstep. Where are you,* he thought. *I know you're here.* Subtle, and nearly undetectable, someone was definitely there. He crouched into the shadow where he'd been standing since detecting the sound. Raben was a pool of dark in the grayness of the night. His thick robes softened the outline of his body as he flattened himself against the wall. His eyes darted from corner to corner, scouring the room for his uninvited guest.

Heavy floral drapes fell from thick posts, covering the walls and brushing the floor. He examined every fold of the coarse material, looking for any unexplained bulge or irregular turn. In the center of the enormous grand room sat several impressive pieces of furniture, a sofa and three chairs. Carved of single pieces of dark wood, their robust frames blocked Raben, hiding a large portion of the room from his sight. He peered at them, letting his peripheral vision report if there was any motion while he waited for the sound to repeat itself. Next to him, as with every other wall in the central chamber of the house, shelves sat full of figurines and collectibles, many of them mementos of a life well spent on the seas. They were well organized, and pleasing to the eye, but the confusion that they offered the thief as he waited for his visitor had drawn his eyes several times to an odd shape or abnormal shadow. He forced his eyes back to the furniture, choosing a piece that had been painstakingly lathed into an artful curved chair that left the sitter comfortably reclined. Behind it, an eyeglass and a particularly impressive detailed map of the oceans surrounding Reman were arranged in a glass-faced cabinet for display. Allowing himself to be momentarily distracted, Raben searched for Liveport, though it was impossible in the poorly lit room. He strained to make sense of the sketch, his curiosity needing to understand the meticulous draft. He poured his attention through the glass door of the cupboard, but succeeded only in creating a dull ache just behind his eyes. Giving them a rest, he scanned the room, and as he did so, he heard the sound again. He opened his eyes wide, focusing in the direction that the footstep had come from.

There! He watched as the black misshapen shadow of a freestanding set of shelves slowly gave birth to the murky impression of his adversary. He examined the figure as it moved with a graceful stealth, painstakingly placing one foot after another, heading directly at him.

Hells! Just burning perfect. He'd been in the house of Lord Von Hessing for less than a few moments and already had company. First suspecting that the sound might have been a guard, and knowing how difficult it was to get into the house, Raben was surprised to find another thief skulking through the place. He doubted that there was another thief of his caliber in all of Liveport. It was a less than comforting feeling for the thief to know that there was another skilled member of his profession so close at hand.

Worse yet, his pockets were still light. He hadn't stolen anything yet. Observing the figure slide from shadow to shadow, a notion struck him. *Probably an elf. Slender,*

graceful... Raben flexed his hands as he thought. ...
Civilized. We can probably work a deal. Never resigned to
a single option, he slowly unsheathed both of his weapons.
A knuckle at a time, he drew the blades out, using time and
patience to remain unseen. His right hand held a slender
sword just over a reach and a half in length, its blade
colored darkly with black wax. In the other, was a reach-
long hooked sickle that glinted red from the metals from
which it was forged. He kept them both at the ready, but out
of view, placing them in the folds of his robe where no light
source, however weak, could betray him.

The creature deftly made its way across the room,
stepping carefully, using every advantage it could find in
order to remain noiseless. Once it reached the thick rug
that sprawled across the middle of the wooden floor, the
figure quickly cut two squares of the material free with a
short blade, and used them beneath its feet, sliding rather
than stepping. Raben patiently waited on the newcomer as
he closed ever nearer, impressed by the being's stealth. He
waited until he was sure that his whisper would be heard.
When there was no doubt, he began.

"Excellent night for a tour of so fine a home." The
being froze, and much to Raben's surprise, became almost
entirely invisible. "Don't you agree?" he asked, whispering
the question. He stared hard at where the being stood,
or had stood, and his stomach tightened as a slight panic
began inside of him. He was unsure as to whether or not
the "elf" was still there. *The damned thing was just there.*
Sweat beaded on his forehead. *Sure as blazes didn't leave.*
Magic? Unwilling to appear rattled or give away his
position any further, he fell silent, waiting for his opponent
to offer something to their meeting. *Just answer.*

The sound of a blade clearing its sheath caused Raben
to turn suddenly in a new direction, and there, a good
twenty-five paces from where he'd last seen the creature, its

4

silhouette was crouched with a thin curved sword gleaming across its knees.

"Yes," whispered the being, responding to Raben's question. It stood up and was maybe two and a half reaches in height. *Definitely an elf.* Again it quietly spoke. "I had heard that humans made poor thieves, but you are truly deplorable." The elf walked easily and confidently across the room towards Raben. It didn't even bother staying in the shadows. While it made no noise, the intruder now seemed to totally disregard the need to remain hidden.

Insane! Raben spun his sickle in his hand as he raised it from his robes, catching it easily in a ready position. *We'll both be caught and hauled in, and stretched publicly by the locals!* The elf was less than ten paces away, and he could feel sweat on the palms of his hands as he gripped his weapons. The unorthodox courage that the elven thief was displaying worried him. *Here I am, in the grand room of the home of the richest and most well respected noble in all of Liveport, and I am being forced to deal with another thief. A crazed thief! I might be able to kill him, but not before enough noise would bring Lord Hessing.*

The idea of inciting a battle in the well guarded manor of a renowned warrior was not what Raben had in mind. Not to mention the fact that a noble like Hessing was bound to have worthy guards around to protect him from the riff-raff that would stoop to thieving from him. *The man was a former war captain. Hells!*

A sweet smell filtered its way towards Raben and struck him suddenly with the delightful smell of fruit. *Perfume. Hells! It's a greeching woman too.* His eyes swept down her form. *Hells!*

"Shall I call you by name, or can you assume I know who you are? I do know who you are." The whispering elf couldn't have more effectively paralyzed Raben. "You still have a debt to pay, rogue, and you are exceedingly difficult to find." Even though it was being whispered, every word struck him as if it were being screamed. "We consider the effort you've forced us to go to, a testimony regarding how well we've trained you."

"Freezing Hells," he muttered. "You're a Guild hunter?" Raben lowered his weapons, knowing that he couldn't win here. A deep-rooted feeling reminded him that Guild hunters were the fiercest warriors in the entire Guild. He couldn't remember ever having seen one fight, but now was not the time for a practical demonstration. *We're already doomed to get caught. Crazy wench!*

"No. I'm an informant for now. I figured that by talking to you here, I would have your undivided attention." Raben heard the sword quietly sift through the air just before he felt the tip of it under his chin. He could feel the point working its way into his skin. He winced. "It is time you prayed, thief." He swallowed hard and felt blood, or sweat, or both run down his chest.

"I thought..." the thief took a few quick breaths as her blade pressed into him harder, "...I thought you were only an informant for now." His voice rose slightly, and he flexed his hands around his weapons. His leather gloves creaked from the stress. The smell of fruit was so strong that he marveled that any thief would wear such a perfume. *It's making me sick.*

"Shhhhhh," She calmly warned. "I am. You must go see the arch-priest named Ulmer. He is ours. If he doesn't hear from you soon... then, thief, I'll become a Guild hunter." The sword dropped from under Raben's chin. *How did I get into this?* He didn't remember at all.

"Which church does...?" The thief's head whipped from side to side. She was gone. "Just like that." *Greeching Wench!* He wiped the sweat from his forehead as he sucked in several deep breaths. *Hells! Go to a boiling priest. Greech!* "I've got to steal something and get out of here."

Raben was aware that a major artifact of the Dayquest was being held by Lord Von Hessing. It was some kind of priceless weapon made personally by a long forgotten and ancient priest of Talvo, the greatest war god of them all. He didn't remember where he'd heard of this quest, or Hessing, before. He simply wanted to steal the sacred weapon and fence it to the Guild, which could in turn, demand a ransom for the artifact. Now that there was another thief in the house, a powerful member of the Guild no less, all he wanted to do was get some valuables to pay for his way out of Liveport before the underground religious organization caught up with him again.

Raben had a fuzzy recollection of what had been done for him at the Guild. He could picture a few moments of his training, but all that really came through when he tried to recall his time there was a negative feeling. *I'll sort this mess out when I get out of here.* It wasn't that Raben didn't want to pay them for the services they'd rendered. He'd learned much there about fighting, stealth, and magic. The problem was that every time they got hold of one of their own, they demanded servitude in order to forward the Guild's strength. This usually manifested itself in the ruthless butchery of prominent enemies, which was usually dangerous, if not impossible to escape alive. One of the things that was most impressed on Raben's mind: do not cross the Guild. *I'm no assassin,* he thought. *I can kill for the right cause, and steal, but I'm no assassin.* He shook his head. *Hells! Take something good and go. Focus! Why am I having such trouble getting my mind straight?* He thought of the only thing that had shaken him. *Blazing Guild hunter! Why a woman?* He surveyed the room for a moment, bending his will to the task at hand. He stood, motionless, until his confidence returned. *It would have been a better battle than you think, elf!*

He then continued his slow quiet journey through Lord Hessing's house, passing by the front door and the welcome hall. *Just the front doors would be worth a fortune.* They were carved wood, inlayed with some type of precious metal. It looked like silver. A faint smile played on the thief's lips as he momentarily entertained the notion of removing the rich lord's doors, but decided that he hadn't the time, or the nerve, for such an involved comic effort. His mirth turned grim as he remembered his elven visitor. *Some other time, when I'm not being hunted.* From the entry hall he ascended a stairwell that carried him right to Lord Hessing's bedchamber. Raben could hear the huge man snoring from the corridor outside.

Lord Hessing was widely loved in Liveport for his generous contributions to the city and his participation in the Free Liveport Navy where he'd captained several ships and gained a name as a ferocious fighter. Anywhere he went, he was recognized, and for good reason. He was nearly three and a half reaches tall, layered with dense rippling muscle, and armed with at least three good swords. The man was an army unto himself.

Slowly leaning into the doorway, Raben watched Hessing sleep. *He's greeching huge.* The thief crept into the room, looking around intently as he slowly placed his weapons back into their sheaths. His arms stretched out away from his body as though he were walking on a tightrope; he was so concentrated on silence. A wallet was easily visible on the lord's night table, as were a number of sheathed swords next to it. Raben edged toward the table, taking one step each time he heard the noble snore. After listening to Lord Von Hessing snore for a short while, the thief was poised to take what he wanted. He reached under his robes and brought forth a container of black dust from the many pokes and vials in his belt. Sprinkling it onto the money pouch and swords, he did little more than mouth the words to his spell. The wallet glowed ever so slightly.

A magic bag. Very interesting. Raben stared at the glowing wallet for several moments. *Very interesting indeed.* He reached a hand towards the lord's coin pouch and hesitantly let his gloved fingers close over the top of the small sack. He looked over to the lord and listened again for the snoring. *Regular and good. Sweet dreams, Lord Hessing.* Raben smiled. He slowly lifted the magic bag from the night table. He picked it up with his left hand and immediately after it cleared the table, his right was beneath it to control any noise it might make. He raised it up in front of himself and began to tediously tuck it into his thick belt. Suddenly, there were coins out. *What the greeching!* The bag was gone. It had vanished. Silver spilled past his hands, and for one moment Raben tried to catch them all, but only succeeded in slapping a few away from him. As the coins crashed onto the floor, and a few he'd slapped hit Lord Hessing in bed, Raben jumped away from the nightstand, drawing his weapons for the second time that night. *Greeching Hells! Damn this night!*

"What's this?" Lord Hessing leapt straight up, and was already standing on his bed. *Great Hells!* The enormous man already had a sword. "I hope your life has been worth the twenty silver you wanted to take!" yelled the noble as he sneered savagely and rushed forward off of the bed. His sword was cutting straight down. Raben's blade shot out across its path, but the brute force of the blow numbed the thief's hand and knocked his weapon onto the floor.

Raben yelled as his sickle arched upwards into the huge man, but the blow never landed. Lord Hessing lowered the pommel of his sword, blocking the thief's attempt, and then shouldered him with all of his weight. Raben fell backwards out of the noble's bedroom, into the hall. He allowed the momentum to carry him over and then tumbled back onto his feet. "Hells." He had lost his sickle. Lord Hessing bellowed and charged out the door. The thief screamed as the warrior charged him, and just before the raging lord could cut him down, Raben dove into his legs. The huge man stumbled over him, giving the thief time to jump up and run. He sprinted back into the bedroom, scooped up a few coins, grabbed all the weapons by the nightstand, and then leapt out of a window. Just as he began to fall, he felt his robe stretch and tear.

"Gul assama," said the thief in the language of magic, his right hand quickly weaving through a short arcane pattern, letting a few pieces of silver fall. Just before hitting the ground, he slowed in the air. And, as if he were stepping down from a stage, he stepped lightly onto the ground. Looking up, he saw Von Hessing holding a scrap of cloth.

"I'll get the hair off your head next, you scum!" The noble hurled his sword at the thief. Raben nimbly dodged out of its way, reached out, and caught it as it flew. Guards leaned out of other windows with crossbows, but soon found that they had no target. The thief had gone.

As he stared at the building, Raben let his eyes slowly rise up it. The thing seemed too tall. So tall, that all of the beautiful artwork that rimmed the massive roof couldn't be seen from the ground. The Cathedral of Arsonin was a gargantuan structure located right in the middle of the city. It had been built with the look of centuries-old classical arches and huge, smooth, archaic pillars, which were interesting when one considered that the cathedral had only been there for a few years. *Every church has to look and feel centuries old.*

The church had been constructed when Arsonin, the god of ambition, decided that he would also like to be patron of merchants. It is recorded that Arsonin discovered that the goddess of merchants was being offered greater riches than He was receiving from His worshippers, and in response, He bent all of His will to battling Her. A short war ensued, thieves and bandits against merchants and pacifist friars. She'd had no chance. It had been a slaughter of Her followers. After destroying Trellia, goddess of trade, Arsonin and his priesthood attempted to gather all of the merchants and thieves of the realm under one banner. Many were the thieves that had already worshipped the ambitious Arsonin. Initially, this created a conflict of interest for those thieves that had victimized merchants, by forcing those bandits to attack only merchants which were not part of the following. As the god of ambition's influence

11

spread, mainly through large rewards to the loyal, the union of merchants and thieves evolved into the subtler, far more organized version of thieving, the Guild. The thieves gained the ability to openly worship a god of their trade while merchants that joined the Guild enjoyed immunity from bandits. Soon, church leadership identified the merchants and thieves that did not follow Arsonin. As the Guild grew in strength, these nonbelievers were either forced into the religious organization, or were hunted.

Great was the need for good hunters and assassins by the followers of Arsonin. A large number of merchants were members of private guilds and refused to give in to the pressures of the god's followers. They could not be left to chance. Raben had been trained for just such duties.

Never being much on religion, Raben rejected that there was any greater force to work for beyond himself. Without knowing what he could be alone, and feeling that the word 'power' was easily used only by fanatical cultists, he was unable to accept such a restrictive set of principals as was offered by the gods. He much preferred the use of magic, which was his alone to wield. He couldn't recall the Guild ever forcing him to join the following of Arsonin. *Right now I don't even remember how I ended up at the Guild to begin with.* It seemed as though he was supposed to express some type of loyalty to the god, however, which made him uncomfortable. *I hope they don't expect me to lead a prayer or cite some forgotten scripture.*

"It's getting towards midday, Uncle. We should go in." The boy looked up with sincere caring in his clear brown eyes as he interrupted Raben's thinking. The thief had forgotten about the boy while studying the ornate cathedral. *Damned kid. The Guild must really be in need.*

The night before, Raben had gotten in late from his visit to Lord Hessing's, and by the time he made it down to the common room for breakfast at the inn in which he was staying, the boy had been waiting. "You do remember that we have…" the boy paused for emphasis, "…have to go to church today. Right, Uncle!" Something was slightly strange about the look in his eyes. A look that indicated a maturity or understanding of the world that was wrong for a boy of nine or ten years. *Like I must have looked at your age.* Without looking into the child's eyes you'd see only a brown haired boy, a little sloppy and dirty from being in the street. Looking directly into them, however, you could see that he was somehow dangerous. *Have you killed a man?* Not wanting to offend the Guild yet, Raben had nodded and followed the boy here.

"Yes nephew, let's get this over with." The boy leapt ahead as Raben answered, and held the door open to allow the man to enter. The inside of the building was a stunning mixture of beauty and horror. Fantastic murals covered the white walls with depictions of lordly men with great heaps of gold and silver, and beautiful women by their sides. Crimson carpet stretched out before them and stopped only at the foot of a dais upon which polished marble statues stood. The statues were men, well dressed and stately, caught in the throes of death as they let their own blood by slashing their inner thighs with some type of curved dagger. Raben eyed the statues as he bit the tip of his tongue in distaste.

"They are the Merchants of Yargo," said the boy in a matter-of-fact tone. "They sacrificed themselves to Arsonin that He might protect their business and help their ambitions to grow. Their want for wealth in Arsonin's name was greater than their need for life. They live with Him now." The boy gestured towards a square door to the side of the room. "This way, Uncle."

I hope to never need or want such protection. Raben followed slowly, more warily than he had when he passed through the front door.

"Father Ulmer, I brought him, the man from the inn." The boy beamed as the large priest patted him on the head.

To say Ulmer was fat did no justice to the size of the man. He'd taken no pain to avoid his enormity, and seemed only to have celebrated it daily, by eating whimsically and in great volume. His bald head seemed far too small perched on his rounded shoulders, as did his arms which seemed just barely to protrude from his torso. He grunted with the effort of turning in his chair to look at Raben. The work that it had taken was already building beads of sweat on his brow.

"Thank you, son. Now, let me look upon him alone." The boy left and closed the door behind him. Ulmer stared intently at Raben, trying to bore into his mind with his sight alone. "Enter man. Don't be alarmed. I won't eat you." Ulmer snorted a laugh. "Spin for me. I wish to know my new charge." Raben spun slowly as requested, his hands touching his new weapons. "Long black hair. Strange hair for a man so pale. And green eyes." The priest smiled, his cheeks nearly blocking out his eyes. "Do you have a strong name?" *Name? I don't have a name. Only the Guild knows.* Raben shook his head while thinking. Ulmer took it as a no.

"I'll bet the ladies like you. I never had such luck. Having devoted myself to the faith and all." Ulmer surveyed Raben in a way the thief had never before been scrutinized. Just under three reaches in height, medium build, average looking, Raben had never drawn much attention, but Ulmer's eyes moved over every knuckle of his body. "Very nice. You're a swordsman?" Ulmer's fat left arm gestured vaguely toward Raben's weapons.

"Yes," the thief answered. *That would explain the three swords I have on my belt.* "I was Guild-trained with numerous weapons. I prefer the sword and sickle." He

14

unsheathed one of his sickles and held the curved weapon up for display.

"Nasty weapon, that," giggled Ulmer. "Well I think I have a use for you." The fat priest sighed, suppressing his humor. "You've heard of The Dayquest, yes?" Raben shook his head that he hadn't. He had, but everyone has different information. "Mmmmm. It's a group of gullible knights and lords who feel that they are prophesied to lead a new era of prosperity and good to the realm." Ulmer's face curdled. "Ridiculous!" The large priest boomed. "Only one man can be that. They all trek for vanity's sake. They have been taught that foolish little poem and all believe it is a foretelling. It's imprudence at best." Ulmer pawed at the sleeves of his brown robes, pulling them down from where they'd bunched up under his arms.

"I've been in Liveport only a day or two, and have never heard this prophecy. What is it, if you don't mind my asking, and have the time?" Raben waited as the priest prepared to answer.

"It is simple. Memorize it. It reads thusly. 'The sword shall draw the foemen. The hero shall valiantly fight. The faith shall conquer evil. And all will be as it was.' The words were spoken by Kizzer Anaxim at the First Fall. There is more to it than that, but it is pointless and tedious to bear. At any rate, he spoke to give hope that times might one day reach back and be as they were in the Centuries of Growth. They are recorded in the Chronicles of Talvo in Remembrance Chapter four, verse sixteen." Ulmer breathed heavily after exerting his voice for so long.

"People live by these simple words?" Raben thought for a moment. "That seems rather absurd. When you said prophecy, I expected hours of recital, not a few lines." Raben tossed his sickle in the air causing it to spin, and caught it again. *They could at least make them rhyme.* The thief smiled at this thought. "You were going to tell me what I had to do? I have pressing business."

"Do you?" The priest sat forward. "Your pressing business is what I tell you it is. Never forget who we both work for. I can have your next breath be your last." Ulmer slammed his palm down onto the arm of his chair. "Your pressing business is to find out who all of the members of the Dayquest are and the route they are taking. Follow them, and once they are under way, you will then proceed to kill them off. From what I understand they shouldn't make it far. Start slowly. Join the trek if you can, and let them guide you to their destination. Once you are sure of it, finish them. You will be further advised at that time." Ulmer sat back in his chair. "Is every thing clear?"

"Yes," Raben answered, his irritation obvious.

"Yes…your Highness," corrected the fat priest.

"Yes, your Highness." The thief stared straight into Father Ulmer's eyes. He tossed his sickle in the air causing it to spin.

I could be a cobbler, Raben mused to himself. *Mend people's shoes, make boring conversation.* The thief watched in passing as a young man sitting by the street began to repair an old boot. "At least then I wouldn't always have to watch my back," the thief voiced his thought as he shifted his backpack to a more comfortable position. It was odd to him that he had been discovered last night in Hessing's home and then again at the inn this morning. *Perhaps I am not so skilled as I thought.* The thought forced him to smirk in irritation.

After his meeting with Ulmer, Raben had immediately returned to the inn and picked up everything that was his. It seemed about time to move. He looked a little odd with his two large travel satchels, a bedroll on his back, and five swords. Two were tucked under the bedroll and strapped across his back while three more hung on his belt, but few people were searching for him, so he passed without notice as he strode out of the inn and into the street. Besides, it seemed to Raben that anyone that wanted him was able to get to him easily enough as it was. With this terrible revelation, he resolved almost at once to leave the city and flee this mess, never looking back. By the time he'd picked up his gear and started for the South road, however, he began to become intrigued by the situation.

Where was the Dayquest headed? What was at the end of it? Why did the Guild have an interest? Why me? These

17

were questions that suddenly seemed to need answers, and obtaining answers was something for which Raben was extensively trained. *I'll figure this out and then leave.* It seemed to him that only the rich and the noble had much to do with the Dayquest, and so, he would have to have something to do with them. It would be simple enough, after all. The rich are always so busy putting on airs and counting coins in their head that they would never notice him until he was already gone. All he needed to do was find someone who might point him in the right direction, and the way that the government of Liveport was structured made that easy enough.

Each city in Reman had an officer whose duty it was to unite the power of the rich and politically powerful, and also to orient the new rich and powerful to the city. Such a person would be acquainted with every development in the city and any thing or person that was gaining influence. Raben needed to find this man. But first, he needed to prepare.

The tailor he visited was thrilled to see a rich man in need, and quickly arrayed Raben in a silk shirt and pant set, along with a satin over-vest. Raben had never before worn such accouterment, but found it tremendously comfortable. He smiled easily and paid with Lord Hessing's money. He then had his long hair braided and tied off with a midnight blue thong, as was the dominant style in Liveport, and spent an additional silver to be cleanly shaven. Some rest, a bath and an hour to properly dress and preen left Raben looking rather stately. He inventoried his gear and decided to take only minimal weaponry. His sickle, he sheathed tightly to the outside of his right leg, and the nicest of Hessing's swords, since he'd lost his own, he wore very prominently atop the sickle on his right side. Wearing both weapons on the same side pushed the hilt of the sword out away from his belt, but served to hide the sickle from view. In the black silks and midnight blue satin, Raben felt ready to join the world of the rich. He strolled comfortably out into the streets. He strutted along as he had seen so many other nobles do, carrying an almost visible contempt for those he weighed with his eyes. When he happened upon a courier that he felt would know what he wanted to know, he lowered his guise enough to appear hospitable to the laborer.

"Fair day, Goodman! Might I ask you a favor of time?" Raben questioned the simple man, wasting no time. The man nodded, while setting the large chest he'd been carrying on the ground. "Where might the most expensive eatery in Liveport be? I have a great need to entertain a lucky lady this eve and am new to this city." Raben brought forth a silver piece and flipped it to the man. "I hope you'll tell me true."

"Aye, 'tis the Golden Capon. That'll impress yer lady, sure. You can introduce her to every lord and knight in the city, sure, but be careful, they may take her to dance instead of you." The man grinned at his own wit, as Raben humored him with a laugh. Pointing up the road, the man gave Raben directions, and soon after, the city's newest lord arrived.

He was seated immediately and offered a glass of Lizarael wine, which he accepted. He looked at the printed menus, which were the first he'd ever seen, and sipped cautiously at the stout vintage. He edged around the table enough to where he could see the entire room. Only a few men were there, but all of them struck Raben as good targets for his real trade.

After receiving the recommended house special of oven baked capon with diced onions, Raben began to feel even more comfortable. The chicken was fantastic. The thief couldn't remember having ever eaten something so delicious. He hadn't realized how famished he was until the elegant feast lay before him. Raben ate as though he hadn't in weeks. *Everything has been so crazy lately. Did I even eat yesterday?*

He finished his meal and was sitting back in contentment, when the door flew open and none other than Von Hessing swept into the room. *Well, this is greeching perfect!*

Hessing strolled up to the bar where he clasped hands with each man there and greeted them by name. Sweeping his heavy cloak from his shoulders, the noble laid it across the bar. Then the huge man turned around and looked directly at Raben. Last night the thief had been heavily shrouded, but now he felt as if he were in danger just for having been there. A knot formed in his stomach as he lifted his hand to give a weak wave to the enormous noble, but Hessing would have none of it. He walked over to Raben's table, clutched his hand tightly in his own. "Well met," he said. "My name is Von Hessing."

"I am..." Raben coughed politely and took a sip of wine. "...Sir Braen Nerab." Raben looked at Hessing, half expecting the huge man to reach out and grab him by the throat. "I have recently arrived in Liveport to establish a home and business." Hessing began to ask the obvious. "I plan to run a training hall, and security company." Raben waived the waitress over and ordered another glass of wine, and one for the noble. "My only problem is that I can't find the city liaison in order to establish my needs."

"Well Sir Braen Nerab, you have just done so. I am one of three such officers in Liveport." Hessing smiled and offered his hand again to renew their previous introduction.

"That's great!" *Just greeching perfect!* Raben shook the man's hand again. "Had it not been for this stroke of luck I might have searched until dusk, or even had to wait until tomorrow." *What a pity that would've been.* He sat back as the waitress placed new glasses of wine on the table. "You know, I believe I heard mention of you when I served as part of the army in Lizarael to the north. Weren't you a sailor, or perhaps the admiral of a fleet?"

Hessing looked at Raben shrewdly before answering. "I was a captain, but that was long ago." The noble sipped at his wine, nodding his approval for the full red.

"Nonsense! You look like you could lead an expedition to sea this moment." Raben waved towards the distant and vast ocean that surrounded Liveport on three sides.

"I could never find the time, I'm afraid." Hessing took a long draught of his wine. "I'm always busy with one thing or another."

"And none of it fun?" Raben laughed almost to himself. "You mean to tell me that with a sword like that at your hip, you don't do anything to get your blood going?" Raben capped the hilt of his own weapon with his hand, covering it from view. "Come now, I won't believe any such thing from a man with your look."

"I mostly greet and aid new nobles and persons such as yourself, but of late this Dayquest leaves me little time to focus on anything else." Hessing could see Raben's obvious and feigned confusion. "You've never heard of the Dayquest?" The thief answered that he had not. "It's a knightly trek to obtain the 'True Knowledge.' We don't know what that is; we are simply given those words off of an archaic map that was recently unearthed in an old temple outside the city. So we will follow the map and find out where it leads." Hessing sighed. "It's probably a hoax."

"You said we. Are you part of it?" Raben finished his second glass of wine, as did Hessing.

"I don't necessarily want to be, but Dorian, the priest who holds the map, seems quite certain that I am the Prophesied, and therefore, that I must go." Hessing ran his fingers through his thick mane of dark hair. "At any rate, the city will force me to go. My civic duty, I suppose." The enormous warrior rose from his chair, towering over Raben. "Perhaps you should volunteer."

"No, I am no crusader." Raben raised his eyes to look at the massive man. "The map is guarded well I hope." The thief stretched his back, flexing his arms over his head.

"The priest and his order have it in the temple of Talvo." Hessing suddenly regarded Raben darkly, his eyes narrowing ever so slightly.

"It couldn't be safer then, I suppose," answered Raben.

"Perhaps," he shot back, "and perhaps not. A priest was murdered only this morning, though not in the temple of Talvo, thank the luck." Hessing had already begun to walk away as he said this. *Where's he going? Is something wrong? The sword?*

"A dead priest." Raben had to raise his voice to ensure he'd be heard. "What was his name?"

Lord Von Hessing glowered at the thief, and turned away as he answered.

Something had gone very wrong in the Golden Capon. Hessing had been contentedly talking to Raben, and then, for no apparent reason, he walked away as if angry. Raben thought through the entire conversation as he walked through the streets of Liveport. *Hessing hadn't looked at the sword. What had greeching gone wrong?* It was dusk, and the white walls of the city's buildings glowed orange with the last light of the day. The thief simply could not figure out what Hessing had reacted to. "Maybe Ulmer was a friend of his." He turned onto the street where he was staying.

The Copper Pot stood near the southern edge of the city near the shore, and was less than spectacular. Raben had been in a hurry when he'd checked into the little inn, but now thought it amusing for him to be returning to this place in satin and silks. The walls had cracks between the vertical slats that allowed the light to stream out into the street. As he stepped up onto the porch he could see that almost no one was in the common room yet. He stood motionless and watched the patrons talk and drink. *Nothing out of the ordinary.*

Raben passed into the alley on the right side of the building and counted three windows back. Speaking two short words of magic, he quickly floated up to his second story window, where he pulled himself into the building. Moments later, he reemerged. Floating back down to the ground wearing long, dark, hooded robes, he secured a number of small weapons on his arms and legs. Upon touching down, he twisted his sword belt until his sword moved naturally with the movement of his black robe. By the time he exited the alley, he looked completely unarmed.

Passing unnoticed through the city, Raben arrived at the temple of Talvo. Unlike that of Arsonin, the followers of Talvo had built a completely unremarkable structure. It was light colored and blocky. There were no markings or engravings on the outside, no depictions of great victories or terrible losses, just a bare wall with two huge steel doors embedded dead center. It did have a very robust feel about it, though. It looked as if it would be the last building standing were the city to be ravaged by a war. "Perhaps Talvo knows the future of Liveport." Raben sneered at the thought. *How could He know what all of these others don't?*

The thief looked back through the Ward of Worship that he'd just passed through. It was nighttime, and very few others were up and about, but he could still make out the many different churches and temples that stood in honor of the gods of Reman. Slowly making his way back into the ward, leaving Talvo's keep behind for the moment, Raben began to wonder why so many people felt that they benefited from their belief in these gods.

Arsonin! What possible good could He give to you? Riches? Riches that you have to murder for? His followers are forced to murder themselves in order to secure their place in His sight. He thought about the Merchants of Yargo in disgust. *How can you walk into that place every day to offer your faith to a god that would demand that of you?* Raben looked up at the massive church that he'd entered earlier. It towered over him, the detail that had been carved into it even less visible in the flickering light of the street lamps. *Vanity and greed. How many farmers come to you? Or is it all thieves and murderers?* He smiled at the irony of his thought. *Like me.*

Standing next to the cathedral to the god of ambition was a dark little shrine. Its walls were constructed of the same white stone that all of the others were, but it had long since been covered by a web of thick vines and broad leaves. The stone that had once shone in the bright sun was now buried in a deep blanket of spidery vegetation. *Not even a symbol.* Raben chuckled. *That must be someone loved. There must be something.* He moved nearer the small building, but as he did so a feeling of foreboding began to build in him. *Really loved.* He left the mysterious shrine in doubt.

Looking back to the ordinary temple of Talvo, the thief began to wonder how much information could be assumed of the gods just by inspecting the buildings that stood in their honor. *Talvo is practical and boring. Highly defensible. Arsonin is covered in His own vane worship and most of the small detail of the cathedral stands beyond sight. And this place.* He looked back to the vine-covered little shrine. *Speaks for itself.* He spun away from Talvo's keep, leaving it momentarily in the distance. An ivory tower stood in the center of the Ward of Worship.

Polished, unerring. Nearly perfect. He'd never noticed the tower before. So intent on making his way out of his meeting with Ulmer alive, he'd not so much as even looked around when he'd passed through this part of the city. *This is the most regal place in the city.* It had silver or polished steel fluted along the sides of it, inlayed to create arcane designs. *Wards of defense?* As Raben moved around it, he could see the front door. A massive arched portal, carved of an ancient and knotted wood, stood behind two enormous wrought iron plates, upon which burned a brilliant blue flame. No symbol marked the tower. As he walked towards the door, he could see that an oily substance lay in each plate, allowing the blue flames to consume them, offering up the azure light that splashed itself across the ground near the tower. Staring into the flames, the thief felt his eyes beginning to hurt, but as even they did, he could make out the vague, shimmering image of the god to whom the tower was committed. He was tall, and His skin was blue, the exact blue of the flame. He was mighty, and looked as though He would tower over ordinary men. *Strange!* Raben looked away, unable to continue staring at the intense light. *There is much to learn about the gods. Too much.*

Turning away from the ivory tower, the thief was set on making his way back to the temple of Talvo, but another caught his eye. Drawn by curiosity, he quickly walked to it, where he found a simple depiction of a rustic man which had been painted onto the front wall of the church. He was a well built man carrying a yoke from which two buckets hung. Behind him, many animals walked single file along a path. The man appeared tired and poor, yet he wore a smile. "Halkam," was inscribed above the painting. Below it, "leader of those who earn their happiness." *The hero to the common man. Happiness through simplicity. Perhaps I have found a path I could appreciate.* He scoffed at the notion.

Backing away from the straightforward church, Raben decided that he needed to get under way. He walked back to the Temple of Talvo and stood before it, considering for the first time, the impact that a belief could have. *It is driving these people. It is driving me. Everything I am doing is a response to their beliefs.* He smiled briefly, amazed that he could be a pawn of a religion that he didn't believe in. Reaching out, he took the plain iron knocker that had been built into the center of the door of the keep. He lifted it and then let it fall.

The heavy knocker boomed as it contacted the door. A hollow gonging sound echoed audibly in the corridors beyond. Raben waited, feeling a familiar excitement begin to creep through his limbs. *Do I want to do this?* He turned his back to the door and surveyed the street. There were a few people milling around, but nothing seemed to pique his interest. Under one street lantern, a man was leaning against a wall smoking a pipe. Raben watched as the swirls of smoke wound around each other and then climbed above the light of the street lamp. The man stood and adjusted himself against the wall, and then resumed leaning. *Is he watching me?* The man added a little more leaf to his pipe, and slowly slid down the wall until he was sitting on his haunches. *No, he's not.* Raben continued to eye the stranger until he heard someone behind the steel doors.

Metal ground on metal as the enormous steel plates cracked open, letting a dim greenish light escape. From what he could see, the inside of the temple looked every bit as dull and uninteresting as the outside. Straight square corridors passed back into the depths of the building, and not a single decoration was visible.

"You have a need, friend?" The voice was clear enough, but the source was not. Raben leaned carefully into the doorway, squinting his eyes, trying to see through the greenish light. After a few moments, he realized that there was indeed a man standing against the back wall to the left. His clothing matched the wall so perfectly that he was well camouflaged. The green light served to dull the contrast between man and wall.

"Yes...Yes I do. I must speak to Dorian." Raben intentionally sounded meek, and nervous. "Lord Von Hessing sent me with a message that can only be given directly to him...Dorian." He moved slowly into the temple, his hands clasped together in front of him. He began to wonder if the man had heard him. He reached up each sleeve and felt the daggers he'd secured on his forearms. The steel knives comforted him. He knew that he had a lethal means that his opponents weren't aware of. He ran his fingers along the polished surfaces of the daggers, waiting for the doorman to do something. *Come on.* He began to rock from foot to foot, nervousness driving his impatience. Self conscious of the fact that he might look suspicious, Raben brought his hands back out and began to wring them against each other. He blew into his cupped hands as though he was cold. *Is he dead?* The thief stood in the doorway for a few moments more, waiting for the hidden servant of Talvo to react. *Hurry.*

"Let me take you to his cell." The man suddenly sprung into motion, moving so quickly that Raben had to jog to keep up. The huge doors scraped and sent a concussive echo through the halls of the temple as they slammed shut. *This feels bad.* Raben's guide never even looked back to see if he was there. He simply wove his way through the many halls until he arrived at his destination.

They stood before an unadorned wooden door. "Dorian is within. Enter." The man stepped back against the wall of the corridor, opposite the door, and waited.

Raben stared at him for a long moment, noting the distinct absence of movement in the man. He didn't appear to be breathing. The thief leaned closer to the man and listened for a breath, but could hear nothing. Nodding to himself in confusion, Raben gave up on the doorman and turned to the door, to far more interesting business. He pulled it open with its simple handle and looked inside. A gray-robed cleric was sitting up on a short wooden cot. He was bearded, and had a thick, slightly messy, head of brown hair. The priest of Talvo started as the door opened, and then took a deep breath.

"Enter, friend. It must be important if Von sent you. Kindly forgive my appearance, I have been sleeping." The man gestured for the thief to seat himself on a three-legged stool in the corner. Raben lifted it and placed it near the cot. "I am Dorian." The priest's hand raised in greeting.

"Arben," Raben answered, and clasped hands with the priest. "Von has been greatly worried about the Dayquest and asked me to come and have a look at the map." The thief stroked his chin. "He feels that it lacks sufficient detail. I mean that…" He placed his hand apologetically on the priest's shoulder. "…He wishes to be reassured by a close personal friend, who is not of the religion that holds the map, that it appears authentic. I am a limner by trade, and have offered to survey it for him. I have extensive knowledge of ancient maps and texts. He struggles with the idea of staying in the city and furthering its glory, while fulfilling the Dayquest. He is such a dutiful man. He is torn." Raben sighed and rested both of his hands in his lap. *That was good.* The thief was happy with his portrayal of a mousy map maker.

"Well," Dorian breathed the word, seemingly in exasperation, "you're lying." The priest stared blankly at Raben's shocked visage. "Come with me. I feel you are more a part of this than you think." He climbed from his cot and walked out of the room, leaving the thief behind. Raben gaped at the empty cot. *What the greeching? How could you know?*

"Part of what?" *Talvo is the god of war, not truth!* Feeling completely confused and exposed, Raben followed the priest through the temple. Dorian led the way through a number of different passages, and down a few flights of stairs. The thief did his best to memorize the way he'd come in, feeling fairly certain that he'd need to get out in a hurry. When they were walking down a long straight hall he tried to get answers from the hurried priest, but the man would not talk to him. He simply marched on in an almost ceremonious manner. Raben continued to follow, but just a moment before he attempted to speak to the priest again, they stopped walking. Turning to face a blank wall, Dorian pressed three fingers into it, and only moments later the section of heavy brick fell away silently. Raben watched as the priest walked through the hidden doorway. Soon after, he decided to follow.

"This, my friend, is the map you seek." Dorian gestured at an entire wall. "This was the front wall of the battle chamber of Talvo, excavated from an ancient temple that had been lost in the White Mage Wars. Our followers dug out and transported the wall to this temple last year. We have studied it extensively, and no one outside of the following of Talvo has expressed an interest until you." The priest turned and walked right up to the thief, standing only a few knuckles in front of him. "Least of all, Lord Von Hessing." Placing a hand on the thief's back, the priest urged him forward towards the wall. It was a map indeed. Raben stared at it, and saw that there was writing on it, all the way around the outside of the map, for that matter. *What is going on here? I need to leave this city! What do I care about any of this anyway? Why are they pushing me into this?* Raben's eyes locked onto the map despite his thoughts.

"All of that writing…what is it?" The thief moved up and ran his fingers across the writing. He could feel the slight texture that the ink had created. It was warm under his touch. *Almost magic. More advanced than I will ever be. Hells!*

"Some of it is the prophecy written in Ancient League languages that were used a thousand years ago. The rest, we have no idea. The wizard's guild once claimed to have great knowledge of this map and the prophecy, but have remained silent since the map's recovery." *Wizard's guild! I'll bet they know.* The thief ran his fingers across a rune that was particularly arcane in nature. Dorian joined Raben at the wall. "The map is fairly detailed, as you can see. The problem we have is…"

"Where do you start? The gods have fought so many battles on Reman that these forests and mountains might not even be in these places." Raben's fingers traced the line that showed the path of the Dayquest until it climbed higher than he could reach. "Where the boiling Hells do these knights and nobles think they are going?" He turned towards Dorian to hear the answer.

"We don't know, and neither do they." The priest moved to a nearby table, surrounded by five uncomfortable looking chairs and sat down in one. "We've waited for someone to be driven by the prophecy. That individual would be the one to complete the predestined journey and would therefore know where to begin. At least that is what the order thinks will happen. The wizards have claimed that they know where to begin and where the journey will end, but have been less than forthcoming regarding the details. They believe the trek is folly." The priest sat back, and for the first time Raben noticed how exhausted the man looked. Purplish crescents underscored the priest's eyes, which were pink with exhaustion. *So capture a wizard. They are reading the information right off of the map you have here. Prophecies! Ulmer was right. This is ridiculous.*

"Tell me. What is it that you feel I am a part of? You said something as we were leaving your chambers. This prophecy of yours?" Raben shook his head and decided to join the priest at the table. Sitting down, his sword jutted out to his side as he worked to get comfortable in the hard wood chair. *Against my will if anything.*

"Perhaps." The priest's foot lightly tapped the sheath of the thief's sword. "You do seem to be more than you first appear." Dorian got up and moved to a cabinet where he brought out a bottle and two glasses. "Not everyone involved need be the center of the prophecy. Someone

31

will be that for certain, but it takes numerous unnoticed quirks and catalysts in order to ensure that it happens." Dorian poured a glass of wine, and after a nod from Raben, poured a second. "Many want to believe that a prophecy is something inevitable, but it isn't. It must be labored after. Someone must strive for it, and we live in a time with few heroes." The priest took a lengthy drink of wine.

"So you believe that because I came to you that I am the hero outlined by the prophecy?" Raben laughed quietly while Dorian shook his head no. "Good. I'm quite sure that I'm not the stuff of heroes." Raben took a sip of his wine. It was very dry, and left him thirstier than before he'd drunk it. *That would be a terrible end to the day. You are part of our holy quest.* The thief chuckled quietly. *Every holy journey needs a thief along.*

"I believe the writing of The Chronicles of Talvo which warn that evil will first take an interest in the Dayquest, and that in saving the knowledge of truth, the valiant who shall fight will need first destroy the wardens of perdition who will thwart the way of the righteous." The priest sat forward and rested his elbows on the table. He watched as Raben began to gulp his wine, the thirst growing too strong. "I do apologize to you, friend, for I have to be every bit as protective as you would be."

Raben looked to Dorian, not understanding this last statement. "What?"

"I have poisoned you." The priest sat back, leaving his fingers splayed on the table. "And I have poisoned me. Just punishment for so cowardly an act."

"You poisoned me?" Raben stared at him in disbelief, waiting for the priest to tell him otherwise. "You did?" Dorian slowly nodded while closing his eyes.

Raben erupted from where he sat. His chair flew. He dove across the table, breaking it in half, and dragged the priest of Talvo from his chair to the floor. "You and your greeching religion!" Raben pounded his fist into the priest's face. Blood sprayed from Dorian's nose. "You're a priest!" he yelled. "Purify!" He had memories of a priest calling upon the power of the gods to cleanse wounds and neutralize the poisons used in combat. "Purify me, you bastard!" Raben picked the priest halfway up by his collar and threw him back to the floor. Dorian just lay there. "You poisoned yourself as well," he said in disgust, and kicked the fallen man in the side.

"I poisoned my soul," the priest gasped, as his hand wiped blood from his mouth, "when I gave in to this method of killing you." The priest coughed and rolled onto his back. *So you didn't actually poison yourself? You killed me, but will have to live with that stain on your soul! Such a burden!* The thief's face twisted with rage as he thought about the religious man equating the two poisonings that were happening in the room.

Nonsensical screaming erupted from Raben. He tore his sword from its sheath and swept the blade through a massive arc around himself. When it came down he screamed even louder, enabling the blade to cleave all the way through the priest's waist. He felt the blade strike the stone floor beneath the priest as he fell away backwards, dragging the sword with him. He could smell the bitter stink and the smell of salt and iron that emanated from Dorian's innards as they gushed out onto the floor, but Raben lay powerless to move. *The wine. That fool priest has done it. I will die after all.* The thief cried, his body heaving as he silently wept over his own death.

Murmuring voices tumbled through the darkness. There were definitely people speaking or chanting, but they were so muffled that not a single word could be separated or understood from the mass of sound that carried to him.

Raben opened his eyes, but nothing changed. *Maybe I'm dead.* He tried again. He intentionally closed his eyes and then opened them again, searching for even the slightest indication that there was something to see, or that his eyes were indeed open. Completely black. He couldn't even be sure that his eyes were doing anything for him. *The poison. I'm blind.* He remembered his last moments with Dorian. *The priest poisoned me. I died. Is this the Hells?*

The voices grew in volume, remaining muddled yet continuous. Raben tried to focus on just one of the voices, but it sounded as though no voice carried for longer than a short time as it faded, only to be replaced by several others.

He tried to sit up, but his body refused to oblige. He tried to wiggle a finger, but could feel nothing. As he thought about it, he realized that he could feel no part of his body. He wasn't sure if he was lying down, sitting up, or standing. *I am just a soul. I have been killed by treachery, which may befit a man such as me.* He tried to call out, but his voice wasn't there for him either. He couldn't even feel himself breathe. He listened to the voices and let them fill the void around him. They were the only thing that he could focus on. *I can hear. I don't know what I'm hearing, but I can hear. I can't be dead. This cannot be death.*

He didn't sense the passage of time, but would occasionally realize that he'd been listening to the voices for what felt like a tremendous span. He didn't have aching muscles or bones telling him that he'd been locked in the same position for too long, and the voices themselves were ever changing and mesmerizing. Raben found that being adrift in the indistinct voices was relaxing and natural. *This is fine. I could do this forever.* Wherever he had landed, the thief found that not feeling a thing was easy. It was a freedom, this apathy and lack of responsibility, a freedom that he welcomed whole-heartedly.

As he lay basking in the chorus around him, the scent of something sweet drifted slowly into him. He took time in experiencing the scent before he finally recognized that he was smelling fruit. *The Guild hunter! That greeching wench!* He tried to move again, struggling to get an arm or a leg to twitch or shake so that he might use that beginning to get himself out of wherever he was, but there was no response, no feeling. As the scent of fruit grew stronger, the feeling of relaxation fled him. *Trapped, paralyzed, and blind. With that blazing elf woman! I need to get out of here. I cannot have died if she is still here! This is the Hells!* He tried to think back to the night that he'd spoken with her. He tried to think of reasons that she might have overtaken him now. *I've only been doing what she asked. She probably made Dorian poison me. Why? Damn it!*

Raben tried again to discern a single voice from the others, attempting to pick a woman's voice out. He had little luck. The voices were so interwoven that as he focused on a single one, it would join into a second and the two would split only to join others in the same fashion. *How many greeching people are around here?*

Light shot through the darkness. His eyes, which he apparently did have open, clamped shut in pain. White light had poured suddenly into them. He fought to open his eyes again, fighting the brightness by letting them open only into narrow slits, but just as he managed to get them to open, partially tolerating the brilliance that had assailed them, they were covered by a large pinkish hand that came into his vision. He watched helplessly as the broad palm descended on him. He could see the delicate creases in the skin, the yellow fingernails that grew from the stubby fingers. It blocked out the light, covering his eyes almost completely. Raben tried to counter it, but his body was still paralyzed. He could feel the hand. It felt heavy on his face. He tried to cry out. Nothing. The hand lifted slightly and the light returned. It made his eyes burn. The pink palm pushed down again, and returned him to total darkness. Then there was only the voices, and the thick smell of fruit.

Raben jerked awake! *Am I alive? I'm alive!* He sat up, but the pain in his head nearly made him vomit. He lay back down. *Just a dream. That damned priest didn't get me. Fool!* He allowed his head to rock from side to side. To his right was the door he'd come through to get in the secret room, and to his left was a pair of booted feet. Raben looked at them for a moment and then began pushing himself against the floor so he could spin around to see without having to get up. *How the blazes?* He didn't recognize them. The boots didn't belong to Dorian. The priest of Talvo still lay where he was killed, but now there was another man lying dead right next to him. He was dressed exactly like Dorian. *Another priest. Where in the blazes did you come from?* His hands were touching Dorian's head. The man had a massive slash wound reaching from his left shoulder blade down to his waist. *This isn't real. This cannot be real! Greech! Were there people here? The dream! Maybe it was real.* The thought made Raben panic. His stomach clinched painfully inside of him. *Someone was here! The chanting voices. Was that here? Why? Talvo? Why would they save me? Or was it the Guild? I need to leave, now!*

He tried to sit up again, and again the pain was shockingly potent. The world heaved underneath him, but he persisted. Trying to stand, Raben's legs and feet felt foreign to him. He took a step or two towards the cabinet the wine had come from before crashing back to the floor.

He fought to gain his hands and knees. Moaning miserably, Raben vomited. Soured wine and yellowish liquid poured from him. He heaved until there was nothing left and then collapsed to the floor again. After a few moments of lying on the ground clutching his stomach and evening out his breathing, he tried again.

Resolved on making it to the cabinet, he began to crawl. After a tremendous effort, Raben managed to get to the foot of the cabinet. Using it as a support, he pulled himself up and stood, leaning heavily on the wooden armoire. The world disagreed with his decision, lurching under his feet. The thief clung to the cabinet, tearing the doors open. Inside of it sat many bottles and a pitcher. He desperately dragged the pitcher out as he sunk back to the floor. Sniffing at it carefully, he found what he suspected. *Water!* He drank greedily and then fell onto his back, where he lay for some time still fighting the nausea that ebbed through him with each breath.

After sipping the entire pitcher of water, Raben hazarded to sit up again. The pain was considerably less, but the thief was certain that any loud noise would make him severely ill. *Oh, those greeching steel doors.* Just the thought of the noise that the entrance doors made nearly caused him to throw up again. Able to move only on all fours, Raben searched the room for his sword, without luck. After tediously searching the room a second time, he began to think maybe someone had taken it when the other priest had been killed. Then, to his great surprise, he found the weapon in the least likely place, his own scabbard. "How the…who cares?" Raben lay down on his back, unsheathed the weapon, and inspected it. No blood, no dents, chips, or marks. "Von Hessing, you truly know how to pick 'em." *Bet that fool noble is missing this by now.* He smiled, imagining Hessing's anger, waiting for some of his strength to return.

In his search of the room, Raben had discovered parchment and quills. He had not, unfortunately, found any ink. He put great effort into his copy of the map on the wall. He took his time to make sure that every detail was exact, often having to remoisten his quill in Dorian's wet gore. The priest's blood and that of the other man was the only thing that Raben could find to serve as ink. They were still fairly fresh. It didn't seem to him that he had been unconscious for very long. He tried desperately to not look at the men as he poked at their dead bodies with the quill, certain that doing so in his present state would make him sicker than he already was. He scribed out the exact lettering around the map, though he understood none of it. *Looks like magic, but something's wrong. Very advanced, but...maybe ancient. Different.* The thief retraced each letter several times to make certain that he had them all correct. After feeling that he had as perfect a copy of the map as he was capable of creating, he carefully rolled the scroll and tucked it into a hidden pocket inside of his robes.

He then crawled away from the messy corpses of the priests where they lay on the floor, and again gathered his strength. He still had a lot to do. Not the least of which was finding his way out of the temple. *And getting out of this cursed city.* Though his head still throbbed and his stomach lurched with the effort, Raben gained his feet and was able to remain standing. Soon after, he leaned against the wall opposite the ancient map and began casting a spell. "Der ansa Mas engrenon Viri Lossa." His hands shot out before him, and from them came two fluid tracts of fire that snaked up and down the wall, burning it instantly. Raben deftly moved them around on the archaic wall, focusing on the writing and the actual route to be taken by the Dayquest. By the time the spell's power failed, the wall had been scorched to the point that none of the writing could be seen at all, and at least half of the Dayquest route was forever lost.

He lowered his arms and breathed heavily from the effort demanded by the magic.

Now, to get out of here. After a few moments of recollection, the thief realized that he would never remember the path he'd followed to get here. He walked to the door and slowly opened it. It was silent out in the hall. Slipping out into the quiet corridor, he reached into his sleeves and grabbed a dagger with each hand. Keeping them at the ready, he began to make his way up the hall. He remembered the last few turns before arriving at the room, but soon after that, was at a complete loss. He cautiously slipped up to each corner and used the polished edge of a dagger as a mirror to see what was there. After detecting no one, he would slide around the corner and make his way up another square, blank hallway. Soon Raben was passing by doors. He occasionally stopped to listen for any sign of the priests that lived there, but refrained from opening any of them. *I've met enough priests for a while,* he thought. *No need to drag any others into my business.* Eventually, he arrived at a stairwell that went up and down. He pondered going down for a moment before beginning a painstakingly slow ascent of the stairwell.

A circular well, it would be simple for anyone above to see him, and easier still for them to attack. With his daggers at the ready, Raben climbed the stairs drawing no more notice than would a ghost. At the top of the curving stairwell, the thief found still more corridors. He cautiously passed through these, arriving at yet another staircase, which he climbed in the same manner as he had the last. Upon reaching the top of the second staircase, Raben could see that he was near the ground level. He remembered this part. The stone was a lighter color, and was interlinked decoratively. Using his memory of the passages to take him to the ground level, he was suddenly forced to stop. He finally encountered the priests. He heard a large number of them having a discussion, though he heard nothing about Dorian or the other priest that lay dead below.

"I misread two scriptures this morning and thought Sire Ferin was going to beat me bloody," said one of the young men.

"He might, that one. It was he who asked me to come to this practice after he caught me out off position during a battle drill," laughed another.

"Battle drills," scoffed another. "What battle are we preparing for?"

"It's ceremonial these days," said one of the previous voices. "We're simply appeasing Talvo these days. There is not likely going to be another White War."

"That's certain enough," answered another laughing, "but we may as well do the practice so that Mathias here can escape a thumping at Sire Ferin's hands."

Nobody seemed alarmed or the least bit perturbed. They seemed to be casually carrying on as they talked about the morning, and what they planned on doing with the rest of their day, but said not a single word about either of the dead priests. *They must not go down into the lower levels very much.*

Raben sat at the top of the final staircase for some time. It was a much needed rest. His stomach pain and nausea had ebbed away, but he felt exhausted. From what he could hear, it was the middle of the day. Knowing this, Raben suddenly felt the gnawing ache of hunger. Growling inside of him, the thief found the sound to be surprisingly loud. He kneaded his empty stomach as he eavesdropped on the priests. Inspecting his surroundings thoroughly, he found that the doorways that led from room to room had a lip over them that might be wide enough to stand on, or grab on to. They were no more than eight or nine knuckles deep; it would be tough.

Using his dagger to see into the chamber outside of the stairwell, Raben watched the priests for some time. He heard them mention bringing some equipment from another room so that they could have a weapons practice. He waited on them, watching as they prepared to get the weapons they would need in order to conduct the exercise. Once they'd gone, Raben took a deep breath, and sprinted across the room, vaulting himself into the air. Landing squarely on the lip over the door they'd exited through, he stood four reaches off of the ground, steadying himself. He pushed his back firmly against the wall, and waited for the men to return. Nausea swept over him once again. He began to take measured breaths, trying to calm his stomach before they returned. Soon enough, all of the priests marched back into the room bearing various weapons. Immediately after the last man entered the room, Raben stepped off of the ledge. Twisting as he fell, so that he was now facing the wall, he caught himself on the lip and swung himself into the next room. Allowing his arms to graze the ceiling he caught the corresponding lip over the doorway in the next room, and let the momentum he'd built up carry him until he stood on the lip over the door in the room they'd just come from.

He saw that he was in some sort of storage chamber. Five A-shaped racks stood full of weapons and armor, each one about five reaches in height and ten or twelve paces in length. They were loaded with a massive assortment of weapons. Swords and maces, flails and morning stars hung from pegs in the top beam of the racks, while spears and pole arms leaned against the tall sloped racks, their blades just reaching over the top beam. Axes leaned against every wall, being both the choice weapons for the priest's of Talvo and His symbol.

Towering over the weaponry, Raben could see that there was a vent of some sort. It was square; easily large enough for him to get into, but it was at least ten full reaches off the ground. *I should have communed for my spells. That was damned foolish!*

Raben would have preferred to simply hover up to the vent using his magic, but after using a spell, a mage must complete a specific meditation where he visits his host spirits who imbue the caster with the ability of the incantation. Raben had used his ability to levitate to enter and exit the inn unseen, and now had to come up with a more secular way to reach the vent. Looking over the racks of equipment, Raben quickly decided on a course of action. *Who knows when those priests will burst in on me.*

He dropped lightly to the floor at the side of the doorway. Passing quickly through the racks of weapons, he chose a massive polearm. The weapon was about six reaches long, and was capped with a massive bladed head, similar to that of a battle ax. Using the weapon, he easily vaulted back up onto the lip of the doorway. He held the polearm across his thighs for a moment, adjusting its balance, and making sure that his stomach was calm after the acrobatics. The metallic din of the priests of Talvo clashing their weapons together in the next room made Raben's head throb. When he felt steady enough to begin, he leapt over onto the top of the nearest weapon rack. The hanging weapons jingled in response to Raben's weight, but so stealthy was he, that they barely shook. He moved carefully to the middle of the rack, keeping his weight completely centered over the beam, trying to reduce any response that the many weapons might make, thus drawing attention to him. This proved difficult as he stepped around the number of pointed spears and bladed pole arms that were crowding the racks. Once he reached the opposite end of the rack, he looked up and found that he needed to move two more racks to the right in order to be almost directly under the vent. Bending at the knees where he stood, Raben lowered himself to the top beam of the rack so that he could lay the polearm across from the rack he was on to the one to the right of it. After a few moments of adjusting the unsteady weapon, Raben had created a staff-thick bridge. Without the pole arm to steady him, he wobbled as he stood, the racked weapons answering with their metallic response. Holding his arms out to each side, Raben did his best to balance himself as he stepped onto the polearm. Tentatively, the thief lowered his weight onto the weapon. It immediately bent under him, nearly causing him to fall. *The most effective alarm ever.* Raben imagined himself falling into the two racks of weapons. *My head doesn't need that noise anymore than they do.* He quickly stepped across the polearm to the next rack of weapons and once he arrived, he again used the weapon to cross to the rack beyond it in the exact same manner. The thief now stood beneath his only escape route.

The vent was built into the wall just below where it met the ceiling. Raben was four or five reaches off of the ground and needed another four or five in order to reach the vent. He walked to the end of the weapon rack towards the wall that was opposite the vent. He memorized each step as he took it, not wanting to accidentally kick any of the razor edged blades that were propped on the rack he'd need to run on. Holding the polearm, the thief again adjusted it until he was holding it firmly at the bottom end. The blade he kept over him like a five-reach-long axe. He breathed deeply a few times, and waited to hear the priests of Talvo in the next room. Once the clash of another mock battle began, Raben ran the length of the weapon rack using the memorized steps, his feet nimble as they passed amidst the many long weapons leaning against it. He hacked downward with the polearm as if cutting wood, burying it into the top of the rack as well as he could, and then leapt using the long pole to vault from the top of the rack towards the vent. The head of the polearm was securely rooted in the groove made by its blade, securing it against sliding to a side. The haft of the long axe carried him upwards. Raben twisted his body until he was upside down and when he heard the wood begin to give he pushed up and off of the long weapon. It snapped as he began to hurtle through the air, reducing the thrust that he meant to gain from the final shove. *Greeching Hells!* Raben had wanted to flip back over so that he could grab for the vent, but it was his legs that ended up entering it while his upper torso smacked helplessly into the wall below. He began to panic; his legs kicking and arms waving. He nearly blacked out when he impacted the wall. Suddenly his left foot caught in something. Raben hooked his ankle on whatever it was and hung from it for a few moments. His head was throbbing from the pain. He felt blood dripping from his nose. Luckily, he still heard the battle going on in the next room. He slowly pulled himself up into the vent where he lay for quite some time. His foot had found one of a few widely spaced bars that had apparently been placed to deter their use as hallways. *Don't know what in the Hells they were trying to keep out of here. Must have rats the size of wolves.* Raben wiped blood from his mouth. He could feel pain burning in his face. His head was pounding from both bashing into the wall and the residual poison still coursing through his veins. He cupped his face in his hands. He could feel his nose swelling. He'd clearly broken it and maybe loosened a tooth or two. *No time.*

He climbed through the vent system as quickly as his battered body would move, and soon discovered what it was for. He was covered in soot, and smelled like a campfire, but after pulling himself through the char-filled tunnels for a while he stopped caring. He arrived at an exit. He nearly crawled right out of the opening, plummeting to the ground outside. Were it not for the sunlight that suddenly struck him he might have blindly crawled out of the vent. It was easily forty reaches off of the ground, but that was nothing his rope and darkness couldn't correct.

Raben rested at the top of the chimney vent until night had set in. Every now and again he would have to push himself out to breathe as a long menacing cloud of smoke and fumes would pour out past him. For the most part, however, it was the most restful time he'd had in the last couple of days. He marveled at how useful a grappling hook would have been if he'd known that those bars were in that vent. He wondered if anyone had found Dorian and the other priest. *Who was that other priest? What had killed him?* Raben thought about many things that had transpired of late. Most of all, he wondered why he was still in Liveport. *Hadn't I resolved to leave here once or twice?* He scratched his sooty head. He really had no clue why he hadn't left yet. Then he arrived at a worse problem. *When did I get to this city? Where was I before here? What have I been doing?* Raben applied himself to it, and after a long while he realized the frightening truth. His skin prickled and tightened around his abused frame. Nausea erupted from the rigid knot that wound in his stomach. *Blazing gods! Who am I?*

Sitting in his dingy room at The Copper Pot, the thief slowly took inventory of everything he owned. Item by item, he removed them from his travel pack, inspected them, and then set them on the nearby rickety table. Placing the last of his daggers in a neat row, he looked at his entire material possession, and felt confused. He knew where he'd gotten none of this equipment except the silks, the Dayquest map, and Hessing's swords. He could somehow recall that he'd been trained by the Guild, but could not picture a single instructor, nor a single lesson. The idea hung over him like an ethereal debt that he'd picked up without knowing, yet required a very substantive payment. Every time Raben looked back to remember his time with the Guild, he came up with nothing. He knew only that they'd taught him. Nothing more.

Mindlessly grabbing up one of his sickles, he tossed it spinning up into the air. It spun quickly, sending flecks of reflected light playing about the room. As it fell back to him, Raben dexterously picked it from the air. Over and over, the thief spun the weapon into the air and let it fall easily back into his hand. Soon he became bored, and juggled two with one hand. He was working on getting a dagger into the mix when he realized that he was avoiding the problem at hand. Catching his weapons, he held a sickle in each hand. He paced from the anxiety that his lack of memories brought. He had no real recollection of anything.

47

No childhood, no training, no father, no mother. Nothing. It was as if he'd just been born on the streets of Liveport. That thought made him smile in spite of his mood. *Born on the streets of Liveport! After all I'm...How old am I?* The smile vanished. *I'm Raben. That's all I can say about myself. I'm Raben and I can kill.* He gripped his sickles so tightly that his knuckles popped. *Greeching misery! This is simply not possible. Someone knows these answers. Where can I go?* The thief tried to figure out somewhere that he could go for help. *I'm tied to this damned Dayquest.* He paced briefly, slowing to a halt as he recalled Dorian's words. *The mages once claimed to know a lot about the map and the prophecy. Maybe they do know that. Maybe they know about me. Maybe I just need to sleep. Maybe it was an injury. A battle, or when I whumped into the wall in the temple. No.* He could remember the past two days with perfect clarity. *There was something wrong before the temple. I was just too busy to notice.*

The only person who had known his name was the woman from the Guild. *The only one. Besides me, it's that greeching wench and her fruit stench. If she even does. Never even said it. Can we assume I know who you are, or whatever she said. I can't find her, bloody Guild hunter.* Raben retrieved his whetstone and started sharpening his sickles. *I don't need to find her. She's eventually going to come to me.* The scrape of his weapons on the stone irritated him, sending shivers up his spine. *She'll probably come to me when it'll greech me good and hard. Perfect!*

Having arrived at the understanding that he could do nothing further at the moment to gain information about himself, Raben picked the Dayquest map up off of the table. Tossing his barely-sharpened sickle and whetstone onto the bed, he sank to the floor, spreading the map out before him. He poured over it, letting his fingers slowly feel their way across its surface as if to suddenly gain a full understanding through his touch. There was something he wasn't seeing and he needed to know what it was. He was compelled in a way that he didn't understand. He was being pushed by something, making this quest paramount, even more important than his own survival. He stared incessantly at the words that ringed the outside of the map feeling that they were the key. *They look like magic. This map, who I am. Blazes! I don't want to go deal with wizards.* Suddenly, it was dark.

Raben started when his candle burned out. *Someone's here!* He quickly slipped over to the table and picked up two daggers. Sweat instantly built on his forehead. He felt a little weak from the surprise. He hadn't fully recovered from the events in the temple of Talvo, and now he shook slightly as he waited for the oncoming attack, but nothing happened. After standing in the dark for a short while, he felt convinced that he was still alone. It was quiet, and nothing seemed to be moving. He lit a hand lantern and inspected the candle. The wax had doused the wick. Raben shut his lantern and sat back down in the dark, his daggers within easy reach. Breathing deeply, he tried to calm down.

Letting his mind free itself of thought, he meditated on his spell casting. It came very easily. Soon he felt the presence of his host come upon him. He focused himself on learning the method to each spell he was allowed, and reveled as he felt the language of magic etch itself into his thoughts. His hands moved unconsciously as they wove through the somatic portion of the spell in practice. A grin spread across the face of the man as he completed his learning, as he felt the power of his magic pulse through him. A short span after he'd started, Raben felt strong again.

He used one of his spells to cast a ward of security on the door and only window in his room. An aura of magic hung like a curtain just inside each portal, and if any living thing larger than a mouse tried to pass through it, they'd learn what little protection skin was against magical fire. Raben then repacked all of his belongings tightly into his travel pack and slipped into bed. *At least I can count on me,* he thought. *After all, I am all I have.* He sneered cynically into the darkness and laughed quietly for no one to hear.

The agitated complaint of a large beast of burden jolted Raben from his rest. He leapt from his bed, sword in hand, and moved near the window, careful to avoid his ward. A merchant was whipping the stubborn thing, insisting that it make its way up the dusty street, but the bulky ox had other designs. It let out another complaint. Raben shook his head slowly while breathing out a deep sigh. He left the window, pulled on a soft, clean, black robe, secured his daggers on his arms and legs, strapped on his swords and sickles, picked up his pack, and started for the door. He smirked briefly as he dispelled his wards, finding it ironic that he should again have the opportunity to foolishly be his own downfall. For a change of pace, the thief decided to take the stairs rather than levitate out the window.

He had prepaid for three days, but felt the need to be constantly moving. Not to mention the fact that he had a lot to take care of and he wasn't really sure where he'd end up. *After all,* he thought, *wizards are a testy bunch. I might end up on the bottom of the sea.*

Raben purchased a few pieces of local fruit to eat as he passed through the city. He used the exchange to gather his bearings, feel normal, and find out where a mage's guild might be.

"That'd be the cursed fang that sickens the land near t'Northgate," complained a vendor at the city bazaar. "Them greechin' sorcerers." He stopped, as if doused with cold water. "Pardon my tongue, but they aren't usually up to no good." The man was rustic, had a pair of wool overalls, a long-sleeved wool shirt on, and jaybird blue eyes. Farmers were famous for being superstitious, yet having a slight truth to their tales. "But if it's them you want, they'll be just a couple of streets inside of the Northgate." The farmer ran his hands through his thinning hair in exasperation, and nodded as Raben laid a few coins on the cart between them.

Continuing his trek through Liveport, Raben looked at everything, really inspected it. For a waterfront city, it was surprisingly clean. The air smelled good, filled with the salty smell of the sea mixed with the many eateries that specialized in the local catches. Seagulls glided overhead, screeching out their competitive calls, always facing the water, only flapping their wings when the constant breeze provided by the ocean let up, or when racing to steal bits of fish that local sellers tossed into back alleys. The streets were well kept, and the people looked generally happy. *Must be because they have such a view each day.* Peering down a few of the larger thoroughfares, it was easy to see the deep blue horizon line of the sea. Liveport was surrounded by water to the east, west, and south, and all of the roads looked as though they would eventually end on a beach.

Whitewashed buildings stood perfectly straight along the side of each street, and the alleys were well maintained. Very few of them had excessive refuse in them. He could see how the Ward of Worship loomed over all of the other buildings in Liveport, and that second to them were the inns and eateries of the noble district. "Nice greeching place to live, I guess," he said to himself, reminded that he belonged nowhere. *Might be worth seeing the Ward of Worship in the light.* He shook his head, discarding the idea. *No need to go back so someone can recognize me. Doorman from Talvo's keep would probably walk right up to me.* He looked at the many open faced shops that lined every street that he walked along. It seemed inconceivable that so many different businesses could exist, rather than only the best of them. He figured that eventually there had to be a few shops that represented the lowest cost, nearest, and highest quality. *After that, why would others even be there? Loyalty.*

He looked back over his shoulder at the Ward of Worship, easily picking out the cathedral to Arsonin and the ivory tower of the blue god. *They all need to have their faith and loyalty. Yet, what do they really have?* He looked up each of the alleys he passed, and though clear of rubbish, he could easily find beggars and hobos that slept there. *I suppose every city must have your sort. I may join you one day. Easier than what I'm doing.* He watched a particular beggar, a young man, sit up and stretch his back after a contented yawn. The man casually climbed to his feet and began asking for a pittance from nearby vendors and passing townsfolk. *You'd argue that I needed to see you on a cold day, I'm sure.* Raben continued on.

He left the bazaar and the marketplace behind, and began passing by quieter, more obscure locations. He saw that Liveport had a number of lending houses where the rich must operate their finances. A large domed building, almost as large as a number of the buildings in the noble district, housed a trading house that obviously owned a number of ships, based on the placard that hung by their door: A well dressed man standing astride four ships as though they were charging stallions. *Hmmmm. Wonder what it takes to get started in a business like that?* Raben guessed that it was something that he had very little of. *Money.* He passed by the trading house and soon could see the building that he was looking for, tucked in among a number of unmarked, quiet buildings.

As soon as the mage's guild came into view, it became obvious why it had a bad reputation. The wizards of

Liveport had foolishly decided that the four-story building that should house their studies be the only black structure within the city. In every other way it matched the other buildings surrounding it, but it loomed ominously and seemed fierce and evil next to the white of all of the others.

The door was a polished and stained plank of Hack Oak. Hack Oak was a dark colored wood that was famous for its strength and density. Smiths loved it for its long hot burn in the forge, and builders loved it for its strength. These wizards loved it, however, because it was easily stained dark enough to not be contradictory to the rest of the black building. *This city is littered with valuable doors.*

The knocker on the oak door was a length of wrought iron that had been bent into some arcane rune. Raben lifted it, and after a brief inspection, set it firmly against the door a few times. The result was silence. The heavy knocker made no noise at all when it struck the door. *Ofcourse, leave it to wizards!* Raben let the knocker fall to its resting position. *A silent knocker...fools.*

Nothing could have prepared the thief for what happened next. The door opened, and a gaunt man appeared inside. Before Raben could even speak, he looked the thief over, pulled his green robe tightly about himself, screamed a high pitched note for as long as his lungs could last, and then slammed the door shut. The thief stood, having changed nothing about his person while this went on. He was starting to become immune to strange things, he was quite sure. Raben turned around to see if he, alone, had witnessed the odd occurrence, and found that he had. Nobody else was in the street. It was early in the day and near a main gate of the city. *How could there be no one?* Raben turned to face the door again. *Maybe these are the wicked folk. After all, everyone else seems to think so.*

Cautiously lifting the knocker again, Raben decided that keeping a hand on his sword made him more comfortable.

Before he let the knocker go, he heard arcane mumbling behind him. *Spell!* He recognized the type that it was. *Attack!* His sword preceded his body as it twisted to face his opponent. Gathering the momentum of the spin, Raben hurled the reach-and-a-half blade at the mage he now saw. Hoping for nothing more than distracting the caster's spell, he dived to a side of the door, just in case the spell had been completed. Rolling up to his feet, the thief saw two more wizards materialize in the street. He had no time to marvel at the fact that he'd skewered the first with the thrown sword.

Daggers flew from each of his hands. He heard one man yelp as he was struck, but the other continued casting confidently. His words carried forcefully, echoing through the street and nearby alleyways. Raben tumbled across the dusty street to the body of the first mage. Yanking his sword free of the still-warm corpse, he prepared to charge the casting wizard. A brilliant flash blinded the thief just before the convulsions hit. He felt his hand searing on his sword hilt as his body spasmed. He balled up and fell on the ground. So painful and continuous were the knots forming in his muscles that he couldn't even yell out. Suddenly, it was over and Raben could breathe again. Despite the pain, and the smell of his own burnt flesh, he felt fear most of all. He heard more casting, and lurched to his feet, unable to get a real view of the caster through the yellow-green spots in his eyes from the lightning. He raised his sword and charged. Just as the wizard was finishing his spell, the thief lashed out furiously and swept the mage's head from his shoulders with a lucky swing. The headless sorcerer fell lifeless to the ground. The ball of fire meant to consume Raben passed by him and hit the front of the mage's guild. The explosion was terrific. Splinters of the once great Hack Oak door blew out across the street, peppering both Raben and the remaining mage, who'd been wounded by the thief's first dagger throw. The thief let go of his sword and immediately two more daggers appeared in his hands.

The wizard, however, had raised his hands in submission. He was staring at the sword floating next to his attacker. Shocked to see the blade hanging in the air, Raben tumbled away from it, but as he regained his feet the sword still hung in the air just a few knuckles to his right. The exact same distance away from him that he'd released it. Raben reached out and grasped the weapon, then let it go again. The blade continued floating. Cautiously, he approached the mage, not knowing which to give a more wary eye to, his opponent or his own sword. Even as he walked, the blade, Hessing's blade, floated along side of him as if ready to strike. In anger, the thief ignored the hovering blade for moment.

"I only wanted to talk to you greeching fools!" yelled Raben as he pushed the wizard over backwards. "Now you've made me kill!" Foamy spit shot from his mouth as he yelled. "Fools!" *Everywhere I go, I run into these self important fools. They think they know everything about me, and everything that is going on. All they know is battle and death. And I am learning quickly.*

The wizard bled from tens of small wounds. His green robes shredded from the explosion. He was middle aged with graying brown hair that was almost waist length, as was the fashion of the wizards. His eyes were a bizarre shade of purple that only the mages seemed to posses. *Looks dead.* He was thin and pathetic looking prostrated on the ground before Raben. The thief plucked his sword from the air almost fearfully, and leveled the blade at his victim.

"What's your name?" He leaned in as he asked, letting the blade close towards the man's chest.

The wizard hesitated briefly. "I am called Venit."

"Why in the blazing Hells did you attack me?"

Again, the wizard hesitated, looking thoughtful before answering. "He…" Venit motioned his head towards the decapitated wizard, "…thought you were the dark before day, the evil to precede the Dayquest. He said his religious brothers knew of you." The wizard shook his head. "Before I could voice an opinion to the contrary, he transported us into the street."

"I'll give you two options." Raben held out two fingers to demonstrate the number of options. His middle finger flexed leaving only one. "You either die on my sword, or submit to a spell I'll cast on you." He started casting without waiting for an answer. A few moments later, Venit looked up to the thief, his eyes glazed over, and smiled.

"Forgive me for my rudeness." Venit smiled again. The grin, a result of the enchantment he'd just given in to, looked like a mockery of friendship. "How exactly can I help you?"

"Much better. Take me to the most knowledgeable of your order at once!" Raben barked.

"That," said the mage pleasantly, "must be me, for I am all that is left at the moment. Everyone else is out of the city for a council, or," he gestured to the carnage in the street, "has been most grievously slain." Venit clasped his nimble, bleeding hands together. "That's a good thing for you that the highest of the order wasn't here, friend, or you would surely have perished in the battle."

"What floor is the library on?" The mage pointed to the top of the building. "Any enchantments I need fear?" Venit shook his head. "Pick up the bodies and do something about the door." A nod. "And get someone to heal us," finished Raben, as he passed into the mage's guild.

Soon Raben was picking his way carefully through innumerable volumes of ancient texts and reprinted books of learning. He moved from volume to volume reading each book's spine, trying to find something that might indicate helpfulness. He had no idea what he was really looking for, as he'd hoped to have some ancient, age-wizened wizard offer him the answers to his dilemmas. Much to his dismay, he realized that many of the books had titles that seemed completely unrelated to the contents inside. Perhaps they were the authors, or some kind of artistic touch, but they served only to slow the thief down as he researched.

"Ah! There you are, friend! A healer." Venit ushered in an elderly woman. She was hunched at the shoulders and appeared to need a cane, though she had none. Her wrinkly face looked leathery from years of use. Her hands reached out to Raben, and after only a few moments he felt much better. After she'd chanted for a short time, and traced her fingers along the many wounds that had marked his skin, the only evidence that he'd been in any battle at all was the dried blood on his ripped clothing. Venit looked equally improved. In fact, he'd gone and put on a new robe while Raben was getting healed. Taking the healer by the arm, the mage showed her back out of the room and presumably out of the building. A short while later, he returned with food and drink. "Well then, while you eat, why don't I get what you're after? What topic were you researching?"

"How long do we have before the other wizards return?"

"Four days."

"Chronicles of Talvo: Remembrance 4:16

Kizzer Anaxim looked up from the sacrifice made by his brethren, being mighty and righteous, and spoke to the peaceful peoples that remained in the land.

'A day will come to you, when you wish to recall that time that is only spoken of in tales told by your mother's mother's mother. It was a time of peace and joy and simplicity. You will want to know how that time began, and how it can begin again. You will have to embrace the light of day and the best among you will have to join a quest. It will be the Dayquest. This crusader will depart from the very gate of the first temple of man, and pass through the trials that only the truest can pass. But beware! Evil will first take an interest in the Dayquest, and that in saving the knowledge of the truth, the valiant who shall fight will need first destroy the wardens of perdition who will thwart the way of the righteous. This darkness will root itself in you, and will act among you. It will go with you even as you seek the light, and bear your own thoughts and armament against you. Have faith, and know the result is good. The sword shall draw the foemen, the hero shall valiantly fight, the faith shall conquer evil, and all will be as it was. In perfect remembrance.'" Venit handed the book to Raben after he finished reading it again. "There's a picture of the temple and some of the holy weapons in here as well."

Raben looked through the tome. It was fairly new and in good condition. Obviously a copy. "A priest poisoned me because he was sure that I was the evil spoken of here, and then you attacked me on the same premise." Raben raised his eyes to look at the wizard. "Why?"

"Well, there are parts of the history that goes along with the passage that few commoners have ever seen," Venit said as he leaned forward and flipped through a couple of pages. "Like that."

Staring for a long while Raben did not understand at first. "Greeching bloody Hells! That's the sword!" He stood up and unsheathed Hessing's sword. "This sword! It's not even mine. I stole it from…" He held it out in front of himself as if he were parrying an unseen blow. "Oh flaming damnation!" He dropped it, letting it crash into the floor. "I killed a priest with the thing. I'm sure to be punished by the gods." He sat back down heavily and with thumb and forefinger, rubbed his eyes. "Damn." *My sword. Hessing's sword. I can't believe this is it! The artifact. The sword! I didn't even want to steal it. Why did I take it? Damn it all!*

"Cheer up, friend. Destiny is destiny. You are prophesied. You obviously feel bad about stealing the sword." Venit scooted his chair next to Raben's. *I don't care that I stole it, Buffoon! I care that it is part of this whole mess, that it is dragging me into the middle of some damned prophecy.* "Give the sword back if you can. That would change the outcome, I suppose." He waited silently for a response from Raben. "Or perhaps we've all misjudged the situation and you are actually the valiant and not the evil. What do you think?"

"Can you hold this place against intruders?" Raben reached down and picked the sword from the cold stone floor. *Greeching boiling Hells! I need to see him. Now! Give it back, or get some answers. He'd better know why in all the Hells I am suddenly involved in this greeching mess!*

"Yes. I could hold this particular building against an army." Venit stood and crossed his arms over his chest. "Something about you, however, completely disarmed our protective wards at the front door."

Raben regarded the wizard momentarily. "Let no one but myself into the tower until I return." *Blazing noble. You can have the greeching sword back.*

Jogging across the city, Raben wrestled with the idea of being either "the evil" or "the valiant." None of this made sense, especially when he considered that he didn't even know who he really was, or where he'd come from. *How could I appear out of nothing, and then suddenly be the object of some ancient prophecy? I wasn't the first to show interest in the prophecy. They already had the quest in the works. The text said evil would be interested first. But I have the sword. I stole the sword. That seems evil, but isn't. I didn't know that this was the sword. The one sword that was in the prophecy. I was just looking for...what? I was there for this thing. I don't even know why. Hells! I'm certainly not valiant. I don't give a greeching damn if they find the True Knowledge or not. Hells!*

It was late afternoon and the city was bustling. People seemed to get out of the running man's way as if a charging bull preceded him. In no time at all, Raben was standing in front of the large home of Von Hessing. Without waiting, he hammered his fist on the beautiful front door. It opened almost immediately, and two guards stood just inside. "Hessing," was all that the blustering thief said, and the guards, with no further instruction, led him to the noble.

He was scribbling furiously on one of a stack of scrolls that littered his desk. The large sea captain looked ridiculous crouched over the tiny wooden desk.

"It has taken you longer than I expected." Von Hessing didn't even look up from his work.

"Do you even know who I am?" Raben asked. *Why aren't you shocked to see me?*

"The sword hadn't taken a life from anyone in centuries. Once someone kills with it, that person is bonded to it until death." Hessing rose up behind from the desk, but moved in no threatening way. "To kill you at the Golden Capon would have been a terrible mistake. We need the sword on the quest, so I just had you closely watched since then." A wry smile formed on the noble's face. "Once you stole the sword, I knew you had a part in the quest."

"You've known that I was some part of this nonsense for days?" Raben was yelling, incredulity fueling rage. Suddenly, Von Hessing seemed to be the person to blame. "Why didn't you tell me?" The thief pointed out the window to the city spreading out before them. "Everyone that can swing a sword wants to kill me, and are very nearly succeeding! All of them are convinced that I am the greeching evil of you're damned greeching prophecy." Raben leapt over to the window throwing the shutters open. "I'm the greeching hero, you asses!" His yell was heard for several blocks.

"Settle down, thief. I'm the hero. I am the valiant that is spoken of in the prophecy. Everyone assumed, perhaps incorrectly, that the sword would go with the valiant. An oversight. And yet…not. You're going too." The noble wore an unpleasant mask, but his irritation was being smoothed over by the poor manner in which his guest was receiving the news.

"Going where?" Raben closed the window and turned to face Hessing. He felt a little calmer after yelling, but still continued glowering at the warrior.

"The Dayquest of course," Hessing remarked, as if he'd expected this outcome all along. "You're the bait." The huge noble laughed quietly as the thief's scowl deepened. "You and the spoils from your dashing thievery are going to draw the enemy to you rather than me, and therefore ensure that the quest is successful."

"Bait? To the Hells with you, Lord Von Hessing. Why would I go just to be the greeching bait? The bloody sword shall draw the bloody foemen. Fool!" Raben produced a sickle, which he held tightly while he considered killing Hessing.

"Two reasons, thief." Von Hessing sat back down behind his desk and reclined in his chair. "First, it is said that the True Knowledge at the end of the quest restores any man to find it. Perhaps you'd not be remembered as a thief and murderer if you found it, though I doubt you'd care overmuch if you were remembered through the ages as a savage murderer." The noble sat forward, placing his hands flat on the desk. "But the real reason is this. That sword you decided to steal will draw every enemy for a thousand leagues right to you, over and over again, until the quest is completed. You can either further that end, or live a long and fruitful life, ever hunted, ever sought, forever tortured."

"I'll throw the sword in a ditch, or sell it to some fool knight," responded Raben, but he knew he couldn't. He knew in his depths that he couldn't part with the weapon. *Gah! I hate this! Why me? Why? What is this?*

"You can't, and if you die, you'll be trapped in the sword to serve its magic for eternity."

"Unless the Dayquest is completed?" Hessing nodded. Raben knew it to be true. "Hells!" The thief walked across the room toward the door, turned around and stood still, glaring at Hessing. A long silence passed while the two men stared at one another. Raben's eyes dropped from the intent gaze of the noble to the floor, where he contemplated his situation. Another long silence passed. "I just had a battle in the streets with half of the mage's guild. Everyone will know of it soon, and I'll be openly feared and despised. How can I even get into the Dayquest? So many nobles, and knights, and all of their righteous garbage." At that moment, the door to the room opened up, and a guard filled the door.

"The sheriff is here, and he wishes to capture him," the guard said, while pointing at Raben. "He says this fellow killed several wizards in cold blood and was seen by hundreds fleeing the scene to your home." The guard waited in a neutral stance. "He has a large militia with him."

"Tell the sheriff," Hessing instructed, "that I..." he slowed down his speech and looked from the guard to Raben and back, "...have already taken this villain into custody and am presently forcing him into servitude of the city." He looked at thief and nodded deliberately. Understanding, Raben sneered and nodded back almost imperceptibly. After the guard left Hessing decided to follow in order to reinforce his will. "The sheriff will need it," he said, "and no one will be that upset about the wizards." Hessing was out of the room for a while, and at one point the thief could hear the muffled argument being carried on between the noble and the lawman. He also heard heavy steps just before the door swung open.

"The sheriff is gone." Hessing said as he returned. "He's not happy about it. He swears you'll be the death of me."

"The death of you, huh? I think all of you people will be the death of me. How am I protected in all of this?" Raben had sat down under the window to listen to the sheriff and his men leaving. He looked up to hear Hessing's answer. "How will I be safe from them?"

"You will be my personal servant. My sword bearer." A narrow grin slowly spread on Hessing's face.

"No! I mean what actually protects me from all of these idiots who think I'm the evil, and not the sword. Every one of them will want the fame of gutting me because they think I'm the evil from your damned prophecy."

"First things first!" Hessing growled. "I think you are the evil! You've lied to me, stolen from me, and killed those I know. You deserve no protection, nor the honor of going on this quest." Hessing marched over and stood just in front of Raben, looming over the crouched form. "But, if you demand extra security from the knights and nobles that will be forced to tolerate you, then take comfort in the knowledge that you have the only map of the Dayquest in your possession." Hessing began to turn away, but immediately swiveled back, this time with a sword in hand. "But, if you so much as threaten one of the members of the Dayquest, I will lead them all to your slaughter." Hessing waggled the sword over Raben, holding it in both hands. He moved slowly, as if he were contemplating Raben's execution.

"Don't worry, your highness. I wouldn't hurt any of the chosen." The thief's voice was thick with sarcasm. He crawled out from under the man and asked, "So how will this work? Am I your prisoner or can I prepare the way I would like to?"

Von Hessing lowered his great sword and explained that Raben had to stay in his house for the next few days, and then they would call the meeting of the Dayquest. The noble mentioned that the meeting was the launch of the holy quest from the ancient temple outside of the city. Though the temple was the actual beginning of the quest, there was a ceremony involved, and the townspeople would send the questers off from the gates of Liveport. Raben was shocked to find that they already knew where to begin. He'd thought that he alone had discovered that information in the wizard's copy of The Chronicles of Talvo.

Hessing showed the thief upstairs and gave him a room. "Two guards will follow you everywhere." The noble

Jason J. Bilicic

looked to his guards as he spoke, pouring his authority into his gaze. He then looked back to his prisoner's room, intent on the window. "Don't leave the house. I'm sure the sheriff left crossbowmen to kill you."

"How do you know the sheriff has crossbowmen out there?" Raben peered out of his new bedroom window, searching for guards. *Nothing.* "I don't see anyone."

"It's what I would have done."

66

Life at Von Hessing's house was the most comfortable that Raben had ever known. There was a cooking staff, a working bath, plenty of room, and every piece of furniture had more padding than the thief ever knew was possible. He was almost able to forget that he had somehow thieved his way into the center of the mess he was in.

Every morning a servant would bring a tray of meticulously prepared succulent foods to Raben's room upstairs and then return later to collect the dirty dishes and inform the thief that his bath had been prepared. Raben would luxuriate in the hot water, lounging as he had never done before, taking in every moment and holding onto it until the water began to cool down. He would then climb from the massive tub and find his freshly laundered robes and shined boots outside the door. Slipping into those he would then check his gear, out of sheer habit, and perform a few practice sequences with his weapons, though they were only half-hearted while so much lounging and relaxing was to be had. Afterwards he would sit on Hessing's back porch which overlooked the noble's garden and drink the light beverages that the servants prepared. It was magnificent. Hessing trapped him in paradise, and then seemingly disappeared so that the thief could enjoy it.

He rarely saw the noble for the first two days, and hadn't seen him at all on the third day. On the morning of the fourth, Raben lounged on the back porch, listening to the birds in Hessing's personal garden, waiting for the fantastic lunch that would inevitably be prepared by Dodge, the house cook. He'd asked for, and been presented, a needle and black thread and was just finishing the stitching of the many slashes and cuts in his oldest robes. He only had two robes left that hadn't been thrashed in combat; he was wearing one set. His two guards were presently lounging just behind him on either side of the door. Raben had them sharpening weapons, which they seemed more than happy to do, though the thief questioned the quality of their work. They had neither armor, nor shields, and seemed to Raben to be more of a status symbol than capable warriors. The swords they carried were short and pointed, and were only for close combat. Each time they unsheathed their weapons, they carried them as though they were leaden. Raben was certain he could dice them in seconds. All three men were content and deeply involved in what they were doing. So much so, they never detected the silent stranger.

"Pardon me good sirs…" A muffled tear interrupted the quiet, followed by a loud, fleshy pop. An arm and a ripped-up, partially attached shoulder flew past Raben, streaming crimson until it landed in the grass before him. "…have you seen …" The rest of the shredded guard followed. As Raben dropped from his chair, tumbling out into the lawn next to him, it was obvious that the guard thrown before him had no throat left. "…anyone with a map to Rhokar?" The second guard just barely cleared his weapon of its scabbard as the creature grabbed his head and yanked it viciously to the side. His neck cracked like a dry stick and the skeleton dropped the guard to the ground, limp.

Raben gaped at what stood before him. It was a lich, a sentient human skeleton. There was no skin, only bleached, white bones. It had armor of a sort. Black steel plates with intricate silver runes and writing were melded right into each of its arm and leg bones, protecting it somewhat from

68

frontal assaults. A huge triangular piece was attached to its chest with a standard painted on it: A brilliant white moon rose full behind a dark and withered leafless tree. Deep in each of the lich's unnaturally black eye sockets, a small purple flame flickered. The lich focused its lavender and black eyes on Raben.

"A map to Rhokar. Gul Thannon wishes to have it." The creature's voice sounded like the echo of a strong voice with a light hiss of air trapped within it. The thing reached out its blood soaked right hand and its segmented fingers opened up, showing little patience for waiting. "Perhaps, I'll let you live."

Gul Thannon. Dear Gods! Gul Thannon. The god of murder and blood sacrifice and the priests of Gul Thannon were legendary as torturers and were thought to be myth. Gul Thannon had not been in the realm for centuries, but now Raben was staring at a very convincing argument for his return.

"I have no such map." Raben's voice trembled as he blurted out the lie. "The only copy that we of the Dayquest had was destroyed by a thief." Raben reached under his robe and freed his sword, holding it before himself in readiness. *Blazing misery. Please get me out of this one!* This thing had just used its bare hands to dismember the two guards. Glancing at the mangled men heaped on the ground in bloody piles, Raben felt somehow responsible, though he didn't know exactly why.

"Lie not to me, brother," the creature answered. "You've done well in obtaining the map. Now give it to me." The creature glided lightly over the ground, his bony feet scraping along the stone porch.

Brother! Raben fought back the urge to vomit. *The evil that precedes the good.* Raben fell back before the lich, growing more and more ill by the moment. *Brother! Of Gul Thannon!* Raben wretched as the creature dropped

69

down the steps one at a time. The clicking sound of the bony feet striking the steps sounded like pebbles being dropped from the roof. Cleaning a string of spit off of his lip, Raben continued backing away, keeping the sword up between himself and the skeleton.

He risked a quick look over his shoulder to judge the distance to the garden, when he saw a flash near the porch. Cringing as he thought of the wizard's lightning, he ducked his head and prepared to fall. A high pitched cracking sound filled the garden area as the lich's head twisted hard to its left. Looking up, Raben saw that Von Hessing was behind the skeletal monster in brilliant silver armor. The warrior swung his heavy blade again, cranking the creature's head to the other side.

The lich, seemingly unaffected, spun around and reached right through Hessing's polished silver armor into his flesh. Blood gushed out over the skeleton's white bones, coating them in slippery scarlet as it lifted the enormous man off of the ground. The tortured scream that erupted from the warrior sent chills through Raben. Rushing forward, the thief knew he had to do something. He got behind the creature and swung at its head, smashing his blade into the monster's black helm, but succeeded only in causing its skull to rock to a side, as Hessing had. Then Raben hacked at the spine and ribs, but his sword found a steel plate much like the lich had on its front. Sparks flew from the deflected blow. Resolved on defeating the creature, the desperate thief swung at the skeleton's legs which were unprotected from behind. As soon as the sword cut through the creature's right leg, the bone exploded. Slivers of bone and the force of the explosion blew Raben onto his back. Hessing hit the ground with another scream as the skeleton toppled over its now-missing leg. Raben jumped back to his feet and charged the lich, holding his sword over his head with both hands, but before he was able to swing, the thing hissed and disappeared. The thief spun almost uncontrollably, searching for it. Several times he spun, unwilling and afraid to allow the skeleton to strike him unaware.

Between shallow, labored breaths the noble asked what the creature was.

"A messenger of Gul Thannon," Raben answered, as he turned another full circle. Hessing passed out. "Help!" Raben screamed until his throat hurt. After a few moments, the guards who were stationed in other parts of the house arrived.

"Back, filth!" They forced Raben away from Hessing at sword point. Raben quickly undercut the first guard's blade letting his blade scrape along it until he could rap the man's fingers and disarm him, and then just as rapidly, knocked the second guard's weapon to the ground as well.

"I don't have time for this!" Raben yelled. Pain grew from the many wounds that had been cut into his chest by the explosion. A slight odor of decay rose from him. The smell of rot. *Oh Hells!* "Get a greeching healer!" One man ran back into the house while the second began removing the noble's breastplate. The heavy piece of steel now had a hole the size of an apple through it. Hessing, himself, had a gruesome swollen purple tear in his midsection. Oddly, it had already stopped bleeding and looked days old. More horribly, the wound already reeked of death and infection. Raben walked away from the noble, stepped over the devastated body of the guard, lying in pieces on the grassy lawn, and fell to the ground. *We've both failed, noble, and before we even started.* The thief passed out.

Raben opened his eyes. A white ceiling. *In a bed.* *Quiet.* He tried to roll over, but thick restraints held him down. *Thirsty.* "Hello?" His voice was weak as it threaded out of his throat. "Hello!" He shouted, making his stomach and throat hurt. "Anybody!"

"What do you want, fool?" The guard had started the question even before the sound of the door could be heard. Raben couldn't see the door or the guard, but knew someone was in the room.

"Where am I? Why am I tied down?" Raben tried to remain calm as his senses screamed from the vulnerable position he was in. *Damned noble had me locked up. Last time I save him.*

"You're exactly where everyone goes that attacks a prominent citizen in Liveport and then gets slaughtered by the demonic minions of the dark." The man's voice was coming from above Raben's head as he lay tied on the bed.

"I'm in a jail?" *I can't get the slightest luck.*

"No." A woman's voice. She walked into view with twice the grace of any cat. *Oh Hells!* She had shiny shoulder-length brown hair and large lemon-shaped brown eyes that were not uncommon to elves. "You're in a Guild holding." She smiled. She was gorgeous. The smell of her familiar perfume crashed over Raben. "You're following an odd path, Raben." Hearing his own name raised an eerie alarm inside of him. He'd never heard it before. "We're having a hard time keeping track of you."

"Are we?" Raben hazarded sarcasm. "I'm trying to do what Ulmer asked. Nothing more." Raben's eyes strayed away from the woman, focused on her pointed elven ears, and then looked straight into her eyes. "I'm part of the Dayquest. If you let me continue, I can bring you the True Knowledge of the ancients."

"We know. We want you to continue. After all, that's the only way that you can learn what you really want to know." She shrugged slightly. "And, unless we are quite mistaken, you do wish to know, don't you?"

Does she know who I am, or is she just baiting me? I need to ask her. Will I look like a fool? Damn them! Damn her!

"Who am I?" He spoke without really thinking, the impulse to know being too much to bear in silence. "Where am I from?" *She knows and is making me beg for it. Enjoying the fact that I suffer the way I do. She must love seeing me get pounded and poisoned and shredded by Thannon's skeletal pets. Oh how I would love to turn the tables.*

"I don't know anything more than your name. Raben Cyren Everinthius. I was told only that, and to inform you to seek after the True Knowledge, for that will aid us not only in knowing what it is, but complete the man who finds it as the priests promised." The woman leaned in and untied Raben's left hand. An unseen servant handed her a cup, which she placed in the thief's free hand. "Drink this." Raben did. "You were given what is surely the most obsessive need for completion. The need to know who you are." *Raben Cyren Everinthius. Something maybe. Who would know something more? An ancient sage, or maybe a magistrate of some city would have some record of those family names. Land owners maybe.*

"Who did it? Who did this to me? I need to know. Am I the evil?" Raben attempted to sit up, but the woman softly held him to the bed. *If I could get up from this bed and get my sword.*

"You are." She leaned in close to Raben's face. "I can't tell you who. But I'm sure you'll soon begin to guess." She was so close to Raben's ear as she whispered the last of it that he could feel the tiny hairs on her cheeks lightly grazing his own. He breathed in her perfume, enjoying it for the first time. He closed his eyes to concentrate on being close to her, but she said nothing more. She was gone. *Again.*

He couldn't remember falling asleep. His head throbbed as he forced his heavy drugged eyes to open. "Must have been the drink she gave me," he croaked.

"Sir, he's awake!" The man's shout brought Raben to full alertness. He jumped up in the bed, landing on his feet, quickly ascertaining that he was unarmed. *Who the blazes?*

"Stand back!" He'd yelled it out before recognizing his surroundings. He was in Hessing's house, back in his own makeshift bedroom. The man before him backed away with his hands raised. "How'd I get here? Greeching Hell!" Raben felt he was losing his mind. *I never know what's going on. Greeching Guild!*

"You were lost after the battle. We carried his lordship into the house and when we returned you had gone. We found you this afternoon in a ditch behind the house." The guard pointed behind himself.

"I'd gone!" Raben screamed. "I was unconscious, you blazing fool! I fell in the yard after the battle. I certainly didn't collapse in a greeching ditch." The thief glared at the guard. *Idiot! I saved your bleeding life, and this is my thanks. A ditch.*

"We thought your falling was an act, and after we returned and couldn't find you there..." The guard backed out the door leaving Raben alone in the room. The thief

75

fumed. *It's not only that I have no past. I don't even exist.* Heavy footsteps echoed into the room ahead of the noble.

"So you did live," Hessing said, sneering as he limped into the room. A broad bandage was wrapped many times around his waist, where the lich had wounded him. *How did you ever survive that? Luckier than you deserve.* "I see you're feeling alert and wakeful." He nodded vaguely at the thief, conveying his apathy towards Raben's condition. "We need to go." Hessing waved for a servant to immediately fetch his boots. "I had wondered if you'd stay comatose forever, or maybe just had your soul taken by the creature." The noble shot a quick glance at Raben. "No more than you deserve." *Were you hoping that I'd lost my soul?* A guard aided Hessing as he pulled a shirt of leather armor on over his head. "Quickly. Climb down from the bed and pack that arsenal you have over there. We need to go. Now!" Hessing sent everyone out of the room. He adjusted his armor as they left, but as soon as he and Raben were alone, he lifted his gaze to the thief and bore into the man.

"Where were you, thief?" *Where was I? I'm touched by your concern for me. I'm fine.* "I asked you where you've been?" repeated the noble impatiently, as he furrowed his brow. *There's the jackass I've come to know.*

"I have no idea." It wasn't a complete lie. "Where are we going?" Raben stepped off of the bed. His head throbbed as he moved, and his body felt stiff. He didn't want to do anything, but arguing with the noble would take far too much effort. He began packing his weapons.

"The members of the Dayquest have been waiting since yesterday, for the hero and the guide." Hessing looked at Raben sternly. "Last time to tell me the truth, thief. Where were you?" he asked again. "I'll find out one way or the other." Raben gave the same answer. The noble shot a dark look at the thief, shook his head, and walked out of the room. Moments later, a guard walked in holding a

new black robe over his arm. Raben eyed it suspiciously
for a moment before taking it. It was very nice, and had
more than twenty pockets inside. *Did Hessing have this
made? Good taste for a sailor.* Raben put on the new robe,
strapped on his many weapons, slung his pack, and walked
out to meet the noble.

"Let's get there, thief," Hessing announced as he began
to march ceremoniously towards the door. He now wore
a gleaming breastplate atop his leather shirt. *Oh Hells!*
Servants held the door open for the two men, their faces
joyful and expectant. "The warriors will be parading by
now." It was the beginning of the Dayquest, the promise of
a better life known only to a long forgotten time. *How'd I
get into this?*

"Yes," agreed Raben, "let's get this over with." He
passed by the servants eyeing them distastefully. They
glowed with the jubilance of the Dayquest, and smiled
at Raben as he walked past, believing that this crusade
would improve their lives, though they really knew nothing
about it. "Perhaps if your master does find the knowledge
he seeks, you won't have to do this anymore. Instead of
holding doors open for overstuffed nobles, you could open
your own business, or preach the will of the gods."

"We're happy to serve a good man." Raben could
tell that the servant meant it. The thief walked out into
the street to catch up with Hessing, and was greeted by
the cheers of hundreds of townspeople. A great mob
surrounded the noble's home. They cheered at Hessing
and Raben, making a path for them as they strode down the
street, and then threw flowers and ribbons over them as they
passed. Raben smiled as he absorbed the situation, smiled
at the townspeople who were cheering and tossing flowers
for the thief and murderer. He observed the faces of each
of the people who appeared so excited to send the quest off,
wondering what they would do if they knew the truth. In

his mind, a great many faces twisted in disgust as they heard the news.

Soon, the two heroes were at the head of an enormous mob, making their way to the center of the city where the bazaar normally sat. Today, however, there were no carts or shops open in the market place.

The only structure there was a raised stage, upon which stood a dozen glorious looking knights in a myriad of fantastic shining armor. Each had a number of massive weapons that they would occasionally lift from their sheaths and holsters to artfully swing before the cheering crowd. Poles with streamers had been set behind the stage, indicating the many houses of the city that were funding the Dayquest and its crusaders.

The enormous circle of people surrounding the stage fluidly opened for Raben and Hessing to enter and then absorbed the hundreds of newcomers. The thief and the noble slowly made their way up onto the stage, doing an excellent job of hiding their recent injuries. Upon their arrival, the cheering gained in strength and volume. Just behind them, a plainly robed priest bearing a battle-ax walked onto the stage followed by an unarmed, thin, old man wearing little more than the dingy tattered remains of what had once been flame-orange robes. The cheering continued, but wavered slightly at the less than spectacular participants of the quest.

"Finally," boomed a rotund man who stood before the crowd at the very front of the stage, "we have arrived at the time that our best will go forth and bring back to all people, the True Knowledge!" The cheering became deafening, trapped as it was, in the small square of the city. "Let us make merry to send them forth!" The man raised his arms and dropped them as he signified that the merriment should begin, and as one, the crowd began to sing a rousing song. Raben did his best to tune out the noise as he followed the small train of men who'd begun exiting the stage and passing through the crowd. Sixteen men long, the line snaked past thousands of excited townspeople and towards the Northgate. They waved at members of the excited mob as they marched through the city. *This cannot happen quickly enough.*

As they approached the Northgate, the Mage's guild stood ominously, watching. Though no living thing could be seen in the windows of the building, everyone near it felt that they were being observed. Today, however, the darkness of the mages had no effect. The singing crowd only gained volume as their numbers swelled and the excitement grew.

Standing between the massive pillars that held the northernmost entryway to the city, known as the Northgate, each member of the Dayquest bowed, gave a short display of their skill with a weapon of choice, and exited the city.

Most of the knights looked about the same as they made show of their prowess. Three of them, however, took great pains to be original. Sir Arris, the son of one of the strongest merchants in Liveport used two swords in one hand, holding them opposite each other, and was still able to wield a long sword in his free hand. He carried himself with such grace that the thief wondered if he hadn't been trained by a less savory instructor than the typical knight received. Raben watched, impressed, as the man arced the blades through an intricate pattern, which allowed all of the blades a chance to strike. At the end of the show, the knight hurled his blades into the air, and yanked free another short blade. When the three he'd thrown fell back to him, he caught them all with little trouble, thus arming him with four blades, all held at the ready. The crowd erupted into an excited round of applause. Raben watched the graceful knight as he left the stage, aware that he would have had a terrible time mimicking the performance. *Perhaps Sir*

Arris, you are in the wrong line of work. The thief feared the skill he'd witnessed, but looking at the plain robed priest and the old man that stood next to him, and seeing them enthralled with the performance, he felt that he must be alone in distrusting the knights.

Sir Peltrist used no weapon at all, but rather moved his hands, each of which held a plume. When he was moving the fastest that he could manage, the blue and red plumes blurred into a purplish color. Having complete control of the blurring plumes, he then wove them through a number of complex designs. Raben thought this was perfectly foolish as he watched the knight swing his colorful feathers at an imagined enemy. He scoffed, and, so it seemed, did the old man in the tattered robes. *Perhaps if you must dust Talvo's keep before you receive the knowledge you could be the savior of all men.* Peltrist walked down from the stage after considerable applause. For a moment it looked as if he might give an encore performance, but much to Raben's relief, he only bowed two more times and then left.

Sir Caman, the son of a magistrate, merely told a story. It was a lengthy telling about his family and the responsibility that they had assumed in Liveport and ended with the assurance that he would bring back the True Knowledge. Just as his story ended, he held out his hands and a loud cracking sound cut through the air. He'd brought an explosive powder, or some type of prop. *Fool.* Raben shook his head at Caman's display, watching the man rub his burnt palms together as he exited the stage. *What a fool.*

After several others had done their part to make a circus of the Dayquest, Lord Norman Tress juggled colored clubs, Raben watched as Hessing stood before the crowd. The noble brought his sword out and held it blade up across his body. Reaching out to the tip of the blade, he ran his palm along the blade, cutting into his hand. He spoke as his blood fell down his arm.

"I, the prophesied, swear by my blood to deliver the forgotten times and True Knowledge back to Liveport, and all of Reman!" The crowd erupted wildly after the proclamation from the well respected warrior. Hessing sheathed his weapon and walked away, leaving Raben to follow him before the cheering mob. *Greeching perfect!*

The thief looked to his left, at the remaining two men, which were the dirty-looking old man and the plainly dressed priest. *The rabble has been left behind.* The priest smiled at him, apparently understanding, but not caring that none of them could follow up Hessing's performance. *He's leaving it to me. Perfect!* The old man in the tattered robes simply shrugged as though he were indifferent. *Greeching perfect!*

"Do either of you have a need to play knight, or are you on this quest because you were forced?" asked the thief, his irritation growing with each moment of urging that came from the eager crowd.

"I was sent, and don't believe I have any skill these folks would enjoy," said the brown robed priest. "Perhaps I could wave my axe a few times." He smiled. *He's enjoying this.* Looking into the man's face, Raben could see the earnestness of the priest's offer, but sensed mirth bubbling up in the man. *He thinks this is funny. Greech.*

"I'm here because I have no other place to be, not that any other reason I have is any of your business," rasped the old man. "Impress them if you want, but by the time you've convinced them that you belong with those metal covered idiots out there, the quest will be over." The old man folded his knobby hands into his grungy robes and waited along with the thousands of onlookers for the thief's decision. *Metal covered idiots, indeed. Let's get out of here.*

Raben thought for a moment longer, and then walked out of the city without having performed anything at all for the masses. Seeing this, and the other two less than exciting members of the Dayquest, the crowd began to disperse. Raben held up long enough for the priest and his companion to catch up with him, and together the three of them caught up with all of the knights and nobles.

"That was impressive," said the old man, from behind the thief. "I've seldom seen such a powerful performance as that. The knights got a few of the people to clap and cheer, but you managed to make all of those folks walk away. They left," he said, and then clapped his hands together loudly, "just like that."

"Never mind him," cut in the priest. "It's obvious that none of us were trained for that sort of thing, and even if we were, we have the good sense to not parade this solemn and important mission before them as though we were players acting out a valiant quest. This is serious work that must be done. Come along," said the priest, as he caught up with the thief. "We can meet the challenge together, because I doubt the nobles would lift a weapon for the likes of us." The old man snorted his agreement and Raben was forced to nod. "And that was one blazing good showing back there." The priest chuckled and the old man laughed quietly behind as they walked.

No sooner had the three of them arrived within earshot of the knights, than one of them called.

"Bring forth the map."

"Yes!" Agreed Hessing. "Let the quest begin!" Raben looked down and away from the rich crusaders as his face betrayed the disgust he felt at having to be in their company. He realized he was looking almost directly at the man in the tattered robe, and felt some relief when he saw that the aged man had a similar expression. He looked to the priest. *Well priest, these are your chosen. Your god has put these men*

82

here in order to journey for your church. You should fear for the success of this trek.

"Don't worry," the priest said. "They may be able to order you about, but we are all here for a reason. Only continuing can show us what." *Perhaps.*

"The map!" called one of the knights. It was Sir Caman, the story teller. The priest nodded for Raben to go to the knights. Turning his head, the thief could see that the old man agreed. *The map. You want the map. The skeleton thing from Thannon wanted the map, but I get to carry it. And the sword. All of the enemies will come to the sword. Perhaps there are a few other things that could draw suffering to me. Perhaps I should carry a leper on my back through the whole journey.* Noting the length of time that Raben was taking in responding to the nobles, the old man spoke.

"In my time, it seems that pushing men like this will only lead men like us to greater injury," said the old man. "But," he announced, "it is a wonderful bit of fun to do." The old man laughed, and in such a wild manner that the thief couldn't help but watch, but the comic seizure was short lived. He stopped abruptly. "Go. We'll attack them if they decide to hold you prisoner."

"Hells," Raben muttered, looking at the two men, imagining them in a melee against the thirteen knights.

"I have the map!" Raben called out as he carefully removed it from his pack. "Let's begin." He glanced back to the priest and the old man as he headed for the nobles.

Three against thirteen.

"Without the proper understanding of why we're going. Without the proper..." Raben had listened to the old man mumble for leagues. In his tattered orange robes, he looked homeless and pathetic. "Our deaths," he said softly, "will come without explanation." After a few more leagues of listening intently to what he was softly uttering, Raben began to feel that he was either a seer, or completely out of his mind. "Deaths, many of them, many of us. The ground already knows. No fear until they come, no time once they're here."

Raben had been forced to walk in the back of the line as a concession to the knights who insisted that they walk ahead of him in order of nobility and knightly rank. At the beginning of the day, when the thief had refused to relinquish the map to them, he and Hessing persuaded them into believing that the map was his sole and primary function in the quest. It took a great deal of assurance before Caman, who was the self appointed leader of the quest, agreed that Raben should fulfill his purpose. He was to be the map's bearer and keeper. Distrustful of the thief, the nobles had insisted that Hessing look on it too, and make all of the decisions jointly regarding their course. When the thief wasn't needed, he was to walk in his place, at the back of the line. Not surprisingly, the brown-robed priest and the urchin, as the warriors had already taken to calling him, were also trailing the expedition.

"A great moment will come, and each of us will face death," the urchin said. "Even you!" He spun, his hand raised and he pointed a finger right at Raben. "You will die." *Crazy, and not a very good seer.*

"Thanks for the uplifting news," Raben answered. He stared at the urchin for a while. "Do you have a name besides urchin?" The orange robed man's hand fell to his side, momentarily releasing Raben from the dismal prediction.

"Urchin is good. Better than a name in this company." Looking forward, Raben and the old man watched as the knights marched. Each of them had told a boastful story in which they'd all exaggerated their own exploits, or stopped the quest to demonstrate their prowess with a weapon. Each of them except Hessing. Raben respected him for that. He seemed to be distancing himself from the many sons of rich nobles that paraded along in their shiny armor, holding their freshly forged, unsullied weapons. Hessing had certainly fought and spilled blood in his long career as a sea captain, but unlike the youths around him, he did not seem eager to do it again.

"When we reach the end of this journey…" they could hear one of the nobles proclaim. His name was Jagon. "…there will more than likely be some hideous beast, or another. It will stand before us and only the righteous will be able to strike it."

"Now this," mumbled Urchin, "is the way to begin a tale. Vague yet riveting."

"I will stand before the foul thing," the knight proclaimed to his audience.

"And cry for my wet nurse," Urchin said. "Because I have never in my life been in a battle, nor will I at that point even remember what this pointed piece of metal on my hip is even for." The old man shook his head, a smile stretching across his wrinkly face.

85

"These men seem to have little regard for the truth of their words," observed the priest.

"Perhaps," agreed Raben, "but there are those who know a little about real life in this quest as well." He looked at the old man and then let his eyes drift back to the priest.

"Oh? Who is that? You?" Another grin spread on the old man's face and Raben could see a number of dark gaps where teeth had once been. "I think not." Urchin laughed and then pointed forward to the priest. "Him maybe. Yes. Him. Not you."

"Tell me wise Urchin, why you think he knows so much about life where as I do not." Raben smirked as he asked. The thief had not enjoyed a conversation that he could remember, but this one intrigued him. He liked Urchin. *More than he seems. And a little bit crazy.*

"You said real life before." Urchin laughed again. "I think there is a difference." The man reached into his torn up clothes and brought out a small pouch. After rummaging through it for a moment, he pulled out a small item and tossed it to Raben. Snatching it from the air, the thief looked at it.

"It's a fine pebble," he said. "Looks like a rabbit." Urchin nodded. The priest in the brown robe slowly fell back until he was walking abreast the other two men.

"Yes," he agreed, "either a rabbit or a lying noble with horns." All of them laughed. Raben was reserved and felt his mirth pulling at his belly while the priest gave a quick bark and suppressed the rest. Urchin wheezed as he laughed as though the joy he felt was escaping through the gaps in his teeth. The old man fought to control his mirth.

"Well," Urchin said. "Which is it?"

"Do you mean what is it really, or what is it if we're imagining what it could be?" The priest lifted the rock from Raben's hand and inspected it. He stared intently as if the small rabbit-shaped stone might come alive and hop away.

"What's your name? Have you met Urchin?" Raben looked over to the priest as he inspected the rock further.

"I'm Thantos, and I know Urchin well," he answered. "It could be a fanged creature." The old man shook his head, brushing his wispy gray hair from his face in irritation.

"Is it a rock or a rabbit," he said impatiently.

Raben looked forward again. Hessing walked by himself while the other knights, walking ahead of him, were embroiled in a debate of their own regarding who would be able to strike the creature at the end of the trek. Watching him intently, it seemed to Raben that the noble was going over a number of things in his head. He waved his arms slightly as if he were practicing a speech. *Accepting the many rewards and thanks from the people at the end of the journey I'll bet.*

"Tell me the answer to your riddle in a moment, Urchin." Raben quickened his pace to catch up to Hessing. He heard the old man rambling that his riddle was not "some joke to be taken lightly." Waving him away for the moment, Raben decided to intrude on Hessing's thoughts.

"Talking to spirits, or have you an invisible friend?" Raben tried to keep the edge from his voice.

"Leave me be, thief. I have no want to talk to you." Hessing looked away from Raben to the East. "There is nothing we can possibly say to one another." The noble looked flustered and guilty, as though he had been doing something that he shouldn't.

"I think," Raben said, "that we had better come to an understanding of who we really are before we suddenly need to defend one another." The thief walked for a short while before speaking again. He waved forward to the knights. "They cannot be trusted. They seem to have come on this journey to do nothing more than talk about what they wish their exploits to be in a fantasy world. This world will take them apart."

"And I should trust you?" Hessing growled. "Why in all of Reman would I do that?" He started forward to the other warriors. "Give me one good reason why I would take the word of a thief and murderer over that of the most prominent men in all of Liveport."

"Because I will come out of this alive," Raben stated. "Because you will too." Hessing looked back in disgust and Urchin laughed, apparently able to hear the conversation between the thief and the noble.

"If you come out of this alive," Hessing said, pointing at Raben, "I'll finish you off myself!" The noble brought out his massive sword, but never raised it. He turned to walk away instead. Urchin continued laughing.

As Hessing stomped away, Raben fell back to walk again with Thantos and Urchin. "Greeching nobles! They think they have every answer, and listen to no one." Raben turned to Thantos. "I was only trying to make peace with the man."

"Were you really?" The priest asked the question like a mother would to a rebellious child and he held out Urchin's stone. Raben took it.

"By the way!" interjected Urchin. "That noble does have all the answers. He does." He grabbed hold of Raben's hand and picked the stone from it. "He is the center of this quest."

"That's what he told me," Raben said. "I'm just a bystander in this mess."

"I'm only here to find artifacts for the church," Thantos said. He hunched his shoulders. "I was sent by my sect to bring anything that might further verify that the old stories and exploits of the chronicles are true." Thantos looked to the other two men. "Seems strange for men of faith to need proof of their teachings." They all nodded. *If anyone really believes in it.*

"I came to see how everybody dies," Urchin said. "There's only one hero in the prophecy. That means there are too many of us." The grim statement muted the men.

They walked the rest of the day in silence. By sunset, the city was many leagues to the South and the Dayquest settled down for its first night in the Plains of Shao.

The Plains of Shao were expansive fields of tall grass that stretched through the interior of Reman for hundreds of leagues. In the Southern plains, where the group was camped, the final battle of the White Wizard War had been fought hundreds of years before, burying the first temple of Talvo. Only a few leagues north of their campsite, the recently unearthed temple stood in ruin.

A nomadic people, who called themselves the Shao, were the first people to detect the temple while digging a grave to bury one of their dead. Horsemen and warriors, the Shao were quick to offer the information to missionary priests of Talvo, who often made conversion trips to the Shao, in exchange for long spears. It was the temple that would be the official starting point of the Dayquest. The starting point that gave value to Raben's map.

He studied it intently by lamplight before carefully rolling it up and sliding it into a hidden pocket inside his robe.

"One of the three of us should keep a watch." It was Thantos.

"Sure," answered Raben. *I'll bet the nobles had this same conversation.* He laughed. "I'll go first, and wake you later." Thantos nodded and walked over to his bedroll.

"Here," said the old man. The rabbit shaped stone landed near Raben's foot. "Think on it." Urchin walked over near Thantos and lay down.

Raben sat up for hours. *Damned stone rabbit.* He let the fire burn down to coals, and stared up at the sky intently, seeing the stars that shined there for the first time.

"Thief! I want to see the map." Raben awoke to the voice of Von Hessing. Thantos was sitting nearby in meditation. The thief watched him. The man's dirty blonde hair and perfectly manicured beard made him look as though he too could be one of the knights they traveled with, but his heavy brown robe with its absence of decoration reminded Raben that Thantos had been ignored by the nobles just as he had. *He lives by the religion that has sent me on this blasted quest, yet he is unlike all of the others. Seems trustworthy.*

Urchin was hovering over a large pot, which was heating over a fire. "Like some food, thief?" The old man proffered a ladle of steaming liquid. "Don't you have a better name than Thief? Seems a bit of an insult." Urchin laughed, his mirth whistling through his teeth in the morning air.

"It's better than a name in this company," Raben replied, smiling. He unpacked the map as he slowly made his way over to Hessing. As soon as the noble was within hearing distance, Raben called out impatiently. "We're not even to the temple yet. Why do you need to see the map again?" He dropped the map near Hessing, who was still laying on his bedroll.

"I like to be informed," the noble said. "Have you figured out any of this writing?" Hessing traced a few of the runes with his fingertip. He focused, much to the thief's amazement, more on the writing than on the map. *So there is something about that writing. It must draw people to it. Me, then him.*

"No, not yet." Raben sat on the ground near the huge warrior. "I didn't have much time to further study it while I was under house arrest, and your guards weren't very well educated." Raben leaned back on the tall grass. Hessing snorted a short laugh.

"Make no mistake! I despise you, Thief, yet I do see that these fools," he gestured to the knights, "are going to end in ruin." Hessing sat up on his bedroll. "I will finish this quest successfully. And you will do your part as the sword. After that, we'll settle our differences." Hessing picked up the map and handed it back to Raben. "Perhaps if you prove yourself to the cause of good, I won't feel compelled to shave your head from your shoulders." The lord rested his hand on the pommel of his sword, which lay on the ground next to him.

"Not many women are charmed by you, are they?" Raben asked. Caught off guard, Hessing laughed a booming wave of sound that carried over the Shao. Raben smiled, tucked the map into his robe, and stood.

"You're as big a fool as I am, Thief," Hessing said. "The reasons for your killing were your own. We all have that. I have killed. It seems I will kill again." Hessing let out a long sigh. "Though we cannot trust each other, let us at least trust that we each kill for a righteous reason." The noble paused. "For the quest."

"Agreed," Raben answered as he walked away. *It's a beginning.* He needed to find some strong allies in the group. Raben had an upsetting feeling inside that was convinced that this trek was going to be harder than anything he'd done so far. It seemed that something inside of him could see something terrible in the near future.

Wandering away from the party, he removed his robes, unsheathed his sword and sickle, and began a practice.

91

Holding the weapons and fighting imagined foes made him feel better, stronger. He moved fluidly, allowing his body to shift easily through the fighting stances he knew. *Where did I learn this? How far back can I remember?* Raben kept his lethal dance in motion as Urchin and Thantos approached. *Liveport? Von Hessing's? The house of Von Hessing.* Urchin and Thantos sat down in the pace-tall grass and watched as the thief danced through several mock attacks. *My first thought, first memory, first anything was the moment I noticed the Guild woman in Hessing's house.* He stabbed forward, gutting an imaginary foe, then drew his sickle across its face, before spinning into readiness for another attack. *Not a blazing thing before that.* He stopped, letting his weapons fall to his side. Urchin clapped his hands.

"Not many of those knights could match that performance," said the old man. "You might have done all of that at the gates of the city, rather than skulking out like a whipped dog." Urchin walked up to Raben and held out his hand, nodding at the sickle. Raben handed it to him. "Strange choice for a weapon." Urchin held the awkward blade out in front of himself. It took two hands for him to steady it. "It has a reddish hue to it. What metal is this?"

"I don't know. I've never had a chance to ask anyone." Raben wiped the perspiration off of his face and arms with the bottom of his robes, and then pulled them back on over his head. It felt good to sweat. *I am tied to Hessing. Why?* It occurred to Raben that everywhere he went he'd either run into Hessing again, or found a reason to seek Hessing out. "I thought it might be copper."

"Wouldn't be copper," Thantos said. "Too weak. Maybe you'll find someone who can tell you before the end of the journey."

"Yeah," Raben said, not sure he wanted to know where the reddish sickles came from. "Maybe." *And maybe I'll live to share that information with others.* He gestured that they should start back.

The three men headed to their camp. They quickly packed everything up and walked over to join the warriors, who had just finished breaking their own camp. *Arris. Caman. What makes you so noble? Did your fathers do something important once? Your grandfathers?*

"What do you two know of Von Hessing?" Raben asked, keeping his voice low as he leveled his gaze at the noble.

"Just what I've been told, really," Thantos began. "He was a sea captain that successfully defeated pirates and invaders. Is a ferocious fighter. Started with nothing, and slowly gathered his wealth by doing favors for the rich. That's it. He's an officer of the city." Thantos lifted his hands apologetically. "He seems to know everyone. That's all I know."

Urchin nodded in agreement. "It's hard to really know a man that isn't your brother. What can I tell of you, Thief, in the short time I've known you?" Urchin offered Raben the sickle he'd borrowed earlier.

"You could probably tell me more than I know, after the short time I've known me." Raben sheathed the sickle as his words trailed off. His companions looked to one another confused. "No one is here by accident, and you, old man, would appear to know more than all of the rest of us combined." Urchin laughed, the wheezing noise erupting out of him.

"Perhaps some things, but not about this quest," the old man said. "There are things about this group of men that I'm not sure I'll ever figure out."

"Like what?" asked Thantos.

"Who's lying and who is telling the truth, for one," answered Urchin. "In fact..." he dug into his pack. "...I think that everyone on this trek has lied since it began, or most of them anyhow." The old man continued rooting through his pack. "It is my feeling that merely avoiding a conflict which would reveal something about yourself is a kind of lie."

"I think the three of us have been fairly truthful with one another," Thantos said. "I am quite sure that I have told all truths since we set out. I value the two of you as the only friends I'm likely to have for a while, and will use all I have to defend you should trouble arise."

"I know where the old man is going, I think, and I'm not ready. I'll continue avoiding," Raben said. "But you can count that as truth." He smiled. "I will defend you as well," he said pointing to Thantos. "But not you, Urchin." He laughed, and soon the others joined him. After the laughter subsided, they began moving out, now that the knights had resumed marching.

"Thank you so much," Urchin barked. "See if I help you in the many ways I might. Where is my rabbit stone?"

"I still have it. I'm still thinking on it," answered Raben. The three men set out, using the time they had to examine and ridicule the knights before them.

"That Arris," Raben said. "There is something about him that I don't like. He moves too well for a knight."

"His family has always been famous for hiring mercenaries. They have taken in many warriors in their time, for whatever reason. They send them off, never to be heard from again." Urchin pointed to the northwest. "I hear they have land in the old country and fight wars there almost constantly." He walked for a while, silent, and then spoke again, more quietly. "But I also hear that they are such barbarians where battle is concerned that they eat the heart of any warrior that falls without taking at least one of the enemy with him."

"Where did you hear that?" Thantos asked. "That's ridiculous."

"I'm not sure where I heard that," Urchin answered. "After living as many years as I have, I can never remember where all of the tidbits I gathered have come from. Doesn't matter. Whoever told me heard it from someone else anyhow."

"Now that I've heard the worst story that I'm likely to hear on this whole journey, why don't we just quiet down and get there. Maybe we can gather some real stories that we'll be sure are true." Raben looked from Thantos to Urchin. The old man frowned, but they all continued on without another word.

The day's journey was quick though it didn't feel that way to the travelers. They snaked North through the Shao, leaving an obvious trail of trampled grass behind them. Walking through the tall greenery of the Shao plains felt like an endless endeavor. The horizon never changed, and there were no landmarks to assist the group as they made their way. Grass stretched away from them in every direction in a seemingly infinite green blanket. Though Urchin requested several times that the party rest for a while, the knights and nobles that led the group pushed forward, insisting that the temple was just ahead. Just as the sun began to descend from the sky, they came across several staked markers that the priesthood of Talvo used to indicate the temple's excavation. In no time, the party came upon a massive hole.

The bottom of the manmade crater was the brick and mortar roof of the ancient temple. Through all of known history, Talvo always had temples in the shape of square keeps. Being a war god, his temples were to serve not only as places of worship, but also as forts should any type of conflict consume the realm. This keep was still buried for the most part, but an opening had been punched through the roof. A rope ladder now hung at the top of the makeshift portal to let diggers climb into and out of the temple. From what Raben could see, there were presently no diggers or priests working in the temple. It looked abandoned as he peered over the edge of the gaping hole.

"Are we going in?" asked Thantos. "I would like to go in." He neared the edge of the enormous pit, looking down onto the temple. "What say you?" He looked to Urchin and Raben, hoping to receive the same enthusiasm.

"No thanks," Raben immediately replied. "The gods and I aren't getting along right now." Urchin laughed.

"You go, priest. It looks like a number of the nobles feel that they need to look about the temple as well, though we needed only to find this place so that we could begin the journey from the right spot." Urchin pointed across the hole, where the knights had already begun to lower their own ropes into the pit. "You go ahead and join them. Make sure they are up to no mischief. Meditate in the old temple, and say hello for me." Urchin laughed. "I will keep the thief company. My old bones can't do all that work." The old man did look exhausted. *When did you wear down, old man? You didn't seem so tired before.*

"You are certain," replied Thantos, as he set off around the dig to where the nobles were beginning their descent. "You may have no other chance during this whole journey to see something as magnificent as this. It's dwarf work. I have heard that the skill of the ancient builders was beyond anything that we could even imagine." Raben shook his head along with the old man. *The ancient builders. How exciting can a block of granite really be? What could they do to it besides put their banners up all over it? Talvo isn't exciting enough for me to worry about.*

Raben sat down on the edge of the hole next to the old man, and watched the exploration begin. The knights looked ridiculous trying to climb down the ropes in their heavy armor. Their feet sank into the soft earth and tore huge chunks free, leaving them spinning on the rope with nowhere to steady themselves that didn't send fresh earth raining down on all of those below.

"You know," Raben said, "if I were any of those fools, I'm fairly certain that I would take that armor off before I tried to climb down into that place."

Urchin nodded as he sucked in a deep breath. "It would make more sense. Look at that dolt. He looks as if he is about to plunge into the hole as it is." He pointed at Sir Peltrist who was spinning around the rope after he lost his footing. "He weighs so much that he's sinking right into the soil."

"This looks bad already." *They aren't all going to make it back from this foolishness.*

Raben lost a silver piece to Urchin on a bet that one of the nobles would plummet to his death. None did.

Soon ten of the warriors had surrounded the makeshift opening in the roof with their swords drawn. They debated. It was obvious. They were surely arguing about who should enter first. One of them would start forward before another of them would step up and make a case for why he should be first to enter. Eventually, Caman dropped into the hole and was followed by the knights in the exact same order that they had used as they marched here.

"It's sanctified ground. What the blaze do they expect to find? They enter it as though they know that demons live inside." Urchin sounded tired. He slowly took in a long deep breath and then let it slide back out. He did this several times as he watched the knights enter the temple, and then turned to Raben. "When is the last time you trusted in someone other than yourself, Thief?" The old man was staring at Raben, his eyes red-rimmed.

"Never, that I can remember." The thief looked down into the hole. "You and Thantos are the first people I've ever met that haven't tried to kill me within a few moments of meeting me." He looked over to the old man. "Yet I can't say that I trust you."

"Where are you from?" Urchin urged.

"No," Raben said, stopping the inquiry. The old man laughed, too tired to persist.

The two men stared into the pit. After a while the dust that had been kicked up by the crowd of armor clad warriors settled back onto the roof of the sunken temple. Urchin lay back and basked in the sun, letting it warm him as he rested. Raben looked across the vastness of the plains, trying to gauge it against the distances that were on the map he'd copied from the wall of the temple. This temple was barely north of Liveport, and beyond it was two more full knuckles worth of grassy plains as far as the map was concerned. *We're going to be walking through this stuff forever.* He reached behind himself and tore a handful of the tall grass from the ground. He broke the lengthy blades apart, segment by segment, letting the green stalks fall into the pit, watching them coast downward until they passed from his view. He searched the lip of the hole opposite himself, looking for Hessing and the only two knights that hadn't entered the temple, but couldn't see them anywhere. Jagon and a junior knight named Dearn apparently chose to remain with Hessing, but they must have ranged away from the temple.

Raben took another handful of grass and began working on it. A long time he sat there until finally Thantos, who had been last to enter the temple, came bursting up out of the makeshift entryway.

"They were killed!" he yelled up to them. A deep rumble passed through the ground beneath them, followed by an explosive boom. Dirt and rock shook from the walls of the massive hole, showering the blood covered priest. "Someone is attacking us!" His voice was muffled by all of the falling dirt.

"Greeching Hells!" Raben leapt to his feet, backed away from the hole, took a running start, and leapt straight out into the cloud of dirt that still spewed out of the dig. No one heard him cast. Descending through the dust, he could only see Thantos as he neared the ground. He levitated down and landed easily next to him.

"What are you doing here, Thief?" Thantos' robe had blood smeared on it. "You're going to get killed!" The priest appeared to be sincerely worried for Raben despite his panicked need to flee.

"What in the boiling Hells happened?" Raben asked. "Never mind," he barked. Another shockwave passed through the ground, knocking both men off of their feet. "Stand up and let me cast a spell on you." Thantos was already up and helped Raben to his feet. "Ferro Mis Lesita Ro," Raben shouted, fighting the urge to cough. He reached out and touched Thantos. "Think of going up!" He yelled. They had just lifted off of the ground when another thunderous crack passed below them. Thantos levitated up into the cloud of falling dirt and rock, protecting his face with his hands, and Raben followed close behind. The thief had cast a spell on himself that allowed him to move both up and down and from side to side, while Thantos could only levitate up or down. He would need Raben's help. Rock and dirt that had been blown into the air by the eruptions pelted them until they neared the top of the still growing cloud. Moments later, they passed out of the veil of dirt and found themselves hundreds of paces off of the ground.

"Blessed Talvo!" Thantos called out. "Get me down! Get me down."

"Hold onto me!" Raben ordered. The two clasped each other's wrists and Raben dragged the priest out over the area where Urchin had been. "Think down!" Slowly the two dropped nearer the ground. Raben could feel pressure building in his ears as he dropped down towards the lush grass of the Shao. He worked his jaw in order to clear it. Just as they were about to touch down, Urchin ran up under them.

"There is something over there." He pointed towards the temple. "It's terrible!" He waited for them to set foot on the ground. "My friends, the dead walk over there."

"The knights awoke it! They were looting the temple, taking small artifacts, and suddenly Sir Peltrist was being torn limb from limb by Sir Arris" Thantos said. "His blood sprayed over everything." Thantos wiped his face as if to clean the blood from his memory. "Then this creature came out of the basement stairwell and began shredding its way through the ranks, knight after knight. It seemed like they couldn't even fight it. I fled. I came to find you," he looked at Raben, "and Hessing. The evil twisted Arris into a beast, and then there was this terrible monster!"

"What manner of thing was it?" asked the thief.

"A skeleton in armor," answered Thantos. "It spoke to me. It told me to lead it to Rhokar. It said I was the chosen of Talvo, and would be corrupted to serve the evil." Thantos shuddered. "It tore men in half with its hands. Its eyes! Poor Peltrist! I fled!" Thantos turned away from them. "We need to leave here, and quickly," the priest clamored, "before we all die."

"I know of this thing," Raben confirmed through gritted teeth. He grabbed Urchin and Thantos by the arm and pulled them away from the hole. "You're right! We must flee. Now!" Dragging them along as they stumbled, the thief ran from the temple. "Has anyone seen Hessing?" They shook their heads as they went. "That fool of a noble will fight it if he has the chance."

The three jogged a good distance from the hole and began moving around it to the side where the knights had been. As they did so, Urchin spotted the towering warrior, Jagon, in the midst of a battle. He was fighting some kind of slow creatures. *Zombies.* Walking corpses of rotting dead men, the things seemed about to fall apart as they attacked. The zombies seemed helpless as the men cut them apart. The terrible danger in them was that they seemed not to notice as parts of their bodies were cleaved away. They pressed on, swinging their club-like arms at the knights. Once or twice, a noble staggered back, having been pounded by one of the things. Hessing, however, simply moved amongst them as he cut them all down. Clearing a path through the walking dead, the three men ran away from the pit as thunderous quakes passed through the ground once again launching more dirt and dust into the air.

"Did any of the others get out of the temple!" yelled Hessing the moment he was in earshot.

As the knights neared, Thantos indicated that none had. "Then," said Hessing, "we need to go in after them. We can't leave men buried alive in there."

"They're not alive," said Thantos.

"The messenger is here," added Raben. Hessing looked confused. "The messenger we fought in your garden." Hessing swore as he nodded.

"We need to leave here then!" Hessing was holding a long sword in each hand. He looked right at Raben. "There has to be a way to fight the thing." Hessing started to walk away, his eyes scanning the land before him.

"Let's go." Raben followed with the others. Jagon and Dearn looked terrified. Their eyes were wide open and they held their weapons two handed, as though they might drop them otherwise. Raben brought out his sword and a sickle. *Gul Thannon.*

The group began to run away from the pit where the temple had been. Raben ran up next to Hessing and steered the group north. They jogged for a good while until both Raben and Hessing suddenly stopped in their tracks, halting the others. Slowly everybody noted that they were not alone on the plains. A lone figure stood on the plains ahead of them. Like a scarecrow in the tall grass, it stood motionless. Shivers passed down Raben's spine as he watched it. Though a single creature, it barred their way effectively, the mere notion of what it was freezing the party in place. They watched it, and gasped collectively as the thing sunk into the ground.

"Talvo save us," Dearn prayed aloud.

"Spread out!" ordered Hessing. "Converge from all sides when the damned thing attacks!" The group scattered, each man looking around at the others, wondering who would get attacked first.

Thantos wept as he stood holding his ax in front of him. He'd seen the creature tear through the knights' flesh without remorse. Raben constantly hopped from foot to foot, waiting for a skeletal hand to reach through the soil and drag him under. Urchin crouched near the ground, laying his hands on the earth. The warriors all stood with their weapons held over their heads, waiting for any sign of attack.

"I can't bear this," Thantos sobbed. "All my life I have been afraid that my duties would bring me to an end like this." He wiped his running nose with his sleeve. "I have always feared death. I can't die today. I can't." His voice rose to an almost hysterical pitch. "I can't die. Please promise me." He began to whimper, making slight noises through the tears that fell down his face.

A long time seemed to pass, while the six men waited on the plain in silence. Only the occasional moan from Thantos was heard as they awaited the inevitable attack of the messenger. A breeze picked up, bending the grass as it passed. Each member of the party looked from one to another, expecting to find only a corpse. Their eyes darted from person to person nervously, trying to make sure that all of their companions were accounted for. *Each of them went on this journey to save everyone else and now they each hope that the messenger attacks anyone but them.*

"Perhaps he wanted us to know that he knows we're here," said Hessing. The noble lowered his swords. "Let's get out of here." The noble looked to Raben expectantly, but the thief had no idea what the best strategy was at the moment. *We're in the trap. It has us at its mercy. There's nothing to do but wait.*

"How far can we really expect to…" Thantos shrieked mid-sentence, and fell to the ground. Raben sprinted over to the fallen man, but not before the lich appeared between them. The lich had been rebuilt. Its legs were whole. The priest shrieked in pain and horror and his legs kicked involuntarily. His right leg had been torn off completely below the knee. Every time his leg pumped in pain, a stream of crimson sprayed out onto the waist-high grass.

The thief looked into the lich's dark eye sockets, and saw the lavender flame burning. *Hatred.* The feeling passed through Raben like lust, energizing him. It awakened his every sense and filled him with the need for carnage. He charged the creature, launching himself sword first at the thing. The lich leapt to the side and gripped his robe, using the thief's momentum to slam him into the ground. Hessing loomed behind the lich and began hacking on the skeleton's back, showering Raben with sparks and splinters of bone. The thing clawed at Raben, but the thief kept his sword moving, arcing it wildly in front of the skeleton. The lich darted in once and tried to disarm Raben, but Raben reversed his swing suddenly and sent shards of bone flying.

"We should fight together," howled the creature as it slapped the thief's blade away, trying to grab Raben by the wrist. Its claw came down on his right hand. Raben felt a pop, and felt stringy cords of his flesh being torn from his hand before he saw the lich throw his finger away. His stomach convulsed, and he doubled over on the ground, letting his guard drop completely. *Blazing Gods! My hand!* The skeleton stood over the fallen man, but was distracted before it could finish him off. Hessing had been smashing on the creature from behind, and finally, the lich turned to meet him.

Raben screamed as the pain of his finger reached him. Fighting the searing burn of the wound and overwhelming nausea, he rolled onto his feet and drove his blade into the back of the lich. Three ribs fell out of the skeletal monster, but it paid him no attention. *Greech!* The thief fell away as the supernatural creature grabbed Hessing by his breastplate and hurled the enormous man into the grass. Turning around to face Raben again, the creature never noticed Urchin who had crawled into the battle on all fours. He reached out calmly and touched the lich on the foot. No sooner had his spindly finger contacted the white bone of the lich than it vanished. Raben's sword whistled uselessly through the air, causing the thief to fall. Landing on his wounded hand, the thief yelped before clamping his jaw down.

"Where the greeching blazing hell did the greeching thing go!" Raben yelled as he stumbled back to his feet. Blood was streaming off of his sword hand. Urchin crawled over to Thantos. Pouring a small amount of oil onto the bloody stump at the end of the priest's amputated leg, the old man lit it on fire, cauterizing it. Thantos screamed until he passed out. The smell of burnt hair and skin floated with the streaming smoke that the breeze blew away from the priest. Raben collapsed. *Too much.* The two knights he saw, sons of nobles, had never joined the battle. They stood open-jawed, exactly where they'd been at the onset of the attack. *I hope that gets recorded in the final tale of the Dayquest. Bastards!*

When Urchin began dousing his finger with oil, Raben almost hit him. After a moment of restraint, Raben bit down on a length of rope. Once the fire was lit, tears streamed down his face as he screamed. Urchin held Raben's shoulders, pinning him to the ground as the pain grew in intensity. Hessing grappled and immobilized the thief's legs. Raben called out incoherently as the burning sensation spread through his hand. It felt as if his whole arm were on fire. He screamed out again and then, he too, passed out.

Raben came to quickly. His eyes snapped open at the sound of moaning, and he saw that Hessing was strapping Thantos onto his back with leather thongs and his sword belts, while the other knights were sharing the burden of carrying Hessing's pack. Raben's head had a dull ache, and his finger pulsed with every beat of his heart. He crawled over to his pack and took a drink of water. *Greech!* He looked at his hand, at his missing finger. The brownish wound looked minor where his finger used to be, yet sharp pain tore through his hand and arm with each breath as he looked at it. He tried to move the stumpy remains of his finger but pain lanced through his hand, forcing him to clutch it to his body as he fought the need to call out in pain. *Blazing gods! Just a damned finger.* He sucked in a deep breath. *A sword in the gut would hurt less.* As the pain became bearable, the thief looked at his surroundings. Hessing was nearby.

"Still expect to finish this journey, Hessing?" Raben grunted as he climbed to his feet, using only his good hand. "Seems that Gul Thannon has other plans for us." The thief held up his four-fingered hand, displaying the injury he'd sustained to the dark deity's minion. "Even if He must cut us away piece by piece."

Hessing winced when he heard the god's name. Still unconscious, Thantos hung limply from the makeshift harness on the noble's back. The massive warrior began walking, though the direction he chose seemed contrary to that designated by the quest map.

"I think we have no choice. This is but a taste of what is to come if we do not finish the quest." Von Hessing continued towards the west. It appeared to Raben that the warrior hardly noticed the weight of the priest. He still moved naturally despite carrying another man. *Impressive. Carrying Thantos. He has to be tired. He fought the messenger. The messenger!*

"Urchin!" Raben couldn't see the old man. "Urchin," he yelled. Soon the old man rose up out of the tall grass, gathering his robes around him. "Where the Hells did the thing go?" Raben asked. "Where did you send it?"

"Into the ground," winced the old man, as he wrung his hands together. "I felt a deep rock cavern, and sent it there." Urchin walked over to his pack, picked it up, and threw it over his shoulder. "It's not a permanent resolution, but we seemed to need whatever we could get." Urchin began walking north.

Hessing, Jagon, and Dearn looked at the old man questioningly.

"North is right, according to the map." Without forcing Urchin to further explain what he'd done, Raben began to follow the old man. Seeing that Hessing had been outvoted, the two younger knights soon fell in line. After only a few steps, Thantos began to moan. The group stopped, looking back to Hessing, who still marched westward. The priest looked bluish and extremely pale.

"He needs a proper healer," Hessing called back to them. "There is a town only a couple of leagues to the west." The noble continued walking in the direction of the town he knew about, and Urchin, suddenly worried about the priest, changed course and followed. Raben joined the old man, walking by his side as they trailed the noble. *He could have just told us, the stubborn fool.* After the rest of the group began making their way after Hessing, Jagon and Dearn again followed suit. The party moved through the tall grass of the Shao plain in silence. For leagues they passed through the unchanging landscape, hoping for anything to appear on the horizon as they trudged through the unending plain of grass. As they trailed the noble, searching for the town he spoke of, the sun slowly dipped down towards the horizon.

Mercifully, the town appeared before them just before dusk. Small, it looked less than twenty buildings. Hessing urged them on, and soon they were happy to be walking on one of the town's dirt streets. The buildings were stout. Made out of stone, they appeared to have been built by the same people that had constructed most of the enormous structures that filled Liveport. *Must have been a rest stop for them.* It seemed like a waste of effort to have crafted the buildings, seemingly in the middle of nowhere, for the few people that must have inhabited them. Very few of the Shao people were visible now.

They were shy and cautious. The street emptied quickly as the bloodied men of the Dayquest neared the small town. Fleeing before them, men, women, and children ran as though the party were nightmares arriving from the plains. By the time the group decided to approach a nearby house, hoping for assistance, a number of horsed warriors approached.

The mounted warriors appeared to be enormous as they rode towards the group. Sitting on regal stallions of the Shao, each rider sat a good three reaches above the party. All men with blazing dark eyes, they had long brown hair that ran down their backs, while their faces were free of facial hair. They were strong. Their arms and legs were thick and well muscled from long days of constant work, and each bore a long spear that glinted yellow with the final light of the setting sun. Spears eight reaches in length, the mounted warriors leveled the lengthy weapons, using them to keep the dangerous looking strangers at bay.

"The plains," declared one of the riders, "have been full of monsters and dangers for weeks. All that have passed through the bladed plains have had need to fight their way through. Those that have made it to us have been insane, or evil, and all of them have been killed, for their mercy, or ours."

"You," boomed another of the riders, who was seated on a massive black courser. "You have traveled the plain, and fought the dead." The warrior threw back his head and made obvious the fact that he was smelling the air, and wincing as though he'd sniffed a long dead body. "You stink of the evil that you have been part of. It walks with you, the evil that may once have been your foe. You have brought it with you."

"You cannot enter our village," bellowed a mighty warrior while holding his spear over his head. "We will not allow it, for there is nothing that you can say that will convince us that you are anything but a plague to us and our simple way of life. We offered the temple to your kind, and ever since, we have been under constant attack. Leave, for you have no chance here!"

"We come from Liveport," Hessing called, desperate to interrupt the Shao as they worked themselves into a fearful rage. "To the south." The huge man unbuckled several of his sword belts and then held Thantos aloft as though the priest's body were a talisman of friendship. "We are on a trek for the glory of Talvo and we were set upon by monsters in the plains." Hessing paused while the warriors looked to each other in confusion. *We were just supposed to leave, not persist in demanding their help. Leave it to the warrior to confuse the barbarians.* "We are here only to scck a healer for our friend. We will pay for whatever aid can be provided, and then leave." Hessing lowered the priest of Talvo to the ground, and then raised his hands high into the air, keeping them far from his swords. "You have my word as a warrior of Talvo."

The horsemen, looking at one another, seemed to regard Hessing skeptically. One of the mounted fighters urged his horse forward, the spear he held slipped forward until it was scraping into Hessing's armor. "I do not believe you," the warrior said, looking down at the massive noble. "I have seen many strangers and strange things on the plains of late. Our people have been harried and attacked, many of them killed." The horseman backed his stallion up a step. "My wise man tells me that he senses evil in your party. You must be evil." The mounted Shao tensed his muscles as he gripped his spear. "That symbol," he barked as his spear tapped on Thantos' chest. "The bladed axe of Talvo! It has been in helping Him that our pain has begun. He wants only blood, and if that is the case with Him, then today we will deliver it!" The warrior urged his horse forward and raised his spear, keeping its sharpened tip one knuckle in front of Hessing's unblinking eyes. The noble kept his arms stretched over his head. Raben took one deliberate step forward, moving up next to the lord of Liveport. The Shao warrior, despite being part of a war party that outnumbered the strangers three to one, let his stallion fall back half a pace.

"If," Raben stated loudly, "you do not back away from him further, and help us, I will kill you all!" The Shao went wide eyed at the proclamation and then laughed in both shock and disbelief. About twenty strong, they had little to fear from the wounded party before them. The spear was backed away from Hessing's chest, but Raben could see the man was preparing to thrust it forward. Hessing stood his ground like a stone, his stoic expression chiseled onto his face. He did not respond to the Shao's aggression in any observable way.

"We are not evil," the noble said. "Hear me. I journey in the name of Talvo!" *No! Fool! Blazing Hells! Aren't you listening to what they have said!*

The Shao warrior before Hessing began to turn away from Raben and Hessing, but instantly spun back with his spear in motion. No sooner had he looked back towards the two strangers than he fell off the back of his horse, one of Raben's daggers buried to the hilt in his skull. Before the dark-haired plainsmen hit the ground, the thief lifted off of the ground, floating before the Shao. His mouth fell open and he lowered his chin to his chest, hovering in the air as if possessed. Each of the mounted warriors was frozen in his attack.

"Help us, or die." Raben held his sword out next to him, and let it go. It too hovered in the air. He unsheathed two of his wickedly curved sickles, and waited for the Shao to decide. "You are right, we are evil," he sneered. "And the only way you're going to survive us is to quickly aid us and send us on our way. Another attempt to attack us will leave your village in ashes, your children and women dead, and your horses as food for the army we are mounting."

The horsemen slowly backed away to a safe distance, terrified of the maniacal evil before them. Once they'd backed up beyond the range of a thrown spear, Raben landed, and helped Hessing resecure his human cargo. The thief spun quickly, making sure the Shao kept their distance before he assisted Hessing with the priest. Thantos moaned miserably as they scooped him up from the ground. Raben glared into the noble's eyes as the priest lay in the warrior's arms. "They would have killed you, fool. Why didn't you do anything?" He was disgusted with the noble's inactivity. "With your arms in the air like that, you wouldn't have even touched your blade before you were spitted like a pig."

"I trusted that you knew what you were doing," Hessing responded. "You are the sword, and I was low on options.

111

You did fine, though I think you are hard on the reputation of the Dayquest, and Talvo."

"And you two," Raben whirled around to face the other nobles. He was livid and hadn't even heard Hessing's explanation. "Are you ever going to help, or shall we expect you to freeze in every battle while waiting for the hideous minions of the evil gods to hang their coats and hats on you!" The thief scowled. "Useless bastards!"

Raben paced, pulsing with rage. He ignored the body of the Shao warrior lying in the road. He was in pain, and needed to figure out what he was doing. His finger was pulsing with continuous searing pain, so much so it eroded his anger. *Greech!* The party had been shredded in a single day of travel. They wouldn't survive many more attacks. *Think. Think. Think. Calm down.* Raben kept himself in motion, worried that if he sat down he might fall asleep. *I am the sword. Thanks a lot. Next time I'll just leave you to the slaughter you invite upon yourself.* He paced back and forth across the dirt street, desperate for anything to draw his attention from his burning hand.

They stood in the road for quite some time, waiting for the Shao to offer up some healing. Hessing unstrapped the priest again, and lay him back down in the street. Thantos moaned again as he was moved. The other two nobles seemed to be having their own quiet discussion. They bothered Raben. Something was wrong with them. They were of no use and seemed to stand away from everyone else in the party, including Hessing. As the sun set on them, both Raben and Hessing became extra alert, fearing that the horsemen might attack in the darkness, but Urchin insisted that he could feel them and they were nowhere near.

"No one is."

Raben stared at the priest, watching his chest rise and fall, willing it to continue, until finally, a simply clad man approached. He wore breeches and a basic brown leather tunic. He carried a sack over his shoulder. In the waning light, one could tell that he had dark hair and dark eyes, but nothing more. He simply tossed the sack to the group and ran. Hessing picked up the bag and slung Thantos over his shoulder with a grunt.

"Let's go." No one argued and they headed silently out of town. Raben marched mechanically behind Hessing, listening to Thantos murmur. The noble handed the bag to the thief, and now cradled Thantos in his arms, carrying the suffering priest tenderly. After the long walk back into the plains, Hessing set the priest down, and bade the knights start a fire. Inspecting the contents of the bag, the noble seemed satisfied. He called Urchin over to him as he set a number of dried herbs and powders on the ground. The bag had been well stocked. It even had a wooden peg leg in it. Raben sat down, using his pack to prop him up. He watched Hessing boil water while Urchin started mixing the items of the bag together. Before any of them had been administered to Thantos, Raben was sound asleep.

He awoke in the middle of the night. Urchin was on watch. *Now I feel safe.* Raben smiled to himself. The thief began to climb to his feet.

"If you need to pee, everyone else has done it over there," said Urchin as he noticed Raben. He was pointing off into the plain. "If you just want to talk, then make me some tea." A sack landed near Raben. "The water's already heated. Just stir the leaf into it. I have nothing to sift it out." Raben made a face. "Hard times demand making do."

After stirring up the leaves and boiling water, Raben carried the mug to Urchin who was sitting cross-legged in the tall grass. "Here."

Taking the tea, Urchin thanked him. "You know, I can see more than people expect I can, even before they decide to tell me." Urchin flicked his tea, testing how warm it was and trying to get the larger tea leaves out.

113

"I had guessed that. So what do you see when you are looking at me?" Raben wasn't sure he wanted the answer, yet he remained, resolved to hear what the man had to say.

"You're certain you wish to hear this?" asked Urchin. Raben nodded slowly. "I see the rabbit. You're not the rock, though the rock is the stuff you are made of. You are the rabbit. I can't read your past. It's not protected against me like a wizard's might be. It simply isn't there."

"Wait," Raben said. He raised a hand to halt Urchin. "Are you telling me that I'm..." Raben stopped to make certain he wanted the words his mind was choosing. "...that I'm not human?"

"Hells and dirt!" Urchin swore. "Don't overreact! Whether or not you're human is a hard distinction to make." The old man took a sip of tea. "Is the rabbit still the rock? I think so, but once you've resolved that it's a rabbit, it can no longer be just a rock, or perhaps more vital in your case, it will not be perceived or remembered as just a rock." Urchin blew on his tea, sipped it, made a face, and set it down.

"You're not helping me," Raben massaged his head with both hands. "Be plain."

"You're a creature of magic. Someone or something has created or magically changed you. You weren't born a human as I was." Urchin waved his arm broadly around himself. "You were just created and placed on Reman not unlike a statue."

"Oh greeching blazes!" Raben spat. "You expect me to believe that this isn't real." He pinched his own flesh. "It's not magic." He stood and turned away from the old man.

"You are human, but how you became human was through magic, for some reason, to complete a very specific end, so it would seem." Urchin got up and stood with Raben, staring out into the darkness of the expansive plain.

"Assuming I am this magic being that you claim I am, what end am I to complete? The Dayquest?" Raben turned to Urchin. *Oh hells!* The thief could almost see Urchin's mind working.

"I don't know, but I do know that you aren't the hero that is needed to complete this quest," Urchin said, pulling his orange robes tightly about him. "That, you are not. You have a lot to do with what you were given, but it isn't being the sword to the Dayquest, I think. No, your task is more important. Greater or more terrible."

"I have the sword," Raben said. "The sword that draws the foemen. I do have to be here. And I have the map." He reached into his robe to make sure the map was still there. It was.

"Have you read the prophecy that these warriors follow?" Raben nodded that he had. "It says that the sword shall draw the foemen, but it never says that the sword goes with the valiant. They assumed it did. Why in all of Reman would they want to attract the foemen to the quest itself? Better to throw you and the sword into the sea and let the followers of evil swim to the bottom in search of you." The old man walked to where his tea was and picked it up. He sniffed it and took a deep drink. "Why are you here?"

"I was told I had to go," Raben thought through the past week, "because I had the sword." *Why am I here? Who am I? That's why I am here? This is my only shot at finding out any of the answers to all of the questions you keep asking me.*

"By who?" Urchin tossed the rest of the tea into the darkness. "I don't actually have all the answers, but I do know this. You are not part of this prophecy, and everyone who has no part in this prophecy will be killed."

"Urchin," Raben replied, "if I don't complete the quest, I'll never be more than the last few days. I believe that I become complete if I obtain the True Knowledge that is sought after. If I turn back…"

"I know," said the old man. "I know. Everyone has a reason for continuing. Most of us have no idea how to stop."

"Who could make this happen?" asked the thief, tapping his hands on his chest. "A wizard?" Raben sat down in the grass.

"Not a wizard, I'd say." Urchin walked away after he answered, leaving the thief alone. Raben leaned back and stared at the stars. *Why am I here?*

The following morning, only Hessing, Raben, Thantos, and Urchin remained. Raben and Urchin had awakened Sir Jagon to take a watch, and then gone to sleep. He and the other noble's son had left in the night. They'd taken nothing, not even their own packs. The group searched for their trail, but found nothing. It was as if they'd vanished with the breeze.

"Strange, or dishonorable," said Hessing. "Guess it doesn't matter which. They have realized their cowardice and fled from the troubles of Reman." Raben was shocked by the warrior's apparent apathy towards his fellow nobles. *You nearly died to save the priest, and don't even flinch when two of your rich friends vanish without a trace.* The thief pondered this until he was interrupted by Thantos.

The priest sat up, and attempted to jump to his feet, shocking everyone. "Don't be alarmed, I woke up earlier, much to my own surprise, and called on the power of Talvo to heal my leg as well as possible. It feels fine, no pain. The thief ought to find his missing finger much the same way." Raben flexed his hand, and was shocked at the absence of pain. He'd become so used to the throbbing pain in the single day he'd borne it, that it felt more alien not to have it. "At any rate, I see that someone has had the forethought to purchase a peg leg. My power can bond it to me permanently, so I'll not be the hindrance I must have been."

Urchin made his way over to the priest and clasped hands with him. "It is better than I can tell you to see you back to normal, my friend. Your life was nearly ended." Urchin gestured to each of the members of the group. "These are the men that saved you, and must trust each other to the end, whenever it may come."

"I am honored, and will carry on so long as any of us has the will to continue," Thantos said. The priest then looked to the other members of the party, inviting them to join him in his pledge.

"As will I," said Hessing. "So long as I breathe."

"Until the end, whenever that may be." Raben did his best to sound cavalier, but couldn't completely bury how he really felt. No one seemed to mind. *You're not part of this prophecy, and everyone who isn't part of the prophecy will be killed.*

Urchin said nothing. He only looked from man to man, his mind still working.

"Wake up," Hessing hissed. "All of you! Wake up!" The three sleeping men sat up, and looked through sleep-hazed eyes for the noble, but there was no fire. "Get up! Let's go." Hessing sounded out of breath as he quickly issued the order. "The enemy is upon us. To the north." Panic swept the party as they did their best to pack up their things, fumbling in the total darkness of the moonless night. Raben was up only moments after the warning, and already had his weapons at the ready. Urchin was still trying to get his bedroll tied up.

"Damned bed. Should just leave the flaming thing and it can deal with these gods and prophecies and swords," he complained. *The sword. The sword shall draw the foemen.*

"Hessing!" Raben waited in the dark until the warrior was near him. The man's armor made enough noise to let anyone searching know where he was. "Let's go. The sword brings them." The noble grunted that he understood. "Urchin! Thantos! Lay down and stay here." Raben sprinted through the night. After only a short distance, he stopped and listened to Hessing catch up. The noble crashed through the knee-high grass, his armor creaking and banging, his weapons bouncing off of the steel plates that protected his legs. He sounded like a troop of soldiers at a run. Raben stopped him with the force in his voice. "Damn it, man."

"What?" Hessing was breathing hard. He ducked, worried that the enemy might be near at hand. "What?"

"Stand still," Raben said. He pulled out a dagger and cut the clasps on Hessing's breast plate and chain mail skirt. Both pieces of armor crashed to the ground. The thief then swiped his blade through the bands of leather that held the huge warrior's armor onto his legs. Each of the heavy plates tumbled noisily to the ground.

"Greeching fool! What're you...?" Raben's hand covered Hessing's mouth, silencing the man. The massive warrior trembled with pent up rage. Raben could feel it building up inside of the man. *Come on Lord Hessing. Calm down!*

"When you fought onboard a ship, I'll bet you didn't wear all that garbage," Raben hissed. "You're so damned loud that they'd still find us were they blind." The thief dropped his hand from Hessing's mouth, and continued sprinting through the night, not waiting for the long-winded response that the noble would surely have. Now Hessing was silent as he followed. *And greeching mad! Pity the unfortunate soul that ends up under his sword.* Raben smiled at the thought as he dashed through the thick grass of the Shao. Both men ran with weapons in their hands, ready to strike at any moment.

After jogging through the night for some time, Raben felt he was in position to attack, sensing that he and the noble must have run a broad half-circle around the assumed position of the enemy. Whether the enemy knew they were there or not was irrelevant. Raben expected that the other two members of the party would never just lie in the dark during the battle, and would therefore be able to hit the enemy in the back while he and Hessing distracted them.

"I hope you're ready," whispered the thief, "because I doubt we are all going to make it out of this." Looking to his side, Raben could barely tell the enormous noble was with him. Shallow almost imperceptible breathing was the only indicator that anyone was nearby.

Raben and the warrior stood still, listening for anything to move or make noise. Slowly, a foreign sound grew before them. The constant crunching of grass, as if a large group of creatures methodically marched over it, made its way gradually towards the men as they lay in wait. Raben judged the sound. When he guessed it was the right time, he stuck his two blades into the ground and raised his hands. "Jer Ta Annak lae Ras Koom," he repeated the words he'd first learned outside of the mage's guild. A small sphere of fire leapt out of his hand, moving north. It zipped more than one hundred paces away before it swelled into a massive thirty-reach ball of blue flame. Raben watched a number of creatures vaporize within the flame before it dissipated, and by the light it produced he could momentarily see a number of others. They were men. Slow moving. Deliberate. Unnatural.

"They're just zombies!" Raben turned to sprint away from their current position. *They're so slow that we can move away and pick them off from a distance.* He was about to take off when he saw the flames. Not two steps in front of him hovering at eye level were two lavender flames. *Oh Hell!* Raben didn't see the blow that smashed into his shoulder. It blew him from his feet, sending him hurtling through the air. He landed on his back and tumbled over to his feet. He crouched there, looking for the flames. His shoulder slowly reported the intense pain, sending dull waves through him that splintered into piercing tendrils of pain in his chest as he sucked in hurried breaths. He felt the ground move under his feet, and leapt forward into a somersault. *Hells!* His shoulder slowed him. He ended up facing where he'd just been standing. His sword and sickle were stuck in the ground nearby. He plucked them from the ground, but was reluctant to use them. He wasn't even sure he'd be able to lift his sickle. *I need a damned club to smash on it!* The lich's bones resisted blades too well, and the only time he'd scored a great hit, the thing had exploded, causing him more pain. *Damn.* The thief began to sense his imminent defeat.

"What the hell? How the greech do you fight it?" Raben wondered aloud searching for Hessing. A glancing blow bounced off of Raben's left shoulder. The thief whipped around wildly, cutting a zombie in half. Another rotting creature clubbed his arm, forcing him to let go of his sword. The sword leapt up of its own accord and began dicing the zombies. It moved as though being wielded by a master, never missing an opportunity to shred the slow moving undead as they pressed on towards the thief. Raben fell back behind the magical blade, relieved that it seemed more than a match for the zombies. *Hessing.*

Two powerful hands grabbed onto Raben's shoulders from behind and he felt himself being lifted off the ground. He kicked wildly to no avail. He was turned around until he was facing the lich, the now-intense light in its purple eyes showing through its nose and mouth, bathing the thief in pure malice. The creature slid its hand up Raben's shoulders so that they clasped his neck. Raben closed his eyes, and cast a quick spell. *Protect me. Help me. Someone.* Suddenly Raben's neck was free of the creature's hands. The thief reached out and his sword was in his hand. The lich leapt on him, but bounced off, ineffective. It could not physically touch the thief. The skeletal warrior of Thannon howled in frustration while Raben gaped at the success of his spell. In only a moment he understood the extent to which the spell was acting, and used it for as much as he could get.

"Now, my friend, perhaps you'll tell me why the greech you're so intent on causing me pain." Raben's voice soundcd cvery bit as twisted as the voice of the creature before him. "What good is the map to you?" He held his enchanted blade before him, waving it from side to side. "Answer before I grow impatient and end your twisted existence."

The lich laughed. "The only weapon that can harm me is held by the valiant warrior, and he is indisposed." The hollow voice of the lich grew in volume as it spoke. "You, my brother, are doing all that we need done. You're simply slower than He wants. Lordship is impatient when it comes to conquering. I would think you'd know that." Undaunted by Raben's display, the skeleton walked up, and stood only a pace in front of the man.

"Perhaps he should come and deal with me in person rather than sending an inept servant," Raben sneered as the words poured from his mouth.

"Fool!" The word was thunderous. "The True Knowledge will bring Thannon back to Reman in force, and you will be eternally punished for this insolence. You are going to see what torture we have become capable of." A sickly laughter began, but soon ended.

Raben arced the only sword in the realm that could harm the lich in a sweeping circle through the lich's neck. The skeletal messenger did nothing to defend itself, expecting the weapon to bounce off harmlessly. The thing's head separated from its body and split, then caught fire and erupted into thousands of bursts of lavender flame. Raben had guessed at the effect and was thrilled to see the fragmented bones deflect off of the magical barrier that had warded him from the creature's touch. *Good thing this greeching thing doesn't carry a weapon.* The ward only protected Raben from direct contact of undead creatures. A blade would have killed him as if he bore no protection whatsoever.

A flare of some type was launched over Raben's head and soon blue light bathed the plains of the Shao. Raben could see Hessing lying on the ground. He was unconscious, but not bleeding. The flare kept burning overhead and the thief heard creatures crashing through the grassy field. He turned to defend Hessing, but found only Urchin and Thantos running toward him.

"The lich took us unaware, but I killed it for good," Raben said as they neared. *I hope. Damned Thannon can probably create another one tomorrow. And this one will have a sword.* He bent down and slapped Hessing. The man woke up instantly. He stood up and his eyes were clear, as though he'd never slept. *Is that how you will survive this journey?*

"The sleep must have been an enchantment." Thantos walked up to the massive knight and cast a spell. "Nothing wrong with him at all. Must have been a spell."

"Where's the enemy? What happened?" Hessing looked at the blue lit field of battle.

"The lich is killed. He defeated it," Thantos said, pointing at Raben. "The zombies are slain. Urchin and I destroyed many of them up near camp." The priest swung his arm around and pointed south toward the campsite. "Talvo granted me great victory and power." The blue flare overhead burned out leaving the party in impenetrable darkness. Urchin quickly struck up a lantern.

"How did you kill it?" asked Hessing. "It's immune to weapons."

"Not this one," answered Raben, holding up the sword he'd stolen from the noble's house. "I took its head right off of its greeching shoulders." Raben swung the sword through the night air in demonstration.

"Well, if that's the kind of thing that that sword is going to bring. If those are the foemen," Hessing took Raben by the shoulders and looked down into the shorter man's eyes, "I'm glad the sword is yours." He stared for a long moment while Raben tried to decide if it was a compliment or an insult. "If I'd had the sword, we'd be dead. You resisted the spell." Hessing let go of the thief and walked back towards camp.

"The sword may have been the reason I resisted the spell," Raben offered, feeling uncharacteristic sympathy for the warrior. Hessing shrugged and kept walking. Urchin and Thantos immediately crowded near Raben to talk. They brought out and lit more lanterns to walk by.

"That was incredible. We could see the explosion of purple fire from over there. Your death. I was sure of it." Urchin took Raben by the arm and escorted him back to camp. "I think," said the old man, waving to Hessing, "that his manhood has been bruised. I doubt he's ever been the weak and helpless in battle before, and worse yet," Urchin clutched Raben's arm tightly, "to be saved by a thief." The old man laughed wildly. At one point it was so overpowering that he fell to the ground while air whistled from between his teeth.

"You, my friend," Raben offered a hand to pull Urchin from the ground, "are twisted."

"Indeed," agreed Thantos.

"Not at all, not at all," argued Urchin. "It is good for us to have a little humility, and therefore understand our vulnerability. Not to mention, it's blazing funny." He laughed again, and accepted Raben's hand, pulling himself to his feet.

The four men packed up the camp and decided to move at night, rest at dawn, and then resume at midday. It would keep them alert and wary during the times that the enemy was most likely to attack, and allow them to rest at a time when the enemy must hide. Very few undead were able to walk beneath the warmth of the sun.

"Where are all the zombies coming from?" asked Raben.

"It takes an evil priest, or a powerful minion of an evil god to raise them," began Thantos. "The messenger could bring them up and it would be easy to find the dead around here to use. The Plains of Shao were the battlefields for every major battle in the White Wizard War. Thousands and thousands died here. These grassy plains have a long history of undead troubles. Ghosts, ghouls and worse." Thantos brought a book out of his pack, flipping to a page near the center. "There are several chapters in the Doctrine of Priesthood that deal solely with the Plains of Shao, and the massive presence of unlife there."

"Just greeching fantastic!" Cussing made Raben feel a little better. "Does anyone have any good news?" Raben looked from side to side at his companions. Silence.

"Actually," Urchin said, breaking the silence, "no." The man laughed. Raben was irritated. He focused on marching, as did the others.

At dawn the Dayquest halted and made camp. Last night's attack loomed in the thief's mind. Raben immediately dropped to the ground and meditated for his spells. His magic had been the only thing that had saved him from the lich. His host spirit immediately commenced teaching him, and the thief was sure that he had a greater number of spells than before. He could feel the greater need for concentration and practice as he focused on the magics that entered his mind. This thought excited him. He was proud of the fact that he'd used his magic to defeat the lich the night before, and was happy believing that he was rewarded with greater spells and power. Thantos too, prayed for his spells. He finished almost exactly when Raben did. Hessing volunteered to take the first watch, and the other three men slept.

By midday, everyone had slept and taken watch.

"Well, I'm starving. We're not going to take one more step until I have a chance to make something to eat, so you," Urchin said, pointing at Hessing, "don't imagine you're going to order everyone to march until I say so." The old man pulled two pots from his pack and began building a fire.

"Did you pack a whole kitchen in there old man?" Hessing asked as he walked over to Urchin. "Were you a baker?" The aged man looked up at the towering noble, irritated by the sarcastic touch that Hessing had in his voice.

"No," he answered, "I was not a baker. I simply enjoy food."

"And there was no chance," Raben interrupted, "that a woman was going to feed him for the rest of his life." The thief laughed while Urchin twisted his face with disapproval. Hessing simply walked away, not allowing anyone in the party to see whether or not he enjoyed the joke.

"That poor fellow needs to laugh a little more," Thantos said, looking to Hessing. "He seems so serious all of the time." Looking from Urchin to Raben, the priest lowered his voice to a whisper. "Something about him bothers me. It's as if he merely tolerates us."

"That's because he does," Urchin chuckled. "He needs his sword, and your religion. And me?" The old man shrugged.

"You're the baker," Raben suggested. Urchin nodded. The thief watched the old man sprinkle a rusty powder into one of the pots he held out over the fire. "Now that we're alone." Raben nodded at Hessing, indicating that alone meant that there were no lords and knights around. "What happened in that temple, Thantos? I never really got the whole story."

The priest's mood shifted instantly from jovial to dark and bothered. He paled in remembrance, and only spoke after many labored breaths. "We walked through a number of hallways. Sir Arris and Sir Caman were leading us. We came into a great altar room. It was…" Awe spread across the priest's face. "It was incredible. You should have seen it. The walls were covered in glorious depictions of real heroes from ancient day. They were remarkable." Raben and Urchin nodded, the old man stirring a pot as he added several herbs to the steaming water. "In the back of the room was the entry to a catacomb, I think. I didn't get too close before the attack started. The messenger appeared before us, in the stairway to the catacombs, and suddenly Arris was attacking Caman. No reason, no warning. He just went insane! He tore him apart with his bare hands. The lich was just behind him, controlling him. Caman fell to the ground, bloody and shredded." Thantos stopped, his hands clenched. "He never had a chance to do anything. Then a melee broke out, and undead began attacking from every direction. One of the knights exploded. Clawed horrors ripped him in pieces. Blood coated everything." The priest reached his hand up to his face, rubbing his cheek. "It coated me." He paused as he wiped remembered blood from his face. "They screamed to retreat so I ran. I ran all the way out. I was terrified. I just didn't expect to have any of that happen down there, and I've always feared that I would end in a deep dark place, having served no purpose. I cannot die until I have served to my fullest. It seems," Thantos said, as he looked intently at the ground, "that I fear death too much. I'm not ready to face whatever lay beyond, and I have apologized to Talvo each day since the temple, asking his forgiveness for my cowardice. It would have served no one for me to die down there that day. By escaping, I can fight a battle that will make a difference. More of a difference," Thantos mumbled, "than adding myself to the ranks of the walking dead."

"My friend," Urchin said, his voice gravelly and old, but soothing, "you did the right thing by fleeing. The quest still continues. You provided a hope that it might succeed rather than an ending before it began."

"Yeah," agreed Raben, lamely. "Besides, we'll need your skills more and more as we go forward. Healers are quickly gaining value in my eyes, and one that carries an ax," said the thief, smiling, "even better."

"Enough dwelling on the terrible things. I don't wish to remember any more of that than I have to. Let's discuss lighter things. Where are you from?" Thantos asked, not specifying it to anyone.

"I have no idea," Raben said, trying to humor the priest. "I guess Liveport. My earliest memories are of there. I have done nothing in my life that seems worth telling until I mixed myself up in this."

"Me too, actually," Thantos said. "I suppose that means we can pry into this old man's life and listen to him prattle on endlessly while he fabricates the legendary things that he has seen and done with his hundreds of years of life." The priest smiled weakly.

"So that's what you want, huh? Your betters to tell you a story? So be it. Stir this!" he ordered, handing a long wooden spoon to Thantos, and showing him the exact rate at which the water should be swirled. "I have traveled all over these lands, but as a youngster I traveled with a number of merchants. They sold many strange things. Carpets and silver items. Lanterns of every size, for every purpose. Glass. Blown glass! Huge vessels that took four men to make and move." The old man used his arms to illustrate the size. "This big, at least."

"Wait," Raben said. "Were these your parents? They were merchants?"

"No, no," sighed Urchin. "My parents were killed many years ago. They tended a large forest for years and years. Longer, in fact, than many men live. They farmed huge Gulphorns that reached nearly to the heavens, trimming them and making sure they survived each winter so they would stand for centuries. They had to bring down diseased branches and keep bears from sharpening their mighty claws on the bark. They could speak to the massive animals. They raised some of the greatest trees ever known in all the realms. One day, however, an evil sect of priests and wizards that must have worshipped one of the dark gods invaded the forest. They captured animals and defaced the trees, offering the living flesh of the forest to feed the plague of their vile magics. Well, my parents could allow no such thing, because they followed the way of nature, and they protected it with all they had." Urchin stopped his tale long enough to look into the pot and make sure it was cooking as it should in Thantos' care. Satisfied, he resumed. "They were powerful, my parents, and normally would suffer no more than the effort it took them to dispose of ruffians that moved into the woods, but when they began to fight the cult, for that is what the worshippers of the dark gods called themselves, they found an unforeseen opponent." Urchin stood up and held his hands over his head, while twisting his face into as hideous a mask as he could. "A great demon, they had, and it bathed my parents in fire, roasting them alive. Still, the forest itself was brought to attack the dark worshippers, but as the last of the priests and vermin perished, so did my parents to the fires of the demon." After saying this, the old man paused, looking down into the ground, searchingly. Slowly he raised his eyes back to his audience. "They did what they were to do, but I never saw them again. I fled the forest, fearing an evil that was powerful enough to slay my parents, and unable to tend the ancient woods. Lacking the knowledge." Though he seemed to have much more to tell, he went silent. Only a moment afterwards, Hessing came walking into camp.

"Is your stew finished yet, old man?" The noble leaned down and took in a lung full of the savory odor. "You can smell it all across the Shao." With that, the stories ended, and the meal began. After everyone had eaten their fill, the party prepared to resume their march for the rest of the day.

"We must make good time," Hessing announced as they began their march. Urchin grumbled unhappily after the proclamation, but kept up as the men moved rapidly through the tall grass. The day passed quickly as the group focused on making good distance with the remaining light, and at dusk there was only a quick meal, a few moments of discussion where the watches were assigned, and then everyone went to sleep. All went well through the night as the party enjoyed a peaceful sleep under the stars.

In the morning, they all gathered around the map of the Dayquest and agreed on a general path to the north and east. They had been winding all over the plains since the trek began because of the attacks and the priest's health, so now they directed their attention back to the Dayquest. For two days they trudged through the unchanging grass of the Shao. It was tediously boring, but it allowed everyone to rest and lighten up. They tried to discuss the scene at the temple where the knights had been killed in more depth, but Thantos was unable to do so without becoming upset. *I have seen the minions of Thannon, my friend. I understand.* Hessing wanted to hear about Arris' sudden conversion into a monster, but after trying several times, Thantos had to stop. Emotion and panic overtook him with the memory of the attack. He stopped walking, and shook with each passing memory. Once Thantos recovered, the group gave up on the topic and resolved to make greater distance away from the temple and the terrible start to the quest.

On the third morning Hessing decided that they would soon need more water. Storms had been forming to the west, but never offered anything more than occasional and distant thunder. Urchin divined for water by touching the earth, and then led them. He moved seemingly at random, turning erratically and with apparently very little control. He ambled drunkenly for most of the afternoon and through the evening until finally he and the party were forced to rest. On the fourth day, he resumed his awkward march, and quickly brought the party within sight of a farm.

A weather beaten gray barn stood in the middle of the plain. An equally aged and mistreated house stood near it.

Just beyond the two structures, a pond glittered like a green eye, reflecting the hue of the sea of grass that surrounded it. Nothing else was visible. As if to explain the shape of the buildings, a distant storm thundered across the plain. A few dark clouds were already passing overhead of the company.

"This place looks terrible," Raben said. He shook his head. "Not surprising if roaming bands of the living dead trample through every night." *Just the sort of place we would end up holding out against a storm.*

"Strange," commented Hessing. "No fences or any signs of pens, or anything." The warrior brought out his sword and checked its edge. Satisfied, he put it back in its sheath.

"The soil here is marked with evil." Urchin had fallen to the ground. "But the water up ahead is fresh and unspoiled." He climbed to his feet. "And that's what we're here for, yes?" The old man appeared eager to make it to the pond he'd discovered.

"Yes, but are we going to die getting a drink?" Raben rested his hand on his sword. "Something feels very wrong here. Does anyone have anything that can help discern whether or not it is safe to go near this place?" The group had nothing. "This water had better be greeching good."

Thantos prayed quietly to Talvo as he began to hobble towards the house. The party slowly and cautiously approached the farmhouse. Nothing was heard. No animals or people. Were it not for the cool breeze that whispered through the grass, the plain would have been totally silent. Just as they reached the house, the sun was blocked out of the sky by a black could, which hung low with rain.

"Tell me," whispered Raben to Thantos, "that this isn't an omen. We are begging to get killed by coming here. I can feel it." *If you aren't part of the prophecy you will be killed. By making foolish decisions you will be killed.* "I'm not knocking on the damned door."

Hessing climbed the stairs of the porch, as if to prove that he was immune to the foreboding circumstances around them. Boards creaked as he walked on them; some of them bowed under his weight causing him to step gingerly as he approached the door. He raised his gloved hand and knocked on the door. By the third knock, the door fell into the house with a wooden crash. All of them jumped. Raben was holding his sword, and Hessing leapt back, both swords in hands, and crashed through the floor boards of the rickety porch. He was standing on the soft dirt underneath, his waist being gouged by broken boards. Never the less, he stood alert, waiting to see if anything was going to come howling from the house to attack him. Nothing. The huge warrior pulled himself up out of the hole he'd made. Lifting his shirt, he inspected the minor scrapes he'd gotten by breaking through the wooden planks.

Raben ascended the stairs while Hessing was pulling himself free and looked into the house. Surprisingly, there was furniture and all the comforts of a well maintained home. The only indicator that it was not well maintained was the knuckle of dust on the floor and the ivy that grew through a window and across the ceiling. He stepped into the house followed closely by the noble. Both of them held their swords at the ready.

Puffs of dust fled from their footsteps, rising into the air. The house had a main room, a kitchen, and two bedrooms. It was well furnished, including three beds. Nothing looked amiss at all. It simply appeared to have been abandoned.

"I'd have been happier if the place was all wrecked and burned," said Hessing. "This is more odd for being perfect." As if to ease his wants, the noble slowly placed his booted foot on the back of a chair and pushed it over. It thumped into the wooden floor, sending a curtain of dust into the air. "This is very strange."

That's for greeching sure. "I wonder what's in the barn," Raben mused, unable to rationalize the condition of the house. As he and Hessing came back through the abandoned home, Thantos and Urchin had just barely entered.

"Anything?" Thantos asked.

"Nothing. The place is perfect, save for the dust. We're going to check the barn. Come on," ordered Hessing. He marched past the old man, his boots pounding on the creaky floor. "Maybe we'll find something." *Like a good battle to return us to normal.* Raben, too, would have preferred that the house not look so undisturbed.

The door to the barn was barred. *Not many barns lock from the inside.*

"Since when does a barn need to be locked from the inside?" asked Thantos. "It's not as if the cows need their privacy, though the undead problem in the area could necessitate the need to lock your livestock up."

Urchin slowly lowered himself to the ground just outside of the barn door and touched the soft earth. For a moment the old man fell into a deep meditation, but only moments afterward, his eyes shot open. The old man's mouth opened as though he would scream, but his stomach convulsed, bringing its contents up and out. After heaving several times, Urchin passed out cold and fell heavily to the ground. Thantos rushed to the fallen man. Raben and Hessing looked at each other. *No way. This is a terrible idea.* Raben shook his head while Hessing gestured that they had to explore. The thief shook his head, but unsurprisingly, the noble was insistent. He gestured emphatically at the door. *Why do this?* Hessing pointed to the door and again waved the thief to it. *Why bother with reason. We'll eventually end up doing what he wants anyway.*

Raben knelt and removed his pack from his shoulder and began digging through it. Soon, he brought out an exceptionally slim saw, which he handed to Hessing while he searched for other tools. Bringing out a lock pick set and a chisel, the thief rose to his feet.

"Okay, let's get in there," Raben whispered. A flash of lightning lit the sky, and thunder followed. *Open your eyes, you great oaf. The gods are warning us against this.* He looked back to Hessing, hoping that the thunder had borne some sort of sense to the man. The noble only nodded as he gestured to the barn door.

The two men walked up to it. Raben took the saw from Hessing, and inserting it in the gap between the crude barn doors, he lowered it until it connected with something. He removed the saw and lowered it half a reach, inserted it again, and raised it until it contacted the same thing from the underside. Lifting up hard, he checked to see if it was a drop bolt. Unable to lift it, he concluded that it must be a sliding bolt.

He reinserted the saw above the bolt again, and began cutting what he hoped was a wooden dowel of some sort. Rain began to sprinkle them with moisture. Saw dust began to fall from his blade. *Yes! Through in just a moment.* He sawed faster and suddenly the saw passed through the bolt and the heavy doors shifted slightly, having been freed from the lock. Thantos left Urchin in the thick grass and shifted to where he could see.

Hessing reached past the thief and pulled the doors open. *Fool!* Raben tumbled backwards, putting distance between himself and the open door. *Doesn't have a clue what's in there.*

The barn was almost empty. The floor was chewed up earth, warm and fresh smelling. Thantos went wide-eyed when he looked in. Every three reaches or so, for the entire length of the barn, were rows of six to seven head stones.

"This is a blazing grave yard." Thantos backed away from the barn, bending down to drag Urchin to safety.

"Worse still," Hessing said, easily plunging his sword into the broken soil. "It looks like no one here likes sleeping." He looked to Raben. Thunder rolled across the plain. The sky was nearly black above them. "We're in trouble."

Rain began to fall in sheets. In only a few moments it fell so hard that the group couldn't see the house from the barn. Raben and Hessing lead the party back to the house through the downpour. The noble was carrying the unconscious old man over his shoulder. Once all of them were on the rickety porch, they realized that water had been their problem in the first place. Propping skins and flasks up on the stairs in front of the house, they let the storm refill them with fresh water. Moments later, they entered the house. Urchin came to and demanded a description of the insides of the barn. Thantos told him.

"Why are there graves in that barn?" asked Urchin as he peeled his soaking robes off. "And why is Thantos terrified? I hope it isn't because I passed out. The ground was so unhealthy. I couldn't help myself. Thantos, have courage." *Perhaps he is still worried about dying at the hands of the dead.* Raben was surprised that Urchin hadn't answered his own question. The drenched old man laid his robes flat on the floor to dry, and sat naked in a dusty chair causing a small cloud. "It's strange, but…"

"Better question," said Raben, unwilling to force the priest to air his fears. "Did the inhabitants of the graves lock themselves in the barn?" He followed Urchin's lead and laid his robes out as well, but only after lifting a throw rug from the floor, thereby finding a dust free area to place his sopping wet clothes.

"Fiery Hells! You mean those graves aren't full of dead people?" Urchin wrung his hands together. "I thought at first that we may have come across a plague grave yard. I'm just about tired of dealing with the undead."

"There is only one type of dead that use graves often enough to keep the soil rich and soft," Thantos said quietly, his voice lacking strength.

"Vampires." Hessing sighed the word in a familiar way.

"Have you dealt with such things before, your lordship?" asked Urchin. "You sound as if you have. You also sound as if it wasn't a very good time." Urchin reached down to the cushion of the chair he sat in, and flicked a ball of dust.

"There was one time, while on a ship that such a creature was aboard," Hessing said slowly, remembering. "We had begun to find dead bodies on board with no apparent wounds. We tossed a couple overboard before noticing the small punctures. Bite marks. One of the passengers told a hideous tale about blood sucking vampires and that clenched it. After that, fear and panic spread through the ship." He crossed his arms and leaned against the wall, staring at the floor. "By the next day all of my row boats had been taken by fearful sailors, and a few more people had intentionally thrown themselves overboard rather than risk meeting the creature. We called a meeting in the noon sun and resolved to search the entire vessel. One of the men," Hessing turned to the wall and wedged his fingernails between two wooden planks, "found that some of the boards in a cabin wall were loose, and when we pulled them down it came at us." The noble curled his fingers like claws. "It tore through the first two men in a mere moment, not unlike the lich did, and I fell back. A particularly brave sailor leapt onto the thing and held its arms for a brief time. During that moment I placed chains and manacles on it. He and I dragged the terrible monster out onto the deck under the sun and it caught fire instantly. Damned near half the ship went up with it. Once I reached shore again, I read everything I could on them. Never really thought I'd face such a nightmare again." Hessing fell back against the wall and let out a slow breath.

"So they really drink blood?" Raben asked, touching his throat. "If you read so much about them, then what is our best course?" Urchin and Thantos joined Raben in looking to Hessing.

"Sunlight is the best way to kill them. A stake through the heart is said to kill them as well. Fire," answered the noble though his voice leant no confidence. "Everything was a legend or a myth. There was no official book on killing vampires, only thousands of distant remembrances and exaggerated stories about a few people who'd known someone who'd seen one."

"Greeching perfect!" Raben padded softly over to the fireplace causing dust to rise through the room. He looked down at the obvious tracks he'd just made. "Do they just float around, or can we safely assume they don't come in the house?" The thief cracked a chair into pieces and placed them in the hearth and after a quick spell, a fire burned in the house for the first time in a long while.

"They sense life, and thirst for it," Hessing said.

"If no one has been alive in the house for years," answered Thantos, "then the vampires have had no reason to enter." The priest was sitting in the middle of the floor in his wet robes, clutching his legs to him. "Based on the number of open graves in that barn, there is no way we can fight them, day or night." He looked to Hessing to be contradicted, but Hessing only shook his head.

"Then what can we even do to stay alive?" asked Urchin. "To the Hells with fighting them." His hand shot out emphatically. "We're on a quest that's more important than this barn out here. What do we do now?"

"I have a spell that might," Thantos stressed this point, "might work." He brought his book from his pack. "It makes a person appear dead, but says nothing in regards to whether or not it works in a way that would fool undead." He set the open book on the floor. "But it could be an option. I can get everyone."

"Are they sentient?" asked Raben. No one answered. "Like the lich. Can they talk and make decisions?"

"Yes," answered Thantos. "They are among the most intelligent undead in existence."

"That does nothing to cheer me up." Urchin picked up his robe and held it near the fire.

"Does anyone have any idea on how to battle or escape these creatures?" Raben walked to his pack and brought out a sickle, which he began to flip and catch.

"No," Thantos answered.

"Nothing we can do here." Hessing stared at the floor.

Urchin shook his head without looking to Raben. "We'll just have to wait and see what happens," he murmured.

The fire was kept burning as the party took turns stoking it with broken furniture. The rain subsided somewhat, falling lightly or not at all. Eventually Raben put his robes back on. Despite being warm and tired he couldn't stop pacing and thinking. *There has to be something.*

Several times, the members of the group brought an idea only to realize they didn't have the resources or the time to do it. *There must be some way to defeat these things. If not, they would have taken over all of Reman by now.*

"One of us will live," Urchin said, eventually.

"What?" Thantos asked, having been awakened from thoughtfulness.

"One of us will live." Urchin turned away from the fire. "The prophecy will be completed. One of us will complete it. At least one of us will escape here alive. One of us has to make it to the end. None of us is here by accident. Those who were have been taken already." The old man looked from the priest to the fire.

"It isn't me," replied Thantos. "I am not the object of the prophecy. We must do our best to make sure he escapes." Thantos pointed to Hessing. Urchin remained silent. Raben contemplated that idea. *It says nowhere in that greeching prophecy who will finish it. It might be none of us. It might be me. The only person who has claimed that he is the center of this mess, is greeching Hessing, and he'd be dead if not for me.*

"We'll all get out of here, or none of us will," said Raben. A familiar feeling of power began to radiate inside of him. He'd felt it before. "I'm going to the barn." He stood up and checked his weapons, making sure they were all in the right places. He looked to the others momentarily and headed for the door. "You guys stay here." *I have beaten tremendous odds so far. I'll get us out of here. Just like the temple of Talvo.* "Do these things use weapons or claws?"

"Claws," Hessing said.

None of the others tried to stop Raben or join him. *They think I'm the prophecy.* Raben could neither smile nor frown. He didn't know what he wanted at that moment. He cast a spell on himself. *The same spell that got that greeching lich. Now the bastards can't touch me with their greeching claws.* Raben gave silent thanks that undead didn't use swords as he descended from the porch and walked across the yard. The rain had slowed to a constant drizzle. Raben pulled his robes tighter around himself and surveyed the area. *The door is closed.* Seeing it, Raben stopped. He shook uncontrollably. *I knew they were there.* He was certain the group hadn't closed the barn door as they left, so the vampires must have. *Just kick the door in and get to work!* He calmed himself as much as possible and walked up to the door. Two or three times he reached out to open the door, but each time he froze as fear gripped him. *This is a phenomenally bad idea. Where in all the blazing hells did I get this notion from?* Almost of its own volition, his leg kicked out and the door flew inward. Dim light shined within.

Raben stared into the barn. A group of seemingly normal people were huddled around a dying lantern. They all stared at him now that he'd kicked the door in. He saw small children that nestled closer to their mothers and a few men who began to stand as if to defend the group, but this was not what he'd expected. *Where are the claws, and anger. Scary. Something's very wrong. They're farmers.* The image of Halkam, the god of the common man, filled his mind. *These are simple people.*

"Are you folks okay?" he asked. He now realized, from their alarmed looks, that he was carrying his sword and sickle. He lowered them. "Can you hear me?" he called. "Are you alright?" The men stood silently, but he could hear the children whispering and crying. "Speak!" Raben waited. The scene seemed wrong to him as he stood before them. He felt exposed, in danger. *Attack! Come on! Attack!*

One of the men waved Raben nearer to them. He heard voices. They seemed to make sense yet they were just quiet enough that he couldn't pick a word out. Now a few of them waved for him to come over. *They're quiet. Just say something. Speak!* Raben looked at them. They were all waving to him. There were many voices, but still he couldn't hear them well enough to answer. He wasn't even sure where they were coming from. The folks were visible before him, yet it seemed as if some of the voices were originating from off to each side. He needed to do something. *This is a trap!*

"Jer Ta Annak…" he started the spell. They kept waving. One of them started towards him. "…lae Ras Koom." The words echoed through the barn as he forcefully pronounced them. The fireball sped into the center of the group and exploded, incinerating the simply clad people who had been huddling there. The barn was immediately aflame. Women and children screamed as their skin cracked and withered. The men, more concerned with their families, called out the names of their loved ones even as they fell, burning alive. The roof of the barn sagged as the walls bowed out from the blast. Pieces of burning material flew out into the night. Suddenly the ball was gone, and only scattered small fires remained. Raben stood, watching. He stared at the carnage he'd caused. He heard a creaking from above him. He quickly withdrew from the wrecked building, and then the roof of the barn fell in, covering the charred bodies of the dead.

Raben involuntarily jumped back further as the barn caved in on itself. He watched intently, waiting for someone or something to come out and attack. Horrified that he believed they might, afraid that they wouldn't. He wanted them to. He had no idea what to do. Were they just farmers? *That's too easy. That was not right.* He cautiously walked back to the house backwards, keeping his eyes on the burning remains of the barn. He carefully made his way up the steps of the porch, never letting his eyes waver from the fallen barn, and then walked into the house. His companions were all poised to attack, but lowered their weapons as they realized it was Raben who approached and not a vampire.

"Well Thief?" Hessing asked.

"I killed them," Raben answered. "I threw open the door, and they were huddled together. They waved for me to join them and I blew them all up. Not even one survived that I could tell." Raben looked back out the door at the blaze he'd left behind. "It was too easy. No fangs or claws or anything." Raben looked back to each of the group members. "We may have been wrong. There might have been no vampires."

Hessing's mouth opened and closed several times as he searched for the words.

"Wouldn't it bother you if that were the case?" asked Thantos. "To know that you just burned a large group of normal people alive." He watched Raben closely.

"I suppose. But either these people were vampires or they slept all day in graves." Raben pointed to Hessing and then to Thantos. "You two were the ones who convinced us that these were vampires to begin with." He pointed to Hessing. "You, in particular, with your greeching story about blood sucking and..." Raben slammed the doorjamb with his fist and moved over near the fire. "Damn you!"

"I didn't mean to say it was your fault," Thantos said. "It just took me by surprise. That's all." The priest held his arms out to his sides apologetically. "We know you didn't go out there to roast innocent people."

Raben sat, staring at the fire, remembering the entire scene. *It was so short, and easy. What do I care if they weren't vampires? I didn't set out to kill a bunch of farmers. If they spent their days sleeping in open graves, they still needed to be killed. Wouldn't it bother me? I didn't see any of you leaping up from where you were cowering to come with me to fight them. No! They were vampires, and you were terrified.*

He got up and broke a cabinet into pieces.

"They never came into their own house?" Raben asked, looking to Thantos. "These weren't normal people. They would have come here if they were. Not locked themselves in a greeching barn full of fresh graves."

"Yes!" he said. "They were vampires." Thantos sat down one the floor, and rested his head on his knees. *Very convincing!* Raben sneered into the fire. He'd done what the rest of them hadn't the courage to do. *It's their fault if it's anyone's.*

Urchin came over and sat with Raben.

"How would you feel if you knew they were just people in that barn?" he asked. He kept his voice low. Raben had to lean towards him to hear the question. "How would you feel?"

"I don't know," Raben answered. "After all that was said, I don't feel at all responsible for it. I just did what was necessary." The two men could hear Thantos weeping. *Weep priest, and grow a stronger will while you do so. I went out there to do what none of us wanted to do, but you can cry if you want. Perhaps you've already suffered enough. Cry.*

"No!" Urchin interrupted. "Forget about responsible. How would feel about the people. Even if we didn't care," the old man said. "We all thought they were vampires too. How would you feel?" Urchin reached out and touched Raben's arm. *This is nearly as strange as the barn. How would you feel? Damn me if you want.*

"I don't know. I don't think like that." Raben pulled his arm away from the old man and tossed another piece of the cabinet on the fire. It looked like a shelf.

"Try," urged Urchin. "How would you feel if you'd just murdered normal people?"

"I," Raben began. *Greeching old bastard!* "I don't care," he yelled.

Hessing and Thantos immediately looked over to Raben. Thantos had tears in his eyes that reflected the firelight. Hessing looked angry. Urchin waved them off, and both men returned to staring at the floor. *What the Hells is this? Did they plan this? Why is it such an ordeal? I did what you all wanted me to do!*

Urchin leaned in and whispered into Raben's ear. "You're definitely the rabbit."

Raben got up and walked over to a window that had a view of the barn and knelt down. It was still burning. *That fire is probably visible for leagues as flat as the plains are.* He watched it for a long time. The flames persisted despite the rain that still fell lightly. His legs fell asleep as he watched the small flames consuming the barn. It eventually stopped burning, sizzling out as the rain began to fall with more strength. Raben could make out a few areas that were still smoldering, but no flame was left. He walked over and sat next to Hessing. The noble was breathing deeply and regularly. He'd managed to fall asleep. *Lucky greeching noble.* Raben listened to the man breathe, and was beginning to drift off himself when he thought he heard something. His head shot up, and he listened. Slowly he became sure. Urchin was sprawled out before the fireplace, and Thantos was sitting in meditation in the middle of the room. Someone was lightly knocking on the door.

Raben sat perfectly still. His eyes were riveted to the door, waiting for it to open. He heard no one on the porch. *Hessing had sounded like a horse walking across that porch.* The knocking continued, just loud enough to be heard. The windows were useless. Neither had a good view of the door, and Raben couldn't get there without making noise anyhow. He reached a hand out and shook Hessing. Still sleeping. He shook the noble again, and sat, paralyzed, as the warrior slid from the sitting position onto the floor where he lay, still asleep. *Oh Hells! Magic!* Thantos had slumped over forward, and Urchin was softly snoring where he lay in front of the fireplace. The knocking ceased. Raben eased his sword out, knuckle by knuckle, and waited. Every muscle in his body tensed, making it nearly impossible to sit still. He adjusted his legs, getting them in front of him, and rocked forward into a crouching position. The knocking started again. He sucked in his breath and raised himself, ever so slowly, until he was standing. *Why must all of these things happen to me?* He looked over at Hessing. *That bastard sleeps through everything.*

He moved his right foot forward and applied weight to it, making sure that the floorboard wasn't going to creak. Once he had the foot planted he brought his other foot forward and tested his next step. Board by board he crept towards the door. The knocking stopped, and so did Raben. He froze mid-step, balancing his weight on one foot. He raised his hands, holding his sword up in front of him. The knocking was louder when it resumed. *Impatience. Why knock? Just kick the damned door in, and be done with it.* That's what Raben had done. *This is maddening!* He walked to the door, and grabbed the handle firmly. Before he opened it, he was reminded of the barn door. *Greeching foolish!* Raben positioned his sword so that he could quickly stab anyone that might attack. He pulled the door open.

Darkness. *Movement!* Raben backed away from the door. "Wait!" hissed a black silhouette. Footsteps. *Behind me!* The floorboards creaked. Raben ducked instinctively as a claw dug into his left shoulder blade. He reversed his grip on his sword and stabbed behind himself. He missed, but something hissed and the claw was gone. Raben kicked backwards but nothing was there. Freezing pain permeated his back, making it difficult to breathe. His left arm fell limply to his side. He tried to suck in a breath, but the icy pain that stabbed through him grew worse as he pulled air.

"Wait!" The hiss was far louder this time. Raben raised his sword threateningly in his right hand. A mist started to fill the house. The thief could see the thin wispy white clouds moving through the room by the light of the dying fire. He took a few quick steps backward until his back was firmly pressed against the wall that Hessing had fallen asleep against. The noble still lay on his side, chest moving rhythmically as he comfortably slumbered. Raben held his sword across his body as he labored for breath. His left arm was paralyzed. He reached down with his chin and pressed it into his left shoulder, probing it. *Oh Hells!* Icy cold.

"Do not attack," said the figure that now filled the doorway. The silhouette was of a man. Two reaches tall with snowy hair on his head, narrow shoulders, and long thin legs. *Too obvious!* Raben looked to his right and left, searching for the attackers he was sure were there. "We are allies. We fight for the same cause." The creature walked into the room where Raben could get a good look. Its pasty white face housed milky eyes with brilliant reflective yellow irises. The predatory glow of the monster's eyes was reinforced by a mouth full of broken, uneven teeth that drew attention to the two perfect sets of fangs which forced the thing to hold its mouth slightly open. *Vampires. Hells! Vampires.*

Raben sucked in another long breath. The cold was diminishing from its original intensity, but seemed to be spreading further into his body. He wasn't certain he could run if he had to. The vampire was only a few steps away from him, the bright yellow eyes peering intently from the deep sockets in which they sat. Raben could make out a number of pale blue veins in the undead creature's forehead.

"We fight for the same side," hissed the vampire as it stepped immediately before the thief. "The living will be dominated." The undead creature pulled its shoulders back as if to stretch. Its head lurched forward. The skin on its chest stretched back and seemed to barely contain the bony ribcage. It growled from somewhere within the depths of its body.

Raben attempted to strike it with his sword, but found that his right arm could barely raise his weapon, which had sunk down until the tip of it rested on the ground.

"What side," Raben rasped, "is that?" He let his body slide down into a crouch. The wall was all that kept him from falling to the floor.

"The side of the dead," the creature said, as it recovered from its stretch. "We are about to begin the war to regain the world we were forced to leave behind, but unable to leave." The vampire bent down and ran a hand over Hessing's shoulders, sniffing the air slowly. It sucked air in past its massive fangs as though it were tasting the air.

"Hey!" Raben couldn't move. "Do not!" he yelled, as he sat watching.

"These are yours?" asked the vampire, standing abruptly. "We understand." It waved a pointed claw and Raben saw a number of creatures leap up off of Urchin and Thantos. Blood dripped from their mouths. Urchin seemed to have been spared from what Raben could see, but the vampires that rose from Thantos' unconscious body wiped excess blood from each other's chins and sucked the red liquid from their clawed fingers to ensure that none was wasted.

"Out! Now!" He yelled. Raben forced everything he had into his voice. "Now!" Pain racked the thief as he recovered from the yell. The cold was pulsing throughout his body. He felt nothing. The vampires began to vanish and pass from the house. Instantly the mist that had filled the house was gone, and only one vampire remained.

"Talk to me," it said. "We can use your strength." It backed away from Raben and sat on the wooden floor. "Your power is not questioned. We couldn't sense you. We thought it impossible to surprise us." The vampire gestured to the barn. "We had no idea another vampire was so near." *Another vampire. Am I dead? A vampire?* Raben focused on the undead before him, searching for some sense of truth. *You think I am a vampire?*

"I cannot join you," the thief wheezed. "I am on a greater mission." *I'm no vampire.* "The most important mission of our order." Raben's breath failed him, and he became unable to talk. His lungs seemed hard pressed to keep gathering enough air to sustain him, much less allow him to press on through the conversation. *Leave. Please leave.*

"I see," it said. The vampire smiled knowingly. Its purple lips spread wide displaying its mouthful of yellow teeth and the horrible fangs. "Then you are the harbinger.

149

We will begin." The vampire stood. Raben couldn't look up as it lifted itself from the floor. "I will visit again." The creature disintegrated into a light mist and diffused into the air.

Thank you! Thank you so much. Raben felt tremendous relief as the creature dissipated. He didn't know who to thank, but was grateful to whatever turn of events left him and his companions alive. The thief's head slumped forward, leaving him helpless to look at anything but the floor. Raben sat there listening to his own breathing as his lungs struggled to draw air into his body and expel it back out. Each breath seemed a reprieve from his imminent death.

Why do all of these damned undead things think I'm on their side? The lich had called him brother. The vampires fear him as a strong counterpart of a war he'd never heard of. *What the blaze is going on? Urchin says I have nothing to do with this whole greeching quest. Hessing says he's the one. Undead are constantly recruiting me. The Guild sent me on this damned trek.* Raben focused on breathing for a few moments, making sure that it was regular. *Think! I'm magical. I'm a magically changed man. Maybe I'm shielded from undead. Maybe they can't smell my blood. Maybe it's because I can cast spells. Maybe I'm the evil after all.* Raben tried to draw a deep breath, but found that even that function had fallen from his control. *Maybe Urchin is lying. Maybe I have a part of this quest. Maybe I was magically changed to complete the Dayquest. Maybe he's jealous. After all, if Hessing's the hero, he'll never get there. The fool gets wiped out in every battle. If I'm not part of this mess then how come I'm the only one who isn't constantly about to be killed? Maybe Urchin thinks he's the center of the quest and wants to discourage the rest of us. Thantos knows it's not him.* Raben stewed on the idea, asking himself the same questions over and over in his mind. *I am the sword. Maybe the foemen that it draws aren't my foes, just foes to the church. Maybe I can use these vampires.* Raben stewed over his predicament for a long time before he was interrupted.

"A fine sight you are, human." Raben heard the female voice, but could only see the brushed leather shoes that she wore. Her feet were small. "I still maintain that humans haven't the first clue on how to survive in the world." *Greeching Hells!* The elven woman's perfume crashed into Raben's senses. *How in the blazing Hells does she always know when to show up? She must have a troop of ghosts that watch me, just waiting for me to be incapacitated. Damn her!*

The thief felt soft thin hands cup his head and lift. He could now see her. She wore a dark cowl that hung over her face, but the shapely graceful body was exactly as he remembered it, and there was certainly no mistaking the perfume. Raben felt as though he were trapped in a thick cloud of the fruity stench. He had irreparably assigned a negative association to the perfume, which may have been appealing were it not for the terrible circumstances in which he consistently encountered it.

He didn't feel the same about the elven woman, however. He'd seen little of her face, but he certainly had a man's appreciation for both it and her body, and he found her voice to be soothing and seductive, though she only used it to insult him and give him orders. *There is something about her.* He stared into the cowl, hoping it would fall back, or that she would pull it back. He wanted to see her face again.

"You haven't learned a thing yet have you?" she asked. "You can't continue at this pace fool, or you'll never finish the quest." She placed one of her hands firmly against his forehead, holding his skull against the wall behind him. "Insulting your body this way and not taking care will lead to your eventual downfall. We trained you against such activities. Quit playing the hero." She smirked as she said it, lending to the notion that she felt Raben had already proven his inability at being the hero.

Playing the hero? I'm certainly not playing hero. Desperate maybe. Damn you! He knit his brows. *I'm just trying to survive this mess. If you have all of the answers, and know my every move, and how to get through all of this, then why the greeching Hells don't you go?*

"You're lucky that I don't easily tire of putting you back together," she said, her sudden aggravation giving an edge to the statement. "If I weren't always on your heels, I'm sure you'd just be dead." She sprinkled some powder over the paralyzed thief. He could smell it, and feel the texture of it in his nose. *Iron. It smells like...blood.* "Not that I would mind too much if you were dead, but I swore to the Guild that I would see you through most of this trek. They want you to succeed even if you don't."

Suddenly she let go of Raben, and his head slammed back down on his chest, leaving him unable to see anything but his own feet.

"You need to figure out how to survive these things. You have been trained with great abilities, fool. Learn them, and lead yourself," she urged. "One with your ability could go quite far if you wanted. I don't understand what your problem is."

He could hear her walking about the room, but couldn't see where she was. She seemed to be inspecting each member of the party, but he couldn't be certain. Her light footfalls could be heard as she ranged throughout the room.

"Your friends aren't doing very well," she said. "If you recover from this, you might want to help them." She sounded like she was smiling, or on the verge of laughter. Then she sounded serious. "Motivate yourself human, or we will find a way. And though I must seem to be a sweet, caring woman, I can certainly find a few unpleasant ways to inspire you to new heights of performance." He never heard her leave, and a while later he had other things on his mind.

Thousands of tiny pin-sized pains began prickling up his hand. Raben sat, unable to move or scream, as the conflagration of his senses spread. Soon it crossed his wrist and was burning his arm. The pain was so intense he'd have preferred being burned alive. *Let me pass out. Oh Hell!* His entire left arm and shoulder were vibrating with the innumerable pricks of fire that accompanied the return of his body's warmth. It felt as if his own blood were acid, consuming him from within. A scream erupted from him the moment he could manage it. He continued screaming until the pain released him. It was dark when it had begun, and by the time the thief could move without his voice ripping through the air involuntarily, the sun was up over the horizon. His voice was stripped bare and excruciating blasts of hoarse sound had been all that was left as they were wrenched from his aching lungs.

Hessing still slept exactly where he'd fallen the night before, as did Urchin. Thantos, however, lay writhing on the wooden floor as if he were trapped in a constant nightmare. *Come on, priest. Our troubles are only just beginning in the real world. No need to dream up other ones.* Raben massaged his body, remembering the tears he'd cried throughout the morning. Once he was convinced that the pain was passed, he tentatively crawled over to Thantos.

The priest was in the throes of agony. Every one of the muscles in his arms was flexed, his teeth were clenched, sweat dripped from his face, and his hands were balled into fists so tightly that his knuckles were crowned with solid white. He would pull his head sharply to a side every few moments as if wrenching it from someone's grasp, and then his mouth would open and his whole body would cease to move as he screamed silently until his breath gave out. *Oh gods!* Thantos had a number of paired wounds, small punctures that had large swollen pink rings around them. Little blood looked to have escaped the holes in the priest's flesh, but Raben had seen the greedy undead lap up Thantos' lifeblood hungrily. *What gods could even allow this?* "Look," Raben snarled as he looked up at the ceiling. "Look at this!" He yelled. The idea of someone actually feeding off of another person struck him, sickened him. *This is wrong. This is the most wrong thing I've seen since I started this damned quest.* He crawled to his nearby pack and pulled out a blanket. Returning to Thantos, he covered him. *They think I'm one of them. To the Hells with these things, these greeching vampires!* "To the Hells!" He fumed for only a few moments until he realized Thantos still needed him, though he had no idea what he could do for the suffering priest. *To Hell with that greeching woman too! Until she actually does something helpful, why would I heed a word she says? She can kill me, but so can everything else, it seems. And it seems that there are enough evils in this world to keep me occupied every single day. Thantos. What can I do?*

Raben tried to lift him into a sitting position, but couldn't raise the heavy man. He was too weakened and Thantos' robes were drenched with sweat. Raben shook him. "Wake up! Come on, now. They're gone." Thantos remained in the realm of nightmares. The thief slapped him firmly across the face. Nothing. Raben arranged the blanket until it was tucked tightly around the struggling priest, and then turned to Urchin.

"Wake up!" Raben called as he neared the sleeping old man. He felt desperate for someone to be awake with him. He shook Urchin. "Wake up, damn it!" Urchin sprung to life. He started to sit up, saw Raben, swung an arm, narrowly missing the thief's head and then rolled away from him until he hit a wall.

"Save us, save us. We're being eaten!" shouted Urchin as he clawed at the wooden planks of the wall. "Oh, Talvo!" He suddenly stopped. His head slowly turned to look back at Raben, who sat motionless, unsure of what to do. "Did they get us?" he asked. "Are we alive, or...?"

"We're fine, I think. Thantos is in trouble." Raben moved near Urchin as the old man sat up. "They fed on the priest," said the thief, nodding at Thantos who was still fighting his dreamed adversary. "They actually fed on him," he stated, shaking his head. "His blood."

Urchin listened while inspecting himself. He checked each of his arms and legs, felt his neck, and pulled his robes off so that he could see and feel his chest. There were no wounds. He stood and turned around, baring his back to Raben. "How's it look?" he asked.

"Bony and white," answered the thief. "You're fine." *Thank the gods!* Raben handed Urchin his grungy orange robe and crawled over to Hessing. The old man tied his clothes back on and followed.

"Any bites on him?" he asked, standing over the noble. Raben shook his head as he inspected Hessing. "Too much silk and satin for the things to bite through," Urchin observed wryly. The old man crouched with Raben and woke the noble up. He tried to pull Hessing's eyelids apart, but had barely touched the huge man when both his eyes opened.

"What the blazes are you doing?" Hessing boomed. Urchin fell backwards. Raben jumped to his feet, alarmed. "Why?" Hessing started to ask, but stopped. "I had dreams." He sat up, rubbing his head. "Sorry, I had these dreams."

"Me too," said Urchin sympathetically. "Rest. Thantos is bit." The old man walked over to where the priest was. "Do you know what to do with him?" Hessing answered that he had no idea, and Raben shook his head again. *Damn this foolish quest!* Hessing shot a glare at Raben as though the noble could read his thoughts.

"Were you knocked out?" Hessing asked. "I'll wager you weren't." The noble stared intently at the thief. Raben stood up and walked to where his weapons were. His legs were wobbly and felt weak. His head swam from the fatigue of staying up all night.

"No." He was instantly irritated with the noble. "Once again, I was forced to do all of the work while you slept." Raben sat down, his weapons lying right behind him. "The vampires came in the middle of the night and magicked everyone but me."

"They must have thought it too harsh to bespell one of their own," Hessing said, venom in his voice. He climbed to his feet and stomped across the floor. "Escaping such an attack once, as you did with the lich, I can call luck, but twice, escaping from the might of Thannon and now the power of the vampires?" Hessing stopped in the doorway to the rickety farmhouse. "You're either protected by the gods of evil, or have their own luck." Boards creaked and cracked under the warrior's weight as he crossed the porch and walked down the steps outside.

"What's got into him?" asked Urchin. He looked over to Raben. "What did you do?"

"Nothing. I think he's realizing that he's not the center of the prophecy," answered Raben as he leaned back on his elbows. "His pride is being cut away. Soon he'll be like the rest of us: Just another dirty beggar being pushed along by the current."

"Have you considered," began Urchin, "that none of us may be the prophesied?" The old man reached out and soothed Thantos, trying to calm the sleeping man, or wake him up. "I know it sounds odd, but we are up against insurmountable danger, and there are only the four of us." He took hold of Thantos' hands and held them tightly. "I don't see how we're going to get through the night, much less continue and complete this quest."

"I think it's my job to get us there." Raben lowered himself to the floor, resting his head on the wooden planks. "I've decided that the gods above have a sense of humor, and it's the thief's job to get everyone there safe so that the quest can be completed. What easier sacrifice to forget when the final words record this quest? And the thief was struck dead, as the True Knowledge was obtained. That's how it will read."

"I think you're just lucky thief. Remember what I said before," Urchin said. "Be careful."

"We'll see, old man. We'll see." Raben tucked his pack under his head and relaxed. He heard Urchin trying to comfort Thantos, talking softly to him, reassuring him that the vampires were gone. The priest continued struggling, his arms and legs flailing uncontrollably. Raben listened to this for a short while more, but soon fell into a restless sleep of his own.

159

"Hey Thief!" A sharp whisper broke into Raben's sleep. "Wake up! Thief, wake up! Your friends are back, and they only want to talk to you." Urchin's voice was shaky as he tried to rouse Raben. "Come on now, they don't seem to be the most patient sort." Raben opened his eyes. It looked like dusk, but he felt as if he'd been sleeping for only moments. He felt as if he were moving in slow motion as he sat up. His body seemed unused to the simple duties he was asking of it. *I just want to sleep.*

"What are you talking about?" Raben asked. He did nothing to disguise the annoyance in his voice. "Why are we still here? Who let me sleep all day? We should have left this damned place hours ago." He looked around the room. *Where is Hessing? Now is not the best time to run off and throw a tantrum.*

"It's only been a short while, Thief. Something is happening," Urchin said. His words came quickly, almost one on top of another. "Hessing is gone, Thantos is still out, and the light outside is fading. I want you awake!" he snapped. "The vampires are attacking!"

Raben scooted across the floor and looked out a window to the barn, or what was left of it. The yard and the barn looked very strange. The thief looked up and saw the clear blue sky, and let his eyes roam out across the endless grass of the Shao plains. It seemed darker than it should. *No sun!* Raben leapt to his feet and flew out the door. *Where's*

160

the sun? He jumped down the stairs and peered up into the sky. No clouds. No sun. *Oh Hell! It's just gone. This can't be.* As Raben tried to cope with the missing sun, darkness slowly set in. Before long Raben was in almost complete darkness. Looking to the horizon, the thief could see the slightest signs of the oncoming dawn. "What the blazes?"

"It's an illusion," said a voice Raben knew. The thief reached down and found no weapons. His skin tightened as the feeling of defenselessness passed through him. The vampire sat on the stairs of the porch, facing the thief from only a few feet away. "With this magic we will fool the humans into thinking it is day, and descend on them when they are unprepared to resist." The fiend smiled, baring his elongated teeth. "It is the same magic that led you to believe that you had destroyed us in the barn." The vampire observed Raben's surprised look. "Yes, that too was an illusion." The vampire rose from the stairs and glided up them. "We understand that you are on a quest, but we need to ask for your help. The eye of Thannon watches all of the creatures of the night. Yet we have divined that you can defeat his agents, for now. So we want you to lead us to a human dwelling. The eye seems not to see you." The vampire intertwined his white fingers before him, as his blazing yellow eyes bore into Raben. "We will cure your priest and offer you the blood of one of our own if you wish it." The thief stood, speechless, not understanding the situation well enough to fight, answer, or run. *Where is Urchin? Is he still alive? Was all of this an illusion?*

"Give me a moment," Raben said. He walked right at the vampire, and much to his relief, the undead creature dodged out of his way. He stepped up the stairs and entered the house. Urchin lay sleeping atop Thantos, who was still being tormented in his dreams. *What can I say? No? Then what? They'll attack eventually. And we can't heal Thantos. He's probably going to die, and with that illusion, these things can trap us whenever, wherever they want. Greeching Hells! Where would I take them? Damn it! Lead an entire army of vampires to humans? Why do these things really need my help?*

He walked back to the doorway. "Heal my priest, and I'll take you." *I might die, but I'll take you.* The vampire that had treated with Raben stepped up to him, offering a hand.

"I am Gabriel," he said. Raben offered a hand hesitantly, and Gabriel clasped it with his. His touch was icy, and reminded Raben of the long night he'd spent unable to breathe.

"Heal him now," he said.

Suddenly Thantos sat up along with Urchin. The two came around so easily, it appeared as if they'd been play-acting. The old man hugged Thantos immediately, sobbing with joy, and telling him how wonderful it was that he was alive and well again. Raben felt a tug of emotions at the sight, but was more worried about the vampires. He snapped his sword up off the floor, and walked out onto the porch. Gabriel was waiting outside.

"Leave us be, for now. We'll leave tonight. Be ready just after dusk," said Raben. *Or else. Or else what? Blazes, this journey is getting worse by the moment. Where's that greeching noble at? And where is that Guild wench hiding at? There are too many enemies around. Thannon is probably sitting astride the roof of this house.* The vampire dissipated into the now familiar oily vapor Raben had seen last night and floated into the night sky. Dawn was only a short while away, and then there was one day to figure out what he was going to do with all of these vampires. *At least a few preparations can be made. Hessing! Where did you go? I could use some of your condescending advice.*

Urchin and Thantos were still celebrating the priest's recovery when Raben reentered the house. They looked up to the thief as one, their joy and admiration readily apparent on their faces.

"Thief is unfitting a name for you, my friend," said Thantos jubilantly. "You continue to save us. Urchin says we all owe our lives to you, again." The priest rose up to his knees reaching a hand to Raben. "Thank you. I saw myself dying all night long. I could feel each part of me giving up on life."

Raben reached out and clasped hands with the priest. Thantos wore a broad grin, and Raben simply squeezed the priest's hand, remaining grim. *I have failed the quest to save your life. Would you have done the same? No.*

"Where is Von Hessing?" asked Urchin.

Raben shook his head slowly to demonstrate that he didn't know. He then let go of Thantos' hand and stood erect, watching the two friends before him, sad that he had nothing better to say.

"We are in more trouble than I can tell what to do with," started Raben. "We have to lead an army of vampires to somewhere inhabited by humans. That was the price of our escape. And," he hesitated, "we leave this evening with or without Hessing. He left in a huff and has either disappeared, abandoned us, or been killed."

The three men sat silently after Raben spoke. The thief sat with his back against a wall while Urchin and Thantos sat just inside the doorway watching the horizon, waiting for the sun to rise.

"Why," Urchin broke the silence, "do they need us to lead them?"

"Because they believe that Thannon can't see me, or if he can, his agents can't defeat me." Raben rubbed his eyes as he answered.

"Thannon would control them. Any of His agents would be able to command the undead to his wishes," observed Thantos. "It is a power that the followers of the dark god have. They are using you to sneak past the eyes of Thannon, yet He's been unheard of for two centuries. Seems strange that Thannon has played such a large part in this quest."

"Not really," Urchin said. "Gul Thannon was the enemy that was subdued back when the Dayquest was first foreseen. It seems right that the god should play such a part when the Dayquest actually proceeded." Urchin looked out the door as the sun began to show over the vast plains. "Besides, Thannon has not slept so much as we would like to believe. His minions were simply more subtle. There are evils in Liveport that go unquestioned every day that weren't there fifty years ago."

Thantos nodded to himself, and Raben thought about the statement vaguely as he slid into a deep slumber.

When he awoke, the sun was shining. Thantos and Urchin were nowhere to be seen, but all of the packs were still strewn about the room. Walking to a window, Raben could see the two out in the yard. Urchin was picking his way through the wreckage of the barn, and Thantos was deep in meditation, sitting in the grass while the sun warmed him. *You almost forget that he has a wooden leg. Unbelievable!*

Raben left the window and grabbed his pack from the floor. He carried it out onto the porch as he rummaged through it. Once he'd discovered some of the jerked venison that had been packed, he set it down and stepped out into the bright sun. Urchin waved him over to the barn, and the thief slowly made his way in that direction. He stopped as he neared Thantos and looked at the man intently. The wounds that he'd sustained from the vampires were just tiny white marks, and his leg seemed natural. The priest crossed it with his good leg with no more trouble than anyone else would. *He puts up with so much.* Raben had really begun to honor and pity the man.

"You're awake." Raben jumped when Thantos spoke.

"So are you," said Raben, agitated.

"I know what to do with the vampires, my friend." Thantos nodded as if confirming himself. "I have spoken to Talvo and our route is shown to me. Two days we will walk, or nights I suppose, and we will come on the town of Nestor's Ferry. There, the vampires will be dealt with."

"How?" Raben sat down in front of the priest. *That easy? Could it be?*

"I have no idea, but you must believe, for it is through the will of Talvo that we are even on this quest." Slowly the priest's body straightened and seemingly grew while he sat there. Thantos looked at Raben in a way that made the thief wary, guilty. The priest had the look of the very powerful. His eyes were commanding, his presence potent with authority. "You are the reason we are here. You are the guide for this quest. I trust you, as does my Lord. Be confident, and you shall be rewarded in the way you seek." Thantos stood and walked away from Raben, climbing the stairs and going into the house. Raben sat staring at the spot where the priest had just been, thinking about what happened.

Thantos says I'll be rewarded. Urchin says I'll die. Why can't I decide this one on my own? Why does everyone have to have an opinion on what the outcome of my life will be? Where is that fool of a noble? Raben took a deep breath and meditated for a while. He tried to reach his host, to feel the power of the spirits that granted him magic, but he'd cast no spells, and the spirits had no need to answer.

He opened his eyes and Urchin was walking towards him. Raben watched as the old man neared. Urchin looked happy. He had his mischievous gap-toothed smile and a spring in his step that hadn't been there for a few days, at least.

165

"Whatever you did in that barn," the old man turned and looked at the fallen building, "made the earth feel a lot better. No vampires living in this ground." Urchin smiled and laughed quietly. "It must have been impressive, whatever you did."

"You're sure you'd be able to sense them?" asked Raben. Urchin looked at the thief in a way that indicated that the question was a foolish one. "I wonder where they are then."

"Maybe you really did kill them all, and the illusion was that they still had many left." The old man looked at him sideways. "Or maybe the whole quest is an illusion and you're sleeping in an inn in Liveport a week ago," snorted Urchin, his laughter catching up with him. He wheezed uncontrollably as he doubled over. "Or maybe you don't exist at all, and this whole thing is an illusion to show you… " Laughter whistled through the gaps in his teeth. Tears ran down his face. "…why you don't want to live with us in the first place." The old man convulsed from his own mirth for a long while.

Raben got up while the old man was occupied with his fit, and walked back into the house. *Don't greeching exist! My life right now is just a game for someone else! I have no answers yet, but I will, by the gods! Get rid of these damned vampires, and I'll get my answers, with or without Talvo and his quest, regardless of the old man's wild predictions of my death. This is my quest. No one else's!* Raben reached out the door and picked up his travel pack. He rolled up his bedroll, and meticulously placed everything in the backpack. He then strapped on all of his weapons. It was the first time he'd armed himself so heavily since he'd left the city. *Feels good.* Looking outside, Raben could see that there was only a little more daylight left before darkness and the vampires returned. *Need to get out of this house. Now!*

Getting Thantos to accompany him, Raben walked around the yard, looking for any sign of Lord Von Hessing, or the direction that he might have gone. The two walked a huge circle around the house and barn, passing by the pond that had first drawn them here, but found nothing indicating Hessing's trail. Just like the two nobles that had survived the temple, Hessing had vanished without a trace.

"It would be almost a day old by now," said Thantos. "His trail."

"Yeah, I guess," agreed Raben, "but it seems totally unlike Lord Von Hessing to just slip away and leave us to the trek. He believes he is the center of the whole prophecy. I don't think he would walk away from his chance to accomplish something of this importance. Especially if he can become famous in the meantime."

"Yes, but it has been a hard trip, and there have been so many times that each of us has been helpless to do anything but watch what was to come," said Thantos. "I have never in my life been at the mercy of others as I have since we left Liveport. And for someone such as Hessing it must be many times more difficult to deal with the feeling of vulnerability than it is for someone like me."

"What are you saying? That Hessing is somewhere feeling sorry for himself? That he is taking time to pity himself and figure out why he is not the greatest warrior in Reman? Why he must depend on others to get him through the most difficult trek in the history of man?" Raben shook his head at the thought of Hessing feeling self-pity. "His whole life is duty and this greeching quest, he'd die if he thought the whole thing wasn't all about him."

Thantos and the thief walked for some time, searching around the pond. Its water looked fairly clean. You could see the bottom at considerable depths. There were even a few fish in the pond that would peek through the water to suck up the bugs that floated on the surface. This happened quite a few times leaving perfect rings on the pond, which would expand away from their center until they washed quietly up onto the shore.

"Maybe," said Thantos, answering the thief's observation of Hessing, "that's exactly what has happened." Thantos looked over to Raben, but he was looking at the sun. "On second thought. I don't think so. Hessing is far too obstinate to quit for such a reason." Not really hearing what Thantos was saying, Raben let his eyes slide from the horizon back to the house where he would soon begin leading an army of vampires.

"Come on, priest. Night is coming."

Raben stood at the base of the porch stairs as the final light of day slid out of the sky. Thantos stood on the porch behind him, and Urchin was sitting on one of the steps. All three of them stared intently at the barn despite the fact that the old man had insisted that the vampires no longer rested there. Raben looked down at his hands. He flexed them both, looking at his missing finger. He wondered how much more he'd have to give before this quest was finished. He reached in his robes and adjusted his weapons as the wooden stake he'd hidden rubbed against his ribs. He'd pushed two stakes through his belt not wanting them to be visible to the army he was about to lead.

Urchin had dug an old rusty ax out of the barn wreckage, and while Thantos and Raben had searched for signs of Hessing, he had hacked the railing down on half of the porch and made stakes in order to fight off the undead. When the two returned, the old man insisted that they carry the stakes. Particularly Thantos, who had already been so viciously attacked by the creatures. So now all three men had the sharpened pieces of railing tucked away. Urchin held one openly. He brandished it before himself as though it were a sword of immeasurable power.

Thantos was the first to point to the ground Raben was standing on as the mist began. A fire was burning inside of the house and its light spilled out of the doorway and two windows, illuminating the yard. Dark mist slowly rose from the earth, moving on air currents that none of the three witnesses could feel. Urchin shifted uncomfortably on the stairs as the haze that rose from the soil eddied on the invisible currents. It seemed sentient as it swirled, meeting other wisps of mist, and coalescing into a thicker, darker form. Soon, the vapor had thickened into an oily black smoke, still churning and rotating in the evening air. Raben stepped up onto the bottom step of the porch. Urchin sat right behind him clutching his stake tightly. The smoke began to boil in itself, rolling and folding over wave after wave of oily smoke in massive funnels of motion.

"Bleeding Talvo!" Thantos swore. "How many are there?" He backed away from the edge of the porch until he stood in the light of the fire. "I never imagined that there could be so many of the things. Vampires are so powerful! What can we possibly do with all of these?"

"Have faith in your god, priest," said Raben. "It's His idea we're about to follow through." The thief reached into his robes and felt the stakes he hid there. Afterward, he rested his hand on the pommel of his enchanted sword. It comforted him as the living smoke grew angrier.

The men watched as a tumult erupted in the yard. The smoke fell into itself creating a tunnel to its heart. A roar of voices began, tortured and desperate. They said nothing, but screamed in what could only be pain. As the group watched, Gabriel slowly materialized in the tunnel and walked up and stood before Raben, seemingly undisturbed by the storm of thick smoke and dismal noise just behind him. The vampire stood, flattening his black silk shirt, waiting. He looked rather noble standing there. He was perfectly clean-shaven, his long white hair was pulled back in a very well kept ponytail, which he'd pulled forward over his right shoulder where its length fell across his chest. His clothes were silk, both tunic and pants. He had a crimson satin vest on, which served to make him look even paler than he had before. His bloodless lips were parted in a smile, which displayed his terrible yellow fangs. His reflective predatory eyes beamed with the firelight that streamed from the house.

The storm lessened as the seething miasma of undead energy slowed and then ended an instant later, leaving the plains stunningly motionless. Innumerable black beings were crouched near the ground behind Gabriel. No skin could be seen through their heavy cloaks as the undead sat balled up on the plain. It was as if a giant had painstakingly placed hundreds of implausibly identical obsidian boulders in the tall grass. *There are so many. Talvo, please lead Thantos well. This is insane!*

"We are assembled and ready, whenever you are." Gabriel's voice hissed only moments after the storm ended. "Shall I call you Master?"

Raben stared at the glowing eyes of the vampire. Gabriel was only a few paces in front of him. Every instinct in the thief told him to run. He'd felt his fear creeping up on him all day long, but now that the vampires were here, he was being crushed by a terror he could never have imagined. *This thing can kill me. Kill me! That fast. There are hundreds, maybe thousands. Think! Stop this!* Raben flexed his hands, and then let them rest on his sword. *They follow me. Shall I call you master? Yes.*

"Yes," Raben breathed. Two deep breaths. "Call me Master." He pointed in the direction of Nestor's Ferry. "We march on foot. Stay out of my way, and none shall touch or talk to us, save you." He nodded forward to Gabriel. "And you!" Raben barked, "will only deal with me." *Convincing?*

The vampire bowed before Raben, and slid out of the way in order to let the thief begin the march. *Good enough. He just floats on air. No feet. Focus. He got out of the way. Good enough!* Raben waved Urchin and Thantos down off the porch and told them to begin walking. After they'd begun, he turned to Gabriel.

"You are my servant, yes?" Raben's voice sounded forceful. More than he'd expected. Again the vampire bowed. The thief held his sword over his head. "This weapon can skewer me. It is the best way to kill me. What is the best way to kill a vampire? I will be forced to deal with those who attempt my friends." He waved to Urchin and Thantos as he sheathed his sword.

"That," hissed Gabriel, "won't be necessary."

"Tell me." Raben's sword was back out, and Gabriel fell back. The vampires behind him rose slightly from the ground. "I care for you no more than any other. These," Raben's voice grew hateful, "mortals are merely a part of my mission. I will slay you and all the rest if I must! Answer me!" He whipped the tip of his sword through the air with impossible speed.

"Yes," Gabriel's airy voice was low. "Sunlight, that sword, or fire." Gabriel bowed. "Master." *This sword. Good. It is the way I would like to see you die. At least I have that much going for me. Sunlight and fire. Leave.*

Raben waved a dismissal to Gabriel as he walked away. The hair on the thief's neck stood on end as he turned his back on the undead army. He looked forward, focusing on the fact that these monsters feared his sword, and tried to push the terror away. Urchin and Thantos were standing a short distance away, waiting for him.

"Where do you think the noble got off to?" Urchin was asking Thantos. Raben heard him answer as he approached. The priest sounded terrified as he answered. His voice wavered with each word.

"I don't know. It wouldn't be surprising if the vampires had him, or if he was now one of them," Thantos said. *No wonder you're afraid, priest.* Being killed by the undead was the one thing that Raben knew horrified the war priest.

"Thief," he called out, as Raben came nearer. "Are you okay?"

"Yeah," he said shakily. "Let's get moving." The other two joined Raben as he walked through them. "You're sure about this plan to take them to this town?" the thief asked. "There are a whole lot of these things behind us." Raben looked over his shoulder, expecting to see a crashing wave of claws and fangs tumbling over the plains. To his surprise, he couldn't see a single undead.

"It was a vision from Talvo," answered Thantos. "It must be right, though I must ask forgiveness. I doubted too, when I stood facing them. All I wanted to do was run." He turned to Raben as he walked. "How could you stand there, and talk to it like that?"

"I nearly pissed myself," admitted the thief. "It was a chore to get each word out. Even now, I feel like they are about to pounce on us." Raben's pace quickened, and though it was difficult, the other two managed to match him step for step, and not complain a single time.

They remained silent as they walked through the night. The vampires were never seen nor heard by the companions as they traveled, but any one of them had only to stop for a short while and the cold fear that preceded the vampiric army would slowly revisit them. After resting only a couple of times, Raben decided that he'd rather march for the remainder of the night without pause than be so close to the unholy army that relentlessly pursued him. Confirming that Urchin, who seemed to need respite most frequently, felt the same way, the party walked continuously through the darkness. With the very first light of the approaching dawn, came Gabriel.

"Master." The hiss of the vampire's voice shot chills through Raben. "We must stop for the day." Gabriel bowed low and then stood silently. The creature seemed too still, as if neither wind nor rain would alter a single thing about him. *He is death. He is part of nature. The terrifying part.*

"We will march a short distance longer," Raben said, intentionally defying the undead. "You and the rest can sleep here, and then find us this evening. Tonight, when you arrive, keep all of the others away from our camp, and only you approach. Anything else will result in your death, and I don't wish for these two to be frightened." The thief made a show of laying his hands on the sword at his hips.

"Yes Master," said Gabriel, and then dissipated into the night. Even as he vanished, relief flooded through Raben, who continuously fought the need to collapse when conversing with the vampire.

"I have never been so near such evil," Urchin said. "It seems to me that these things are worse than the skeleton that attacked us." The old man spat. "Something about them feels more twisted and unnatural.

"The skeleton was a creation. These," Thantos waved back to the army, hidden in the grayness of predawn, "are people, who've been warped and perverted until they only exist by feeding off of blood, and humanity." The priest sounded stronger, as if he fed off of the oncoming daylight.

"Humanity?" Raben was confused. "How do they feed off of humanity?"

"They gain their," Thantos thought for a moment, "civility from the blood of humans. Were they to eat of an animal, or each other, they would go insane, or even die. It is something about what makes us that keeps them alive through our blood. That is why they hunger for it. Were we to feel our rational sense begin to fade away, I'm sure we would go insane as well, and be forced to combat its passing." *I know how correct you are, my friend. Each day I hunger just to know who I am, and where I came from. I suppose that that is not totally unlike what these creatures suffer from. Perverted away from normal men into thoughtless, driven, needy beasts that live only to fulfill the want to sustain themselves. How like me, and every other man.*

Urchin spat again and grunted his disgust.

"How in all the blazes do you know this?" asked Raben. "Seems that you've gained knowledge since the last time we pooled information regarding these things." The thief shot a curious look at Thantos, realizing that the priest was certainly acting with greater poise than he had in days.

"I could feel it when they were feeding on me," responded the priest, as he touched his neck. "I could feel them eating my soul, gaining of it. They take more than blood, and they can give it back." Thantos stopped walking as he focused on his understanding of the vampires. "I don't know what you did, Thief, but I do know the very moment that you won out against them. I felt my desire, my aspirations, my faith come back to me. They were taking more than just my blood, I tell you." Thantos paled as he remembered the attack at the farmhouse. "Let us look to the day." The priest turned and walked towards the dawn, cutting short yet another difficult memory of the journey. *How many terrible memories can you bear before you collapse? You are stronger than all of us in some ways. Far stronger.*

"Urchin, you're always feeling things through the ground," said Raben. "Do you understand this? Can you figure a way to use the information to battle these things? They are terrified of the sun and fire, but Thantos has a very powerful knowledge of them, I think." Urchin leaned in close to Raben. He started to answer, but stopped. He chewed his lip for a moment as he thought through his response.

"There is a reason they didn't feed on me." The old man took a very slow breath. "I think I can put all of my energy, if you will, into the ground. The things found nothing they'd call life to feed on." Urchin looked to Thantos, who was a short way off. "That left only him, and they did much to him, because he was the only thing that they found that would feed them. It seems to me that you are different from normal men, and Hessing, despite falling in every battle since the beginning of the trek, also seems to be very well protected."

"Is he at risk of…" Raben liked the man, but there might be a danger. "Could he be one of them? Or could you feel it, or do you think…" The thief looked at Urchin and tried to let his thoughts carry to the old man. "Would he need to sleep in the ground, or a coffin?"

"I don't know," answered Urchin. "I don't know."

The two of them caught up to Thantos and walked with him until they decided to make camp. The grass was almost waist high and they decided that it would be safe to sleep without a watch, since the greatest threat that existed in all of the Plains of Shao was the army that they were leading. Urchin immediately unrolled his bedroll, ate some jerked venison, and lay down to sleep. The sun was warm when it finally lifted over the horizon, bringing hope to the group. Urchin got up and used a blanket and the tall grass to create a makeshift lean-to so that the mid-day sun wouldn't wake him up.

Thantos knelt down in prayer, and meditated. Raben watched him for a while before borrowing Urchin's idea with the blanket. It was difficult to fall asleep with the sun rising. Something about trying to make the body rest as the day was just beginning seemed difficult. It seemed like a long time had passed when Raben finally felt sleepy, despite his exhaustion. His mind was racing through the recent events. Hessing disappearing, the army of vampires, Thantos' understanding of the vampires, and what part Raben was supposed to play in the journey washed through him over and again, forcing him to give each his attention, though no resolution was forthcoming. Only after he'd exhausted the topics, each ending in the same confusion with which they'd arrived, was the thief able to entertain the idea of sleep. Just before slipping into unconsciousness, the thief heard Thantos.

"Allow my companions to survive the wrath you have designed for the vampires. They are good, and as you well know, they have a large part to play in the future of so many lives. They battle whole-heartedly, and only for the cause of good."

And only for the cause of good. Raben fell asleep as the sun climbed into the sky.

The heat was too much for the thief, and as soon as he crawled out from under his wobbly tent, he found that Thantos was already up, or was still. *He'd been praying when I went to sleep.* The priest was sitting in the grass, his robes hanging open in the hope of cooling himself.

"Did you sleep, friend?" Raben asked. Thantos nodded and smiled weakly. "Urchin is still asleep." As he stood, the thief could feel a number of knots in his muscles. He'd fallen asleep with all of his weapons on. He vaguely remembered waking up and getting rid of the stakes and swords, but he'd warn his sickles and daggers all morning long. He took his robes off and stretched, leaving the sheaths on still. He moved through several practices, weaving his arms through trained patterns as if he were holding weapons.

"Talvo chooses his allies well," commented Thantos as he watched Raben shift through the exercise in his smallclothes. "You must have thirty blades on you right now. I wouldn't have thought it possible to wear so many without looking the part. What keeps them silent?"

"The belts that hold them," answered Raben unclasping one and tossing it to the priest, "are made of silk, not leather, and therefore do not squeak or bounce. You stretch them around yourself." Raben pulled one away from his body and then let the strap rebound back to his skin, silently. "In my line of work every noise can be the end of you. So these are necessary."

"The church should pay more attention to what is happening in other communities of combat. We have nothing of this sort. We could certainly use such things as this." Thantos stretched the belt and tested its strength. "Very impressive. Where did you get these?" The priest caressed the belt, feeling the smooth material. He then shifted his attention to Raben, looking to him for the answer.

"I haven't the first idea," said Raben. He turned away from Thantos. "I have told all of you nothing of myself since we left Liveport. That's because I have no idea." Raben unsheathed a dagger and held it by its tip. "I can throw this thing and hit a man in the eye at thirty paces, yet I have no clue where I learned to do so." The two men fell silent, the words looming. *You must believe me.*

"That's extraordinary," said Thantos. "Do you remember anything? Childhood." Raben shook his head. "Then you just know how to do what you do? Magic, fighting, everything?" Thantos stood up, and returned Raben's belt. "What do you remember?"

"I have memories of being trained, but I am starting to wonder if they really ever happened," Raben answered. "My very first memory was in Liveport. Hessing was there. That's how I am tied to him, wherever in the blazes he even is. I just woke up in motion. I was already doing things, so far as I can tell, and then. Poof! I became aware."

"Do you remember your name? Thief is hardly the best title to live by." Thantos stood behind Raben, while the thief struggled with the situation. Raben sheathed the dagger he'd been holding and flexed his hands while he stood. "If you don't wish to tell me these things I understand. You called me friend, and I believe it. I can't imagine what you're going through. No man could tell you a thing about your situation, and I won't begin to try, but I want you to know that I believe you, and will help you."

"The name I have is Raben."

"You only know your first?" asked Thantos warily. "Have you any idea what your family name might be? Or a clan name, or anything?"

"The rest was once spoken to me by an enemy, but I think it isn't mine," Raben said. He stared into the distance, looking back towards the army of undead that would come to find them after nightfall. "Raben Cyren Everinthius." The name hung in the air. He'd never said it aloud before.

"A name and no memory. Strange to say the least. How do you think it happened?" Thantos asked. "Was it an injury, or an accident? I mean, how did you lose your memory? Do you know?" The priest reached down to his knee and reflexively wrapped his hand around the wooden peg leg that he'd attached to his amputated limb.

"No," Raben answered. "I thought it might be an injury for some time, but after really thinking about it, I know it wasn't. I've had some things happen to me since I became aware that have begun to explain to me where I have come from, but I still have many things to figure out." The thief turned slowly until he faced Thantos. "So far as I can tell, I just appeared."

"From where? How?"

"I'm not sure, but that is what I aim to find out," Raben stated.

"Who do you plan on asking, and how?" Thantos asked. "This seems hardly ordinary. How do you plan on doing it?"

"I plan on holding them at sword point, and forcing the information from them," Raben answered, a humorless smile spreading across his face as he tore his magical blade from its sheath and pulled it through a massive arc before him.

"Sword point, huh?" Thantos mused. "Who is it you plan on holding under the sword? Who would know enough about you to ease your need?"

"The gods, my friend."

"Have you ever heard of Meriss?" asked Thantos.

"The goddess of morality," answered Raben. "Why? Have you decided you're uncomfortable living for battle?" The thief looked over to Thantos. The two said very little since Raben had announced he'd like to question the gods. Somehow it forced the two men into silence, as if something truly terrible or tragic had been said. Urchin was snoring loudly. *How can he sleep in this heat?*

"Also the goddess of family," said Thantos. "The priests of Meriss teach that you can keep in touch with the spirits of long dead family members," he added, pointedly. "Even speak to them, some say."

"Why is this important right now?" asked Raben, finding the conversation strange considering the straits they were in. *The last thing I want to do is bring more dead things back to life. With our luck they would attack us rather than help us in any way.*

"I was thinking about your name. The church of Meriss knows every family lineage. It's a power that they have. They can follow any lineage for a fee. They do it for free for all of their followers, but since neither of us would qualify as family men, we'd have to pay." Thantos looked to Raben, waiting for an answer. The thief thought about it for a moment. At first it seemed ludicrous, but as it sunk in, the idea gained validity. *Yes! That would be fantastic. This man. So selfless. Incredible.* Raben had never known anyone that had genuinely offered themselves to him. Offered to make his troubles a priority in his life. The priest had, in one conversation, gained a loyalty equal to his altruism.

"Thantos, if we had the time to go somewhere, earn the fee, and find these priests, I think I'd take you up on it," Raben said, a genuine grin spread across his face. "Would that there were some of them nearby, or on the way. If ever there is a chance, my friend, I want you to be there."

"We may be able to," shot back Thantos. "After all, we're hardly taking to the map so far. Perhaps this is part of the True Knowledge. I believe that the True Knowledge is awarded to those who accomplish the Dayquest because of the numerous things they learn along the way. By the end, you've discovered exactly what you are supposed to have found." Thantos looked over to Urchin who coughed for a moment, and then rolled over and continued to sleep. "That's amazing," the priest said, pointing at the old man. "I could never sleep in this. Maybe," mused Thantos, returning to the more serious conversation. "Maybe Hessing is completing what he needs of the quest."

"I never thought I'd miss that fool, but he made me feel calm," said Raben. "He was my way of knowing an enemy. If he could fell it with his sword, I should fight. If he was having no luck, I knew that magic was the weapon to wield." The thief chuckled. "I hope he comes back. He'd have no idea what to make of me hugging him, and welcoming him back."

"I should say not," Thantos agreed. The priest stood. "I'm going to try to sleep again. Rest Raben, you need it." Raben nodded as the priest walked away. He watched him, marveling at the man. Everything that Thantos lacked in courage, he made up for in compassion and understanding. *There is much to trust in you.*

The thief looked off towards Nestor's Ferry, and wondered what could be there. *How can anything deal with these creatures? Can we really hope to escape this mess without dying?* Raben could feel forces at work. Something huge was going to happen tomorrow. He just hoped it would be what Thantos hoped, and that they all lived through it. He crawled into his bedroll, mentally and physically exhausted, and slept.

"He'll get up if I kick him," laughed Urchin. Thantos joined him. Raben lifted his head as he heard the noise. He'd slept peacefully for the first time in a long while. The sun was well into its descent towards the horizon, but a little time still remained. "Wake up, and dance for me, Thief!" called Urchin. "Thantos tells me you were taking off your clothes earlier and showing off."

"Old man, I seem to recall you taking your clothes off in the farmhouse," answered Raben as he pulled his blanket from the grass and tightly rolled it. "You even turned around and waved your bony ass for me to inspect." All three men laughed.

"I thought a vampire may have bit it," Urchin wheezed. The three of them continued their fit. Raben rolled from his bed, drawing deep breaths. After regaining control, he began to eat a mug of stew that Thantos held out to him. As he ate it, he repacked his equipment, taking great pains to make sure each of his possessions was properly secured. The other two had apparently done so already. They stood, waiting on the thief, as though the journey were only moments from continuing.

"Take your time," Urchin said. "After watching you sleep for quarter a day, we can't help but expect you to take another quarter to wake up and prepare yourself." The old man laughed, and after he wheezed for a few moments, Thantos joined in. Raben ignored them.

"So," the thief said, after the laughter had died, "what is the plan? Anything special?" He waited for the other two to join his more serious mood. "Do we just walk there and everything else is taken care of, or should we be using this time to our advantage somehow?"

"It has been left unclear," said Thantos. "We just go, so far as I can tell."

Urchin burst into laughter. "Well, then to the Hells with it anyway!" Raben and Thantos watched the old man for some time, not understanding the old man's humor. *I wonder if he understands it. Maybe he's just insane.*

"You, my friend, are truly odd." Raben watched Urchin respond with a rude gesture.

"I agree," said Thantos. The priest then walked away and sat in meditation. Urchin suggested that Raben hone his skill in combat, and practice with the old man. The thief agreed. The two of them sparred for quite a while. Urchin used only his hands. He was no match for Raben, but insisted regularly that the thief would be dead already, on the first hit in fact, if he were really fighting.

Sooner than any of the three of them wanted, the sun set. The mirth had retreated, and the tension grew. The sun fell below the horizon, leaving a crimson cape behind it in the sky. The red faded to a dull pink and dark purple. Ominous blue replaced that along with deep gray, and then the black of night. Stars glimmered like hope in the beginning of a night that felt blacker than most.

"Shall we resume?" asked the hissing vampire. Gabriel appeared right in front of the thief. The question had been heard before the creature was even visible. Raben did a surprising job of remaining calm, though he felt none of it.

"Yes Gabriel, we shall continue now." The three men began walking, knowing that the vampire would disappear into the air and follow. They could feel the cold of the vampires behind them. It quickened their pace. *You will be gone by tomorrow at this time, so enjoy your last walk through the night.* Raben sneered in the darkness as he imagined Gabriel exploding into a thousand flaming pieces, as the lich had. That, and innumerable other malicious images filled the thief's imagination as he marched mechanically through the night.

League after league, they pushed on, not resting even once as the night wore on. The group knew neither exactly why they were heading to their destination, nor how it would turn out when they finally did get there. All they knew was that turning back was not an option. They trudged over the plains of Shao, pushing their bodies to continue, even as they began to feel exhaustion overtake them. Never once did one of them complain or suggest resting, for distress at the feeling of the vampires. The grass stretched endlessly through the dark before them, leaving them only with the need to put one step in front of another until they made it somewhere. By the time they actually arrived at Nestor's Ferry, Urchin was nearly falling with each step, and Thantos gave a grunt of effort each time he pushed his peg-leg out in front of himself.

Raben saw the town before the others. They were too focused on just making it. He was looking at the few lights that even allowed him to know the town was there when he heard Urchin call out, and grunt as he fell. Thantos and Raben stopped and moved to the fallen man as quickly as they could.

"Don't fret, Raben," Thantos said. "I've been saving something just for this moment. Hold his hand." The priest mumbled an incantation as he held onto Urchin's hand. Raben had been first awakened by the yelp that Urchin let out, and again brought to consciousness by hearing his name used so casually. *I may never get used to that.* Thantos began calling some manner of spell through the power of Talvo. He chanted for a while, longer than any spell Raben

185

had ever cast. Then Thantos brought his hands up the old man's arms and let them rest on Urchin's chest.

The old man's eyes shot open, and Raben thought he was dying. Urchin sucked in a deep breath. Suddenly Raben understood. A rush of power struck him. It swept like heat up his arms and flooded his chest with energy. He felt invincible. Any exhaustion that may have eaten away at him throughout the night was now banished from his body. He felt ready for anything. Urchin leapt to his feet.

"By the power of Talvo indeed!" He called. "Let's get this under way."

Thantos was on his feet and looking hale. Raben stood, amazed at the vibrance within him. "Yes! Let's!" Calling out a few words of incantation as he yanked his sword from its sheath, Raben let the power of magic surge through him. He held his weapon over his head and spoke one final word. The blade was consumed by flame. The sword was now almost three reaches in length and flame ran the blade like liquid, little bits of it blowing in long swirls as Raben waved the blade in exhilaration.

The three men jogged toward Nestor's Ferry, but were a considerable distance away when they noticed the cloud descending on it. The same oily black smoke that had poured from the ground at the farmhouse now floated slowly and purposefully downward onto the sleeping town. The group jumped forward at a full sprint.

Screams greeted them in the town. Wretched calls erupted from the vampires that fed on the citizenry, and cries of sheer terror could be heard from everywhere.

"Thantos!" Raben yelled, "What in the greeching Hells is this?" He couldn't believe what he was seeing and hearing. Men, women, and children were being slaughtered before his eyes, eaten by the undead that he brought here. "No!" he screamed as his sword swept into a vampire. The creature howled pure malice as it dropped the women it had been feasting on. It whirled to Raben, but never had an opportunity to do more. The thief lost control; his blade hacked mercilessly through the undead, and then struck again sweeping an arm off of the already severed torso. Still the head screamed. Raben hacked at it until it was silent, and unrecognizable.

Losing sight of his companions, Raben attacked at random, hewing vampires apart with his flaming sword, pure rage, and guilt. He had brought massacre, in the name of the gods. He became unaware of the battle beyond the opponent he was facing. Once his adversary fell he moved to the next monstrosity. The undead were always feeding. Children, babies, whatever. They seemed not to discriminate, nor did Raben. He slew everything that neared him. He became unable to discern the vampires from the living. His blade simply tore through anything that stood before him. He could never have counted the number of deaths he caused in the time that the battle raged. He was wounded more times than he remembered or cared. Blood ran freely, marking a trail behind him, but none could follow it, because the streets were scarlet with the blood of those who'd formerly lived in them, the innocent that he had sacrificed to the vampires. It was during his rage driven bloodlust that he happened across Gabriel.

"Master, the humans are slain to the last," the voice dared to hiss.

"You!" bellowed Raben. "You have done your last in this world, Gabriel!" He screamed the words. His blade whipped around so quickly that a fan of trailing flames lit the street they stood in.

"Wait!" came a voice so powerful that Raben and the vampire fell from their feet. The ground shook and the buildings swayed with its power. "Gabriel, of the world of death!" Thantos moved into the street. His clothes were shredded, his skin was torn. It looked as if he'd lost an eye from the bloody gash down his face. He limped to the center of the road and continued. It was his voice, and Talvo's power. "You are commanded and bound to the will of Talvo!" The vampire flew across the street as if pulled behind a horse. He bounced on his back and slammed into a building, where he was suddenly pinned as if staked there. "You will disband this army, which you alone have inspired, and do what His Greatness fills you with in order to atone for this heinous crime!" The vampire howled as Thantos spoke but his words and high-pitched scream were lost in the power and sheer volume of the priest's command. Gabriel's shrieking ceased and he collapsed to the dirty road. Raben regained his feet, and charged the downed vampire.

"Raben!" The voice still held its power, but did nothing to assail the thief.

"Everyone was killed!" Raben screamed. "What the Hells did we do here? We led the army here, Thantos! What the greeching hell good is this god of yours. We killed them all!"

"Friend, I do not know, but can assume that we saved more lives in the long run." Thantos' voice slowly fell in volume. "I don't know." The priest, Raben could see, had indeed lost an eye. A thin, dark, bloody slit was left where his eye had been, and a trail of flesh and blood ran down his cheek mapping the path his eye had gone. *Damned fool of a priest. How can a man follow a faith so blindly?*

Silence befell the town as the sun began to rise.

"Gabriel!" commanded Thantos, his voice carrying through the now-quiet streets. "You will return to this spot, the very moment that the sun has set! Flee now to your dark sanctuary!" The vampire dissipated on command, leaving the two men in the street.

"Thantos, where is Urchin?" asked Raben. He felt terrified at what had happened, what he'd seen, what he might have done. "Where is he?" *I could have swept his head off and never even known it.*

"I haven't seen him. Talvo claimed me and I acted without consent. It was His power that you saw." Thantos gestured up to the heavens as he spoke. *So I wasn't the only one killing people without thought. Damn it all! Is this why we came here?*

"All of this," Raben waved to the bloody street, littered with the dead citizens of Nestor's Ferry, "seems to be His power." *I made the deal. I brought the greeching things. I should have led them anywhere but here. I should have just killed that bastard Gabriel!* "Leave me priest. See to your eye." *My mistake was trusting in religion to make this right.* Raben limped up the street, finally becoming aware that he had an injury to his leg. Street after street was littered with bodies and blood. *If anyone survived this attack, it was because they were evil.* The thief looked upon the dead. Every one of them looked innocent and normal. No knights, wizards, or priests. *Just farmers, their wives, and their families.* They all lay in the street, their flesh ripped and torn away so that their blood could be drunk like cheap wine. There were so many!

Orange robes! Urchin's body lay amidst several others. Raben tried to run to it, but only fell. He crawled the rest of the way to the old man. Urchin wasn't breathing. There were no wounds on the man, but he wasn't breathing at all. Raben slapped the old man's face. "Come on!" He shook him by the shoulders. "If you greeching leave me, I'll…" Raben didn't know what. He hit the man full in the stomach, his anger and fear teaming up on his ability to remain calm. "Urchin, you skinny fool of a man!" He yelled. "All you ever did was lay on the greeching ground and get dirty. By the Hells, you'd better stand the greech up before I cut off one of you're damned fingers!" Raben fell forward onto Urchin's unmoving body. *Damn it all! Damn*

Talvo and his greater vision! The thief sobbed silently, not knowing what else to do.

He let out all of the anger and guilt if only for a short while and embraced his latest suffering: sadness. He cried for Urchin, who lay dead in the street amidst a hundred other people who didn't deserve to die, but did. *Because a god made it so.* His tears flowed easily as he wept. The sun was well over the horizon when he finally stood back up. He lifted Urchin's limp body from the street. The sun-baked road stunk of iron. The blood that filled his nostrils made his boots stick to the occasional paving stone as he walked out of Nestor's Ferry. Stopping at a now-abandoned general store, Raben broke through a window, and stole a spade. Once out of the city, he carefully set Urchin on the grass, and dug.

He cried off and on. He moved the earth with determination, despite his body's need to collapse and rest. Once he'd dug far enough, he carefully lifted the old man's body into the hole. He said goodbye, wishing the man a fair journey, and a peaceful afterlife. He felt as if there should be more to say, something more he should do, but images of the dead flooded his mind, pushing any further sentiment or ceremony away. After staring at the body of his old friend, trying to arrive at something profound, and failing, Raben began filling the hole. He heaped the dirt back into the grave, and once that was done, he immediately left the grave behind, and entered Nestor's Ferry to find Thantos. *Goodbye friend.* Raben had only taken a few steps into town when he fell to the ground. He wanted to get up, but after several unsuccessful attempts, he gave in, and lay there. He'd lost too much blood, having never dressed the wounds he'd sustained in battle, and now hovered on the brink of unconsciousness. *Take me too, Talvo. Bring me with Urchin, and the thousand others that died today.*

Raben let his eyelids slowly shut as the need to sleep closed over him. After only one shallow breath, he passed out.

The sun woke him. It was straight overhead, and was too hot. He opened his eyes, and realized where he was. He exerted all of his strength, and pulled himself to a shaded area on the side of the street. Once there, he collapsed, again losing consciousness.

"Raben, wake up," said a soothing voice. The voice of a woman. *Oh no! How? Damn it!* The Guild hunter stood before him, her lithe body covered in tight white silk pants and tunic. Her large eyes looked sympathetically at Raben, while her pointed elven ears emphasized her exotic nature. *So beautiful.* The perfume she always wore washed over him. He welcomed it after the stink of blood that filled every street of Nestor's Ferry. Raben lifted one of his arms, weakly. He couldn't sit up. *At least I'm not bound.* The thief was still in his clothes, though they were shredded and covered in blood. He could see his boots nearby, the soles caked with the blood of the innocent. *How many people died so that the gods could be entertained?*

"What happened, Raben?" she asked calmly. "You were supposed to be completing the Dayquest, and suddenly you're off fighting a war with vampires." She folded her thin arms under her bosom, emphasizing the feature.

"Not with," he coughed as he said it. "Against." He lifted his right arm, but it barely moved. "Fought against." *Damned things followed us for two days. A whole army of them! Or did you fail to notice that from your comfortable seat.*

"No, no," she said. "We saw you kill the people of the town." She shook her head. "We're not angry, Raben. We just want you to get back to task." She walked away from him and stood by a curtain that seemed to separate the room he lay in from another. Drawing it back, Raben saw Hessing. The noble was blindfolded and strapped into a chair. Massive leather thongs held his arms and legs to the wood. "Unfortunately, we've been forced to use your growing admiration for your companions as a tool of motivation. If you don't get back to the quest, we'll kill him."

"How'd you get him?" Raben tried to think through the events surrounding the farmhouse. *The vampires would have sensed them. Hessing wouldn't have gone far. The day was illusion. Did he leave at night? Was he there at all? Oh Hells!*

The elf walked over and leaned down to him playfully touching his nose. "Yes, we are that powerful." She turned away from him. In an inconceivably fast motion she produced and buried a dagger in the chair next to Hessing's head. "Never forget that, and never try to guess our means, Raben. It will only leave you feeling more hopeless than you already do." She narrowed her lemon-shaped eyes, and scowled as she said it, peering into the thief's bloodshot orbs.

"Helpless," he said, repeating her in a way that suggested that he was anything but. "How can I be helpless? You are merely a dream." *What are you?* Feeling as though his world was falling down around him after the attack at Nestor's Ferry and Urchin's death, the thief used a desperate ploy. He lied. *I need to know.*

"Is that what you think?" she asked, taking her chin into one of her soft slender hands. "Well let me assure you that we are far from a dream, if that word could ever apply to you and me." She looked at the battered thief, her sympathy obvious. "Nightmare is more fitting for our lives, and yours," she said, leaning down until her nose nearly touched his, "is far worse than mine." *Nightmare is more fitting to our lives. Our.* "Never doubt us."

193

"Doubt you!" he barked. "How can I doubt you? You are the first person I ever met. I am your prisoner even as I strive to figure out what I am even doing, and half of the time, I'm not sure. Fear not! If it is important to you to know: I do not doubt you!"

"Good," she responded. "It does matter. Perhaps more to me than some." The Guild hunter smiled as she turned away from him. Raben couldn't help but appreciate how handsome she was as she walked away from him.

Stepping to the center of the room, the Guild hunter began chanting a spell. Raben was far too weak to resist the spell's affects, and was soon asleep.

"Raben?" Thantos' voice was full of surprise. "Are you awake?" The thief opened his eyes and could only see white. He lifted his hands and felt material. There was something on him. A linen sheet. *A death shroud!* He tried to call out and roll, but there was wood to either side. *I'm in a greeching coffin.* He sat up, and Thantos already had his arms around him. "Great Talvo! It's okay, Raben. Hold on!" Thantos lifted the thief from the coffin and helped him to a nearby pew. Calling on the power of his god, the priest called aid for Raben. The numerous wounds on the thief's body tingled as the power worked on them. Raben sat, unaware of the church around him. Thantos continued chanting, causing the gashes and cuts on Raben's body to close and heal.

"Water," Raben croaked. After finishing his spell, the priest ran to a nearby pitcher, bringing the whole thing to Raben. The thief drank, took a few deep breaths, and drank again. "Thantos," he said, and passed out.

He awoke again. The priest was still there. "Thantos," said Raben. "Thantos, we killed them all. We killed Urchin. My enemies have Hessing." He raised himself onto his elbows. "You're all that is left. Run before you're killed." *This quest is a death sentence. None of us will survive, my friend.*

"Rest, friend," soothed the priest. "I will not leave you." He brought Raben another pitcher of water. The thief drank it greedily. "I found you on the side of a street. I thought you were dead. No," corrected Thantos, "you were dead. I checked with a spell. You were dead, and then, after I carried you to the temple and was performing your funeral, you awoke." Thantos backed away from Raben. "I've never been so surprised in my life."

"Bring me water too, you damned idiot," interrupted a voice. Raben turned away from Thantos to see the speaker. It was Urchin. *What the Blazes. It can't be.* The thief blinked hard several times, but the old man still filled his vision.

"What the Blazes," Raben muttered. The old man was covered in dirt, from head to toe. He was lying in a cot, not three paces from where Raben lay. "Holy gods!" exclaimed Raben. He rolled from his cot, falling to the floor. Pain shot up his leg, and his head throbbed. "Urchin!" He crawled to the side of the old man's cot. "You were dead. I saw you. I checked. I greeching buried you." *How the blazing Hells can this be?*

"Yeah, I know. I woke up from my magic, and nearly suffocated," said Urchin as he smiled. "Luckily, the earth and I have an agreement. I take care of it, and it'll take care of me." The old man reached a dirty hand to Raben and smiled again, his gap-toothed grin giving the thief some relief from the misery that had beset him. "I kept most of those damned vampires from saving themselves in the ground, I did." Urchin raised a fist, signifying his victory.

"I killed innocent people," Raben said. "I went berserk and killed everything in my path." His head fell to his chest. *I lost all control, and the Guild knows it. For all I know, they are the ones that make it happen.*

"Including yourself, friend," stated Thantos. "You were dead. Seems I was the one to escape this time." Raben, remembering, suddenly looked to Thantos. The priest had a brown eye-patch over his right eye.

"What got your eye? Vampires?" Raben shook his head. Just thinking about it made him nauseous. "Doesn't surprise me. They move too damned quick to fight."

"Actually, it was a component necessary to cast a spell. It was the only way I could see where the true leader of the army was and gain command over him, in Talvo's name," said Thantos without regret. He reached up and felt the eye patch, shifting it slightly on his face until it was comfortable.

"You tore your own eye out?" Raben asked in complete disbelief. *That's grotesque.*

"You saw what they were doing," Thantos said. "Because of us, there were survivors."

"Were there?" Raben shot back. "I walked through the streets immediately after the battle and saw the bodies. There were hundreds." Raben shook a fist at Thantos. "Hundreds!"

"There were hundreds, Raben!" yelled Thantos, "but," he took a deep breath, "how many would have died if that army had just walked all over Reman on its own?" The priest of Talvo moved nearer to Raben. "What would have happened if Thannon had gotten control of all of those vampires?" Thantos asked, gesturing vaguely to the destruction that surrounded the temple they were in.

"We could have done it differently," said Raben, lamely. *Damned gods and religions finding a good way to look at it. Greeching Hells!* Raben crawled back over to his cot, and climbed in, with help from Thantos. *This quest has been anything but glorious. I wonder if all of them are this way, and the people who record it just don't want to write something so terrible.*

"What time of day is it?" Urchin asked. It was midday. Raben rolled onto his side and slept some more. *After all, it is the one thing I really want.*

It was a good sleep. Raben woke up feeling better. He remembered the events of the past day, or was it two days- he didn't know- and felt a little removed from it. Urchin was up already. He and Thantos were sitting at a table playing some kind of card game. Based on the coins they were using, Urchin was winning. The old man was still covered in dirt. *He probably wears it like a badge.* Raben smiled to himself.

Sitting up, Raben could see a window. It was dusk outside. *Now I'm probably nocturnal for life.* Neither of his friends noticed him as he sat up. The thief climbed from the bed and moved to the window. He looked out at the streets of Nestor's ferry, and saw people. They were moving around in a normal fashion. Average people milling about, walking to an inn, enjoying the warm night. *Illusion. They act like it never happened. Maybe it was less than I thought. How can I be sure?*

A door opened behind Raben. His hand shot down to his sword, but it wasn't there. He reached up his sleeves. Nothing. *Damned priest had seen every weapon I had, and taken every one off.*

"Brother Thantos," said a robed figure with a rich deep voice. "Gabriel is here." The moment the announcement was made, the thief saw Thantos look to his cot. Not finding the thief in the cot, the priest immediately moved around the room.

"Raben," he started when he saw the thief, "can you handle being near him? The vampire?" Thantos held both of his hands out as though to stabilize the thief at a distance. *Gabriel here? What in the greeching fires is going on? Does the god of war accept the blood sucking minions of Thannon in His own greeching temples?*

"Why would he come here?" asked Raben. "Aren't we in a temple to Talvo?" *These gods are less scrupulous then men. At least men can fuel a feud and keep their priorities straight.*

"I commanded him to fulfill the wishes of Talvo, and Talvo has sent him on the quest with us," said Thantos. The priest wasn't looking at Raben when he said it.

"What!" shouted the thief. "You can't be serious!" *I'm leaving! I'm done with this foolish greeching quest.* Raben moved to start picking up his things. He could see them all lying near his cot. He prepared to tell Thantos that he was done with the Dayquest. He was resolved on packing his things and leaving. Pursuing his past through Meriss, the way Thantos had suggested sounded far more fruitful, and longer lived. *That'll get me further toward what I want than this damned craziness anyway.*

He opened his mouth to say it, but something happened.

"That'll be fine. Bring up Gabriel," he said grudgingly. "Just let me get armed first." Raben's anger grew inside of him. *Something is wrong. I have no control. I want to leave. I can't.* He tried to run to the door, but his hands kept strapping weapons on. He attempted to scream out, to tell Thantos that his temple was being defiled by the presence of Gabriel, but all he did was nod to the priest once his weapons were on. *I have no control of my own body, unless I'm doing what they want. Who the greech are they?*

"You are a greater man than I could have imagined," Thantos said. "I saw how you wanted to kill the vampire out in the street. I saw your rage." He walked up to Raben and held him by his shoulders. *Your eye! That eye-patch makes you look horrible.* "You have a big heart. You are a gemstone amidst the coal." Thantos squeezed the thief's shoulders. "Bring Gabriel up," he commanded. The robed figure in the doorway left to do so.

Raben could have laughed, or cried. *I'm being honored for being manipulated. I wonder how many times I've done exactly what I didn't want to do. The barn. The front door of the farmhouse. The temple of Talvo. How many others? I need to find answers.* Raben strapped on his last sheath and then covered himself in a new black robe that had been provided for him. *I wonder what my companions would think if they knew the truth. That I would have abandoned them several times already.*

The door opened and the vampire entered. He still wore his perfect silks, and bright red vest. He still looked noble, but Raben no longer feared the vampire. He only felt fury. Raben hungered to kill Gabriel. The creature was so arrogant, and yet, had so quickly been dominated. There was no doubt that the vampire was immensely powerful and could be used, but sending him on the quest? *How could a god be so foolish?*

"I see your companion has awakened," said Gabriel as he surveyed the room. His voice hinted at mockery. "I trust you are feeling well." The vampire was looking right at Raben, but the thief said nothing. "Are we to leave this night, or shall we hold over yet again?" Gabriel shifted his attention to Thantos.

"We'll leave tomorrow night," Thantos replied. "What did you figure out?"

"The only real power in The Shao Plains, besides the vampires, is a lone-standing tower of a white wizard," began the vampire, his hissing voice pouring through the room unnaturally. "He is reputed to have participated in the wars, and to have found a way to stretch his mortality. There are no towns or hamlets near the tower, so going there will be quite obvious." He gestured to Raben. "I believe a visit would benefit him greatly. His turmoil is consuming him." Gabriel shot a glance at the thief. "The white wizard might save his life."

"Why would a white wizard help him?" asked Thantos severely. White wizards were well known for their destructive magics and manipulative ways. They had caused one of the most infamous wars that could be remembered.

"Evil knows its own," answered Gabriel, with a smile. "He is malformed by magic. No less twisted than I. A white wizard will be his best bet." Gabriel walked over and sat at the table with Urchin, who still held a handful of playing cards. The old man immediately stood up, and walked to Raben.

"Let's walk outside, Thief." Urchin passed Raben, and moved to the door. The thief wrestled with the idea of leaving Thantos with Gabriel. He trusted that the vampire would take every opportunity to complicate the journey. *He has command of the damned thing, I guess.* Raben walked out the door with Urchin.

The two exited the temple of Talvo, leaving the blocky building behind. Urchin wove a course through the town until they were no longer on streets or in alleys. He had taken Raben out of Nestor's Ferry. The two walked through the grass they'd been walking through for days. After a short while they came upon a dark spot on the plain. The grass had been torn away, and now only earth remained, upturned and fresh.

"You buried me right here," said Urchin. "Do you remember?" The old man chuckled as Raben nodded. "You took my old bones, and hurled them into this pit, and covered them over with dirt. Gave me a proper funeral." Urchin laughed. "It saved my life, Thief." The old man knelt down next to the fresh grave and pushed a hand into the dirt. "Yep," he confirmed. "I would have died without your funerary services." Another quick laugh.

"What did you do? What were you doing?" asked Raben. "There wasn't a wound on you. You just weren't breathing." Raben felt defensive. "I didn't know what else to do, so I buried you." The thief sat in the grass next to the kneeling old man.

"Stop telling me why, fool," snapped Urchin. "You saved my damned life. I had spread my energy into the ground so that the vampires had to travel far in order to rest. Many died because they didn't understand what was happening, and the sun got 'em." The old man sunk his other hand into the dirt. "Many still lived. I couldn't withdraw my energy, so I lay dying." Urchin looked over to Raben. Only a faint reflection of his eyes and the white in the old man's wispy hair could be seen. "When you buried me, the energy that was in the ground came back to me enough for me to live again. Once I got out of the grave, a few townspeople found me and took me to Thantos." Urchin looked back down to the ground. "The priest healed me."

"Why are you telling me this?" Raben asked, shaking his head. "Are you afraid to tell Thantos?" The thief took a deep breath and sighed. "Do you think he would somehow begrudge the way you survived?"

"No, he knows all about it now. When the folk had told him how I crawled out of a grave, I had to let him in on my ability. He already had a good idea." Urchin pulled his hands out of the grave, bringing handfuls of fresh dirt. Raben could smell it. "Thantos sees the world in good and evil," said the old man. "He wants to turn that vampire to good. Thantos believes that this town needed to be destroyed, and that only people who were somehow deserving of death were killed in the attack. He thinks that is why the townsfolk are so easily able to go about their lives since the battle." Urchin stood, and Raben joined him. The two looked at the horizon as a pale blue sliver of the moon rose. Raben could barely see the smile on the old man's face. The moon over Reman only came out for a few days each cycle, a cycle being about twenty-five days. This was the first night, and Reman would bathe in bright blue light for the next few. "Thantos seeks to do the same with you. He doesn't know if you're good or evil, but he wishes to help you end up serving good." Urchin started to walk through the tall grass again, letting it slide off of his legs. "Thief, there is no good and evil, except in certain, very obvious cases." Urchin turned around to look at Raben, who still stood a few paces back, staring at the moon. "What there is, is healthy and unhealthy." Urchin held his arms straight out to his sides. "The land knows the difference. Rain is healthy, wind is healthy, and those vampires were certainly unhealthy. Just to feel them nearly killed me at the barn." Urchin slowly spun with his arms out. "You Thief, Raben, are not healthy." *What? Me?* "It doesn't make you evil, it just means you're not healthy. For a couple of days we have sought the best means to restore your health. Your body is fine. Your body is the healthiest any has ever seen, but your energies, your spirit. Those Thief, are in trouble."

"And what exactly are you proposing we do?" asked Raben, his voice carrying an edge. "Follow the damned vampire to one of the most legendary destructive forces known to Reman so that we can ask him what the greeching hell is wrong with me?" Raben drew his sword and held it, feeling its balance. "The damned wizard will probably answer everything, and blow me into cinders." Raben swung his sword, and was shocked to hear Urchin laughing. "What, old man?"

"You whine and cry, and expect the worst at every turn, and maybe for good reason, but you've got to look at this from the one perspective that matters to us all." The old man sunk into the ground. Immediately afterwards, Raben could smell fresh earth. "You're," Urchin was right behind him, "still alive." The thief spun and his sword spun with him. The old man reached out a hand and blocked it. His skin seemed impervious to its razor-sharp edge. The force of the blow caused Urchin to rock to a side, but he held the blade still with his bare palm. "And you're learning every single moment." The old man pushed the sword away. Raben stood, frozen, unsure. His mouth hung open. "And even if you never really figure out who you used to be..." Raben's mouth fell open a little more. "Yes, Thantos told me your story, and even if you never figure out who you used to be, you have more than all of those poor people who were slaughtered at the hands of the vampires." Urchin knew he had Raben's full attention. The thief didn't make a sound. "You still have a chance to figure your problems out, and a few friends that will follow you to do it." Urchin lifted his hand to Raben's chin, and closed the man's mouth. "No element of the ground can harm me. Including your steel." The old man walked past Raben. "You'd have better luck punching me."

"That was amazing! That swing should have swept your ugly head right from your shoulders." Raben lowered his weapon, looked down at it for a few moments, and then slowly followed Urchin.

"Pay attention!" the old man snapped. "You need to quit whining and worrying. Do you understand?" Urchin waited for Raben to answer. Eventually, he saw the thief nod in the dark. "And try not to kill the vampire before we've met the white wizard," Urchin added. "I think we need his power to ensure our safety when we're there."

"Yeah, yeah," agreed Raben halfheartedly. "That greeching thing needs to be cut in half." The two started walking back to town. "You know old man? I have the ugliest mother anyone has ever had." Urchin looked at the thief through darkness, confused. "Are you going to tuck me in at night too?" Raben let himself laugh and Urchin wheezed, and some of the weight of their troubles fled.

Once they arrived back at the temple, Gabriel had already left. Thantos was putting on some new robes that he had been given. They were white with a deep brown sash. He had a brown eye-patch on, and his boot was clean and new, his peg-leg freshly oiled and polished. He looked like a priest for the first time since Raben had met him.

"Well, aren't those nice clothes, Brother Thantos. Are there any for me?" asked Urchin. "While I do cater to the dirt, I suppose it would be more comely of me not to wear it throughout the rest of the journey." The old man looked Thantos up and down, and then turned to Raben. "You know what?" he grinned. "Everyone in this room has new clothes except me." He barked a quick laugh. "Aren't I the bum in this crowd?"

"These are for you, friend." Thantos brought out a package. Untying the yarn that held it closed, he brought out a lush olive green robe. "The locals had no orange fiber or dye. I hope this will do. A bath can be pulled for you, if you wish to rinse off."

"That robe is better than this." Urchin shed his robes. Remarkably, the man and his smallclothes were perfectly clean underneath. "No need to rinse. The dirt doesn't stick." As he said it, Raben heard the small bits of dirt that had covered his face and arms fall to the floor, clattering almost inaudibly on the stone. "Well then," Urchin sighed, "that's much better." The three of them looked clean and comfortable, if a bit battered.

"We're going to head to the white wizard tomorrow?" Thantos directed the question to Urchin, nodding deliberately. *Very subtle. You're certainly a priest.* Urchin shook his head as the priest's gesture gave him away. "He lies northward."

"Yes," replied Raben. "We are going to the wizard. It's on the way, as far as the quest goes, I suppose." The thief walked to his pack and pulled the map out. "Maybe now we can get on course and stay on course. From the onset of this quest we've been pushed from place to place by battles and pursuit. How will we ever finish if we never follow the trek as it is given us?" Raben traced the course he wanted to take on the map with his finger.

"We have conquered great evils, Raben," stated Thantos. "Do not discount what we've accomplished while on this journey." Thantos sat down at the only table in the room, watching the thief. "We are still on a holy quest, and from what can be seen, we have overcome tremendous troubles that would have one day plagued all that wish to live a peaceful life. It would have been a travesty were that army of vampires not dealt with.

"Well, the quest can't continue until tomorrow night at any rate." Urchin jumped over to the table and seated himself opposite Thantos. He gestured Raben to a chair. "We have to show the priest how normal people prepare for long journeys.

"I don't know how to gamble," said the thief. *At least not with money.*

"Great!" exclaimed the old man, grinning. "Neither does he. You both have until sunset tomorrow to figure it out." Urchin waved him over and Raben sat down for the night.

The packing was done, and their supplies were renewed. Each member of the party had three new sets of robes, a pack full of food, and Urchin had, along with all of the cooking equipment, most of the money. It was a couple of hours after sunset and Gabriel had just arrived. The four of them stood in the street in front of the temple while Thantos issued a few suggestions to the priests he was leaving behind. He was trying to stabilize the small order of Talvo in Nestor's Ferry because all of the high-ranking priests of the order had been killed when the vampires had attacked.

"Okay, that should do it," Thantos said, nodding to a priest who stood in the doorway to the temple. He waved to Urchin and Raben. "Let's go." They started out of the city. Gabriel walked in front of the three men. This seemed to be the most comfortable arrangement, and the most practical. *Better than having the damned thing behind us for the whole journey.* Raben gladly accepted the plan, having terrible memories of the journey to Nestor's Ferry.

None of them actually knew where the white wizard's tower was in the Shao Plains, and considering it was a single building in the massive sea of grass, the chances of just happening across it were abysmal. Gabriel, however, said that he could sense the power of the wizard and therefore served as guide. He ambled almost whimsically in front of the party, leading them in a generally straight line, northward. It was the same direction that the quest had to go, so everyone seemed fairly content to go. The vampire said nothing all the way through the night, he never even turned around when the party rested. He simply stood in the blue light of the moon, waiting until he was ordered to resume. He would then continue to stroll through the black, cool night.

"Does he need to feed?" asked Raben to no one in particular. "Or did he get enough already?" The thief surprised himself with the question as he realized what the quest had done to him. *What in the blazes!* He found himself considering things differently, worrying about details that ordinary people couldn't fathom. *Will we be able to get Hessing back from the Guild? Does the vampire need blood to continue? Am I human, and if so, why am I here, and what am I supposed to be doing?* He looked to Thantos, interested in seeing if the priest had even fully considered that the party was being escorted through foreign lands by one of Thannon's most terrible creations.

"He is going to eat animals. He says he can go a long time feeding on animals, now that he has fed on humans," Thantos said, deadpan, letting his voice demonstrate his disgust. "If he gets terribly in need before the quest is over, I will milk my own blood. I will require no such service of either of you," added the priest. "He is my prisoner. I will be responsible for him."

"Just let him die," Raben said. Urchin grunted his approval, nodding. *Feed him your own blood! You tore out your greeching eye to capture him, and now you'll feed him your lifeblood.*

"I cannot," stated Thantos. "He has a part to play, and Talvo wants him to play it." The priest adjusted his pack. "Besides, the brothers at the temple told me that the True Knowledge might free him from his undead bondage. At least we will have saved his soul." *Well then maybe the brothers at the temple, or Talvo himself, should feed the greeching thing their blood. How good of them to suggest the manner in which you might assist him and then leave you to become his food.* Raben remembered the night at the farmhouse. He had seen vampires rise from the priest, his blood falling from their chins, only to be lapped up by others of their kind. *He shouldn't be allowed to live, much less receive your sympathy.*

"His soul deserves torment, Thantos." The thief's sword leapt from his sheath and into his hand. "And if I had half a chance, I'd make sure he got it."

"Maybe." The word was a challenge. "You can't be certain," argued the priest. "What if he was a noble that simply got bit? After the disease set in, he required blood, and so it began. His soul may be every bit as valuable as mine. I won't abandon him for having terrible luck." Urchin and Raben exchanged glances. "Saving a man's soul is a far greater task than fighting his body. If you sweep his head from his shoulders, it will be you that condemns him to die as he is, rather than helping him to improve."

"Thantos." When Gabriel said the name, he drew the hiss out at the end of the name. "Due to my capture, I am forced to tell you that a dozen of my brethren follow us still." The vampire stroked the satin vest he wore as he looked back across the plains to the south, gazing over the land that the group had just covered. "They are some distance back, but I can now sense them as they near. I can forestall an attack, but cannot keep them from trailing your party."

"I thought that you broke them of their bond to him," said Urchin as he pointed to Gabriel. "Are they going to follow us forever?" The old man wiped his wispy hair from his face as his cheeks flushed red. "The thief is right about him." Urchin shot a heated look at the undead.

209

"They are independent. They do what they wish," answered Gabriel, disregarding the old man's insult as his glowing yellow eyes raked across the plains. "Feel contented that they did not go back to the town. Without the three of you, the town would suffer tremendously." The vampire smiled, letting the blue moonlight shine eerily off of his fangs.

"They can't go to the town, I sanctified every piece of ground in it. It would burn their skin to even take one step into Nestor's Ferry," Thantos said angrily. "We're not going anywhere populated, so it might be best to let them follow. They may become disinterested and give up on us." Thantos looked to the statuesque vampire for affirmation.

"I don't think so priest." Gabriel shook his head slowly, his grin spreading. "Vampires live forever, so boredom is seldom a reason to give up the chase. They can waste years at this single endeavor, and not feel it one bit. Only feeding will draw them off, and after the amount they were able to do back at that town, they have a long while before they will be forced to fall off their pursuit." The yellow eyes of the undead creature turned suddenly, blazing at Urchin. "Maybe they have a personal stake with someone in particular." The vampire's hissing voice broke into a malicious laugh. Paying it no heed, Urchin took a step nearer the creature.

"Will they fear the white tower?" asked the old man. "As they should?"

"Do I?" Gabriel laughed again. "I happily walk towards this tower. Whatever wizard occupies it will certainly not care if I am about. The Shao Plains have always seen undead. Ever since the White War, it is the living that are rare in this grass. You are more noticeable out here."

"Let them follow," announced Raben, "and you," he pointed to Gabriel, "will forestall nothing." The hideous fangs of the undead vanished. "Let them come for us, and I will give them reason enough not to follow." *If we argue long enough, they will overtake us before we've gone anywhere.* He leered at the vampire. *Is that your intention? Are you holding us here so that the others can catch us, take us unaware?*

"Thief, what are you saying?" interrupted Urchin. "Where does that attitude come from?" The old man threw his hands into the air. "What the boiling Hells is going on with all of you?"

"I don't know," Raben answered honestly. "I just hate being chased, I guess. The longer you stand back in fear, the worse that fear becomes. Thantos can save Gabriel's soul if that's possible, but if these things mean to force us from the quest again, then I'd rather just have it out and be done with it." The thief rested his hand on his sword.

Thantos said nothing in response and Urchin only nodded. Gabriel waited a few moments to see what else would be said, and then he nonchalantly returned to the trail, leading the party towards the tower.

The party walked in silence, expecting an attack, but nothing happened. They marched throughout the night, resting occasionally to eat the food that the temple had packed for them, and let their bodies regain some strength. Urchin seemed to handle the hike far better than he ever had before, never grumbling for rest, or stumbling as he walked.

The sun cast its first faint highlights into the sky and Gabriel's voice immediately shot through the party.

"Thantos." The vampire's voice preceded his appearance, shredding the calm morning air. "It is time to stop, and rest."

Thantos waved him away, dismissing him to go. Gabriel vanished. The priest turned to the party, preparing to say something, but his eyes widened and he pointed back through them to the grasslands to the south.

211

Looking back, the three men could see the train of creatures gliding over the plain. The vampires were like ghosts as they flew over the grass, causing not a single blade to bend or move as they passed. They headed straight for the party. Raben moved to the forefront and raised his sword before him. The vampires each landed on the plain, thirty steps away.

They were human, or used to be. Their clothes were simpler than Gabriel's. Most of them had basic tunics and breeches made of wool, all black or brown. *They were probably farmers in their previous life. Now they hunger for blood.* They were unkempt and dirty looking, which seemed strange after the regal mannerisms of Gabriel. They stood, silently. *Somehow familiar. Were you at Nestor's Ferry?* Raben ground his teeth together as he tried to remember the battle at the small town.

He held his sword high over his head. "This sword slew many of your kind in Nestor's Ferry. More than twelve," he said. "Leave us be, or you'll fair no better than the others who crossed me." The fear that had preceded the vampiric army at the farmhouse was not present with these twelve. Raben felt as though these were hardly a threat. They didn't move with the same predatory grace that Gabriel did, or seem nearly as intelligent. *But I have seen you before.* He stared at the creatures where they stood, scrutinizing them. *Where have I seen you?*

"Release Gabriel, or be devoured." The one who spoke had long black hair that fell over his shoulders and down his back. He was little more than two and a half reaches in height, and dressed in a black vest and trousers. *Familiar.* His voice was thin, trying to carry over the vastness of the plain. It held none of the power that Raben had come to expect from the supernatural beasts. *These might as well be average ruffians threatening us.*

"Attack!" yelled Raben. "Attack now, or flee the sun!" *These are not the same creatures. They are pitiful.* They lacked all that there was to fear in Gabriel, who single handedly provoked sheer terror in Raben before he was captured by the priest.

"We do not fear you," called out Thantos. "These creatures," he said under his breath, "cannot be vampires." As he finished saying this, the dozen undead creatures dissipated into the air. Raben spun quickly, looking for them. Urchin crouched near the ground, almost disappearing into the waist-high grass. Thantos peered forward at where the creatures had stood, his ax in his hands. The group waited only a short time, before the sun crested the horizon, making it impossible for the vampires to return.

"That was odd," commented Urchin, as he stood up. "Those were not nearly so ferocious." He looked to Thantos, who seemed about to speak.

"I don't know," was all that the priest said. "Maybe they're not fully vampires."

"It makes me feel a little better to know that they are not the same mindless things that we faced in the city," said Urchin. "Though it strikes me as strange that they could be so timid. I would think something as terrible as vampirism would be an all-consuming affliction. I would even expect it to be worse in the beginning." The old man shrugged and then began unpacking his bedroll.

"It is indeed supposed to be," added Thantos. "Many people, according to the Chronicles, that were infected would go insane and die before they even began to have blood cravings, and once the cravings came, they were unstoppable. Rabid animals in need of blood and carnage. Those that we just saw match no description I've read."

"Maybe," hypothesized Raben, "our friend Gabriel was raising a new breed of vampire. Perhaps he was helping them to convert more easily, thus swelling his numbers."

213

Raben looked to Thantos who nodded thoughtfully. "He was trying to mount a war on the living."

"Just order the damned thing to cure them," Urchin said matter-of-factly. "Didn't you say that a vampire could give back what they took, or some such thing?" The old man busied himself, trying to prop his blanket up on the tall grass in order to block out the sun so that he could sleep in the shade it created. "Stands to reason that a vampire would know how to not be a vampire, even if it meant ending its own life." He stopped what he was doing and looked directly to the priest. "You," he paused, "know how to kill yourself."

Urchin continued with his sleeping arrangement, paying no more attention to the conversation. Raben leaned into Thantos and spoke softly.

"Would that work?" he asked. Having no answer, Thantos only held his hands up helplessly and shook his head in confusion. Raben laughed. *If that's the solution, this world is crazier than I thought. That old fool says more than he knows.*

Thantos and Raben prepared their bedrolls, and talked a little about the dangers they may encounter as they neared the white tower. After Thantos finished highlighting a few of the creatures that white wizards used to have as guardians, Raben decided that keeping a watch might be a good idea. "I'll go first," he said. Thantos happily agreed and lay down.

There was nothing to keep an eye on. The plain reached out in every direction until the horizon cut it off. Raben was amazed that there was not a single thing in all that he could see that interrupted the Shao. *How many leagues have we walked over this grass? This is the best place to have a war. Nobody would be able to sneak up on anybody else.* He had no idea how far he could see, but the air was clear and the ground was flat. It made the thief feel safe and insignificant.

He was a tiny spot in the vastness of the Shao plains. Raben disrobed and practiced with his weapons in the sun. He fought with his sword and sickle as he hadn't for days. *It's almost as if this sword is in my hand before I even think to fight.* He held the sword, Hessing's sword, in front of him in the light. *If you die,* he could remember Hessing saying, *then you'll be trapped in the sword to serve its magic eternally. What the greeching Hells does that even mean? I need to ask more questions when I have the chance.* Raben sheathed his sickle and held the longsword with both hands, concentrating on it. There was an energy in the weapon. It almost vibrated with power. Small ripples of force were ebbing off of the blade. A white flash blinded Raben. He dropped the sword. Another flash. He clutched his head in his hands. It wasn't pain or surprise. It was knowledge. *Twenty-nine. I've killed twenty-nine living things with that sword.* Again Hessing's words formed in his thoughts. *The sword had never killed anyone until you stole it. Twenty-nine.* The number seemed unreal. Raben could remember battles, but he always lost control and raged without thought. *As if someone else was in control. There are so many times. Not just ideas! There are actions, murders, battles where I haven't been in command of myself. Who is? Who am I?* He picked up the sword and understood it. For every life he took, the sword was able to fight on its own until it killed an equal number. Feeling the sword's power, Raben reached out to his side and let the sword go. It hung in the air, floating at the ready. *Twenty-nine. Once someone kills with it, that person is bonded with it. How in all the Hells did he know? Greeching noble!* Raben sheathed the sword, and walked over to where Thantos lay. *The priest will never be able to sleep in the midday heat anyway.* Raben kicked him lightly to wake him up.

"Your watch," said the thief. After a short while, Thantos began sitting up. That was enough for Raben. He went to his bedroll and climbed in. It took a while, but he eventually fell into a light sleep.

Rain pattered on the blanket over his head, and in one spot, it dripped through the makeshift tent, splashing a light spray on the thief's face. It felt good. The air was cool, and the smell of the wet grass was strange and somehow wonderful. It smelled earthy and fresh, and carried the light vegetable scent of the grass. The thief had never smelled such. He filled his lungs with it, feeling as if it were cleansing his body just to breathe. *Healthy. That's what Urchin would call it.*

Raben rolled over and realized that it was later in the day than he would have guessed. Dark clouds were blocking the sun, but Thantos had already gone back to sleep and Urchin had the watch. The old man had removed his green robe, and was standing in the rain, letting it soak him. Though the drops were small and few, for now, Urchin stared up into the cloudy sky and let them spatter his face, patiently, expectantly. The old man looked truly happy. *He's a thousand year old child.* Raben smiled. *I wonder how old he really is. Sixty? No, seventy.* Urchin stood experiencing the rain for a long time while Raben watched. He would occasionally look down from the clouds to reassure himself that nothing was sneaking up on the party through the vastness of the Shao, then look back to the heavens, and wait. The drizzle gained in strength, becoming more constant. A light breeze began to blow, intensifying the chill of the rain that was splashing onto Raben.

As time passed by, darker and darker clouds moved overhead. *This storm can only get worse.*

"Urchin!" Raben called through the rain. "Were you going to wake us up, or just let us wash away?" The thief crawled out from under his lean-to. Urchin remained staring at the sky as he answered.

216

"What would you have done differently? There are a thousand leagues of grass in every direction." The old man waved his arms as the rain gained in strength. "It's a force of nature, Thief. Enjoy it. You sure as Hells can't outrun it." Raben, however, did not share the glee that Urchin was feeling. The thief crawled back underneath his now failing shelter, and tried to think of a way to escape. Everything he thought of was incredibly farfetched or outright foolish. At long last, when his blanket was nearly soaked through, and smashing the grass that held it up, he resolved on an improbable solution.

Raben cast a spell of levitation, but rather than indicating himself as the target of the magic, he chose the blanket. *It worked!* The thief laughed at his discovery. He pushed the blanket up into the air, and the fabric simply floated. It stayed exactly where he put it, completely unaffected by the weight of the rain, or the breeze. He then cast a dweomer on the blanket that infected every object that touched it with a light magical aura. The spell was designed to track the gadgets and components of a wizard's inventory, but Raben was without options and therefore hoped it would cause the rain that dripped through the blanket to seem magical. He couldn't tell if it was working or not. *Magical rain. This is a waste of good magic.* Finally, the thief cast a spell that protected his body from magical attack. Upon completing the spell, Raben held his hand under the rain that was now streaming through the drenched fabric overhead. It splashed on his hand, or very near it actually. He felt nothing. It wasn't touching him. *It worked. That actually worked.* He laughed out loud, and threw his pack over his shoulder. *I've never really experimented with anything. I need to figure all of this out.* He grabbed two of the corners of his blanket and walked it to where Thantos was laying, pulling it through the air. The priest was soaked, and didn't even look up as the thief approached with his discovery.

"Hello priest," said Raben happily. "Quite a storm, huh?" Thantos scowled up at Raben through the rain. "You wouldn't happen to have a spell that protects you from magical assault would you?" Thantos didn't answer. "Magical assault," Raben said louder. "The rain is magical."

Thantos sat up and discarded his blanket. It could become no more wet. He reached over his head and spoke while the rain poured down on him. Upon finishing, he resumed glaring up at Raben, the rain still drenching him as it fell. The thief smiled and pulled his floating blanket over Thantos. Letting it go, he spoke.

"We need to change clothes now." Raben immediately threw off his robe and pulled a new one from his pack. Putting it on, he became dry and totally protected from the rain. After watching the thief for a short while Thantos followed suit. He waited a few moments to make sure the results were similar and real.

"How'd you do it?" Thantos asked, as he rubbed his clammy hands together. Raben explained the process. "Brilliant and wasteful, but I'll not complain." The priest toweled the water out of his hair, and then offered the cloth to Raben who did the same.

"There is a drawback," said Raben. Thantos looked to him. "I have no idea how long this blanket will levitate." He smiled and Thantos simply shook his head.

The two of them sat and watched as the storm grew in fury. Rain came down in great torrents, and pounded on the blanket. The men stood and watched in awe, as their visibility was cut to nothing. Urchin was completely out of view. Thunder began to roll through the sheets of rain, though no lightning could be seen. They could feel the vibration of its force in the ground, and the water that had built up, which was soon ankle deep. A wind began cutting through the downpour, causing Raben to pull the corners of the blanket down, forming a sort of domed enclosure. Occasionally a drop or two would navigate its way into the shelter, and being nonmagical, splatter on one of the men causing great irritation.

Suddenly, the storm lessened. Moments later, it stopped altogether. Raben could see the wall of rain as it continued across the Shao, but not a single drop still fell over the party. Urchin was still standing in his smallclothes. The man was completely drenched, his meager hair plastered to his skull. *I'm surprised he didn't drown in that. Crazy fool!* Looking at Raben, Urchin must have thought much the same thing.

"You're dry!" he shouted. "How in all the Hells did you manage that?" The old man bent down and picked his slogging robe from the ground and approached Raben dragging the soggy clothing behind.

"There was a sun spot right over there, and it never rained in it," answered Raben, pointing at the still-floating blanket.

"Why didn't you tell me? I damn near froze my manhood off standing in that storm." Urchin spread his robe over the grass to dry it. "I hate the greeching rain!"

"You told me to enjoy it," countered the thief.

"Hells!" groused the old man. "That's only because I thought there was no other option." Raben laughed, and after a few moments, Urchin joined in. Thantos walked up and stood next to Raben. The priest was dry, but holding his sodden boots. "Oh!" announced Urchin. "Tell the priest, but not me." Thantos looked shocked having missed the previous conversation, which only incited more laughter. He joined in once it started.

"Thantos," Gabriel hissed, appearing a moment after he spoke. "It is time to continue." The vampire stood amidst the group, waiting for the priest to respond. He was later than usual. The sun had set quite a while earlier, and the vampire usually appeared only moments after the daylight faded over the horizon.

Thantos looked at the fanged creature. The undead's yellow irises were particularly bright, reflecting the light of the moon. "Are your weaker companions going to attack us tonight?" The priest gestured in the direction they'd last seen the twelve vampires on the night before. "They hadn't the nerve this morning. We've been expecting them for some time." Thantos walked around the vampire, until he stood behind it. "We've been waiting for you as well."

"The others," hissed Gabriel, "are now ahead of you. I believe they are trying to arrive at the tower before you. I apologize for myself. I have been following them since dusk to be certain." The vampire was facing Thantos. He hadn't turned or moved, he simply was. "I am bound to you." He gestured to the men standing around him. "None of us can change that. I serve you." *I hope you don't expect us to embrace that fact.*

"You serve Talvo, and the next time you decide to follow your friends across the Shao, you will tell me before you depart." Thantos pointed to the north. "Lead on." The priest stood unmoving until the vampire complied.

Gabriel turned smoothly and began his casual walk through the grass of the plains, taking the party ever closer to the tower of the white wizard. The scenery of the plains didn't change a bit as the party hiked through the night. By dawn they had covered a considerable ground, yet the Shao looked exactly the same in all directions.

The day passed without incident, and each member of the group kept watch in turn. Thantos prayed, Raben practiced with his weapons and meditated on his spells while thinking through his own inescapable dilemma. Urchin did nothing that could be witnessed. Anytime that the other two would awaken for any reason, the old man just sat on the ground looking uninspired, yet he constantly claimed that he was perfectly at ease and needed nothing to pass the time.

Gabriel presented himself on time the following night, and so resumed the routine that would draw the group through the next three nights. The vampire would arrive at dusk and report on the other vampires, constantly insisting that they had passed far ahead of the party, perhaps to ambush or dissuade the white wizard from dealing with the humans. The group would then walk through the repetitive leagues of grass of the Shao, seemingly covering no distance whatsoever. Each day, in the mid-afternoon a storm would pass, drenching the ground and giving the party their generally accepted wake up call. After the rain, they would talk, discussing what they wished to attain from the wizard, what creatures might be around him, and how they could deal with the vampires should they encounter them again. The monotony calmed them. They had become so accustomed to battle and terror that the boredom of the trek was welcome relaxation.

Soon the humor inherent to each of them began to bubble out, and the group felt light hearted and passed each night discussing small things like where they would live if they could be anywhere in Reman. Of the three of them, only Urchin had lived outside of Liveport. The old man described distant lands and each of them voted on whether or not they would want to live there and why. The group decided that they would find a place to be near one another after the quest was over, or even travel to some of the places that Urchin had described as beautiful and uneventful.

"You're sure we're getting somewhere old man?" asked Raben. "We're four nights out of Nestor's Ferry, and from what I can see we could be no further away than the first night." The thief plucked a handful of grass from the ground and tossed it at Urchin.

"We are," answered the old man, somewhat dolefully. "In fact, we are near the forest, but I think once you're in it, you'll wish you still had another season to walk through the Shao."

"What forest again?" asked Thantos. "I hate all of the names for these places. I can never remember them."

"It's called the Narwood forest, or Leafwood. Some call it Nalman's wood, after the first man to die in it." The old man looked at Thantos, arching his bushy eyebrows. "The trees never grow leaves, and yet they never rot and fall over either. They stand bare in a think carpet of ferns and brambles." Urchin entwined his fingers and stretched his hands before him. "Men say that the trees live, and kill intruders while others say that's myth. There is something amiss in the forest, but…" he crouched to the ground and lay a hand on it, "…it isn't unhealthy."

"Sounds like a place I'd rather not live," commented Raben. Urchin snorted his agreement. "But how can we be at this forest of yours?" asked the thief. "I thought the tower was in the plains."

"I don't know. I know nothing about the damned wizard, but I'm telling you. We are near the Narwood forest. I can feel it," Urchin said, pointing northward. *Why do you sound so upset about getting here if it's so healthy?*

"Gabriel!" Thantos called out. The vampire materialized just in front of the priest. "Gabriel, where is this tower?" asked the priest, commandingly.

"Less than a league," answered the vampire as he pointed north. "At the very gates of Nalman's wood." Thantos nodded and the vampire disappeared. Immediately, Gabriel was ahead of the party, continuing the march to the tower. "Remember," said the priest, "white wizards gather their power from spirits. I can block them." He turned and walked onward followed by Raben and Urchin.

The moon was waning though still bright enough to supply the group with light to see by. Each of them had no idea what to expect, but they were scanning the land ahead in search of the towering spire that would house the most powerful man that lived on the plains.

"The tree." Gabriel's calm voice came unexpectedly, causing the party to jump. Raben already had weapons out. After taking a deep breath, it was obvious. Looking to where the vampire was pointing, a small black tree could be seen in the night. It stood alone, breaking through the grass and standing some fifteen reaches high. There were no leaves from what Raben could see, only narrow dark branches that hung out over the grass like clawed fingers. After having seen nothing but grass for a week, the tree bothered him. *It looks wicked. Urchin says it's healthy.*

"There is a man sleeping beneath the tree," stated the vampire. Narrowing his eyes, Raben could see no man. Thantos and Urchin were leaning forward into the night in order to see the man that the undead had indicated but nothing more than the tree was visible. Gabriel waited a short time and then vanished from sight, melting away into the night air.

223

"Well, how should we proceed?" asked Thantos. "Gabriel wouldn't have been so direct about pointing the man out if he weren't important. Perhaps even the wizard."

"This isn't how I expected it would be," said Urchin. "I envisioned us knocking on a door to a splendid tower, and having an archaic man of unparalleled knowledge laugh at us. Not finding him lying under a tree." The old man shook his head, grumbling as he did.

"I think I'll go over there and talk to him," began Raben, "and if he seems threatening then I can assure him that my powerful allies are within range of attack." He looked from Urchin to Thantos. The priest nodded. "If everything looks good, I'll call you over." Raben eased his pack from his shoulders and dropped it to the ground. "You get ready," the thief said to Thantos, "and if anything even seems to happen, separate the mage from his spirits. And you old man," Raben looked over to Urchin, "do something that would merit being called a powerful ally." The thief smiled and soon Urchin answered in kind.

Raben checked his weapons, making sure that they were loose in their sheaths, and could be pulled quickly should the need arise. He looked to the tree and then to each of his companions. Urchin reached out to Raben's shoulder, holding it firmly.

"Be cautious. Every wizard I've ever known has had a disregard for life." The old man nodded at Raben as he let his arm fall. "Destructive, they seldom see the result of their actions before the dead are being hauled away." He looked away from the thief for a moment, and then turned and walked away.

"Do you think of me as a wizard with no regard for life as well?" Raben asked Thantos.

"No." The priest looked right at the thief with his good eye. "That's not the way I look at it. It's not how I see it. You're a weapon for someone, from someone. I'm glad you're not my enemy." Thantos looked down at his open hands. "I don't hold you accountable for the death that surrounds you. You appear to have little choice in the matter. If it weren't you, then someone else would have been sent in your place."

But I'm still a death sentence. Dangerous. Raben started to walk toward the tree. *Appear to have little choice. I have no choice in this. None! Traveling to a wizard who has probably dreamed of killing fools like us for centuries. Some great decisions we make.* He thought about sneaking over to where the man was supposed to be lying, but after thinking about the way a mage renowned for violence might respond to being surprised, he opted to walk to the tree openly. His legs brushed noisily as they battered through the tall grass. His weapons clicked in their sheaths, the grass forcing him to step high over the thick vegetation. *I've never noticed how loud we are as we walk through this stuff.* He looked down at the dark sea of grass. *Everything is louder at night.* He neared the tree, and could see a dark form under it. It was nothing more than a black stain on the ground until he was much closer.

As he closed to within twenty paces away, he could see the distinct shape of a man. Each step he took was more deliberate than the last. He felt as though fear and need were arguing within him. *This wizard is supposed to be able to help. The greeching advice of a vampire. Another bad idea! At least this one is mine. Walking up to a white wizard with no protection. A fine idea to claim as my own.* He cut short a quick laugh as he forced himself to take another step. *There is no way a man of power would lay out here without defense. I might as well carry my own headstone so that it can land wherever my ashes fall to the ground.* He looked to the figure, hoping the man would jump to his feet. *Too eerie.* He lay there. *I'm walking into a ward!* He stopped. He felt certain that there was a spell. *Something has to be protecting this guy. No wizard would be so foolish.* Raben looked overhead. Nothing. He quickly turned so he could see behind himself. Nothing. He took another step forward. Nothing. He breathed in slowly and forced himself to take another step. He kept his legs in motion, slowly carrying himself to the being beneath the tree. *Get up!* He was less than ten paces from the dark form. He could hear the labored breathing of a sleeping man. Raben closed his eyes as he took another step. Another. He didn't want to see the magical shield just before it incinerated him. He took another step. He was five steps from the man. He could see the wisps of white hair, the unkempt beard. Raben could even make out the man's chest as it rose and fell with his breathing.

"Hello?" called Raben. No response. He took in a breath, and tried to hear the exact volume he wished to call out. *Loud, but not too loud.* "Hey!" he called, cringing even as the word left his mouth. *Damn it! Don't make me walk over there and lean down into my death.* "You!" He shouted.

"Great spirits!" The man screamed. He scurried on his hands and knees away from Raben. "Back spirit! Don't make me snare you!" The man's voice was screechy and high pitched. "Surr Kadz Narn!" *Magic!* He spat the words. Raben froze. *Thantos has him locked away.* The spell created no effect.

"I just want to," started Raben as he lifted his hands to indicate that he bore no weapons.

"Impossible!" Screamed the wizard, as he jumped to his feet. "You can't just stand there!" He kicked his satchel where it lay on the ground. The bag bounced off of the tree, and rolled to a stop.

"We just want to talk…"

226

"Frissni Kalda Vaok!" yelled the mage, gesturing angrily at Raben. Again the thief stood unmoving, waiting for the result of the incantation. "Burning cats!" The mage stomped up to Raben. He had a wand of some sort in his hand. The thief tore his blade from its sheath.

"Stand back, mage!" he shouted. "I only wish to speak with you. My friends guard you! You cannot affect me with spells!" He pointed his sword at the advancing wizard. "I don't wish to kill you." The old sorcerer stopped his approach.

"Who sent you, demon?" asked the wizard with visible disgust twisting his face. He sized the thief up, scrutinizing him where he stood.

"No one." *Not that I know of anyway. Hells, old man! Settle down before we are both blown to the fires.*

The mage stared at Raben silently. He lifted his wand, pointing it at Raben. The thief shook his head and lifted a sickle from its sheath, gripping it in his left hand. He then held his ornate sword out to his side and opened his hand. The blade floated as he expected it would.

"You may knock me from my feet, but you'll die with me," said Raben as he pulled another sickle from his belt. "I wish to ask your help, not battle you." The thief tensed as he let his body settle into battle readiness. "Decide soon, wizard, because if you don't wish to help me, then I need to find someone who will. I don't have time to wait for you to figure out how quickly you will die if you try and attack."

The sorcerer lowered his wand, and his chin fell with it, lowering his old head to his chest. He spoke a muttered word and moments later the sound of wings could be heard from behind him. "Don't fear," snarled the wizard, looking up at the thief's alarmed expression. He and Raben waited. The sorcerer walked to where he'd been laying, only three paces in front of the thief, and lifted the veil on a lantern. Light poured from the lamp, bringing green back to the dark

227

grass, and giving humanity to the black form of the wizard. *A man after all. Even the greatest wizards on Reman must fear death at some point or another. Especially you, my old mage. A vampire told me that you had worked to find a way to prolong your life. Not the pastime of one who would quickly put that same life on the line fighting the likes of me. So what sort of man are you?*

He looked ancient. His face was riddled with the wrinkles of long years. He had sporadic wisps of white hair on his head and on his face, particularly his eyebrows, which pushed further off of his tanned face than his beard. His lips were thin and tight, drawing deep creases against his whiskered cheeks. But what really caught Raben's attention were the old man's eyes. They were clear and bright green. They looked nothing like the eyes of any old man he'd ever met, especially a man reputed to have lived for hundreds of years. They held youth and energy. *He has a quick mind.* Raben respected him already. He felt that the man had power and knowledge. *Dangerous.*

The sound of wings grew louder just before the creatures landed within the light of the lantern. *Urchin! Thantos!* The creatures bore the unconscious bodies of his friends. *Blazes!* They held his friends easily. They had four arms apiece and each arm had a clawed human hand at the end. Their horned heads were expressionless as they came to a resting position. Stone gray skin covered their genderless bodies. *They look like living statues.*

"My companions! Put them down!" Raben shouted the command, never looking from the stone monsters to the mage. The old wizard nodded and the monsters dropped the sleeping men to the ground. "What in the boiling Hells are those?" asked Raben as he moved towards his friends.

"They are called stone demons," answered the mage, his old voice cracking as he spoke. "They are statues that I have invited the souls of the damned to inhabit. Rather against their will." He waved to the statues. "It took great power, but they are impervious to nearly all attacks. They make fantastic guards," said the mage. "Most of the damned time." He eyed Raben as the thief bent down to his friends. The stone demons stood over him, unmoving, as he checked Urchin and Thantos. Raben's sword floated between he and the demons, keeping watch where the thief was afraid to. He trembled slightly as he worked just beneath the horrible beasts, never having dealt with an enemy of the old sorcerer's power.

"Let them awaken," ordered Raben, keeping his voice even.

"I think not. If I am to deal with such a possession as yourself, then I shall need collateral to guarantee my life," stated the wizard. He held out his hands, allowing them to portray a scale. He moved them until they were even. "As long as I am fine, then so are they."

"I can kill you now, if you like," Raben offered angrily as he shed his fear. "Your demons won't stand in my way." He looked up at the unmoving statues. Their neutral expressions looked wrong to the thief. He thought that they should be snarling.

"Perhaps," the wizard responded. "You might kill me. You might even kill the demons. Based on what I know of you, you might even live." The mage walked up to Raben and stood next to him. He pointed to Urchin and Thantos as they slept. "But they won't. I'm certain."

Hells! What he knows about me. The words passed through Raben's mind over and over. *What does he know about me? Greeching Hells! How can he know anything about me? Lying bastard!* Raben's hands shot up from his sides and his sickles crisscrossed around the mage's neck. The thief could sweep the man's head off with no more effort than shears cutting through silk.

"Not smart to kill the greatest mortal that walks this land," the old mage advised. "You might rid the whole of Reman of the only helpful resource it has." The sorcerer then sighed dramatically, emphasizing the simplicity of the thief's decision.

"If you harm them in any way," said Raben, "you'll end up as a damned soul. And I," he spat, "will snare you, and rack your soul eternally." The only response the wizard gave was a slight nod. "Good."

The ancient wizard waited for Raben to release him from the sickles and once he was free, he waved his stone demons away. The creatures bent menacingly over Urchin and Thantos, plucked them from the ground, and sped off into the night. *Never even checked his neck. You have, indeed, seen much, been in a few scrapes.*

"We'll walk. It's not far." The mage bent down and picked up his satchel from the base of the tree. "What do you need?" asked the wizard. "I'll not have my time wasted with foolishness, so you'd better be direct with whatever it is." He began walking away from Raben. He stopped, staring in the direction he'd been heading. "Don't test me."

"I have heard you are a wizard of some power," Raben said. "I need to know more about me. I am wrapped in some magic or another that I want you to explain." The thief put his sickles away, but let the sword float next to him as a warning, and a comfort. "There is something manipulating me, and I need to identify who, why, and how."

"I'll need you to submit to spells, if you can." The old man turned around and glared at Raben. "You'd be totally at my mercy." *Something tells me that you are completely incapable of mercy.*

"I know all of the spells of offense. I'll remain awake through all spells cast on me, and if you start one that might harm me…" Raben left the words hanging.

230

"So you do know some magic. Then tell me," ordered the mage. "How did you dispel my ward without setting it off back there? I must know." The wizard waited until Raben caught up with him, waited for the answer. His mouth was puckered into a scowl, and his bony hands were balled into fists. "How?"

"I stepped through it," Raben said distastefully, "or it was miscast." The thief looked down at the bent old mage. "Because I did nothing to dispel it." He started to move past the old man.

"Wait!" the old man barked. His hand grabbed Raben's arm. "You did nothing?" Raben nodded slowly, looking down at the wizard's thin hand. "Nothing?" The old man's voice dipped, searching for certainty. Again Raben nodded as he reached a gloved hand across his body and picked the wizard's grip from his arm. "Come on!" groused the old wizard as marched away.

The ancient sorcerer led the two men through the tall grass of the Shao. Raben watched him closely. The mage gave no indication that he cared that Raben was there, nor that he feared the thief in any way. He walked across the plain ahead of him without so much as a backward glance. They hiked for a short while before arriving at the foot of a dark structure. Raben couldn't make out its size or shape in the darkness. He could only feel that the free air of the Shao had ended and a solid form was before him. As he peered into its deep obscurity, he saw the dim reddish outline of a door forming.

The light intensified and soon a warm firelight was clearly showing a door in the dimness of the building's wall. The wizard stood ahead of Raben to the left, and seemed unmoved by the light of the door. He remained still when the door began to open letting the red light pour out into the Shao. After only a brief span of time, the wizard stepped into the door way, his shadow stretching across the plain

231

until it faded into the countless blades of waist-high grass. When the wizard was just inside of the door he stopped and turned back to the thief.

"You may enter," he said emphatically. The reddish light diminished considerably allowing the mage's shadow to dissipate. The door was still glowing with a dull reddish light, but after the power of light that had just been there, it seemed only a remembrance to Raben's eyes, as though he'd just looked into the sun and had lasting spots plaguing his vision. He blinked for a few moments before accepting the wizard's invitation.

He took only one step inside of the building.

"You never fail to surprise me," she said. Her perfume flooded into his nostrils. "You go days making me proud. Your every decision perfect, your prowess growing with every passing moment, and then suddenly," she steepled her fingers before her lips, "you do something that forces me to wonder how the race of man has survived for as long as it has." The Guild hunter stood only a few paces before him. He lay on the ground before her. It felt like stone. "Have you nothing to say?" She shook her beautiful head, her eyes narrowed angrily. "This cannot be the result of just trying to finish the quest that we have asked you to complete."

"What, in all of the blazing, fiery, greeching Hells, are you talking about?" Raben asked, his voice carrying all of the genuine confusion and irritation that he felt. "I haven't the first damned clue how I even got here, wherever in the Hells this is, and I certainly don't need you to tell me that this is not the result of trekking for the True Knowledge." The thief grimaced as he tested his arms and legs. Neither was bound, so he sat up. "And just so that you can report it to whoever it is we serve, that neither of us can identify, the members of the Dayquest haven't the foggiest greeching idea of what they are doing, nor where they are going, so until you are ready to leave this quiet and protected shelter that you seem to be able to magic me into, I suggest you keep your sermon to yourself." He scowled up at the beautiful elf, smug in his tirade.

She strode up, and stood over him, allowing his outburst to end. She knelt down almost on top of his legs, her lithe body within an arm's reach of his own. A smile played across her face. "I see," she snapped, taking his manhood into her hand roughly. "Perhaps there is something that you need to keep in mind." Raben restrained himself from calling out as she let her grip tighten. "You are merely the soldier in a battle that you will die not understanding. And before you even try to decide what part I should play, you might," she added even more pressure, earning a pained grunt from Raben, "want to find out exactly what it is that we are already doing just to keep your foolish corpse walking." Her lips spread into a glorious smile. "Now do you think we can come to an understanding, or should I finish you off in a manner that is more noticeable to your senses?" The thief nodded, his eyes beginning to tear. "Good." She let go of him and rose back to her feet in a fluid motion. He gasped, taking in one deep breath after another.

"You need to gain a better perspective of your role before you end up dead," she said while he recovered from her motivational speech. "You have little to gain by bucking against us, my pet. There is no chance for you to either force them to divulge their identities if they do not wish to, nor can you gain inference on yourself by going to anyone but us. In fact, it would take a god for you to obtain any worthwhile information on who you are, and that is exactly why you will gain the True Knowledge, because unlike the rest of the people who are questing to gain the True Knowledge, you have a personal value invested in it. They do not! To them it is a golden chalice that they will wave before congregation in order to become rich and famous."

"Do you actually believe that?" Raben asked as he rose gingerly to his feet, "or have you been programmed to say this to me?" He could remember the last time he was with her and she had used the word 'our' as she had described their situation. *We both are working for the same people, and we both need to know more if we are going to do anything but inflict their designs on the world.*

"I am free to do as I please with you," she responded, her voice lacking its usual confidence. "You belong to me." She looked at him momentarily before turning away. "You are mine. And should you displease me, I could end your life with no more than my wish to do so."

"Are you convinced not even of that small detail?" he asked, trying to use her incertitude against her. "Or are you as much a pet as you claim I am?" Her eyes blazed as she spun to face him, her hand reaching down to her sword. But the answer never came. Disgusted, she waved her arm wildly, as if brushing him away, and as she did so, he plunged into darkness.

Raben was lying in a well-lit chamber. His eyes popped open and he was unsure if he'd been magicked or knocked out, but he was sure that he was coming out of something. His head pounded. *I just took a step in, and now... Was I asleep?* He sat up, shaking his head slowly. The old white wizard was standing just where he'd been as the thief had taken his first step through the door. *He looks exactly the same.* Everything looked the same. It seemed as though he was the only thing in the whole room that had been affected. He looked around for a moment. *Is she only in my imagination? How can that be? She was in Hessing's house. Hells!*

A fire was burning in a hearth opposite the door and several very well cushioned antique chairs were placed in front of it. A large rug covered the stone floor, patterned with concentric circles of red and blue, which had been stitched onto a field of gray. Tapestries covered the walls. Each drape was an epic remembrance of the white wizards, showing them in the midst of combat wielding fire and lightning as other men might handle a sword. The wizard's home was warm and comfortable, and not what Raben expected.

"What happened?" Raben demanded. His voice seemed coarse to him. He needed a drink. "How...did I end up down here?" The thief rubbed his head, trying to drive the recurring soreness away. *Why does this have to happen to me?*

"I'm not totally certain." The white wizard scowled down at the thief. Raben lay there for a time, trying to feel out what had happened, but it had been far too instantaneous. His mind hadn't even registered entering the tower before he'd been talking to the Guild hunter, and then his return to the white wizard had been even more sudden. Raben felt lucky that he was sane enough to even begin trying to figure out what happened to him. The wizard continued to glower at him. Both men did little to contain the confusion that was vexing them. It had been a disease in Raben's life since he'd awakened in Hessing's house. Confusion was a daily event for him. The aged wizard, however, had obviously seen little of late that he couldn't immediately explain. His anger mounted as he stared at the thief, filling his eyes with fiery contempt. *He will figure something out.* Watching him, Raben could see that the mage took the unknown as a direct challenge. The ancient sorcerer was on his way to becoming livid based only on the fact that he didn't already have an explanation for what he had witnessed with his own eyes. *That is why I needed to see you.* The thief waited patiently, hoping that the old man would break his silence and begin describing a solution to Raben regarding his situation. But only an intense quiet resulted. Finally, sensing that no answers were forthcoming in regards to what had happened only a few moments before, the thief tried to redirect the conversation.

"How do you keep the light from spilling out?" Raben asked as he waved to the door. "I walked from darkness into a perfectly lit room in a single step."

"It's a simple ward against light, turned into the room," answered the wizard, irritated with the question. "It blocks the light as though the light were a spell being cast out the door. Restrains it to this room, so that my lamp lights aren't seen all across the Shao."

"I didn't think you were overly worried about that after your display out there. That red light became bright enough near the end to be seen for leagues," Raben shot back. "Or do you have more wards sprinkled all over the plains after all these years?" He looked towards the old man after the slight, but the mage was lost in thought, and hadn't heard the comment.

"That was one of the most interesting things I've seen in centuries and will tell you about it later," answered the mage, "when I have the first damned notion of what in the spotted night sky happened." The man stumped over to one of the antique chairs and lowered himself onto one of the stuffed red cushions. The curved dark wood creaked slightly in complaint as the wizard gripped the chair's handles, fuming at his own ignorance.

Raben watched the wizard for a time, and then crossed the room and sat down in the chair opposite the centuries-old mage. The white wizard had closed his eyes and sat motionless in the large chair as if in deep meditation. Raben was reluctant to intrude, but there was too much he needed to know. *I have waited to find anyone that might have any insight into what is going on with me, and now that I have found you, you need to take a nap. If you want to try and beat it. If you are so competitive that you have to know or you will explode, then let's get under way. Begin! Cast your spells. Do what you need to do.*

"How long will it take you to figure out what I need to know?" the thief asked, keeping his voice low, trying not to sound impatient. "And where are my friends that I can make sure they are safe?" Raben leaned forward in the chair causing it to creak. "And what do I call you?"

The old man let out a long slow breath. His hands raised before him with his fingers steepled. He pressed them to his mouth, as he took in a long slow breath. He held it momentarily as if arriving at a great decision.

"I am called Kelc," sighed the aged wizard. "I will need at least several days to test a number of things regarding what you wish to know about yourself." He opened his eyes and let the fury he felt pour through them. "As far as your friends," he growled, "they are my prisoners until you are leaving and I am but a long forgotten moment in your ever-growing trek." The mage slowly dropped each finger from his lips and wove them together until both if his hands were clenched into one fist. "And if you try to see them in any way before then I can guarantee that you'll never see them again." Kelc lowered his hands back to the chair. "Now that we understand one another," the ancient man said as he abruptly stood, "I am going to sleep. You can sleep on the floor in here. Do not attempt to exit this room in any way." Raben didn't even have time to blink before the practiced sorcerer vanished. *Hells! I can't wait!* Patience wasn't one of the thief's strong points. *What am I supposed to do in here? Appreciate the art work? Hells! All of these fools with their ability to just vanish when I want to talk to them are beginning to anger me. The next greeching fool that vanishes while I am trying to talk to them is going to get a gut full of steel when they return. Damned strangest part. They all vanish as though I don't matter, yet every one of them reappears sometime later and demands that I bow to them in respect. Hells!* He fumed until his mind began to tire of the constant barrage of murderous thoughts.

"Just greeching perfect." Raben slid down out of the chair and lay down in front of the dying fire. *Damned Dayquest! Damned guild!* It had been a long time since the thief had been alone, and now that he was, the feeling that he was the victim erupted inside of him.

What does all of this mean? How can I be the center of this quest? I can't. Where is that fool noble at now? I don't even like him. Why would the Guild use him against me as a hostage? Now that he isn't with us, being a sword and shield for the party, what would I care if they kill him? That makes no sense. But then, what does? Raben took his sword and sheath off of his belt and laid them on the floor. *This damned Kelc had better be able to tell me what I am and how to fix it. He better not hurt Urchin or Thantos! I wonder how many things he has in this place like those stone demons to defend him, and kill me if I sleep.* He made sure his sword was within easy reach and scrutinized every shadow that the fire sent leaping about the room. Raben grew keenly aware of the dependency he had on Thantos and Urchin.

It would be damned easy to be struck unconscious and get to sleep through all of this greeching mess. I wonder if they're even here. Probably not. He realized how much he had comforted himself in knowing that they were there to talk to. The thief was far more eager to face his unexplained future when he was defending the other two men. They certainly had abilities, but they always ended up seeming so helpless. *But I guess I really don't need any witnesses for the death that this crinkled up old bastard probably has in store for me. Just being here is foolish. She's right, I do end up in the most foolish places. I'd marvel at the foolish things I'd end up in if I was watching me. It would never make sense for me to end up somewhere safe to spend a night. We traded vampires with no cover from the night for a week being held prisoner in a mortar block by one of the wizards that waged the worst war this land has ever known.*

"My enemies must think I'm a fool," Raben said as his eyes followed his own filmy shadow from the fire. "They can always see me coming." The thief lowered his head to the carpeting and tried to calm himself enough to fall asleep. After a long restless period, the fire burned low and then died leaving only dull orange embers, which did nothing to light up the room. He stared at them, counted them. *Sixteen.* He slowly reduced the number as the embers faded and vanished from sight. Eventually they all went cold, leaving darkness behind. With nothing left to look at, Raben's eyes slid closed. Sleep eventually came.

Raben woke up in the same complete darkness he'd fallen asleep in. His head felt heavy, as though he'd slept either far too long or not at all. He waved his hands just before his face to verify that he could see nothing. Feeling claustrophobic, he immediately shot his arms out to either side of himself. His left hand brushed one of the carved wooden legs of Kelc's chairs. He followed the leg up to the cushion, and then used it as a prop to stand up. His joints popped as he raised himself. *Where did I leave my pack?* Raben tried to orient himself to the room based on the time he'd spent not sleeping the night before. *Sword!* He bent over and dragged his hands along the floor until they bumped into his sheath. He traced his way up the hardened and polished leather until he felt the hilt. He drew the blade out letting the sound of metal cut through the room. Standing erect, he held the weapon out to his side and let go. He half expected to hear it crash to the floor, but the only discernible noise was his own heavy breathing. *No light, no sound. This is insane! Does this greeching wizard really live in this dark hole?* He rubbed his arms, and doubled over, doing the same to his legs. *Last time I sleep on the damned floor. Feels like a wagon drove over me.*

"Bastard can probably generate light or fire whenever the greeching Hells he wants to," Raben muttered to himself. "Or else he's adapted to this kind of life like some kind of blind salamander that crawls around in a dark forgotten cave. Hells!" He swore loudly enough for an echo to answer back.

"Or," Kelc spoke, drawing the word out, "I have mastered the art of lighting torches." A flame appeared before Raben. The thief blinked, turning his head away from the bright yellow flame. Kelc stood a few paces in front of Raben holding a burning torch. "I find that the heat that comes from actual fire is more to my liking than the cold of magical fire." Kelc turned away from Raben and walked to a nearby wall where he mounted his torch in a sconce. Raben looked around the room, shielding his eyes from the direct light of the torch. Nothing had changed. He was almost surprised by his sword, which was floating dutifully by his side. "Now, you are an odd and wonderful creature," Kelc announced. *Yeah, so are you. Greeching bastard. How spry you look after a long sleep in your luxurious home.*

What a difference a night makes. Raben sneered at the mage. *Hope you enjoyed your bed. Probably stuffed with feathers. I hope one of your pet rats that you must have around here dies and rots in that wonderful bed.* The thief's sneer lost its edge.

"What has you so happy, old man?" Raben drew a dagger and held the weapon by the blade. It helped him feel that he wasn't helpless. "There is nothing to be happy about so far as I can tell. This dreary dark place you live in does nothing to help." Raben flipped the dagger, catching it by the handle.

"It has been days, Thief. You have slept for quite some time while I have worked tests on you and tried to figure out what you are." Kelc smiled mockingly, his eyes darting momentarily to the spot where Raben had slept. "You have walked and talked and done all that I asked in order that I could figure out how you are able to do what you do. I now know more about you than you do." The wizard pointed at the thief. "Would you like to know, or would you like to eat?" A plate of steaming food appeared on a side table near Raben. Hunger surged inside of the man. *Has he just let me starve for days?* The thief rebuilt his sneer again, and walked to the plate, picked it up and sat down in one of the lush chairs. He used his dagger to eat, slicing the succulent slabs of meat and then spearing them to lift them to his mouth.

"Tell me," Raben ordered. He tucked a steamed onion into his mouth. "Tell me what you learned." *If you withhold a single detail after keeping me locked up and unconscious for all this time, I swear by all that I have, that I will see you diced and served.* Raben stabbed a piece of steaming meat, and lifted it from the plate.

"You must do something for me," Kelc responded. "You see. I learned how to kill you, and while it is difficult, I know I can do it." The old man hobbled across the room and lowered himself into the chair opposite Raben. From such a short distance, the thief could see that the white mage hadn't enjoyed the process, hadn't gotten to rest comfortably as he'd first thought. The wizard looked spent. *All those tests must have taken a toll.* "But I don't wish to kill you needlessly when I can blackmail you and obtain a service."

Raben sat, silently eating. *I knew this was coming. Bastard!* He had expected to be killed when he finally had fallen asleep. *Add a little more to this damned quest. Why not?*

"What do you want?" he asked. "There is little that I have, so I suppose you want me to steal something or kill someone. You have no doubt discovered that that is what I was created to do." Raben stabbed another large piece of stewed beef with his blade and stuffed it in his mouth. He chewed as he stared at the mage. The wizard sat soundlessly, watching the thief. Raben swallowed a few times. "Are you going to tell me? I grow impatient with you and this life, so having either end is fine." Raben filled his voice with controlled anger. *Just spit it out!*

"I want you to submit to a spell," Kelc said, his old voice cracking. "I want you to allow me to encase your will into one specific dweomer." The wizard stood up and waited a few moments before continuing. "I wish to force a quest upon you. I ask that you neither steal nor murder, but only betray those who now control you upon completion of the quest you must now pursue." Kelc took a few tentative steps toward the thief. "You must give in vocally, swearing to do what I ask while I cast the spell." Kelc edged forward until he stood immediately before Raben. The floating sword slowly made its way around the sitting thief until it was between the two men. *Betray those who now control you upon the completion of the quest you must now pursue.*

"What does that mean? Betray those that control you. What does that do to me?" Raben pointed his greasy dagger at the mage. "And what does that do for you?" *Make sense quickly. No one can exhaust me faster than you already do.*

"It will free you of your master's will," Kelc answered. "It will cause their power to pass into a new magic which I will design, and thereby imprison them to do my bidding. That will make sense after I describe your situation a little more. We'll get to that. You will be as normal as you can get, I suppose." Kelc knit his brow. "It should give me considerable knowledge on magical transfers and inhabitation, thus helping me solve the riddle of death, permanently. I am very old, and would like to live a little longer if I can."

"After you have told me all that you know, I will swear," Raben stated flatly. "And, after I have seen my friends healthy."

"I will tell you all I know first," began Kelc. "Then," he pointed at Raben, "you will swear to do as I ask while I cast the incantation on you, and then I will give you your friends back." Kelc shook his head as he looked down at the thief. "You have no option but to accept. I do not accept enemies into my home that I cannot control." The old mage grinned mockingly. "Fortunately, there are ways to control everyone."

"I suppose so," answered Raben. He had no other course if he wanted to get Urchin and Thantos back. Not to mention the fact that he had no idea if he could get out of the wizard's home. *There are probably wards upon wards keeping me in here if he has had days to work on them.* "Fine, old man," Raben said. "Tell me." The thief sat back in the chair and prepared to hear the reasons for his own existence.

Kelc made his way back across the carpet to his own chair and sat down facing Raben. The wizard mumbled a few arcane words and a footstool appeared before him. He nudged it into place with his feet and then offered to provide one for Raben who declined.

"What are you?" asked Kelc to no one. "What are you indeed? I labored for two days to find out if there was magic cast on you, to see if you were magical, to find out if your sword was protecting you. I thought that perhaps you were a mage of such strength that you radiated the magic from the very fabric of your being." Kelc pointed at Raben lazily. "Not the case."

"Let me tell you the true beginning of my want to discover what you are." Kelc's face lit up with the telling of his story. Much to Raben's irritation, the wizard was enjoying being able to recount the past few days. "When you walked up to the tower, and saw that red light. That was a flame ward. The growing light that gathered in intensity until it flashed bright red was magical fire that consumed

246

you." Kelc held his hands out to either side of him. "You died!"

"This is crazy," Raben barked. He stood up, his hands each had a sickle at the ready. "Don't toy with me, wizard!" He shouted. "I've come too far to hear this rubbish!" *I might have been unconscious for a season and now that it comes to telling me the discovery, he can do nothing but make it up as though he were an old granny spinning tales for her own amusement.*

"Sit down," Kelc yelled. "This is the truth. You died, and have died several times that I can tell so far." The wizard lowered his voice. "Sit down."

Raben stood quivering, and then slowly sat back down. He held each of the sickles, debating in his mind which one he would use to kill the white wizard. *This one, you wouldn't expect it.* He glanced down at the curved blades, content with the one he would use.

"Now," Kelc continued soberly, "I watched your skin crackle right off your bones, and then you fell to your hands and knees, still trying to get in the door. Then you disappeared momentarily and then. Poof! You were new again, lying on my doorstep." Kelc pointed to the door. "You knew something had happened, just not what. I had just watched you walk through the worst ward I could prepare, watched you melt into nothing but bones, and then saw you suddenly regain your health in full." Kelc's hands slapped happily on his thighs. "I knew then that you would be the most interesting person I'd met in ages. Naturally I thought you were a mage of incredible power. Again," he said. "Not the case."

"So I pursued the idea that you were magicked for some purpose, but that was not the case. No controlling magics are laid on you. I thought perhaps you had cast such powerful spells yourself that you'd built an aura of magic about you." He shook his head. "I even researched that damned sword of yours in three cities, and, incredible as it is, it couldn't do for you what I witnessed." Kelc reached into thin air and snagged a mug from nothingness. He took a long draught. "In desperation, I cast a menial divination spell. These usually yield no information, but this one actually gave me a new direction and it hit me. You aren't surrounded by magic, you are magic." Kelc sat forward in his chair holding his mug with both hands. "You thief, are not human. You aren't even living." Kelc cackled triumphantly. "You are pure magical energy." The ancient wizard rocked back in his seat. "I cast a number of spells and confirmed this through many means. You are pure magic."

Raben sat stunned. He could neither talk nor move. This wizard was peeling him like an onion, and excitedly telling him that he wasn't even a living creature. *Urchin said as much, or hinted at it.* Raben could feel the truth. There was nothing left to contest. As the white wizard spoke, the thief felt that there was no deception. *I am not even human. I am pure magic. Not even human.*

"Then, more questions came forth," continued the old man. "Who could even do such a thing, and why do it at all, and how do you indefinitely sustain a magic that needs so much energy? You're a complex spell, or many. That, I couldn't discern." Kelc pointed a gnarled finger at the hearth and flames started. "Why you exist was what I needed to answer. I didn't get too may specifics, but after a full day of exhausting work, I found out the most crucial thing. Are you ready?" He didn't wait. "You are what is called a phylactery." The ancient man brought his hands down on his chair with a slap, emphasizing the excitement of his find. He wore a broad grin.

Raben didn't respond in the least. He folded his hands into his lap and simply watched the wizard in shock. He was absorbing the story, but would need days to sort out exactly what he was being told. Kelc continued.

"A phylactery is normally a container that holds a soul for a time. Or a possession, as in a demon or a ghost." The sorcerer gestured to his mug. "You are like a mug for someone's soul, and I believe it to be many someones. You are a sentient vessel that is moving to a set location so that the true you can emerge and do whatever it is you're supposed to be doing. At any rate, just creating a phylactery is tremendous work, and to make one that is sentient and capable is an altogether different task. You are the most fantastic work of magic I have ever seen. Someone has great power to expend considering what it must have taken to bring you into existence." Kelc looked at Raben for a long time, but the thief simply sat inert.

He had nothing to say. He'd known something strange was happening to him. He'd felt that there were times when he was being controlled. *How many times have I thought something was a bad idea yet still I persisted in acting on it? How many times in battle was my control over myself wrested from me and I fought as if berserk killing anyone who neared me? How many times have I been driven in a direction to complete a task I didn't understand? Phylactery! I'm not even me. I'm someone else. I'm a slave to someone else. Not even human. I am a mug for someone's soul, and I don't even know who. I came here to find this out. There must be a way out of this. Must be.*

"What happens if I kill the person who is supposed to fill me, or pass through me?" The thief's eyes narrowed as he asked the question. He could picture the mindless slaughter that he would commit on anyone who tried to control him, though he didn't know who it was.

"We should stop for now," Kelc announced. He threw a book to the ground, a purple ribbon trailed it through the air and coiled up on top of it as it landed. "Read the portion that is marked." Kelc was gone.

"Damn it!" Raben screamed. "Don't you leave!" He threw his sickles. They whistled through the air and sliced into the lush red cushions of the chair Kelc had just been seated in. "Damn it!" Raben leapt from his seat and scooped the book from the floor. The book was heavy. He threw it at the chair knocking it over backward. He tore his sword out and delivered the thrashing that he pledged he would give, hacking at the walls, shredding several of the enormous tapestries. He ranted until his frustration turned to sadness. Nothing he was doing was helping, and had stopped making him feel any better.

"I hate wizards." He walked over to the toppled chair and picked up the book he'd thrown. He read its title aloud. "Fundamental knowledge for casters." Raben stared at the title, which was pressed in silver down the spine of the dark green book. "Exciting." He sat down before the fire and opened the massive tome to the page the ribbon marked.

The basic rules of magic may be divided into a relatively simple number of proofs that will hold true in nearly every instance. These proofs may coexist in a single case, thus lending ability or detracting strength from another as the spells desired affect may dictate. The proofs are as follows.

1. Magic is a bound energy subject to the will of the caster.

2. Magic exists only as a perception of those who understand it.

3. Magics of different natures can be intentionally bound together.

4. Magics can be reversed or dispelled.

5. Magic can be sentient, and thereby consciously carry out a function.

6. *Sentient forms of magic may be able to bind magic.*

7. *No magic is absolute, magic degrades over time.*

8. *Exceeding amounts of magic may destabilize natural law.*

As was previously noted, any number of these proofs may coexist in any single magical spell, creation, or phenomenon. Consult your superior or instructor regarding these differences before attempting to handle a newly encountered case, as such things can be dangerous and have in the past resulted in the deaths of young and ambitious mages.

The book slammed shut. *What the greeching? Damned book!* Raben tried to pry it open, sure that he would learn much that he needed if he could continue reading, but the tome was sealed somehow. *Magic! I'm sick of magic! I am magic.* "Damn!"

He threw the book across the room where it smashed into a wall and tumbled unharmed onto the carpeting. Raben ran over to where the book lay, and ripping his sword from the air next to him, he hacked at the book, but succeeded only in batting the arcane volume across the floor. It was completely safe-guarded against attack. Raben yelled his frustration at a wall, and then wildly attacked the fallen chair he'd knocked over earlier. He hacked it up, dismantling it in only a few moments. Nothing but kindling and shredded red material was left when he finally felt as though he was regaining control.

What can I do? I need to know more. And this damned wizard and his spell. I have to swear to betray those that now control me, live in me. What a lie. How can he control them? Do I need them? Do I even exist without them? Gods above! Is this going to kill me? Maybe that would be for the best. I don't really exist to begin with.

Raben laughed. Not an enjoyable laugh, but a mirthless vent that spanned the short distance between panic and insanity. *I don't exist.* The laughter continued until the thief remembered his friends. He knew that he had to continue at least long enough to make sure Thantos and Urchin were alright. Sobered by the thought of his imprisoned companions, Raben began stoking the fireplace with the remains of the lush antique chair he'd destroyed. *You'd better hope my friends haven't a scratch on them, Kelc, or I won't be the only fool here that doesn't exist.* Raben watched as the fire grew, consuming the chair, green flames sprouting off of the heavy lacquer. He sat in front of it and watched it continue to grow, feeding his troubles into it, feeding his frustration into it, and never noticed that the wizard had returned until he spoke.

"What did you think of the passage in the book I left with you?" Kelc asked. Raben remained sitting before the fire, watching the chair burn. The thief smiled at the thought of Kelc having to buy or magic up another chair. *I hope it is an irreplaceable relic of your childhood. It burned very nicely.*

"I found it somewhat interesting until the book snapped shut," Raben spat. His eyes never left the flame. "I should like to continue reading unless you are going to faithfully report the rest of the book personally." The thief could sense that Kelc was nearing him. "Is that your intent? To make me further dependant on you?" A loud snap in the fireplace shot sparks out onto the carpeting. Raben flicked them back in with his dagger. "Are you my instructor now? Master Kelc?" The thief chuckled after he said the name.

"In many ways," Kelc began, "yes." The wizard was immediately behind Raben watching his chair get consumed by the fire. "There is firewood," said the old man, calmly. *Damn him! Next he'll tell me the chair was hideous and that he was about to buy new ones anyway.* Raben heard Kelc pad away from him.

"Tell me about these proofs." Raben slowly turned around. Kelc was sitting in the remaining chair now. His gaze fell on the thief. The man looked tired and serious. "You're done mocking me? This is not an experiment to me, old man," Raben said. "You will sit there and tell me what I want to know until I'm happy with this. Do not leave again."

"Fine," the old man barked, his high-pitched voice slicing through the room. He took a deep breath. "Let me tell you of the proofs you read about." The old man lifted the book from his lap. The silver title on the spine reflected the orange and yellow flame of the fire. Raben never saw him pick it up, but that was hardly surprising to the thief after spending a day with the wizard. "The first one seems straight forward enough. Magic does what the caster wants it to do. Yes?" Raben nodded his agreement. "The second one is far trickier. Magic exists only as a perception of those who understand it," the old man's voice wavered as he read from the book. He coughed and cleared his throat, and continued after spitting discreetly into as handkerchief. "This one means that people bring magic to bear by willing it into existence and believing in it. But it also suggests that magics can be negated by disbelieving that they exist. So if you were unaware that a spell was even possible, this suggests that it wouldn't affect you. Obviously this is flawed, but it stands true in many cases. Particularly with divinations of the future for instance, and illusions cast to mislead you by your senses."

Kelc looked up from the book, and stared intently at Raben. "Are you getting this?" The thief nodded. Raben was actually at home when the information came to him quickly. He enjoyed the need to absolutely focus. It was what he was built to do, gather information with the utmost speed and assimilate it into his daily life in order to maximize the knowledge. Though he couldn't actually remember being Guild trained, that was the sort of thing he had drilled into his mind.

"Good," said Kelc. "I don't want to have to explain things to you a dozen times." The aged wizard dropped his eyes back to the pages lying open before him. "The third proof says that magics of different natures can be bound together. That seems obvious. Certain spells require that this is done. Yet I cannot easily tell you what the intended meaning of this proof is, I can let you know that magics can be combined, and only those that are completely opposite one another will fail." Kelc unconsciously stroked his chin after the less than satisfactory explanation.

"Hold on, old man!" Raben interrupted. "What different natures are there in magic? Are we talking about some special knowledge or are you saying that the result is the nature of the spell, like fire and water."

"Some create, some destroy, some control, some are illusory, there are many," he said lamely. "Too many to teach you now. There is no clean-cut way to describe it to you. Let us move on before we die of aging. The fourth says that magic can be dispelled or reversed."

"Yeah, I read that," said Raben. "Can I be dispelled then? Can someone simply walk up and I'll cease to be. Gone, just like that?" *If so, then the incredibly powerful force that made me needs to try again.*

"No." Kelc adjusted his robes under his legs. They'd bunched up and begun rubbing his skin. "It would take a user that was more powerful than the one who created you in order to dispel or reverse the magic that you are. Have no fear, Thief. That will never be your downfall." Kelc paused for a short while. "If the caster of you was killed, however, it might dispel you, or it might free you. For that there is no answer until it happens. Magic typically ends once the original caster is slain, but you are sentient and self sufficient, so you might be able to carry on. Hmmm." The wizard returned to silence. "With more time I might be able to figure that out, though I'm not sure that anyone could actually kill the force that was able to originally create you." Kelc shook his head slowly, as his mind tore into yet another challenge. "More difficult than it's worth."

Raben let his eyes wander about the room while he contemplated his own life. *I might die if the caster is killed, or I might be free. Yet this mage asks that I swear to betray those who control me to him after I've completed whatever quest it is that I am supposed to be carrying out for those beings. Am I swearing to die in the end? Yet how can I die? The wizard says I've died already, many times even. I need more information. Who controls me? Who would really want to control me, and why?* "What of the next proof old man? Magic can be sentient." Raben pressed his palm to his chest. "I won't argue with that proof, or the sixth. I have cast spells myself, so obviously sentient magic can cast a spell."

Kelc raised his head in surprise. "You have them memorized?" A strange smile creased his lips, a genuine smile. "I am impressed Thief. The magic that binds this book only allows a person to read it one time, yet you have the proofs memorized it would seem." The mage slammed the book shut. "What is the seventh proof?"

"It says that no magic is absolute, and that magic degrades in time." Raben looked past the wizard at the banners that hung on the walls, spending time admiring the few that now hung in ribbons. In one particularly large one, he could see an ancient man holding a lasso of flame. Obviously a wizard of considerable power, the man was casting the spell around the neck of a shimmering silver dragon. "I suppose magical beings must age and die like everyone else," Raben observed from the proof. "Even you." *What would Reman do if the crotchety old man on the plains were to die and leave everyone to a peaceful existence without wars and destruction? What luck that you've survived.*

"Yes," Kelc answered. "I do expect that I will die one day, but it will be a great fight. That is where the eighth proof comes in. Exceeding amounts of magic can destabilize natural law. Many of my order used to think that this meant that a large enough magical battle could bring about the end of the world. I think not. We had some truly massive battles and nothing was affected beyond those hit by the spells. I believe that this proof means that natural functions can be averted, perhaps almost indefinitely by magic. Hunger, being cold, being warm, tiredness, maybe even death itself though proof seven seems to suggest that none of it can be avoided permanently." Kelc tossed the book into the air where it vanished. "Many of these proofs are subject to interpretation. I don't think any of them has one set meaning at all. As a wizard you find that each old man wants to impress upon his peers one set of profound rules that carries an entire generation of wizards to the height of their power. It works until you work one or two spells, and then you discover," Kelc sighed, "that proofs like those you've just read are the minimal ground work of magic, and what's more, they can be as confusing as they are helpful."

"What wizard wrote those, that you would choose to have me read them?" asked Raben. Kelc didn't answer. The white-haired mage took a deep slow breath, and then let out a measured exhale. "You wrote them didn't you?" Kelc nodded that he had. "Long ago?" Another nod. "To teach other wizards?" No response. The two men sat quietly.

"I wrote them down because they were the eight most important facts about magic that a wizard needed to know in order to remain wary and perhaps live through the White

Wars," Kelc said. "There were countless magical attack methods in those years, and I wasn't sure I would survive, so I wrote these down for any wizard who had to fight in that terrible time." The old wizard's head shot up and his eyes bore into Raben. "The proofs make you paranoid of magic, and they keep you alert when dealing with magic, and it is only those who treat magic as a dangerous weapon that prevail where it is concerned."

"So you want me to survive this ordeal?" asked the thief.

"I don't want something powerful enough that it could create you to prevail," answered the mage. "I believe you are delivering something powerful to the start of a very dangerous quest. It can't be stopped, so an effort to that end would be fruitless. It keeps you alive even after death. But perhaps it can be dominated if attacked subtly at a vulnerable time. And though you are the object of a very intricate and admirable magic, it seems that you intend to fight it however you may, and for my protection and the safety of the masses who would have no idea what to do with another leader, even an evil one, except follow, I must do what I can."

"And that is why you wish me to betray them?" Raben asked. "For fear that you may become affected or enslaved by it?" The thief began to wonder if the man cared more than he wanted to. *The white mages are labeled as destroyers yet you just admitted that you would fight to save people from evil.*

Kelc spat on the floor. "I could never fall so easily, but neither do I have the energy of youth to fight so skilled an opponent." The old wizard clenched his jaw and then relaxed it. "So at a time when I'd rather not be bothered, I will assist you rather than ignore a situation that would inevitably demand my attention anyway."

"I see." Raben smirked momentarily. *He is already imprisoned by them. My masters have long arms, to force even you to attend them against your will. Now if only one of us knew who they were.* "So you know who made me?" Kelc shook his head after a moment. "But you know that I have died?"

"Yes," started the mage. "You died in a temple, according to you. I did a spell that searched through the depths of you. You told me that you died in a temple. You told me that vampires killed you. You told me a skeletal messenger of the dark god killed you. And I saw you, and you told me that you were killed in the fire ward at my doorstep. Each time you thought you'd been asleep. Some of those times you were mysteriously moved around, but always you thought you had fallen asleep." Kelc shook a finger in the air. "You were dead." The wizard looked past the thief. "I believe that the woman you always see has something to do with those who created you, and I have never heard of this Guild you serve." *The woman! You have been in my mind. You really have.* The woman raised strange emotions in him, and he feared telling anyone about her, but now this wizard knew. *She is with me when I die. She has something to do with those who first created me.*

"Hessing? I was created in his house? The woman was there." Raben tried to recall his first night clearly. "She was the first thing I ever noticed. She was my first thought." He closed his eyes. "Yes, and Hessing. Is he part of this?"

"I'm not sure," answered the mage. "I was having a very hard time discerning what was illusion, dream, or reality. "It seems that you have been passing easily between each state without your knowledge. Another testimony to the skill of those that created you."

"We don't know who, or why," Raben murmured. "Damn!" He leapt up from the floor and began pacing. "I am pure magic. Greeching Hells! This has only made me feel more helpless than before."

"At least you are gathering information, Thief. Before now, the enemy had everything. They knew everything and you knew nothing." Kelc let his head rock back and forth as Raben alternated directions before him. "Perhaps you are becoming armed enough to confront them."

"Maybe." Raben stopped walking and faced the mage. "Whoever they are."

"Regardless of who they are, they have created an immortal," Kelc said calmly, looking at Raben. "And I have every intent to prove the theory for myself this very day. Would you like to see for yourself? To know that you are what I have said you are?"

"Yes." He spoke the word from the want to see that it was true, to know absolutely that he was on the right path, but as Kelc leaned forward and spoke, Raben was certain that he'd just stumbled into a trap.

"Good," said the white mage. "Remember that you said that." The old wizard stood up and began casting. Raben cringed with each word, afraid that he was about to be incinerated for the pleasure of the mage, but once the spell was finished, the thief could detect no discernable result. Kelc marched across the room the very moment he finished the spell and threw open a door that had previously been perfectly hidden as part of the wall. "Please come in," he said, his voice full of soothing and kindness.

"Where am I?" asked the boy, as he entered the room. He was six or seven years of age, and had blonde hair, and clear green eyes. They were large, and Raben could easily see the fear and wonder in them from across the room. He wore the common wool tunic of a farmer.

"You are in the clouds," Kelc said. "You are here to rest forever with your family. Turn and face the wall, and we will prepare you to see your Da. Would you like that?" he asked. The boy nodded. "What's your name?" *What the blazes? His father is dead. No! I won't.*

"Reese," the boy said weakly. His eyes had begun to tear when the wizard had mentioned his Da, and now they glittered in the firelight as they crept down his cheeks. *Hells! Leave the boy, you greeching bastard!*

"Okay Reese," calmed the white wizard. "Turn to the wall and we'll take you to see your Da, and everyone else you've missed." The boy turned to the stone wall, fixing his eyes on the dark stone.

"Will Meeka be there too?" he asked without looking away from the wall.

"Yes," said Kelc. "If we hurry. Your sister will be there." The mage turned to Raben and gestured the thief to the boy. *No way!* The thief shook his head violently as Kelc gestured again. *Never! This is worse than Nestor's Ferry! I won't do this just to help you experiment with me. I would never do this even if it meant all of you would leave me alone.*

"Obey," Kelc said. The word hit Raben's ears like thunder, shaking him and removing all resistance from his body. He felt as though he were drunk. His vision was blurring, and his body felt as though he might fall at any given moment. "Bring out your weapon." *No. Will not,* he thought, as he heard the wizard bark the command, but even as he contradicted the mage's desire, he saw his sword before him. He was holding it, waving it threateningly, feeling its balance. *Greech! What the boiling Hells!* "Approach the boy," Kelc declared. Raben began to walk to the child, who was still standing by the wall, staring into the blank stone. *No! Who is this kid? Why?* The thief walked up behind the boy, his sword nearly poking the boy in the head when he stopped. Then Kelc spoke again. "Kill him." *No! Damn it! No!* Raben watched as his arm ripped the magical blade downward through the air. Just as the sword came down on the boy, Reese spun, fearful and in need of knowing what was happening. Raben's weapon cut across his face, tearing one of his bright green eyes from his face. The boy collapsed to the ground instantly in a puff of red mist. *Oh gods! Oh gods! What has he done? I will kill you! What did you do? What did I do?* Looking down at the fallen child, Raben could only see the pool of crimson fluid that grew across the floor, originating from the boy. The same blood dripped from his sword.

"Sit down," Kelc commanded. Enslaved by the magic, Raben walked back over to the chair and sat down. "Sheath your weapon," he said. The thief pushed his bloody blade back into its sheath. Raben wanted to cry while he thrashed the wizard. *I killed another person. A child. Another innocent. How many have I killed? How many is it?* The thief could feel bindings being tied around his arms and legs. They were tightened to the point that he couldn't even move. Then a broader restraint was bound around his chest, smashing him against the chair. "Prepare yourself," Kelc said. And the world came back into focus.

"Damn you, wizard!" Raben shouted. "Are you insane? You murdered that child for no reason!" The thief took a deep breath, but before he could resume yelling, Kelc had invoked another spell. *Damn you!* His jaw worked, and he wanted to scream if he could, but no sound came from him.

"That's better," Kelc said. "Now let me tell you what is going to happen. You are about to die. While you are gone, I will cast some spells that make certain of our little discovery, and when you come back, you will help me to complete the binding spell that you said you would." Raben struggled against his bindings, hoping one of them would split so that he could strangle the mage. "Or I can kill your friends now, and a few innocent folks that you've yet to meet. Decide now!" Kelc shouted. *You will die by my hands. I will kill you!* The thief stopped struggling and sat, waiting for the white mage to kill him. *I die again. What's the difference? Maybe this time I won't come back.* He smiled at the thought of this journey ending. *Yes. Maybe this won't work and I'll be done with this whole mess. Done with wizards and magic and controlling me. Done with gods and their religions and people who can't see farther than their own noses. Done with killing small boys and innocent women. No more vampires or walking skeletons. No more. It would be worth it just to make you wrong.* He smiled savagely at the mage.

Kelc stood before Raben, waiting for the thief to notice that he was there, but when a smile was the captured man's only reaction, the white mage unleashed a tremendous bolt of searing fire into him. Raben flew backwards, landing on his back, still strapped into the now burning chair. He couldn't feel anything, but he could smell his own burnt flesh. Its bitter scent loomed in his nostrils as he faded. He closed his eyes. *No more. Please, no more.*

He saw her. She was kneeling with her hands clasped behind her, as though they were bound. She had her chest thrust out before her, and her face looked strained, as if she were in pain. Her lips were stretched tightly across her mouth and her eyes were clamped shut. *So pale. She looks terrible.* The Guild hunter looked nothing like herself. All of the voluptuousness and confidence had been replaced by agony. She began to shake visibly as Raben watched. *What in the Hells? What in the?* She looked as though she were being shocked. He felt an intense pain, yet couldn't localize it in his body. It simply began inside of him and expanded from within him, passing through every fiber, consuming him piece by piece. *Lightning? What is this?* He kept watching her as she cramped, every muscle in her tightening, bending her to the floor. He looked away but moments later his eyes snapped back to the elf woman, concern for her exploding unexpectedly from deep with him. Her mouth fell open and a rivulet of blood streamed from her nose and ran down her cheek where it dripped from her chin. *Stop!* Another painful spasm wracked him. *Stop!* He tried to turn away from her, but was paralyzed. He let his gaze fall a little, inspecting himself, and found that he wasn't with her.

How? Where am I? He had no body. Though he seemed to be locked into watching the Guild hunter suffer, he could tell that he wasn't seeing her with his eyes, and he also realized that it wasn't his body that was being shocked by the painful force. *Am I free? Leave!* He focused his thoughts on just escaping it all. As he had once before, Raben found that the idea of being free of the physical world was somehow exciting. *I am magic. Magic can be altered, commanded. Leave. Move. Let me go, please!* The elven woman collapsed. *No!* He wanted to help her, though he had no reasoning for doing so. She had been every bit as unfeeling and vicious to him as any enemy, yet she was the only person he'd encountered with whom he felt any commonalities.

Another wave of pain tore through him. *What in the Hells is this?* He bent his will on reaching the Guild hunter and only after an arduous time of fighting off the recurring pain that seemed to regularly assail him did he feel as though he were moving. *I've done it. Magic can be altered.* He drifted closer to her, wishing he had arms to stretch out to her. He wanted to touch her, caress her cheeks, wipe the blood from her face, and do anything that might help her. *We are similar. You are suffering for no reason. Because they tell us we must. There must be a way out of all of this.*

He was just over her. He looked down on her and began to understand the limitations of his state. *This is worse than arriving here like I normally do. I can do nothing.* Watching her, he tried to detect her breathing, but she was completely motionless. *Wake up. Move, flinch, snore. Do something!* She had always been the confident, powerful, driven commander to whom he'd been forced to make account of himself, and even though he struggled with the idea of even tolerating her, she shared his fate. Raben hated seeing her so abused. *Who would she be were she free of their constant wretchedness? Wake up. Sense me! You are not alone right now! Wake up! Damn it!*

The elven woman didn't respond. Frustrated and helpless, Raben willed himself to appear where he floated, willed himself into existence, but nothing changed. *Why didn't I appear to see you like I normally do? The damned wizard used some spell. Kelc! Another trap. One day, mage, you will look up at me as you slide from the steel I've buried in your black heart. One day it will be your rotten soul that I will trap. Why must everyone else always have control over me?* The idea of the white wizard restricting him from being with the Guild hunter was more than Raben could handle. The elf still lay, motionless, on the stone floor. His emotions raged. *Bastard! She's dying! I'll skin you right down to your old white bones and then crack those into pieces and scatter them to the wind!* He tried again to materialize, but again, nothing changed. Another wave of pain assailed him, shooting through him with renewed force. *To the Hells with you, wizard.* The pain hit again.

Raben could feel the effect that each throe had. Every time it struck, he was less and less with the Guild hunter, his present energy reduced somewhat. With each wave, the amount of power that was his to command seemed to be lessened. He could consciously feel his being faltering, and being dissolved with each insufferable episode. *I'm being dragged back. He's taking me back. He kept me from arriving, and now he's putting me back. His test. He forced me to kill that boy with the sword, and now he's killed me, just to see if I will come back. He's dragging me back.* Again the wrenching pain pulsed through him. *No. I will not come back. You are wrong. I must stay here! Gah!* Another pulse.

Knowing what it did, the thief sought a way to resist it, but couldn't figure out how he was supposed to do so. *I'm just a soul. Use will against it? Magical energy?* He tried to float away from the Guild hunter, but couldn't move. *Go!* Nothing. *Damn it!* Another torturous wave crashed through him, pilfering more of his spirit.

He reversed his thinking and tried to bend his will on staying with the elf, but the more he thought to resist the effect of the painful attacks, the more they came. *Hells! What can I do? Everything makes this worse. How can I even begin to deal with all of this?* Time and again, they seared his being, drawing him back to his body, forcing him back to the wizard, stealing him away from the elven woman.

What can I do? He longed for help. He wanted someone to show up and assist him. Give him some answers. Get him out of the situations that seemed to rain unending suffering down on him and those he knew. *Why must all of this happen? What role must I play? Why do we suffer?* He looked at the beautiful woman where she lay, paralyzed, on the floor. *What has she done to deserve her fate? I have never had a chance to do anything but your will, yet I am punished each day for the actions I perform. Does she suffer the same pain, the same imbalance of suffering and misunderstanding? Why?* A massive blast forced him almost entirely back, causing his thoughts to fog, wrenching him from concern and self pity to malice.

You want me, Kelc? Fine! Bring me back!

He kept his eyes shut. *I'm here. You brought me back. She needed me, and you used your might to give me another terrible memory. She suffers even now. Along with the boy. Reese. You're next, Kelc.* He could hear the wizard's spell, hear the incantation as the old sorcerer continued it. He could smell his own burnt skin, scorched hair.

"Dul ondum Reas a manik, Kerram Mak Deviun shos pree Noea Ricza..." chanted the white wizard in an unending stream of magical language, his voice strengthened by the otherworldly spirits of sorcery, belying his age. Raben tried to hear the words, make sense of them for a few moments, but after only a couple of sentences he knew he would never understand the level at which Kelc was casting. *You shouldn't become so involved in a spell that you lose control of your environment.* The thief yanked his sickles free of their sheaths and prepared to attack. His arms ached as they responded to his wants, slowing him, making him wary of his abilities. He flexed them slowly, and then checked his legs. He slowly twisted in the chair, where it lay, blasted on the floor, and made sure that he would have no trouble moving through an attack. *Good.* Once he verified that he was able to get up with relatively little pain, he struck.

His eyes shot open and he saw the wizard only a few paces away, waving his ancient hands through the air, still chanting the complex and seemingly unending spell. Raben rolled over backward, out of the chair, launching himself up onto his feet, ignoring the dolorous pounding that suddenly originated in his head, and the nausea that often accompanied coming back to life. Gathering his balance, he leapt at the wizard, leading with his sickles.

Both weapons bit into Kelc, one in his stomach and the other in his left leg. The white wizard shrieked as blood gushed from the injuries. He then reached through the thief's attack and clutched Raben by the throat. Ignoring the ease with which the mage had dealt with the wounds, Raben pulled the curved blades from the old man's body and buried them again, both in the old man's chest. Crimson flooded down the front of the ancient sorcerer, but he did little more than flinch as the mortal wounds were delivered. *Hells! Die damn it! Oh Hells!* The thief tore the weapons from the old man and prepared to strike again, but Kelc shook his head. So slow and deliberate was the action that Raben froze, cold fear prickling through his body replaced his anger. His arms fell as his courage and anger were dismantled by the unreal constitution of the white wizard. *He's not even fazed. Hells! He's not human! I'm going to die. He needs only to squeeze my throat.*

"Strike me again, and both of your friends will die!" The words came from the white wizard, but they had a force behind them that was clearly supernatural. Cringing as he hung weakly from Kelc's tightening grasp, Raben was reminded of the strength that Thantos had gained from Talvo when he'd commanded Gabriel at Nestor's Ferry. Kelc drew back his arm, dragging Raben as if he were weightless, and then casually flung the thief across the room. Raben bowled into the chair he'd been sitting in earlier, his head smacking into one of the wooden legs, breaking the charred wood into pieces. "Calm yourself," commanded the white wizard in the unnaturally powerful voice. He then vanished, the blood from his wounds suddenly hanging momentarily in the air before it fell, splashing into the pool that had formed at his feet. *Calm myself. I'm going to die. I just killed myself, Urchin, and Thantos. They're dead, and why? For her? She's part of them. They use her to get to me. For the boy. The boy. Thantos would understand. So would Urchin. They would never have let that bastard escape after what he did to the boy. Reese.* The thief reached up and massaged his throbbing head. Dying, coming back, and getting thrown across the room had driven a headache into him that pulsed intolerably each time his heart pumped. *They need to live. I need to get out of here alive. That's all. Just do what I need to do to get us all out of here alive. We can wage a battle against Kelc another day. We just need to live through this moment. Get out of here alive, and then we can decide how best to deal with all of this. The old wizard just wants me to let him cast his spell. I can do that. I'll submit. Do what he asks.*

"Good advice," Kelc murmured from across the room. His old voice cracked, causing Raben to jump from the floor to his feet. "Sit down," said the wizard, "before one of us kills three people." The wizard was no longer wounded, or at least had no blood on his robes. They were clean and wrinkle free. In fact, the mage himself looked as though he'd managed to bathe and groom himself in the short time that he'd been gone.

"What the greech did you do to me?" Raben demanded, trying to push the wizard into talking about the experiment rather than thinking about the wounds he'd suffered. "Where was I?"

"Only you know that," Kelc answered. "I wasn't about to let them get you though. Someone wanted you pretty badly. I could feel it. If they had taken you away, they would have placed you wherever they wanted, and we weren't done here yet." The ancient man walked to the thief and offered him a large bowl. "It's water. You want it, I presume. Your head must be pounding after all that you've

269

been through. Every account of resurrection holds that the newly awakened has painful injury to the head."

Raben took it and gulped most of it down, saving some. He dampened the sleeves of his robes and pressed the cool cloth into his eyes, easing the pain that seemed to be trying to burst from his skull. "I will still do as you asked, wizard. I'll still submit to your spell so long as my friends are alive." *If they aren't, then I will find out how many times I need to bury my blades in you before you finally die.*

"Good," Kelc responded. "I would have hated to kill you after all of the trouble we've gone through to figure something out." *We've gone through. I was made to kill a small child and then watch the only person in Reman that understands me die as well, while being your greeching prisoner. Damn you!* "At any rate," continued the wizard, interrupting Raben's hateful thoughts. "I was right. Though it is no great surprise, I feel a good deal better knowing that all that I have told you is indeed correct. You gain the ability to die from each innocent life you take. Very formidable should you take it seriously. You could kill as many people as you wanted, it seems, and live through nearly anything, so long as your masters wanted you to continue. It appears that you visit them when you are near death. Whenever it happens, you are taken to wherever you go, and they rebuild your body and another person's energy, their spirit or soul, if you will, fuels the spell that makes you. So far as I can tell, the spell will erupt into an explosion of some note were you to die the final time." Raben could hear the aged wizard ambling about the room. "So let's avoid that."

"Who was the boy?" Raben asked. "Why him?"

"Oh," Kelc said. "He was the last living heir to a poor failure of a farmer. The man and his entire family, save the boy, had been killed by undead. We freed the boy from a long lonely life in a very hostile world." *Great! Good to know that we're helping.* Raben wanted to weep, and scream, and kill something. Something that deserved it. *Someone,* he thought as he let his robe fall from his eye and looked at the ancient wizard. *Why must there always be killing?* The thief wet his robes again and placed them back in his eyes. *Why must I always be the one killing?* "It is your destiny," Kelc answered. "You are bringing death." The ancient mage sighed. "Even to me, I fear."

"How is that?" Raben asked, lowering his soggy robes from his eyes. *I hope you're serious.* "How have I brought death to you?" *Good! Maybe you will see Reese in the clouds from your place amidst the Fires.*

"Whatever made you was powerful enough to cause me trouble even though they weren't expecting me," Kelc explained. "It should have been simple for me to retain you here, but you left so quickly, and then the resistance was so formidable that I was nearly unsuccessful in bringing you back." *It was me resisting you, fool! She was hurt. Dead for all I know. But what do you care? The boy is dead and you think you were helping him. Why? How can you be so warped?*

"So I am the bringer of a force that will one day kill you, huh?" asked the thief, leaning forward, ready to personally deal the wizard his imminent death. "After this many centuries, you're finally going to die?"

"Perhaps, yes," answered the old man. "It will come to that if I let it, but before that happens I will take steps to interfere with their plans, whoever they are. I can hardly leave it to chance with you and your friends. Look how well you've done so far," Kelc grated, as he scowled at the thief.

"You aren't joining us," Raben stated. *I'll not have you marching all over Reman, killing people and telling us how lucky we are to have an ally of such power. What could be worse?*

271

"No," Kelc agreed, "but that doesn't mean I won't be doing my part in thwarting such a power. I have my ways." The old mage walked to the fire and stood before it, peering into the flames. "There are other ways to combat this force than hacking at it with a sword or killing you." The wizard quietly laughed. He spoke as if to himself. "Doing that would only bring them looking. You're not worth the trouble."

"Were you through with me?" Raben asked. "Or was I supposed to listen to this?"

"No," breathed the old man. "I think we are quite finished for now. I have some things to do, and then we will place my spell on you, and after that, I suppose I will let you go." Kelc turned from the fire to look at the thief, but no sooner had his eyes made it around than he vanished.

Good riddance. Pushing the damp sleeves of his robe back into his aching eyes, Raben tried to get excited about finally leaving. *At least we'll be on our way,* he thought, but his focus was stolen to other things. He thought of the elven woman. He didn't know what he was supposed to think, but he worried about her, hoped she was fine. He tried to remember each time that he'd seen her, tried to picture her when she smiled. *Beautiful.* He imagined the last few times that he'd appeared, and how she'd gradually been nicer, gentler with him. *You understand, and now so do I, I think. I wanted to help you, wanted to comfort you. I understand what you're going through. I think we are the same. I could come and see right now.* He was wearing his sword. *I could come there right now. Kill myself. I deserve it. Reese.*

The thought of the boy and the gash that Raben had cut into the boy's face permeated his thoughts, forcing their way in, no matter what he used to push them out. The huge green eyes, excited and scared. The way he'd looked when he spun around to see what was going on just before the sword crashed down onto him, taking his life, and reducing him to a lifeless heap on the stone floor. *Why? Damn it! Where are all of these gods at now? Do they want this to happen? Is this part of your Dayquest? Does the god of war want children to die like this? Is this the way You'd like it recorded in your next holy book.* Tears formed in his eyes, but flowed no further than the fabric of his robes. *And then a small boy was hideously slaughtered by a rogue wizard and a mindless thief to prove that the innocent need to die to fuel the powerful. Is that what this all proves? We are insignificant to Your wants. And You want blood. Blood must be the way gods keep a tally on their faithful. You know Thantos has given enough. Does that make him a good follower, or does he need to bleed some more? What of the knights that set out on this quest? Need we bring them back so that they can die again for Your glory?*

Raben wept as he sat, tormenting himself. Lowering his sleeves, he looked at the spot where he'd been forced to kill the boy. *Damn it!* He slid from the chair onto his side, and curled up before the fire, his body quaking with the effort of crying. *I'm sorry.* He thought of the Guild hunter as she fell limply to the floor. *Sorry.* He stared into the fire through his tears, wishing that he could climb into the flames and rise to the clouds with the smoke. *I'm sorry.*

"I swear that I will use any means available to me in order that I should arrive at the residence of Kelc the wizard once the compulsion that moves me on my present quest subsides, thereby freeing me to act in accordance to my given oath." The white wizard had forced Raben to practice the statement hundreds of times, and now that he'd said it the final time he was surprised at how little he cared. Kelc stood just behind him murmuring in a low voice. The language of magic was unmistakable, yet so advanced was the spell being called forth that Raben couldn't retain any of the incantation as he heard it. The ancient sorcerer had been casting for quite a while and rested his hand on Raben's shoulder when he needed the thief to speak his line. The thief expected a powerful resonance of magic to become a tangible force in the room, surround him, and force an ominous future upon him, but as Kelc's voice slowly dimmed to silence Raben felt no different. He raised a hand up in front of himself expecting to feel a static buzz radiate from the magicked air around him, but again was surprised, even a bit dismayed, to find that nothing seemed any different. *Did you even cast a spell, old man, or did you simply want to hear your long winded scribblings repeated out loud.*

"It is done," stated the wizard. Raben heard the exhaustion in Kelc's voice. The spell had drained the old man. The thief climbed up off of the floor where he'd been forced to sit, and brushed off his shoulders. They were covered with numerous dark powders that Kelc had intermittently sprinkled on him throughout the spell. *It is done. What is done? I've just been made into a homing pigeon?*.

"Alright, so now I have to come back to you after I've completed whatever the task is that I am presently set upon," began the thief. "Now give me my friends and we'll be on our way." Raben looked to the only door to the room, hoping that the ancient mage would sprint to it, excited to send the thief and his friends on their way.

"Soon," breathed the wizard. "There are two more things I wish to tell you about yourself." Kelc broke into a coughing fit that lasted for several moments. "One," he rasped, "is that I don't think you're supposed to be the center of this holy quest you're on. If you persist then you will only end up hurting yourself, but if you do not, then the final answers as to what it is you are going to accomplish will remain veiled in mystery." He coughed again, covering his mouth with his hands. "And two." Kelc's voice was stopped by another fit, and he held up one hand indicating that he wasn't finished while he crumpled, wracked by convulsions. He gasped for air. "You," he spat. "You can only die as many times, as you've killed," he wiped his mouth with a handkerchief. "Die only as many times as you've killed innocent people. I've mentioned it before, but wanted to remind you. It is only the souls of the innocent that keep you alive." He sucked in a quick breath, his face twisting with the oncoming episode. "Only the innocent," he croaked. The thief started forward, but the suffering mage waived his hand at Raben in dismissal and suddenly the thief felt the cool breeze of the Shao on his face.

The battered and leafless Nalman Wood stood before him. *Hells! How in the...?* No structure was visible in any direction. Thantos appeared suddenly. The priest

275

was armed with his ax, and was spinning slowly as if surrounded. Upon seeing Raben he stared intently, but did not call out or motion to the thief in any way. Immediately, Urchin appeared, but was visible only moments before his thin body lurched over into the high grass. Raben exploded into a full run, but had taken only a few steps before the old man sat up in the Shao greenery, shaking his head.

"So you lived through the wizard ordeal, eh?" Urchin held out a hand, which Raben used to assist the man to his feet. "Learn anything of use?" The old man seemed unchanged, as if he'd slept for the entire time. Raben found this curious because Thantos still stood, facing the other two men brandishing his weapon as if debating the practicality of attack.

"Thantos," Raben called out. The priest stood about forty paces away. "Thantos! It is us! You are out of the wizard's prison!" *What are you doing? You look insane. Thantos, calm yourself. It is us.*

"Prove it demon!" screamed the priest, nearing hysterics. "I will not fall victim to your treachery again! I will not die. I will not! You have had soothing words, and I know that all you want to do is consume me. If I lower my guard you will fall on me. I know!" Thantos waved his ax through the air. "That is my answer to you. I will not die. You can take your comforting words and burn with them in the fires!" His voice carried across the plains, leaving silence and confusion behind. Raben looked to Urchin, unable to decide on a course. The old man shook his head, and they looked back to the priest as one.

"Talvo be praised! His power is great to have brought our companion to us still in conflict with the strengths of evil!" Urchin called out forcefully. "Talvo is great!" The old man held out his arms and walked toward Thantos as if to give him a hug. Raben followed slowly, and as the two men neared Thantos it was obvious that he'd been through perhaps the worst of them all. He had deep black circles under his eyes, which were shot with red, and his skin was pasty and hung loosely on his thinned frame. "I speak the name of Talvo openly," called Urchin. Thantos poised his ax to strike. "No demon could do so much," continued the old man, reaching his arms towards his old friend. "Talvo is great!"

Raben wanted to assist Urchin, but didn't feel comfortable calling on Talvo, and could think of no other assistance to give. If Thantos had been tortured with illusions, then nothing save very specific nostalgia might convince the priest that these were indeed his real friends, and the thief could think of nothing to say that might provoke a specific memory. *Damned wizard! You had better have had nothing to do with this.* Something told Raben that the white wizard hadn't been the cause of this. It had seemed that Kelc was sincere in his want to have Raben serve him happily. *Perhaps I have to do everything voluntarily in order for him to trap my masters. Maybe Talvo reached down from his keep in the clouds and freed Thantos from the wizard's grips. After all, His followers waged a war against the ambitions of the wizards a few hundred years ago.*

Urchin and Thantos were mere steps from one another. The priest still held his weapon at the ready. His messy hair was blowing away from his face now, showing his sunken cheeks. *He hasn't slept or eaten this whole time. Where was his Talvo through all of this?* Urchin reached out and pushed the axe to the side and let one outstretched hand come to rest on Thantos' shoulder. The priest began to tremble. Tears formed and began to stream from his eyes, and then, without a noise, Thantos collapsed through Urchin's arms to the ground, unconscious.

Urchin tried to catch him, but was unable, and could only watch as the now frail priest tumbled to the earth. *Where have you been, my friend? Where could you have gone that was so much worse than being held captive by the mage?*

"Greeching blood," Raben swore, as he rushed up next to Urchin. "He looks more terrible by the instant." The thief bent down and touched his fingers to Thantos' chest. It barely moved and the usually strong thrum of a powerful heartbeat was almost undetectable. "He's nearly dead, old man. He's taking only meager breaths. He'll be dead if we don't help him soon." The two men looked at each other again, neither of them forthcoming with any assistance.

"There is nothing I can do," Urchin said, sinking to the ground in dismal helplessness. "You?" Raben shook his head slowly, unable to think of anything helpful. "I will prepare a grave for him, that he might join his god quickly after passing."

"That's it!" Raben yelled. "You're going to dig his damned grave! How very greeching noble of you!" He shoved Urchin hard in the chest, knocking the spindly old man onto his back. "You too have been affected. This," Raben pointed to Thantos, "is your best friend in all of Reman, and you are going to go dig his grave!" The thief was yelling again. "Where is all of the effort in trying to save his life, fool? You are not the same man that was captured by the white wizard, and I truly lament the passing of that man." Raben bent to Thantos again. *You lived that long just to die after weeks of torture and deprivation. Damn it! We need to move. Hold on, my friend. There has to be something that we can do. We need to get to a temple quickly. I need to learn how to vanish and appear like everyone else seems to. The wizard could just transport you where we needed.*

"Gabriel!" Raben yelled. "Gabriel, you greeching corpse! I don't care if it's daytime. Your master calls!" The thief slowly rotated where he stood, hoping, for the first time, for the arrival of the vampire.

278

"I cannot exit the shadows," hissed the undead almost instantly. "The sun will destroy me." Gabriel stood within a narrow shadow being cast by one of the bent and sinister looking trees at the edge of the Nalman Wood. "What do you need? I must sleep."

"You must transport Thantos to a temple that he might get healed." Raben ripped his sword from its sheath and set it in the air. "You will do this, or die. Take Thantos to a temple now, and have them use any means that they have in order to restore this man. Cost is no object. If needs be I will pay whatever amount they feel like stripping from me, even if it takes me the rest of my days to earn it. Go!" *And bear him well, fiend. If I find that you have betrayed me, I will hunt you down.* Raben's eyes blazed as he sneered at the undead.

"Bring him to me," Gabriel ordered from his shadow, "and I will take him."

Raben grabbed the priest by the arms and dragged him into the forest. Urchin still lay on the ground, seemingly disinterested in the whole incident. *Damn it. What has been happening? You can only die as many times as you have killed innocent people. Thantos will not be one.* Upon reaching Gabriel, the vampire lifted the emaciated form of Thantos from the ground and held him easily, cradling the priest before him as he would a newborn babe. *I am giving Thantos to his worst enemy. I can't.* Raben began to reach for Thantos in order to get him back. *If I keep him he dies.* The thief stopped. *At least this way he has a chance. Maybe Gabriel will actually dump him off at a temple.* Raben backed away from the vampire. "Go," he said, "and fear my anger should you displease me." Gabriel sunk into the ground, taking Thantos with him.

Now what in the blazes am I going to do with him? Urchin still lay exactly where he'd fallen, and now stared unblinkingly at Raben. *To think of the group that set out on this quest, and now I am all that is left. What has happened? Thantos made it to a terrible place, and now the old man seems not to remember how much he cared about his friends. That's not who you were.* Raben could remember several times when Urchin had celebrated the priest's recoveries from wounds, how he had reveled in the party's triumphs.

"Get up, old man," Raben called out as he walked back to Urchin. "If I can find the map, you and I must carry on the quest. Perhaps we'll be rewarded with more terrific fortune as we try and pass through this delightful looking forest." The thief looked at the Leafless Wood, trying to build the confidence he would need to make it through the allegedly dangerous forest. *It was supposed to be better once we escaped the mage, and now we seem to just have more misery heaped on us.*

Urchin nodded noncommittally as he pulled himself back to his feet. "I'm not sure what happened just there, but I think I'll be alright after I get some sleep tonight." The old man shook his head as he spoke. "I just froze. I couldn't…I just froze." He stared at the ground. "That was quick thinking, calling for Gabriel." He looked into the forest, to where the vampire had been crouched. "Do you think we'll ever see Thantos again?"

"I don't know," Raben said, despondently. *What happened to you?* He couldn't bring himself to ask just yet. Urchin seemed too shaken to burden him with the description that had to follow such a question. "Let's find a place to camp so that you can rest through the night." The thief looked around them, surveying the land. Narwood to the north and endless Shao grasslands in every other direction. "Is the forest safe to stay in, or do you feel it is a risk we shouldn't take?"

"We're fine in there," Urchin responded. His voice was more even, more commanding than it had been only brief moments before. It sounded more unlike Urchin than the sorrowful and hopeless man he'd just been. *My friend, you are anything but yourself. He needs rest before he loses his sanity. He's everyone but himself.* "Let's camp within." The thief's old friend began ambling towards the woods.

When he first appeared and fell over he seemed fine, but then... Urchin had seemed uncaring when Thantos had collapsed, and then was suddenly taking on a mantle of command as he hadn't in any part of the journey before the white wizard. *Let him rest.*

"Good," Raben muttered softly to himself after nearly tripping over the three packs that lay in the grass before him. They were stuffed, and heavy enough that carrying all three at once was difficult for the thief. He slowly made his way in amongst the trees, where he found Urchin laying on the ground, already asleep. The bony old man was curled up on a large fern, smashing the plant to the earth. His head lay on his arm, and he'd balled himself up into the fetal position.

Raben looked at the trees of the Nalman Wood. Knobby dark bark covered the twisted branches that wove about themselves after growing away from stunted and crooked trunks. No leaves adorned any part of the trees, which let both rain and sun pass through to the ground. Thick underbrush carpeted the forest, and in some areas, thick vines had crept up the desolate trees and draped themselves off of the naked branches, creating perpetual shade in which the ferns grew. No birds chirped in this forest, no small animals scurried away from the two men. The Nalman Wood was completely silent.

"What kind of twisted hell really does exist beyond the walls of Liveport?" Raben drew two sickles and began clearing undergrowth until he had a clean circle in which he could build a fire and lay down. The brush was difficult to clear, because all of it was covered with sharp little thorns that cut into his skin effortlessly, one of them needling into the back of his hand through the hard leather of his glove. *I'll bleed to death just trying to make it through the bushes. I don't even need enemies.* Figuring that the only foes he had to fear would be able to detect him for a number of other reasons already, he built a fire fueled with the brush he'd just cut from the ground. *Damned thorns. Least you can do is keep us warm.* A thin plume of black smoke seeped through the canopy of fingerlike branches over him and rose into the sky marking his location precisely for leagues around. Once the fire was burning with some strength, Raben began to dig through the packs that he'd lugged to camp.

Each one was brimming with food and had several sets of clothes, each folded neatly and stacked tightly into the pack. They had a coil of rope each, all of them made of silk, which was tremendously expensive, and at the bottom, every single one of them had a flask of strong drink. *These were packed with caring and success in mind. What in all the Hells? Kelc truly had nothing to do with the condition of any of us. What happened to them? Am I acting strangely to them?* In one of the packs, the thief drew out the map he'd drawn in the temple of Talvo. It was wrapped in a heavy winter blanket. Raben breathed out, confused and somewhat impressed with the courtesy extended by Kelc, who had obviously been responsible for the packs. *So who the blazes tortured these two? Particularly Thantos.* The thief watched Urchin sleep from his place by the fire as he tried to think of a responsible party for the priest's torment. The fire was snapping and popping as it consumed the shrubs, filling the silence of the forest with a comforting sound. Urchin slept restfully. *It seems as though he should be having a nightmare or something.* The old man lay in the fern, sleeping like a baby in its mother's arms.

Raben eased onto his back and stared up into the crisscrossing branches of the trees. They were curved forward from every split in the branch and turned downward. They looked just like fingers the way they drooped. They looked as though they were reaching towards the two men, waiting for the chance to grab them and carry them to the heart of the forest. They left Raben feeling uneasy, feeling as if the trees actually lived. *The myth seems to have real reasoning behind it.* He waited for the fingerlike branches to move, but they never obliged his growing paranoia. The trees stood in their silence. The fire provided the only sound as it burned. After the brush was finally reduced to ashes, Raben could hear his own breathing. *Laying in the middle of the outdoors and not even a breeze.* He controlled his respiration, trying to make it quieter and became acutely aware of his heart pounding in his chest.

"Damn it," he said sitting up. *Too quiet.* He leapt to his feet and pulled his sword from its sheath so that he could hold it in both hands before him. Slowly rotating in a tight circle, Raben spun, watching the trees. *Damned things are alive. I can feel them. They want to attack, to take us away.*

"They love to play this game," croaked Urchin. "The trees." The old man's eyes slid open half way as he said this. "You are letting them laugh. This is what they want to do to you."

"They are closing in on me, Urchin," Raben answered. "If we both sleep, they will clutch us in their greedy claws. Can't you feel that?" The thief rotated until he faced Urchin. His sword was upright, prepared to strike any opponent that might suddenly leap at him. "They are going to attack me if I let down my guard." *He can't feel it. He doesn't sense them. They are healthy. Are they? Yeah. Evil can be healthy. And this healthy forest is going to kill us if we sleep in it.*

"You can't do this. Look at you." The old man let his eyes close. "You have the same besieged and helpless look that Thantos did just before he fell." *Thantos! How dare you! How dare you just lay there while Thantos dies, and then wake up and say that. How Thantos acted before he died.*

Raben dropped his sword. It landed with a dull clunky sound in the dirt at his feet. *This is how Thantos had acted. By the Gods! Did he stand in this forest alone for two weeks?* "Were the two of you together?" Raben looked to Urchin for the answer, but the old man was breathing rhythmically in deep comfortable sleep. *It took me mere moments to fall prey to the trees.* He eyed them suspiciously and then sat down, hugging his sword to his shoulder. *Could the priest have stood in here the whole time? Could anyone? How could he have even survived? More to him than we suspect? Hells! The old man was right. I need to sleep. I'll be useless if I don't.*

Several times throughout the remainder of the day and the beginning of the evening Raben tried to relax enough to sleep, but each time he did the trees began closing in on him. He was at the ready with both of his sickles and his sword floating at his side when Urchin spoke.

"Thief." His voice was thin and dry. "Get some sleep, and I will watch over us." Raben jerked his head around to look at the old man. *Urchin! You old fool! You may as well ask me to sleep comfortably in the campfire!*

"Sleep!" He barked. "How can I sleep in the midst of these damned things? They hunger. I've tried not to feel their desire, but they are worse than the vampires. They want me to sleep. Don't try to comfort me, old man." Urchin had begun to stand up, but now crouched.

"Why don't we pick up our things and move onto the plains?" suggested the old man. "It will do you good. Once night sets in, there will be no moon and to see the stars will calm you." He rose slowly to his feet and slowly started out of the woods.

Raben nodded in the failing light and began packing all of the equipment and food back into the packs. The two men made their way back to the tall grass of the Shao. Urchin was forced to carry two packs because Raben insisted on keeping his weapons at the ready, spinning to face each tree they passed. Once he was near the edge of the forest he jogged the final distance and burst gratefully out into the openness of the plains. Almost instantly returning to normal, the thief whirled around and waited for Urchin. The old man struggled out of the thick undergrowth, shouldering the weight of the packs with great effort. Raben picked one of them from Urchin's shoulder and the two men walked away from the ever-darkening Nalman Wood.

"Sleep here," Urchin said. "I'll keep a watch." The old man sat down and stared into nothingness, betraying not a single thought or activity that might keep him happily occupied through the long night. *At least that seems like Urchin again. Wherever you've been, I'm glad you're back. I'm going to need you, old friend.*

Raben bedded down in the grass with a thick blanket that he'd discovered in the packs, and fell asleep only moments after he lay down. Urchin, staring off into the night, was the last thing he saw as he dozed off.

He woke up in the dark. A slim arc of purple was lightening over the horizon, hinting that dawn was beginning, but there was far too little light to see by. The old man was nowhere to be seen.

"Urchin," Raben said. No answer. "Hey, Urchin," he called out a little louder. Still no response. The thief clamored to his feet and began to search through the predawn gloom. It didn't take long to find the old man. Once Raben neared him, the sound of Urchin's breathing was easy to follow, thus betraying the old man who'd fallen asleep some time during his watch.

285

"Hey, you wretched bag of old bones, wake up!" Raben said as he brushed his foot against the sleeping man. "Get up! We need to move. I'll fix us a meal." Lightly booting him again, Urchin grunted. That was enough for Raben. The thief turned back toward the growing dawn and used the dim light it provided in an attempt to quickly find the packs that he and the old man carried last night.

After finding them, Raben prepared something for the two men to eat. There was some kind of hard biscuit that he'd never before eaten, and a dried meat that had herbs rubbed into it with such a pungency that when Raben rubbed a little water into it to soften it, the smell forced his eyes to water.

"Smells good," came Urchin's voice through the darkness. "So the wizard captured you to teach you how to cook?" The old man's dark form appeared next to Raben and sat down on the ground. The thief could hear grass being pulled, and after a short while, a small fire was burning where Urchin was crouched. "Heat your food, Thief. It will do better for both of us. Cold food makes you gootch."

The thief couldn't help but laugh. "What are you talking about? We've eaten cold meals nearly the entire journey and not a single one of us has gootched. At least not where you could hear."

"Then you haven't been listening very close," the old man said, suddenly bursting into laughter, his mirth exploding through the gaps in his teeth. "Thank Talvo you haven't!" Urchin fell onto his back as the laughter took over. "Just heat it anyway, you fool of a thief!"

Raben dug back through the packs as he laughed, and found a shallow skillet he'd remembered vaguely from the night before, and warmed the spicy meat. While he held the pan over the small fire, Urchin sat back up, having finally gotten a hold of himself. The thief gave him a little time before delving into more serious information.

"Urchin, where did you spend the past week or two?"

"I don't know," the old man answered. He reached out and picked a stick from a pile of them that he'd obviously collected the night before. "It was a strange place to be sure, but the earth felt healthy, so I sat in communion with it almost constantly. I tried to feel you through it, but I couldn't, nor Thantos. Since I didn't think you were dead, I had to believe I was in a different world, or really far away from you on this one." Urchin looked around the two men, as the first pinkish light of the dawn began illuminating the Shao. "It looked just like here, though." The old man looked over to Raben. "Where did you spend this time?"

"In his home. He ran tests on me and told me about my nature. At least, the little he could figure out. He cast spells on me in order to control and test me further. It wasn't bad, really. If he wasn't so powerful, and obsessed with controlling people, he wouldn't be a horrible ally." *I did something, my friend. I can't tell you.* Raben picked a strip of meat from the pan and took a small bite. It was delicious. He'd never tasted anything like it. Whatever spices were on the meat sprang to life in his mouth and filled his nose with the flavor. *Damn.* He immediately proffered the pan to Urchin who took a piece. The old man grunted with the satisfaction of the meal, and the two men finished the pan in silence. *One day I will.*

"So, what could he tell you about yourself?" Urchin asked after they'd eaten.

"He told me that I was magical and that someone else was controlling me, or using me as transportation to some other quest. I'm sort of possessed, like in a sense of…magic." Raben shook his head. "It made more sense when he told me." He lowered his eyes to the fire, watching it diminish.

287

"So are you going to continue with the Dayquest, or do you have something else you have to go and do?" Urchin leaned into the thief. "I hope you aren't going to abandon me just yet, Thief. I couldn't bear it if I didn't have a big strong warrior to escort me along the way."

"I'm going to continue on the quest though it seems to be the road of the damned," Raben answered. "You do need an escort, and so does Thantos, if ever he comes back." Mentioning the priest silenced the two again. The image of the priest collapsing on the plains, fearing his only friends, darkened the thief's mood. *Thantos. What did that damned vampire do with you?* Raben got up and began packing all of his things back into his new pack. He pulled the map from the pack and unrolled it. The path cut right through the Nalman Wood. *Boiling Hells!* "Hey, old man!" Raben called out. "How can we get through that forest? It does things to people."

"We can either go around it, I guess," he said, "or cut down trees each night so they don't loom over us, but that is hard work and we don't have an ax." Urchin looked over to Raben. "Or we endure. It is only two nights that we spend in there. And if it's too hard we press on, and it is only one night so long as we can keep our bearing, and not get lost."

"How long would walking around it take?" Raben looked to both the east and west, hoping to see an end to the dark, twisted forest. *Must everything be so difficult?*

"Days and days and days from what I can remember," Urchin said. He stretched his hands to either side of himself. "The forest reaches far in either direction, like a shield over the Shao, but is not too deep from north to south."

Raben struggled with the idea of passing through Narwood. He knew that time was of the essence. There were enemies that would continue to pursue the group, and extra detours they didn't have time for. *But that forest.*

Shivers passed through him, leaving goose bumps in their wake. *Greech!*

"We endure."

Pushing between the dreary trees was not unlike trudging through a swamp. The undergrowth in the Nalman Wood was thick and cumbersome. If it wasn't a gnarled shrub that was so thick that walking through it wasn't an option, then it was thorns that would easily find their way through the thick robes that each of the men was wearing. Distance was made slowly in the Leafless Wood, and breathing became difficult in the oppressive atmosphere created by the hunkered trees. Occasionally a bare stretch would open before them, allowing them to walk unencumbered, allowing Raben to feel a little less distrustful, but it would only last for a few paces, and then the foliage would resume with redoubled difficulty. The greenery that stretched along the ground through the forest was in complete contrast with the army of trees that stood above it. Fresh and healthy, the shrubs didn't share the characteristics of the trees, which looked neither like living wood, nor dead graying trees, but wholly unnatural. As Raben hiked through the wood ahead of Urchin, he was able to focus only on getting through the undergrowth. The trees were not a factor like they had been the night before, inspiring very little paranoia in him while the sun lasted. *So long as we're moving.*

Anytime Urchin asked for a pause in the journey so that he might rest, however, the feeling that the trees were stalking him, waiting for him to be unaware crushed back into him like a boulder. The thief's chest would constrict and he would choke on the thick forest air. His body would begin to tremble as his mind became certain that the enemy was near. He found himself suddenly holding his weapons, his eyes leaping from shadow to shadow, tree to tree, knowing that he had to strike first. That if he was not ever vigilant, an enemy he did not comprehend would strike and strike hard, killing him before he had a chance to make of his life what he wanted. Once the feeling had set in, it took long spans of hiking, and focusing on the trail to settle him, and that seemed only to work because the trees that were about to attack had been left behind. In their need to be subtle and silent, the trees would never resort to crashing through the Nalman Wood in order to finally capture Raben. No, they would have to wait until the thief came again to rest, and was less attentive to their activities. *Damned things will never get me.* Raben spat on one of the trees as he shoved his way past it, brushing his pack through a fern nearly as tall as himself.

"How can you not want to hack these trees down one by one, Urchin?" Raben growled, eyeballing a particularly good candidate for felling. "They are twisted and hideous. They are mockery of a real forest." Raben sucked in a breath as yet another thorn found its way to his already bleeding legs. "This damned place nips and nips until you've bled your last drop."

"I can feel the forest," Urchin began, as he held his hands out to the tree he was passing. The thief nearly leapt to the old man, restraining him from touching the hideous bark.

"Must be terrible."

"Not at all," Urchin responded. "The forest is healthy, and has a number of natural defenses as we are finding out, but by feeling it as a natural creation of Reman, I can feel comfortable that it is not a forest that feels vengeance the way you seem to suggest."

291

"Mountain cats are natural too, old man, and they would just as happily drag your miserable old body to the ground and eat you for dinner," Raben said. "What's to say that this forest's natural job is not to kill men and water these ugly trees roots with their blood?" He stomped a fern down, creating a walkway.

"Nothing I suppose, but in nature I think that the functions usually get carried out more mindlessly. I slept in this forest," Urchin stated, "and not a thing happened to me." Raben looked back to see the old man shrugging.

"I was protecting you."

"Yes, but in nature that wouldn't matter," Urchin answered, annoyance slipping into his voice. "Once it was quiet and dark, a predator that existed naturally in that environment would have slipped into camp and carried this old man away to its den. But nothing happened." The old man breathed heavily after his body reminded him of the great exertion it was giving just to carry him. "At any rate, the trees have in no way moved to attack, carry us away, or in any way hurt us. Only in your mind has any of that been a possibility."

"Then explain one more thing to me, old man," Raben said, as he continued forward. "Why are their no living things whatsoever in this whole forest? Shouldn't there be groundmunks, and treemice, and birds, and chirpers in here. Why is this such a dead place? These bushes that are shredding me seem to be a good home for small animals. There are even berries on them, yet not even a spider or a fly lives in them. Does that not seem odd for such a natural place?" Raben challenged. The thief looked around at the bleak trees, and listened to a forest with so little sound in it that Urchin's heavy breathing was the loudest noise he heard. "The trees eat them, Urchin. They catch them and suck them dry. They like their silence and kill anyone that threatens it, which includes us."

"You are obsessed," Urchin said between breaths. "And if this is how a man is affected by the trees in the single day we have been walking beneath the trees of Nalman Wood, then I can now understand the insanity that gripped Thantos, having spent countless days in here, if indeed that was the fate that held him."

"What do you think became of him?" asked the thief. "After I sent him with Gabriel." Raben stopped abruptly and turned to Urchin. "What do you think?" *Is he alive? Or do you think that bastard vampire dumped him somewhere without even helping him.*

Pulling up to a stop, the old man stared into Raben's eyes, seeing the slight mania that gripped the thief. "I think we will see him again, actually, but I think he will have changed. That priest seems to be sacrificing everything he has. His leg is off, his eye, and now perhaps his sanity, or a large part of it. If nothing else, he will be a tremendous bit more solemn than he used to be." Urchin stood up straight, watching Raben digest the information, afraid that a crazed attack was forthcoming.

"As long as we see him again," Raben answered and spun back to the trail. "He deserves to finish this damned quest." *If there is even an end to be had, which isn't likely if the whole trail has trees everywhere.*

"That he does," Urchin agreed. "That he does."

As the light began to fade, Raben murmured to himself almost continuously. Urchin remained completely silent, not wanting to contribute to the thief's present circumstance at all. Trying to put the thief at ease may invite a violent reproach, and to agree with the situation would send the thief spiraling into oblivion.

Once it was almost completely dark, Raben announced that they "would not camp until they had escaped the terrible clutches of the trees." Lighting lanterns, they pushed onward. The only way that they knew what direction to head was the line of travel that they left behind themselves. Every few moments they would look back over their trail, making sure that they were heading in a relatively straight line. *Getting lost in this forest will be the end of us. Damned trees. Just keep your distance. I'm getting out of this alive.*

Raben continued to mumble as he walked through the night. It became increasingly difficult for Urchin to keep up. The thief, however, was so driven to continue that he shouldered the old man's pack along with his own and the third that would have been Thantos'. All of the weight of those packs did little to slow him, much to the old man's surprise. He continued to plow through the underbrush, getting cuts from the thorns and the occasional bruise when the brush wouldn't relent, and tripped him. Urchin's amazement grew as he began to truly comprehend the resolve that this forest had given Raben. The old man took an intent look around himself, shining the lantern he held through the tree trunks and the intermingled branches, looking for something that could instill such hatred and fear. There was nothing so far as he was concerned, but he could feel the forest's health.

Raben stopped a while later, and placed all three packs on the ground near the base of a tree, which was the only place the underbrush didn't grow in such thickness. With military efficiency the thief removed food and the flasks of strong whiskey. He gave Urchin several strips of meat and one of the flasks. Without a single word, the two ate their meal, and as soon as they had no more meat to hold, Raben packed everything back into the packs and shouldered them. The old man hadn't even regained his feet before Raben resumed blazing a trail through Nalman Wood. Urchin jogged to catch back up, but just as he did, he realized that the thief was no longer moving.

"What is it?" Urchin asked quietly. He edged up behind the thief. "Why have you stopped?"

"Demons," Raben hissed. "Servants of the forest. I saw them." He slowly moved his lantern, aiming it at a tremendous fern. "They were lying about in that plant there, and when I came crashing through, they leapt up and ran, but I could hear them as they ran. They are going to sneak up on us from behind." Just at that moment a shrub shook a short distance ahead. "See!" Raben hissed. "They are up there right now." The sound of his blade being drawn sung through the air. "I will not die in this place. I will shred this whole forest if I have to," Raben ranted. "I will cut down every tree and kill every damned demon in here."

"Calm yourself, Thief," Urchin urged. "You are no good in combat if you go insane with it. You might kill me that way." Raben didn't respond at all, he simply stared ahead of them into the forest, waiting for the enemy to show themselves.

It came after a long while. Raben had waited for something to move, and suddenly a noise came from behind the men. It started as a light almost crystalline sound. It sounded like tiny chimes, and then grew in volume until it became recognizable as high pitched laughter.

Raben whirled quickly and pushed Urchin to the side, lunging back towards the unseen creatures. He instantly crashed to the ground. Kicking angrily, Raben was bound around his knees. Groping in the darkness, he found his lantern and directed its beam to his legs. Urchin was there, clutching the thief's knees with both arms.

"Are you crazed, old man?" Raben screeched. "The enemy is here and you are attacking me?" The thief yanked his right leg free. "Let go damn it! You're going to get us killed!" *You have indeed been warped by the wizard. Leaving us open to attack by demons!* "Let go! I don't want to kick your head in."

"They are harmless!" The old man howled. "Let them be!" He scrambled to get Raben's leg back in his grip, but the thief kicked at him. "They have done nothing to us at all! They are faeries, not demons. They are good!" yelled the old man, but Raben persisted.

"You're crazed Urchin!" the thief screamed. "Do you see what this forest has done to you? You're attacking me. Me! I've saved your life so many times, and now you attack me?" Raben kicked hard and jerked his leg free. Using the momentum, he rolled to his feet, coming up with his sword in front of him. He bent down and picked up his lantern. Urchin was coughing after being kicked in the stomach during the thief's escape.

"You fool!" shouted Urchin. "If you do manage to hurt one of these things. Then!" he shouted. "Then we are in trouble!" *I can handle demons, old man. You used to trust me where battle was concerned. Hells! You just asked me to stay with the quest just to escort you along. What was that?*

Raben turned his lantern out into the forest, waiting to hear the tinkling laughter again, searching for the demons. *I'll show you.*

"There!" The thief shouted, and began to run into the forest.

"Raben!" Urchin boomed. The thief froze. "Come back!" Raben stood still. "Come back now!" Slowly the thief turned around and looked at the old man. "Raben, you are safe. I have cast a magic to protect us from all demons."

Shocked at hearing his own name, not to mention the power with which Urchin had used it, the thief slowly walked back to the old man. He had somehow returned to his senses. He didn't feel the trees for the moment. *What is happening? Did he really protect us? So quiet.* There was no laughter after the powerful voice of Urchin. The deep silence of Nalman Wood was restored along with Raben's sanity.

"What did you do?" the thief asked. "I feel far better."

"Good!" Urchin barked. "I protected you from this place by immersing you in it. You are magically part of it in a way, now, so the effects of it are not affecting you. I didn't think it would work. I've never reached out to another life form before, only rocks and dirt, but I'd had enough of being kicked so I tried." The old man looked to Raben, his brow furled. "Seems it worked."

"For a time," Raben answered, "but I can feel it returning already. We'd better continue before the demons come back and renew the attack on me, or before your spell expires." The two men collected the packs. Urchin took his back, deciding that if Raben did take off chasing demons through the forest that the old man would like to have his supplies with him.

The two of them continued through the forest until dawn broke. Raben had ceased mumbling to himself, but said nothing to Urchin either. He simply found the trail through the thick growth and made his way forward. The old man didn't mind the silence. He was certain that if anything did get said it would be about demons and living trees, and he'd heard enough of that to last several lifetimes. Thantos had been nearly killed by the suffocating effects of Nalman Wood and Urchin didn't wish to see Raben go the same way.

With the sun, Urchin insisted on stopping for a while. He needed rest. Raben complied, and the two men lay down and ate. Still, nothing was said. After eating, Urchin bedded down to take a short nap while Raben sat watching the trees anxiously. He didn't feel so oppressed now that there was light, but neither could he sleep. His trust only went so far.

Am I insane? These trees don't move, yet they attack. I am insane. Right there Urchin can just go to sleep. Does he not understand the danger? Or am I crazy? I need out of this forest. I need help. I wish Thantos were here. I'd even take Hessing or Kelc. They are living. Before this is over, that old man will agree. Hopefully before we are dead or dying.

Raben awoke having no remembrance of closing his eyes. He saw the sky overhead through the claw-like branches of the Nalman Wood. It was blue, and he yearned to be able to see it without the trees obstructing his view. He wanted to feel wind on his face. He wanted to hear chirpers and birds.

"Well, how do you feel?" Raben nearly cried when he heard the question. His hand lowered defensively. He knew before she leaned over him, before he smelled the perfume. *Damn it! How in the blazing boiling Hells can she be here? I thought you were dead.* Raben tried to sit up but he was staked down. He wanted to hug her, let her know that he'd worried about her, cared whether she'd lived or died, but he couldn't. Each of his hands and feet was tied with rope to a stake that had been hammered deep into the ground. "Come now," the elven woman cooed. "Don't be difficult. It would put a wrinkle in our relationship. After all, we're doing so well. You don't want to make this hard."

"You're not real," Raben said, unable to decide for himself. "You are a dream." She laughed a silvery joyous laugh that made Raben feel joy. When she was done, she grinned. *Blazes, she's beautiful. You exist only in my mind.*

"I am certainly real, dear man, and you know it. As real as you are," she answered. "You are doing very well, but we were having trouble contacting you for a while. Where were you?" She sat on the ground next to him and rested her left hand on his chest.

"I don't know," he said. "I was asleep mostly. The last thing I remember was getting captured by some wizard. I could do nothing against him." One of her perfect eyebrows arched at hearing this. "Then I woke up and one of my companions was near death. I ended up in this damned forest, but it was too much. Without Urchin I would certainly have died from it, as Thantos did." *How did you survive, or are you just a magical creature like me, a slave created by them to do their dirty work?*

"You did die from it, fool," she said, and smiled warmly. "The insanity coupled with the venom of the thorns. It killed you. No man can survive it without powers of the earth or spiritual protections. You have neither." Raben closed his eyes, thinking hard. *Have I only seen her when I died? Is she only here when I am dead? I saw her when I died from the fire ward. Was she there after the vampires? When exactly did the vampires kill me? Damn! She's not even surprised that I know that I'm dying over and over. They must think I know more about me than I do. Not just when I'm dead. She was there when I woke up, was there in Hessing's house, right at the beginning.*

"What do you need of me now?" Raben asked. "You said I am doing well." He struggled against the ropes to no avail. The elf dragged her hand across his chest and up his left arm where she nimbly untied the rope, freeing his hand.

"I wanted to find out where you had been. The Guild is very picky about keeping track of its members, especially those who've tried to escape before," she said, as she lightly caressed his chest.

"When did I ever try to escape?" Raben asked as he flexed his left hand trying to get the circulation back to normal. "I have always done exactly what was asked of me." *Why don't you leave me be?*

"It was before your time," she said. "It was why we had to wipe you clean and start you again. Not important," she finished. *I existed before that night! Maybe there is something to know about me. I have a history.* "Anyway, you are doing well, my pet, but you must make better time from here on out. You have dallied long enough. Your friend Hessing's life depends upon how quickly you can finish the quest you've been assigned."

"I have thought quite a bit about this. It seems strange to me that you have Hessing. He would be more helpful if you released him to assist me with the quest," Raben said. "After all, it seems as though the Guild is powerful enough to get any of us it wants to at any time." The thief reached across his body and began to untie the binding on his right hand. The elf watched and did nothing to stop him.

"Indeed," she said, and slowly rose to her feet. "That might be a fine idea." She walked a short distance away, her lithe body moving gracefully, drawing Raben's notice.

"Why is it that you only visit with me when I die?" he asked. He watched her intently as he waited for the answer. She didn't flinch from the question, nor did she betray any surprise that the question was being asked.

"It seems to reflect that you are somehow failing at your quest, and therefore seems to be the perfect time to look in on you," she answered. "Those that do everything right never excite their masters to interrupt them." *I'm failing.* Raben smiled. *She's as real as I am. I wonder if she shares my fate in the end.*

"What happens if I die the final time?" Raben asked. His fear of the Guild had lessened with the notion that he didn't really exist. He'd decided to push his luck. Someone needed to keep him alive for a while at least, so he figured that nothing too terrible could happen. "As long as I kill innocent people I can live forever, but what if I don't kill anymore, and then die?"

"If you died twice more without killing anyone else, my dear, then you would shatter into a thousands beams of lethal magic and destroy everything within five hundred paces." She turned to him, and smiled. He had both hands free and began untying his feet. "Fortunately for you, you can't help from killing the innocent. It's built into you as a survival trait." She walked up to him and produced a dagger from her sleeve. Two quick thrusts and Raben's feet were free. "So you have been learning about yourself. We wondered if you would do so this time."

"Only what presents itself with time," Raben responded. "It seems that I should be proud to be whatever I am. It took tremendous work to create me." He smirked. "You know, like you, I actually believed that I was living for quite a long time, but only recently realized that I was simply another one of their creations." *Ahhhhh, it worked.* Her eyes widened as he said it. *She is as real as me.* He kept from smiling.

"How did you ever figure that?" she asked, her voice sharing both anger and awe. "When we walked to the temple, I was sure you were hopeless, but now I understand why we keep such a grip on you." *I wish I did. I need to know what I've done before this quest. Wait, the temple? What temple?* "We can hardly afford to have you rebelling against us constantly. That would be maddening, and whether or not you've realized it yet, impossible for you to win." She winked at him as if his hopeless state was her little secret.

"What temple? When?" The elven Guild hunter turned away from him. *She's helping me. Or at least she is talking to me about things other than the damned mission. She is like me.* He grinned with the knowledge that his guess had hit the mark. *Temple? When did I ever see her in a temple? I wonder if she has gone through all of this. If she has walked Reman and been recalled and reborn each time she died.* "You know, we're on the same side. Now that you've seen that I won't attack you, you could just walk up to me and ask me questions rather than always kidnapping me like this." She stood facing away from him. He didn't mind very much. Her body was striking and her clothes were skin tight. "I understand exactly how you feel. You want to do exactly what you're supposed to, but you don't have the information or the understanding of yourself to do it. You spend each moment trying to prove who you are to yourself." She bowed her head as he spoke. *I'm getting through to her. We're the same.* "We're the same, you and I."

She spun to face him, her cheeks flushed. Her mouth opened and then snapped shut. She lifted her hands as if to throw something at the thief, but her hands too, fell back to her sides.

"That, we are not!" she screamed. Her voice was piercing and lasted until Raben woke up.

Urchin was crouched over Raben when awoke. "Thank the blazes," the old man said. His forehead was covered with sweat, and he was shaking visibly. "I thought you were gone, Thief. I thought you'd left me alone in this place. I really thought those trees had killed you somehow."

"Not the trees," Raben said. His voice was dry and thin as it always was when he came back. "It's the thorns. They have venom that kills you unless you have natural protections, which I suppose you have." Urchin stared at the thief, and slowly nodded. "It makes you go crazy until the poison finally kills you." *And then I was magically brought back to life. Like her.*

"How did you figure that out?" Urchin questioned. "You didn't know that before and just didn't tell me? No, then you would have intentionally risked your life. How do you know?" The old man was babbling from the stress of fighting for Raben's life and the relief of him coming to.

"I dreamt the answer," Raben answered, the usual throb in his head beginning. "I died and the powers that be brought me back to life and explained how not to die again." *I am as real as you are.* The meeting with the elf was ebbing from his mind just like a dream. The more he tried to remember, the more that slipped away. *She had treated me differently this time. So beautiful.*

"You died?" yelled the old man. "You're immortal?" Urchin seemed excited. Raben thought that he would be worried or confused, but the old man was not. He sounded thrilled at the prospect.

"Sort of," Raben began. "I have to earn it." Urchin nodded as he stood up, and then walked away. *What the Hells?* The old man walked over to where his pack was, and picked it up. *I didn't explain anything. He used to question everything, and then offer his opinion about every single bit of it. He must have spent the whole two weeks away from me talking to rocks. Turned himself into one. Doesn't even want to know what is going on. He must be losing himself, losing who he was. Forgetting. Damn it!*

"We had better get moving if we have to hack through all of those thorn bushes rather than walking over them," Urchin asserted. "We'll need all the time we can get in order to get you out of here before dark."

What the blazes? He must have really been worried about me dying. Raben nodded and stood up. He felt fine. Better than he had since the white wizard. *That was only two days ago.* He took the water skins from two of the packs and emptied the cured leather bags onto the ground. Urchin stared at him curiously, but did not question. Raben then strapped the two flattened bags to each of his shins, protecting them from the thorns. Nearly every prick he'd suffered had been below his knees. He then wound silk rope loosely up over his knees and then up his legs to about mid-thigh where he tied it off a little tighter. He stood up and tested it a few times. *Uncomfortable, but it works.* Urchin nodded and then grunted his approval. The thief reached down and picked up his pack, strapped it on, and then lifted the third one, strapping it on his front. The two men set off through the forest at the same rate they had the day before.

With Raben not getting pricked by the thorns, the insanity created by the forest was reduced considerably. The thief could still feel the strangeness of the woods, but he didn't resort to complete paranoia or attack. He forced his mind on the dream, or whatever it was, but soon found that he could pull no more from his fading memory. He would rest occasionally, allowing Urchin to catch his wind, and the two even had a conversation. They spoke of nothing important. The old man never asked about Raben, but rather discussed when they would exit the forest, and what would be on the other side. Urchin believed that the land was rolling hills with occasional trees, and some kind of mountains away far to the north and west.

"These trees have leaves?" Raben asked of the land beyond the Nalman Wood. The old man grinned, showing signs of the man that the thief trusted. *It's like a game with you right now. I never know which Urchin I'm going to get.*

"Yes," he said. "There are leaves on these, and there are no thorns beneath, and no demons that come forth to attack you with their menacing laughter." The old man chuckled.

"What were those things anyway?" Raben looked to Urchin. "I was ready to slaughter them. In the state I was in, I felt certain that they were demons of the forest. I would have cut them down gladly, never thinking about it again." He tapped his sword.

"They were faeries," Urchin said. "Magical beings that inhabit forests where no men can walk. They tend to the trees, and protect them if trouble should arise. If some noble were to come to this forest and try to cut wood for a new castle, he would find a great deal of trouble from those faeries you saw," he said, nodding. "You and I last night, however, were safe as safe could be. The faeries could feel my health and would never have attacked the two of us."

"I suppose, but they sure arrived at the wrong time considering what was happening to me," Raben said. "Without you clinging to my legs like a damned spider, I may have killed some of them, and then where would we be."

"Imprisoned in a tree, or dead, more than likely," answered Urchin. "They would have never let us leave. Even if you did get up again. They would kill you over and over, or transport you all over the forest until you were lost beyond hope."

Raben shook his head thinking about it. The night before was clear in his mind. The logic he had been following, however, was completely crazy, but that was what the forest did. The thief stood up and prepared to continue. So did Urchin. Soon they were on their way again, and making great time. Urchin whistled as he walked through the woods. Raben tried to figure out what tune it was, and couldn't.

"What is that tune?" he asked. "Your whistling. What is it?" The thief had been trying to figure out what the man had been whistling for a long while. It seemed familiar yet Raben couldn't peg it.

"I don't know," Urchin answered. "I've just been making it up as I go along. It's just something to keep me occupied while we march." The old man chuckled. "How long have you been trying to figure it out?"

Raben didn't answer as he continued plowing through the underbrush. When Urchin resumed his whistling, the thief became instantly annoyed with it now that he knew the old man had no clue what he was whistling. The thief ignored it and continued on. Luckily for him and his failing mood, the Leafless Wood ended before his patience did.

The people of Kernish were abuzz. From the political ward, which sat atop the hill upon which the city had been built, to the scrubby outskirts where the laborers lived, everyone was talking about the recent events that had been mystifying the local population. It seemed that there had been grave robbery, random attacks to outlying farmers, kidnappings, and murders. Kernish was in a state of panic. Just like nearly every other city in Reman, Kernish kept very much to itself. This was a lesson learned during the Wizards War.

The war originally began as a trade disagreement between two cities. An agricultural city, with a very controlling and rich upper class, Kernish was only as stable as it was calm. With the intrusion of inexplicable events came difficulty keeping the peace. There was little more than a militia in the city. The militia, however, was a voluntary group of armed farmers, those being victimized by the recent attacks, and with the understanding that they were completely overwhelmed by the supernatural forces that a number of them had witnessed, they refused to try and confront the problem in any way.

The energy of panic, sense of crisis, and pure fear were evident to Raben and Urchin from the very first step they took in the large city. The two companions had been walking almost a day after exiting the Nalman Wood. They passed over large rolling hills of short grass until they came across a wide dirt road. Following it northeast for half a day brought them to civilization again. A city that neither man had ever set eyes on before.

Kernish was beautiful. Broad streets paved in stone had trees running along them while each building on the main thoroughfare sat back a short distance giving a sense of calm and nature to the place. The city was intentionally terraced, with the classes each living just a little higher than those under them on Kernish hill, in full accordance with the general financial value or political importance of each family. The buildings were well crafted and made of fine dark wood. Every window was full of flowers and hanging plants, and each door had a knocker and an engraved plate showing the name of the family, or if not that, then the general trade the family performed.

Walking just inside of the city, Raben looked up the main street and was impressed by what he saw. The paved road slowly rose until it ended in the center of the city at a massive white building. He soon learned that it was the Council of Judges, the place where the Kernish magistrates all met daily in order to make decisions regarding the government of the city.

The people of Kernish gave dark and suspicious looks to the two strangers as they passed, but were courteous and polite when either Raben or Urchin asked a question or requested direction on where to go, or what local custom might be.

"The inn es t' Molehill," answered a local in their short choppy speech when Raben asked where travelers might find lodging. "Jus follow t' road t' mid city and ye'll see her." The man walked away abruptly after answering, eyeing the travelers as though they might be muggers.

Raben thanked the dark-haired stranger and continued walking up the wide street. Slowly passing through the center of the city, Urchin and Raben were able to get a good feel for the people there. All of them had dark hair and were stocky. They were polite to each of the men as they passed, but shot dark and leering glances at them after they passed. *No doubt because of all the crazy things that have been going on. Maybe Urchin smells.* The thief laughed to himself. Urchin looked to him with an eyebrow arched. Raben shook his head and chuckled again. *Yes, he smells.* The two men made their way up the main avenue until they spotted a large timber building. The heavy lumber walls sprang up from the ground as though a large portion of the inn was buried, as indeed, it was.

Raben was the first to enter The Molehill. Right past the front door a staircase descended twenty paces down into the main tavern, which was ostensibly underground. A large bar spanned the furthest wall, and was a single log turned on its side and flattened so that it could serve in its present capacity. Numerous tables had large groups seated at them. Each one was a cross cut of a tremendous tree, stained and polished to a glossy perfection. As the two strangers made their way to the bar, they each marveled at the grain of the wood in the tables, easily visible as they passed by. *Impressive. Wonder where they found trees this mighty around here.* The only wood that they'd seen locally was the Narwood, and those trees were spindly.

"What t' be?" asked the barkeep. "Did ya need t' room, or just t' drink?" The man was short, but burly as all the Kernish people seemed to be. He had the customary dark curly hair, and a thick beard. He had a large gap between his front teeth, which brought a bit of a whistle when he pronounced his S's.

"T' room, and drink," Raben answered, doing his best to use the local accent. The barkeep nodded, and spun where he stood. He quickly reversed his spin and placed a large iron key on the bar.

"Two silver a night, or three with t' drink and eat," said the large man, displaying his gap-toothed smile. Raben nodded and Urchin sniffed at the thick head of foam on the mug of ale that had just been placed before him by a serving girl. The thief picked up the large mug that he received and nodded to a table. Urchin lifted his mug and moved to sit at the large circular stump.

"This place is wonderful," Urchin said, "and the beer tastes great." The old man turned his mug up and drank heartily. Lowering it, he used his sleeve to brush the foam away from his mouth. "So natural." He rubbed the polished table, feeling the smoothness of the wood.

"Yes, this place is, but one of the people in it isn't," Raben responded as he traced his finger along the circular grain of the table. Urchin looked up from the table after Raben spoke. The thief described the man he'd noticed earlier. *Not half a moment to rest and enjoy a drink before we have trouble.*

"Looks like all the rest. Short, muscular, dark hair. He's wearing a dark blue tunic that is edged in black, and had a gray travel cloak on," Raben described, keeping his demeanor the same as if the men were having a light conversation. "And," the thief moved as if he were telling a joke, "he's probably the only other person in here wearing a blade." It suddenly dawned on both men that no one in the city had been armed that they'd seen, despite all of the events that had been described in passing conversation. *Wonder if there's a law or something.*

"What's he done to get you worried?" asked the old man, trying desperately to enjoy his drink without interruption. "Everyone in here has eyed us. What has he done special above that?"

"I don't know," said Raben lamely. "I can just feel it. He has looked at us several times with more than passing interest. You in particular. He keeps looking at you as if he knows you." Raben kept an eye on the man, watching the fellow constantly return his attention to Urchin. "Yes, he definitely seems to be looking at you, my friend, and if I am any judge of men, then he will be coming over to talk with us before long."

"Fine then," the old man barked. "Then you won't mind if I sit here quietly and marvel at this place, and enjoy this beer then?" Urchin held his mug as if toasting and then poured the beer into his throat like a man bent on getting drunk. *Go easy, old man. I don't want to have to carry you to the room.*

Raben could not so easily forget the man or pretend that he was not going to be trouble. He drank his beer and had barely made it half way through his first beer by the time that Urchin had ordered his third. The old man was smiling like an idiot and making conversation with himself, discussing the forest and Liveport, and places even further away that Raben had never heard of. The thief occasionally had to nod at the old man in order to placate him, but was unable to join and become excited about the pointless topics that Urchin was discussing. The man in blue was in his mind, as he had been since they sat down.

Urchin had discussed realms ranging from the southern coast of Reman to nearly the cold north before Raben's pigeon finally got up and made his way to the bar. Leaning on the enormous, shaped log, the man spoke for a short while with the barkeep who vaguely gestured to the table where Raben and Urchin sat down. A short while after that conversation, the man walked straight over to the table and stood just behind Raben's left shoulder.

"I'm t' meet ya' here and show ya t' ye room," the man said, forcing the two companions to think through the sentence before they understood it.

"Who sent you?" Raben shot back. "You've been targeting us since we passed through the door." The thief looked up at the man from where he sat. The stranger ignored him, looking at Urchin as he spoke. The thief watched the stranger's hands, but they didn't even motion towards his weapons.

"I work for a friend of ye's and I am t' take ye t' him," he answered.

"That's not helpful at all," Urchin burst out. "Who the blazes has you waiting for us, ruining my drinking, and scaring the boiling blood right out of us, you miserable fool of a man?" The old man steadied himself with both hands and raised himself halfway out of his chair. "Use a name or we'll attack." Raben was alarmed at Urchin's performance. He'd never seen the old man so drunk, or violent. The thief couldn't decide if it was an act or the result of Urchin's intoxication. *You just made us the night's entertainment, you old fool.* The thief smiled. It was worth seeing his friend this way.

"He calls himself T'antos and he told me t' take ye t' him straight away," the stranger said as he backed up a step. *Thantos? Here? By gods! Why not. This is probably the closest city, and Gabriel would have known that. Thantos! He's alive! It will be good to see you, my friend. Very good.*

"Well lead on, you blithering wretch!" Urchin called out as he stood. A number of other patrons looked over to the table as the old man grew louder.

"Don't mind him," Raben addressed a stranger who was sitting at a nearby table. "He's never had a drink before." The thief waved to all of the onlookers. "His first drink. Have a lively evening." Raben held his mug up and quite a few patrons answered in kind. The thief took a quick drink and set down the mug. He followed the stranger and Urchin who was already making his way across the bar toward the front door. Walking up the stairs that led to the door, Raben wondered how easily a stranger might have come by the name of the priest, thus using it only as a trap. *Not likely.*

The three men walked through the darkening streets of Kernish. Nobody else was out at all, despite the fact it had only grown dark a short while before. "Farm community," Urchin commented. "They rise with the sun and set with the sun." The stranger nodded, and quickened his pace at being reminded that it was abnormal to be out at this hour. He took them down the hill slowly, picking his way through small streets, leading the two friends through an area they'd not yet seen.

The large buildings in the commercial area gave way to large comfortable wooden homes which grew smaller as they descended the hill, until finally they were walking through tiny houses, some of which seemed to be on the verge of collapse.

"We've certainly found the worst of the city," Raben said. The stranger nodded. "Lot of crime here?" asked the thief. The stranger nodded again. "Anyone care or do anything about it?" *Probably where I'd end up if I had to live in Kernish. I'm sure my boss would be the lord of the dregs.*

"No." *There's a place like this in every city.*

After a few more quick turns the stranger stopped and pointed into an abandoned shack.

"Before we go," Urchin said. "What was your name?" The stranger looked at him and held out his hand in greeting. The old man clasped it.

"Strad."

Raben walked past the two men and cautiously approached the unstable hut. He drew his sword silently and held it before him. Lanterns from shuttered windows and the glow from the upper sections of the city produced just enough light to see what he was doing. He stepped up next to the doorway. There had been no door for quite a

314

while. Urchin stayed back with Strad and waited for Raben to call for him.

"Put away the sword," came the exhausted voice of Thantos. "It won't do you any good unless you wish to skewer and cook us dinner." The priest wasn't visible but he sounded thin and unhealthy. His voice was full of air as though each statement required his maximum effort.

"Do you not have a light around here, priest?" Raben asked, still holding his sword. "Light a torch or something." *Is he stricken and bedridden?* "Can't you call light from Talvo?"

"No." It was a whisper. *Something is seriously wrong here. Thantos! What has happened to you?* Raben wanted the whole story of what had gone on with the priest shot into his mind. He hadn't the patience to go through the questioning of his friend, yet that was the only way to really learn what had happened.

"Urchin!" Raben called. "Create light. Start a fire. Something." The thief heard the old man pad up next to him and mere moments later a fire sprang to life in the center of the floor revealing the insides of the tiny shack. The walls were cracked and streams of firelight streamed out of the hut, but inside of it, the only thing to look at was Thantos, or what was left.

Raben could see the cracks in the priest's skull; he was so emaciated, his skin so tight. His robe was tied tightly around him and he looked as if a man could easily wrap his hands around Thantos' waist. The priest's good eye stood out in his face because all of the flesh had sunken away, gripping tightly to the bone behind it. *He's a skeleton. The man has nothing left. Merciful gods, let him die. Do you fear death this much? Is it worth living this way?*

Urchin stared in silence, the joy he'd been feeling since the inn smothered by the gaunt, hideous form of Thantos.

"Call on your damned god and heal yourself, fool!" Raben's voice cracked with emotion. "Heal this!" Raben thought of the thorns in the Nalman Wood. *No man can survive without protection of the earth or the spirit. He has protection.* "Call to Talvo, damn it!"

"I cannot!" breathed Thantos. "I swore against him while in torment, and now he ignores me." The priest's voice was eerie, being so much like a hiss. None of the strength of his voice was present. *What have you done? Forsaken your god? You fought with me about upholding a faith in Him, and now you tell me that you gave up on Him? We led an army of vampires to a feast because Talvo told us to? Boiling Blood!*

"You lack any health, my friend." Urchin seemed about to cry. "What keeps you alive if not the strength of your church?"

"I," Thantos sighed the word out. He stopped and his thin bony hands rose to his forehead, holding it as he lay on the ground before his two friends. "Gabriel sacrificed himself into me. I ordered it. I have spent so long in fear of death, and when I had the chance to beat it, I chose to live like this than face it. I cannot die," he rasped, "but nor do I live." Thantos began to cry. His body shook with the effort. The priest mumbled something further between sobs, but it was lost.

"What?" Both Raben and Urchin asked in anguish, nearing their fallen companion.

"I took his place," Thantos said and was then racked with a fit of sobbing. "I am one of them," he said. "Talvo hunts even me now!" *Mother of Hells! What did you do? How could you? We have spent all of this time fighting them. Hating them. You took his place?*

Stunned, the three of them remained silent. Urchin cried on Thantos while the priest sobbed. Raben felt the tears forming in his eyes, but he was as angry as he was sad, and more horrified than anything. *Thantos is a greeching vampire. How did all of this happen? Damn it! Where was greeching Talvo? He gave his life to You! Bastard! As real as I am. There are so many that are that way. Held together by desire. Driven by someone else's will. Yes, I understand more now. Come talk to me now, my fair elf. I will make you more than angry. I understand! I will make you rebel from your chains. We are all held against our wants. If Thantos can fall so far then none of us are safe. I will break my masters, and I will use that power not to prolong that crusty wizard who treated me like an experiment, but to give my friend back a body and soul that is not so perverted that he must cry when he beholds himself.*

Raben reached out to Thantos and took his hand. It felt like the hand of a child. It was so thin and felt so fragile. *We will correct this, my friend. There must be a way. And we will find it. You were ready to help me discover an explanation to my troubles, and I will help you conquer yours.*

"The three of us are going to finish this damned quest together, and we will fix all of this," Raben said. "I am going to find out exactly how much power I have, and all of it will be used to safe guard all of us by the end of this. Do not despair too much!" Raben cried as he said it. *There must be hope. Damn it! No magic is absolute. Power over the dead is magic. Power over me is magic. I am magic. All magic can be changed or reversed.*

The three reunited companions wept until Strad cleared his throat, getting their attention. "My pardons, but yer t' get t' inn, ye need t' go now," he said. "T' watch'll be out soon and nobody can walk about."

"Thanks," said Raben, unable to say more.

"Can you walk?" Urchin asked Thantos. The priest nodded and climbed to his feet. He looked surprisingly stable despite the fact that he had no meat anywhere on his skeletal frame.

"I am empowered," Thantos said, staring at the ground. Raben rose from the floor in silence and exited the shack. He motioned for Strad to lead them back to the Molehill, which he did. Together the group passed back through the back streets of Kernish, arriving at the large inn only a short while before a deep note tolled across the sleeping city.

"T'ats t' nightstroke. None may now walk t' street," explained Strad. The tavern was now empty, as it too closed at nightstroke. The party climbed the stairs inside of the inn until they arrived at a room with a picture of the large key they held. It was impressive for its accuracy in depicting the key.

"Are you staying with us?" Urchin asked Strad. "Or do you have somewhere to go home to?"

"No more," answered the local. "I have sworn to serve and honor the bravery of T'antos." Strad stepped into the room ahead of everyone else and struck a lantern.

"You have a servant?" asked Urchin. Thantos shook his head, unable to lift his head and look at his friends in the eye.

"He serves in order to avenge the death of his wife who was killed by the undead who have suddenly been raised lately," hissed the priest. "He helped me before Gabriel did, and I swore that should he join me he would be serving the cause of good." Thantos stepped into the room. "That was before I turned into this. Now he overlooks it."

"Mercy," Urchin said as he stepped into the room followed by Raben. They all remained silent as they prepared for bed. Raben slept in one of the two cozy beds in the room. Strad and Thantos took the other, and Urchin happily slept while sitting in the center of the room. While the night had been disturbing, the room was quiet, and the city was at peace for now. The entire group slept fitfully until the next day.

Raben had paid for the room and a meal, thus breakfast was prepared for the group as they came down to the tavern. Urchin had been first, and was on his third helping of griddle cakes before the others joined him. Thantos now wore a tattered brown robe with a hood that hung low enough that his face was not visible. He kept his hands folded into the opposing sleeves so that they too remained unseen. He refused the breakfast.

"Are you able to travel in the day?" Raben asked as he ate. "Gabriel couldn't." *That bastard! I hope you killed him as you took his place.*

"I can," answered Thantos. "I'm not like Gabriel in every way. I am definitely altered in that direction, but I am not exactly like him, and I hope that it stays that way. I still need to sleep at night and I can walk in the sun."

"And you eat?" asked Raben, coaxing the priest to finish the sentence. *Food? Or do you feed on…*

"Nothing," answered Thantos. "I am not what you think. I have only prolonged my life a short while. Or gained the ability to function like a person until my physical body fails completely. Once I have rotted away completely, I will be gone from this world to that of the damned." Everyone stopped eating and pushed their plates away. "I have bargained that I might finish the holy Dayquest. I have bargained away everything, including my religion, my body, and my soul."

"Let's leave," said Raben as he stood up from the polished table. "The sooner we finish this foolish mess the better." The others followed the thief as he picked up his pack and strapped it on. Urchin did the same and then handed the third one to Strad.

"This was his, but he doesn't need it anymore," Urchin said.

319

"Not yet," answered the Kernishman. "But he will again." Urchin clapped him on the shoulder and nodded.

The four men exited the inn and walked down the paved central road of Kernish until they were just outside of the city. They then stopped at Raben's request and he pulled the map of the Dayquest from his pack and laid it on the ground for all to examine.

"We are about here," Raben said as he pointed to the map indicating a point far south and west of the final location of the True Knowledge. He looked up to Strad. "Do you know any of the area beyond Kernish?" The man shrugged and shook his head. *How come nobody travels? No one has any damned clue what's out there.* "What about you?" Raben asked of Urchin. "Have you ever traveled to here?" The thief pointed at the map near their final destination.

"No. I traveled more westerly than that. I didn't even know that this whole city was here," Urchin answered. "That looks to be far closer to the ocean, and that means terrible storms by every account when you're that far north."

"This is greeching perfect," Raben swore. "We need to figure out how to best get up there, and based on the first half of this journey, we're in serious trouble if we don't get some helpful information, fast." Raben raked his fingers through his hair as his companions began to mill around in thought.

"Do you feel?" asked Strad. He was holding his hands out as if to steady himself. "Do you feel t' ground?" *Now what?* "Somet'ing is wrong. T' ground!" yelled the Kernishman. Raben felt nothing and neither Urchin nor Thantos responded as if they were feeling anything out of the ordinary.

Raben tore his blade from its sheath and readied himself just in case, and Urchin dropped to the ground trying to feel for the disturbance. He shook his head as he concentrated on the earth.

"T' ground!" shrieked Strad just as dirt began to erupt skyward just under his feet. He dove to a side, but another forceful eruption caught him and spun him head over heels into the air. The party could only watch as the screaming Kernishman was tossed by the force erupting from where he stood. Urchin sat unmoving with his hands pressed flat against the earth, and Thantos stood where he'd been since the group had stopped to read the map. Raben prepared to cast a levitation spell on Strad just as soon as he caught a glimpse of him, but he never had a chance.

A concentrated gust of air pounded into the thief's chest sending him sprawling out on the grass. He began to tumble back to his feet when he felt something wrap around his ankles. Looking down he saw nothing. Immediately he was lifted from the ground and hurled through the air. He yelled himself hoarse as he flew, and tried to prepare for the impact. He crashed into the ground and heard something in his back pop as he somersaulted over the short grass. He rolled over, feeling a sharp pain in his left shoulder.

Raben was desperate to see his attacker, but still saw nothing as he scanned the area. Suddenly he saw a current of air pass through the hanging dust. It looked concentrated and powerful. Stranger still, it looked sentient and fluid. It snaked through the air with intent and direction. It was coming for him. He leapt to his feet, and nearly fell. One of his knees had been injured when he'd landed. He let his sword float beside him and prepared to cast a spell.

"Uthaloa Soom Rathul," he yelled and held his hands out in front of himself, grimacing from the impact of the expected blow. He saw his sword dip through the air and spear into the oncoming creature. He felt his spell pass from his hands, and then he was pounded by the force of it. He flopped over backward like a paper doll, and slid along the ground for thirty paces. His robes had been sliced by the ground, and his back had been scrubbed by the grass and torn by the hard earth. He realized that he couldn't breathe only after he'd stopped sliding. He tried to pull air into his chest, but his chest wouldn't respond. He tried to lift an arm, but as he did he saw that it was fractured and the broken appendage only folded in on itself, jutting bones hanging flimsily by the skin and flesh that surrounded it. Raben lifted his head and looked around. The pain from the effort was excruciating. He saw the creature still moving, but he could tell that his spell had worked. The thing was barely mobile. It moved so slowly that the others were now able to fight it. Urchin was holding a globe of yellow light, and from it intense beams of brilliant orange energy were flying to the creature where they would burst into white hot explosions. Thantos was standing just in front of it raking it with his hands. The dusty air was the only way that the creature was even visible. It was now caked with dirt that had been airborne after the first eruptions from the ground.

Raben felt dizzy. He knew he wasn't breathing. He knew that his body was devastated after the thing had collided with him. He knew he was going to die. He closed his eyes and waited.

"That was impressive," she said. Raben had expected to hear her voice. He had lain in the grass, waiting, almost happily, to hear it. For the first time, he knew what was coming. "You could have escaped the wepwraith you know?"

"My friends would have died, if they didn't anyway," Raben said. He wasn't on his back, nor was he tied. He was standing on the same grassy hill just outside of Kernish upon which he'd just fought the wepwraith. "I don't abandon those that have earned my loyalty."

"So I see." She walked up to Raben and stared up into his eyes. Hers glittered. "You'll die forever if you fall again you know." She took his right hand and placed it on the hilt of his sword. "You need to sacrifice some innocent blood before you have failed yourself and others on this quest. The wepwraith was sent by Thannon. He's not forgotten you, and after the damage that the wepwraith did, another will surely follow."

"Why don't you come and help me, rather than staying in this place? I know you can," he said, his mind turning over the events of his short past, trying to keep the many absurd occurrences in order in his mind. "You simply fear master," he mocked.

"What makes you think that, my foolish pet?" She used his hand to draw the sword, keeping it clenched tightly with her own delicate hand. Together they held the weapon straight up, pointing the blade into the sky. *What are you doing?* He looked up her slender arm at the sword, never realizing that he might have it in this place.

"The first time I met you was not in this place. You were in Liveport. You can walk on Reman when you want to, and you enjoy it, being amongst the real world." He bore into her with his eyes. "Join me!" he said. "We can beat them! Put aside your fear!"

"Fool!" she screamed, letting go of the sword. "You can never defeat our masters!" Her voice died in his ears and he saw that her eyes were telling him something other than what she'd shouted. *What is that? Pity? Help? What?* "It isn't possible!" She stared into him for a time, emotions conflicting in her eyes. "The only time I will come to your world is to kill you," she said. *To kill me? You and our masters need me alive. What would killing me do? End me so that they could rebuild me, again. Does it bring the real me out? Do they have to kill me in order to rebuild me? She will only kill me when it's time to kill me. Not sooner. Not out of anger or desire. At the time they want me dead. And they've told me I need to complete the Dayquest. Perhaps I can have my True Knowledge tell me when they are going to kill me and then I can prevent it. I could just kill hundreds of innocent people and live through the attack.*

"You say that as if it has to be you that kills me," he said. "That would make me sad indeed, for I feel that I understand you. Yet I can speak of battling our masters while it seems impossible to you." *Have they beaten you to the point that you can't even see the better world that sounds outside the door? They treat us like dogs, you and I. There is a better way to live, and if I wasn't constantly assailed by one ridiculous misery after another, then I would show you by example. I would live that life.*

"I believe you do understand me," she said. "I have no more chance to alter my fate than you do," she continued as she backed away a few steps. "So you can speak of defying them, even battling them, and while I have a quest to complete, I will, and once you have gained the True Knowledge for our masters, you will complete yours. That is all there is"

"Is that it? To get the True Knowledge?" he asked. "There is more to us than a quest. Remember! I escaped them once, and I will again. You can come too. Am I only to get the True Knowledge?" he asked again quickly.

She shook her head. *It's after that.* "I can't tell you that." *It's after that. I can try and get the True Knowledge first and then fight her off. Or will it be too late? When?*

"Do you know what I have learned?" he asked her. She looked at him curiously. "I have learned that we can change our fates. I know how," he lied. *Just say that you want to join me.* He yearned to hear it.

"Tell me," she begged as she rushed forward. "Tell me how." *It is her weak point just as it is mine. How do you escape the slavery? It is everyone's true dilemma. Thantos.*

"You had better keep me safe," Raben said. "There is nothing you can say or do to make me tell you right now." He stared into her beautiful eyes. "We can change."

"If I can change my fate, then you'll live," she reasoned. "You must tell me. It saves both of us. We are contingent on each other. You aren't done until I kill you and I don't kill you until you walk from Talvo's temple!" *Yes! Yes! Yes!* The elf shrieked as Raben suddenly blacked out.

Raben looked up suddenly and saw the cowl that Thantos wore hovering above him. Though he couldn't see the priest's face, the thief took comfort in his friend's presence. *How long it seems since we traveled together. Since we left Liveport, only having just met one another. So long ago.*

"So you are immortal," Thantos hissed. "Urchin said you had become quite unstoppable, but I had doubted until I watched you disappear. When you returned you were whole and ready to go." The cowl waved from side to side as the priest shook his head. "I suppose none of us are quite who we used to be. I know that I have changed a little. How do you feel?"

"Fine," Raben grunted, his throat dry and his voice thin, as it always was after he died. He sat up and looked around. His head throbbed as he forced his eyes to adjust. A little dust was still in the air. There was noise behind him. He slowly looked back at the city. A large crowd of Kernish people had gathered near the edge of town and were now standing aghast, as they watched the aftermath of the battle. They called out, but because of the distance and the accent they had, he was unable to make out whatever it was they were shouting. He looked back to the battlefield.

It wasn't much. Some of the soft turf had been torn up, and there were a few deep pits no wider than a well in the earth off to the side of the road. Urchin was up and walking around, and just like Thantos, was seemingly untouched. *Was this entire attack for my benefit? Or did anyone else actually have to suffer the power of that thing.* He didn't necessarily want his friends to be harmed, but it was less disturbing if he could convince himself that horrible creatures weren't appearing from nowhere to attack him alone. *The damned sword I guess.* It seemed to him that he'd overlooked someone. *The Kernishman!*

"What of Strad, and the wepwraith?" The thief spun where he sat, looking to Thantos and Urchin for the answer.

"Strad has some broken ribs, and the," Thantos paused, "wepwraith?" Raben nodded. "It grew smaller and smaller as we all attacked it, and eventually either ran away, or dissipated. I don't know which to tell you the truth." The vampiric priest turned slightly away from Raben as though he were looking the scene over for himself. Thantos had changed so much. It was impossible to picture the optimistic, seemingly naïve, priest that had started the journey by his side. He was now a creature, not a man. *You are a thing. A monster. One that we feared. And you fight with their weapons.*

"You're hands!" The thief said. He cleared his throat. "I saw you attacking it with your hands. Did that work? Is that some kind of new ability, that you can claw things?" *Stay with us, my friend. Don't become one of them totally. I'm not sure I could bear it if I ever have to watch you shred an enemy with your hands and then lean down to drink their blood from their dying corpses.*

"Yes, one of the benefits of being this way," Thantos touched his chest, "is that I can steal other energies. That thing was pure undead energy. It probably added another week to my existence. I'm curious to fight another undead. I would like to know if it works on vampires and zombies. I might be far more helpful than ever before if that is the type of enemy we are still to face." *Good! Sounds better than what I expected.* Raben nodded his understanding. *It seems we have all expanded our abilities.*

"What in the Hells was Urchin attacking it with?" asked Raben. "That old man has more tricks than he lets on." *Not to mention moods. He's been no less than three men since we left the wizard.*

"That I don't know," Thantos said through his cowl. "You'll have to ask him." The priest held out his hand, and with Raben's help, slowly lifted the thief from the ground. "Come now. Strad can walk and the city has asked that we leave. They feel that we bring trouble with us."

"Do they!" Raben roared. He spun around to all of the watching townspeople. *Have we offended you by being attacked on your doorstep, you ungrateful bastards? If only I had enough time to put you all on your backs.*

"No," Thantos said calmly. "They are right in a way. Please let us leave here peacefully," he pleaded. *Right in a way? The sword shall draw the foemen? Good to know that I have endangered them. To the Hells with them!* He spun to yell something, but Thantos shook his head.

The harsh words stuck in Raben's dry throat. *Ungrateful fools. I hope their luck goes on being as good as mine. Then they'll see how it feels when no one wants to help.* The thief turned away from the crowd and walked with Thantos to where Urchin was standing. The old man turned to them.

"That thing just tunneled through the ground as if it were butter," he said in awe. "It moved only slightly slower through the ground than it did through the air. Oh, by the way," he said, offering Raben a rolled up piece of paper. "Here's the map that caused all of this." *What is the real cause of all of this?*

"Thanks." Raben walked over to his pack, which was twenty or thirty paces from where he remembered it. Strad was laying nearby. *Want a map, Kernishman, because I think I've had enough of it?*

"You're on ye feet. Are we ready t' go?" Strad asked.

"Yeah, I think so. I heard you broke a couple of ribs when that thing threw you. Are you alright to march?" Raben pushed a few scattered supplies back into his pack and slung it over his shoulder.

"T' is nothing so long as I don't sneeze," Strad answered. Raben stood and then helped the Kernishman to his feet. "By t' way, did ye t'alk t' t'hem who were looking for ye'?"

"Who was that?" Raben asked as he looked at each of the townspeople who had gathered since the battle. He pointed at the crowd. "One of them?"

"Couldn't tell ye now. T'hey were a moppish bunch," Strad answered. "Looked downright scrappy t'hey did. I feared for ye' when I saw t'hem. Unnatural somehow." Strad looked around for the men, scanning the crowd along with Raben. "I don't see any now, but t'hey will find ye' for sure. T'hey seemed t' serious sort."

"Well that unfortunately is nothing new since I began this journey," Raben said, turning his grim look to Strad. "We've had hard times, and nothing seems to suggest they'll be getting any easier." The Kernishman turned to Raben. "Did Thantos tell you of our journey?" Strad nodded. "Then you are more stout than I would have expected. I've wished a dozen times to be no part of this journey." Raben reached out and rested his hand on Strad's shoulder. "Welcome to the Dayquest." The thief led the newcomer to Urchin and Thantos.

"This ground is not the least bit offended that the monster passed through it," Urchin announced when Raben neared. "Usually the ground is offended when a creature bent on murder uses it."

"Did either of you two see the men looking for me?" Both Thantos and Urchin shook their heads. "Alright. So what does that mean, that the earth doesn't mind being used?" Raben asked.

"I don't know," Urchin began, "but it is surely strange." The old man lifted a hand of fresh earth and let it sift from his palm. "It seems almost enriched from the contact. Like the thing, the wepwraith helped it. I bet I could raise a glorious crop from this dirt." *By all means, let's raise a crop before we go.* "As far as I know," said the old man, pondering the fresh dirt before him, "the thing had to have been called here. The ground sent me no warning, and was not offended by the beast. The only way that could be, was if the wraith thing were called here, rather than coming of its own want. If it had arrived to do violence, the beast would have tainted the ground with it."

"So does that make it a force of nature?" asked Thantos. "Because it didn't feel exactly like a normal undead. Its energy was certainly mixed with something else that I didn't recognize."

The four men stood pondering the creature that had attacked them. It had easily passed through the ground and erupted beneath them with the sole desire of destroying Raben. It had homed in on him with every opportunity, and according to everything the thief would gather from the other men, it hadn't even seemed aggressive once he was down. *Sounds a lot like a spell.*

"Thantos! Are there undead creatures that are born of a single mission, like haunting a house or hunting someone?" Raben asked, as he adjusted his pack on his shoulders. "Can an undead be sent to say, just kill me?"

"There are, actually," Thantos said, his now unnatural voice slowing to a quiet hiss as he thought. "There are spirits whose entire function is one single thing and once they accomplish it they can retire to the world of the dead."

The cowled priest turned to Raben. "I have never heard of one that had to kill a man."

A stone landed amongst the party causing a small cloud of dust to rise from the ground. Then another fell. Turning to the city, they could see the massive crowd gathering stones. Only a few of the people had thrown the rocks, but many more were now picking them from the ground, their faces twisted in anger. They began to hurl the stones at the four men.

"The idea that we have brought their grief has turned to action," said Thantos calmly. "Let's go." The frail man turned and walked away from Kernish. Strad walked just behind him, making sure that none of the stones struck the priest. Raben simply dodged the flying rocks while Urchin picked one or two up and threw them back. He was too weak to cover the distance to the townspeople, but the attempts seemed to satisfy his need to react.

"Where is it that we head?" asked Urchin. "We never had the chance to collect any information on where we are going, so are we just going to guess our way there?" The old man asked the question with excitement in his voice.

"Looks like the only option." Raben shook his head, but Urchin only grinned. *I'm glad someone is enjoying this.*

"It wouldn't make sense if we had it all laid out for us, Thief." He chuckled. "We have to earn every step if this is going to be worth a damn," stated Urchin. "I wouldn't have it any other way, nor with any other company." When no one responded the old man fell silent and focused on the terrain ahead.

The map showed that the final destination was to the north and east, toward the sea. There was supposed to be more trees as they advanced northward, and a large lake between them and the end of the journey. Several small towns were supposedly around the lake, and from the clouds and the specks that came down from them on the map, one could only assume that it either rained or snowed a lot in the northern reaches of civilized Reman.

The elven woman had told Raben that she would kill him after he finished the trek and was exiting a temple to Talvo. He thought a lot about that statement, making sure to keep it first and foremost in his mind. In fairly high spirits, the thief had every intention of changing that outcome when the time came. *And at least we know that we're trying to reach a temple.*

"Thantos, did the followers of Talvo ever live so far north as the map suggests the end of this journey would be?" Raben pulled the map from his robe and handed it to the priest. *How easily we walked away from all of those angry townspeople. We are certainly a different breed. We have seen so many insane things, that none of us even thought about it.*

"It is possible," hissed Thantos. "The chronicles speak of a northern sect that was more barbaric, but wholly dedicated to Talvo. They were among the strongest and purest of our order because Thannon and Arsonin and all of the gods of evil had no following at all in the frozen north. If I recall correctly, they may have even been dwarves. I'm not sure, though. The church focuses very little attention on the history, and more to the future." Thantos unrolled the map and held it down near his waist so that he could see it from under his hood. "Even the white mages couldn't break them, having tried to do so for reasons never explained."

"I wonder if the mages were trying to find what we are," mused Raben. "After all, that was seven hundred years or so after the Dayquest was prophesied. Maybe the white mages were trying to crack this prophecy before anyone else even read it." *Maybe they had a better idea what the True Knowledge was. Even Dorian said that the wizards knew more than they did.*

Thantos turned towards Raben sharply. "Interesting. That would put a whole new spin on the White War. It would increase the reasoning behind targeting temples of Talvo in the southern reaches of the Shao, but that is still a stretch in thinking. How would the northern tribes even have known that the southern areas were being attacked?" Thantos handed the map back to Raben who rolled it up and put it away.

"These are answers we shall never possess," Urchin said. "Let us make some distance while we can." The old man sounded less jovial than he had earlier. *He really seems to be held between the man I knew and a commanding angry man we are all just seeing.*

Heeding Urchin's advice, however, the group marched. The ground was ever sloping as they traversed the endless hills. The turf was good to walk on with its short spongy grass and the sweet smell of the trees that were standing in small bluffs on an occasional hilltop, or huddled from the breeze in a small ravine between hills, filled the air. The sky was clear and though the air was a little cool, the sun felt good to the party as they climbed over hill after hill.

By the time the sun was setting, the group was breathing heavily each time they climbed a hill. The constant need to adjust how they walked with the slope of the ground was wearing on them.

"We must rest," said the old man. "Even the hale Kernishman looks about to fall."

"Nonsense, t' folk of Kernish can walk t'il others have fallen from t'iredness, and still a half day more march on," Strad answered. "But if T'hantos wishes t' rest, I will as well."

"Yes," said Thantos. "Let's rest for the night."

All of the men unrolled bedrolls under the open sky. The thick insulation of the beds and a fire would be good enough. A peaceful night under the stars had been rare, and so all of them wanted to enjoy it as much as they could. Strad had a fire burning by the time the sun dropped below the distant horizon, and Urchin had already prepared a pan and was cooking some kind of venison dish with a few roots that he claimed to have dug up as they traveled. While Strad and Urchin were busy, Raben singled Thantos out.

"The forest," said the thief. "Was it the Nalman Wood that did this to you? I have had no chance to ask, but after traveling it myself, I needed to know if that is what forced you to take this course."

"I wandered for weeks in that cursed place," answered Thantos, his voice little more than a whisper. "I fought with it, and tried not to be consumed. The brush was so thick that I had to hack at it just to take a step, and when I grew frustrated and tried to push through, thorns tore my skin. After a week, I knew I would die in there and prayed for a beacon to lead me to safety, but nothing appeared to me. I was abandoned in the evil wood. I tried to reach Talvo several times through prayer, and never did my lord provide me a sign, or give me knowledge to escape the tightening madness that was consuming me, so I damned Him. I wished sincerely that He end up in the blazes where He might suffer as I have, trying to fulfill this damned journey. I have no spell abilities from Him. He has forsaken me after my outburst, as is right. So I took the only road left to me. I consumed Gabriel, by telling him to possess my physical body, but when he did I fought him and suppressed him. He is inside of me somewhere, but as my slave. He gives me knowledge. Eventually Gabriel and the vampirism will overcome me and you will have to kill me like you would any other denizen of the Hells, but until then, I will strive to complete this quest. It was what I set out to do, and I will not abandon my companions as everyone else has."

"Don't feel alone, my friend," said Raben. "I too have something terrible in me that will overtake me in time. I walk forward with the knowledge that completing my function in this quest will end my life," he continued. "The only real difference between us is that you will get to live on a white puffy cloud and I will end up standing in the blazes."

"I think not, friend. Your story must certainly end, but not that way. You will not be damned, but rather... redeemed." The two of them turned to look at Strad as he approached.

"T' old one says ye' dinner is ready," announced the Kernishman before he turned back, sensing that the two men were in an important conversation.

"Why do you think that I am to be saved from this?" asked Raben. "I have done things that I am certain will have the fire at my heels. I am probably carrying demons inside of me that are going to wage the final war on Reman." *You are now a member of the damned, my friend. You need to accept that there are things we will never be forgiven for.*

"But it angers you to know it, doesn't it?" Thantos snapped back. "You wish to fight it! Even if your reasoning is selfish, you certainly don't want to unleash these demons onto the world, do you?" Raben shook his head. Thantos pulled his cowl back and his bulging eye was focused on the thief. "Don't you give up for one moment, Raben." Thantos' voice slid down until it was almost a growl. "It is the effort to remain good that saves you. You might not succeed at it, but if you want, in your heart, to remain good, you are saved. I failed to do that!" He moved his face near Raben's. The thief pulled away. "Look at the penalty for giving up. Remember it! For in me you can see failure and will yourself forward."

They sat silently for a moment while Thantos pulled his cowl back up and over his dilapidated face.

"Go eat," said the priest. "I require no such sustenance." Raben gained his feet and looked down at the priest who waved him away. He walked to where Urchin and Strad were eating and dished himself some venison. *You have made a decision, my friend, and I will help you with it. I have killed the innocent. You have never seen it. And to tell me that what I want in my heart will save me in the end. I have wanted terrible things. Willed them to happen. Hoped for them. You are no different. We are all very much the same. I will show you. You will see. You will be saved.*

Kernish lay four days back, and all of the hills that surrounded it were a day behind. The party had rested fitfully every night since the attack of the wepwraith. They now walked on a plain of short grass. It was as green and lush as the Shao had been, but allowed for the group to make fantastic time. They could move easily here, and didn't have to clear any ground in order to stop and rest when they wanted to. Each man had elected to carry wood that they collected throughout the day, so that they might have a fire in the night. Urchin had become his cheery self as they marched throughout the hills and onto the plain, complaining regularly, and joking about nearly everything. Strad and Thantos had been nearly silent, only speaking in regards to what direction they felt the party should head and to address simple needs like watches and meals. Raben had talked at length with Urchin about the quest, the ground they wished to cover, and the general path they should use to get there. The map itself suggested entering a winding canyon that would eventually deposit the travelers at the shore of a lake to their north, but Urchin suggested heading straight east until they hit the shoreline, and either buying some sailor's service or simply hiking up the shore. Raben had been thinking about this and a whole torrent of other thoughts.

He tried to keep the laws of magic fresh in his mind. He thought often of the elven woman and how she had been more and more civil to him each time he'd seen her. He missed her as he thought about the time he'd spent with her. She was beginning to share more about herself, and had been forthcoming with useful information that might eventually save the thief's life. He realized, according to her, that if he died one more time he was finished for good. *The only thing that gives me more chances is the killing of innocent people. I can't. I've done enough of that. With or without their control, it still ends up haunting me. How can I?* He wanted to see the Guild hunter again, and he wanted to finish this quest. *There is the True Knowledge at the end of this, and there must be an answer for me. There must. Is that information worth the lives of the innocent?* Raben tried to figure out who he could kill that was innocent but deserving of death. *Is that possible. I need to get to a prison. Or perhaps I need people so sick that they are going to die anyway. One city full of plague and I could live forever.* He felt a chill climb up his spine as he realized what he was thinking. *I need to make it. Damn it! What would happen if I killed myself? Am I innocent?* Raben yanked his sword from its scabbard and inspected it as he walked. *Why does this sword do what it does, and why was it the sacred weapon of the Dayquest? No sane man of god could kill innocent people in order to further his own life.* He swept the sword through the air several times. It passed through the air easily, its balance perfect. *Why did Hessing have it at all? Why did I come to be in Hessing's house with the want to steal this thing?* He shook his head as the degree to which he'd been manipulated became clear. *I have done not a damned thing that I wanted to do until now. There must be a way to not do exactly what they want.* He put the sword away and pulled out two of his sickles. They glinted red in the sun. *I rebelled once before, she said. They had to run me down and wipe my memory clean. It can be done.* Raben began twirling the sickles, releasing them into the air and catching them as they fell back to him. *How can it be done?* A feeling that no one else could help him kept Raben from describing his situation to his friends, or asking them their opinion of his future, or what course he should take to meet it or avoid it. *The elf woman knows more about it. About me. She and I are alike. There must be someone I can kill that needs killed that will satisfy the sword.*

Raben continued to wrestle with his dilemma even as the sun fell below the horizon. The group unpacked their bedrolls as had become the routine over the past few days, and Urchin began preparing a meal while Strad struck up a fire. Raben sat, consumed by the thought that he needed a sacrifice for the sword so that he could kill himself or be killed. He would look up from his deep pondering every now and again, but the rest of the party was absorbed in their own duties.

"Friend," came Thantos' voice. Raben leapt at the sound. It was chilling to hear him hiss so loudly. "We have trouble. I sense my kind." Raben leapt to his feet, sword and sickle in hand. "There are vampires about us. Eleven or twelve." *Hells! I had hoped to never see them again.*

"Twelve," said Raben. "I wondered when they would come back."

"They have fed," said the priest as he inhaled the night air. "And they are strong. They do not have magic though. None are so skilled." Thantos pulled his cowl back. He opened his mouth, and Raben fell back as he saw the long fangs that were customary to the undead. Raising his hands, Thantos also had terrible claws. "Do not," he hissed from his horrible mouth "fear me. I control it and fight for you. Build up the fire," he screamed. The priest's eye was glowing. He had the same predatory yellow glow in his remaining eye that Gabriel once had. Raben was so taken aback by Thantos' appearance, that he was momentarily distracted from the impending attack. *Talvo let this happen. Why could He have ever given you up to this?*

Strad began adding fuel to the fire an armload at a time. Brought back to alertness, Raben jogged to the growing blaze and stood with his back to it, waiting for the vampires to attack. Urchin crouched near the fire where he'd been and felt the ground.

"They are very near now," said the old man. "I can feel the complaint of the earth."

"Never have people had such vile enemies as ye all have," announced Strad. "I know not a t'hing of embattling such monsters." The Kernishman huddled as closely as he could to the fire as he continued adding fuel to it.

"Stay with the thief," Thantos ordered. "He may be the only one who can protect you from this enemy." The priest sounded less and less human as he spoke, ending in a gurgling voice that sounded more beast than man. His body remained thin and fragile looking, but it was now warped and he was forced over at the waist until his arms almost touched the ground when he moved. The undead priest howled with lust and rage as he loped into the darkness. *He is tortured even as he walks.*

Talvo protect that poor bastard. Raben swayed from side to side, keeping his weapons at the ready. Strad sat behind him holding a burning tree branch. *That's as good as the next thing against a vampire, I guess.*

The party minus Thantos heard the battle begin only moments later, but could see nothing of the enemy. Ear splitting screams cut through the darkness as the undead attacked. None had arrived at the fire, but Thantos had seemingly begun the battle in the blackness of the night. *He better know what he is doing. If he dies tonight...* Another scream. It was like hearing a catfight in the middle of the night. It sounded so close because it could not be fathomed that any creature could be as loud as it could when panic and rage struck it. Raben jumped each time the sharp calls reached him. He waited, trembling, for a fanged monster to bear down on him from the darkness. Looking back he saw that Urchin was sitting with his hands planted firmly on the ground chanting. The old man had his eyes closed and seemed to be concentrating so much on what he was doing that he wouldn't have known if a vampire stood a knuckle in front of him. Strad sat shaking, clutching his brand to him as though it were the only heat in the world.

Then a scream rose shrilly behind him, and Raben nearly stepped backward into Strad and the fire. *How in the Hells?* The screeching grew louder as the battle rose in fury. The screaming resumed in front of him, while the piercing howl of the battle behind them was still there. *Just come and attack! This is insane! Insane!* The battle continued out of Raben's sight. He was able to monitor it only by the screeching battle cries of the undead as they attacked, or were attacked. Each shrill sound set him further on edge. Strad was crouched so close to the fire that he looked almost in the flame. He still held his flaming brand, though he appeared totally unable to fight should the need arise. Urchin still sat calmly on the ground in meditation, and Raben found that he had fallen to one knee as he waited, but still held his sword, waiting for the attack to reach him. *What the greeching...?*

Just in front of the thief, the ground bulged. A mound of earth simply began to rise, only paces before him. Raben stared at it, slowly raising himself back to his feet. Unfolding from within the earthen mound, two robust arms emerged. Soon, the thief could make out a shambling man of dirt. He raised his blade, but as he advanced, Raben heard Urchin murmur. The old man was still chanting the same words he had been before, but when the thief looked back momentarily to see why Urchin had suddenly spoken audibly, he saw that the old man was shaking his head violently. Spinning back to the earth-man, Raben held his sword and sickle at the ready, but did not attack.

A high pitched whistle of a scream began, and suddenly a screeching vampire fell to the ground between Raben and the earth-man. The thief lurched backwards, knocking into Strad, the undead's battle cry still ringing in his ears. The Kernishman fell back into the fire and leapt up, landing on his back on the other side of the blaze.

The vampire bore into Raben, swinging its clawed arms, forcing Raben to parry with his weapons. It moved far faster than the thief remembered any of the vampires before. *I wasn't in command of me before.* The undead was constantly pounding away at Raben, and the thief was almost standing in the fire. Suddenly the vampire stopped its wild swinging attack and reached right into Raben's chest with both claws. Raben crossed his blades to block it, but was pushed back another pace. He stepped into the fire and felt the intense heat of the flame begin to burn his robe. He tried to sidestep, but the undead was faster, and held him where he was. Raben leapt straight back over the fire, but that was apparently what the vampire wanted, because as the thief jumped, the vampire launched itself into its victim, overbearing Raben, and landing on top of him. The thief lost his sickle, flinging it into the night, and could feel his leg burning. He was no longer in the fire, but the heat had charred his robe, and was now finally reaching his skin.

Raben reached out and tried to let his sword float, but the vampire clasped his hand with both claws, and pinned it to the ground. *It knows!* The creature bent over Raben, and opened its mouth, showing its long wet fangs.

"I think we're better served if that sword stays put," growled the vampire, its claws crushing the thief's hand.

Suddenly, the vampire lifted off of Raben. The thief immediately rolled over backwards, letting go of his sword and patting his legs, trying to make sure there was no fire. Looking up, he saw the earth-man. It was holding the vampire in a tight hug. Seemingly unaffected, the undead howled and began to attack the immense arms of the earth-man. The earthen being simply held the vampire in its grasp and walked into the fire. An ear-piercing shriek erupted from the undead, and it quickly began to wither. Its skin crackled, leaping into flame like ancient paper. The earth man threw his arms open as the vampire exploded into small flaming darts of blue and orange fire, leaving nothing behind. *Blazes!* The thief jumped away from the campfire as the streaks of fire blew through the night air. After making certain that no other vampires were near, and seeing that his sword was floating beside him, Raben did a final check on his leg. It was red and a little blistered, but hadn't been badly burned. Strad lay on the ground, terrified beyond helpfulness. The Kernishman was gibbering mindlessly, still clutching his flaming brand though he'd smothered the fire with his own body.

Raben picked an extra his sickle up from his pack and yanked another from its scabbard, and waited for another attacker, but the plain was now silent. After waiting for what felt like half the night, Raben finally lowered his guard. At that time, the earth-man sunk back into the ground, leaving only a few patches of freshly culled earth in its wake. Turning back to where Strad and Urchin were, Raben nearly walked into yet another vampire. He yelped in surprise as he attacked.

His blades whipped up into the creature's torso, but his sword hung idle, refusing to attack. His wrists were suddenly bound in an icy grip.

"Raben," Thantos hissed. "They are gone." The priest was no longer bent over. He stood erect and if it were possible, he looked as though he'd just gained fifty stone. He no longer looked skeletal, but robust. His arms had thickness, and his eye no longer bulged as though it were about to fall from its socket. He carried himself with pride and confidence. *He looks like one of them. Cocky. Incredible.*

"How?" asked the thief, shaking his head. He lowered his weapons. *My friend, has Talvo come back to you? Healed you?*

"As I defeated the vampires, I consumed their energy, and it fed me," said Thantos. "I believe that I can maintain myself indefinitely if I have undead to consume." The priest raised his clawed hands. "They can't even touch me," he laughed. It sounded terrible, like a thin high-pitched mockery of human laughter. "If they even contact my skin, I absorb them. Whatever I have become, it is the perfect weapon to embattle undead." Thantos walked away and began cleaning his robes. They were covered in dirt and some kind of black ichor. They were hardly robes; they were so shredded. "It felt good. I felt unstoppable."

Unwilling to share what he thought of his friend, Raben made his way to Strad who was still sitting by the fire, hugging his legs. The warrior had done nothing since the onset of the attack. It took a considerable time before he stopped prattling on about the death he knew was coming, and how helpless he felt. The battle had completely rattled the Kernishman.

"How are you doing?" the thief asked. *If you had any sense in your head, you'd have passed out a long time ago. Better to have nightmares in your sleep.*

"Ye' fight t'hese creatures," he stammered. "I t'hought t'hey were just wives t'ales, and I had no idea what I was get'tin into. I was scared. T' fight t'hese t'akes more courage t'han I have." The Kernishman looked into the fire and began rubbing his arms.

"I hate to tell you this," Raben said, "but you will get used to it." Strad shook his head as the thief said it, but did not answer. The thief rose and walked to Urchin.

The old man was lounging in the grass. He lay there taking deep breaths, a broad smile of contentment stretching across his face. He looked as though he'd spent the evening at a party rather than a battle. His eyes had the whimsical look of pleasure glazed into them.

"That was something," Urchin said. "How did you like it?" he asked.

"The earth thing?" Urchin nodded. "It scared the Hells out of me at first, but once I saw that it was helping me…that was impressive, old man. Where did you gather that power from?" Urchin simply shrugged. "I wish I could discover some secret power like that. How many of them did you kill?" *I wonder if I can learn the magic that he wields. He chants, and does some things with his hands. Is it just magic?*

"Two, and our vampiric priest says that he took three. I did see more, but they retreated after losing half their number without even wounding one of us," the old man added, as he cracked his knuckles.

"Well, I never had a good chance to see them. Was it the twelve raggedy vampires that confronted us on the plain, but never attacked us?" Raben asked. *They seemed so familiar then. Maybe I'd just seen too many of their kind lately.* Nothing seemed familiar or attention grabbing about the undead that the thief had just battled.

"Yes," Urchin said as he nodded. "The white mage captured them and was holding them in some type of spell. He locked me in some kind of graveyard, but I simply sat down and built a sanctuary from the ground, so any creature that he wanted to harass me couldn't. Thantos had spells that let him escape, but he ran to the forest sadly enough. Anyway, the vampires were trapped in the graveyard, and were still there after I was sent back to you. The gods only know how they got out."

"So the white mage would have had to let them go," Raben said almost to himself. "And they knew about my sword." The thief fell silent. *He wanted me alive. Why would he have betrayed me?* "The wizard was helping us in a number of ways, from what he told me to how well provisioned we are, yet it seems that he told these creatures some things that only an enemy would share." Raben stared off into the darkness, looking back to the south, to Kelc. "This makes no sense."

"Don't get too excited," Urchin said. "Maybe the mage knew about my power and Thantos' as well. The undead were so focused on you as the worst amongst us that they never thought to prepare an attack that included Thantos and I. You should have seen them. They tried to walk right past us, every one of them dead bent on getting to you." Urchin nodded. "That wizard was crafty, and was more powerful than he let on. After all, he captured all of us. If he wanted us dead, he could have done it in his tower." The old man sat up and waited for his words to sink in. *The old man makes sense. You have grown, old friend.* Over and over Urchin was demonstrating sides of himself that he'd either kept hidden, or was only now becoming familiar with. It felt very strange to Raben. "Don't worry about him. If anything, he's the closest thing to an ally that we have." *If he's the closest thing to an ally, then we will certainly have little enough time for our enemies.*

"Perhaps," Raben said, unwilling to accept Urchin's appraisal of the situation without further thought.

"I must admit that I feel quite good," said Thantos, interrupting the others with his hissing voice. "It has been a long time since I could admit as much. Since Liveport."

"You feel?" Raben asked, looking at the disrobed vampire. Thantos looked like a man except that his skin was milky white and his finger nails were dark claws. His missing eye and the peg-leg made him seem somewhat comical, rather than beastly. Raben made no comment. "I would have thought you felt nothing, but rather, sensed things. Sort of different than normal."

"Oh, it is different from what I used to feel," he said, smiling. His fangs were gone. "This is more animalistic. There is only need," Thantos held out one hand, then the other, "or contentment." The priest pulled his robes on and sat across from Urchin. Strad was a few paces behind Thantos, facing the fire. "I am content." Thantos held up both hands.

"Don't you miss being a priest of Talvo?" Raben asked.

"I did as I suffered, but I now have a new health and a new method to combat the enemies of good. There is still a part of me that thinks that Talvo allowed me to become this way," answered Thantos. "I prayed every day and sacrificed myself to Him whenever necessary, and it got me killed. Had I died in the glory of combat I would never have become bitter, but I died in a cursed forest, because I was meant to. Because I was left there. Talvo left me there. He is not paying the attention to his worshippers the way the gods of old did," Thantos snarled. "If you read the chronicles, a priest five hundred years ago could call on a god for nearly any reason and receive a boon, or a sign. There is one story where a priest in a small village calls on Talvo for a sign that the weather will be good for a celebration in the war god's name, and He lit the sky with a shooting star. I walk in the quest of redemption for all of mankind under Him and can get no assistance at all." Thantos looked at Raben and then Urchin, malice showing in his eye. "No, I don't miss being a priest. I have regrets like every other man, but living for me, for the first time in my life, feels great."

"There's a notion I understand," Raben agreed. *How good it would feel were there no one else in control. I don't even know what I would do with myself if it were up to me to decide what to do with each day.* "So why finish the quest?"

"I still want to know what lies at the end, and for the first time since we began this journey, I am powerful and can truly help whomever is supposed to reach the end of this to get there," Thantos hissed. "We have all changed since the beginning of this trek, but still, as our reasons change, we each still want to know what lies at the end." All of them nodded, understanding the priest's explanation. For the first time it dawned on Raben that he might not be the only person in the group driven by the need of self, by the need to know what their purpose is in the world. *Perhaps everyone has this, and I have it thrust upon me as the only thing I must do.* He laughed briefly in amazement at the thought that he might have a simpler life than the men around him. *I only have to worry about me while these men seek themselves for others. I seek to rid myself of the others. Thantos has gained freedom, but at what cost? Would I do that? Is that what I am trying to do? Am I already that, just in a different way?*

"I need sleep," Raben announced. He climbed to his feet and walked to his pack. He chewed on some venison as he shook his bedroll out over the grass. The others began following his example. Finishing a few pieces of the jerked meat, Raben lay down and fell asleep.

"I still think we should have marched to the coast and then turned north along the sea," Urchin voiced his opinion as he joined the others, looking forward to the broken ground of the canyons. "It has to be easier than this is going to be."

"Probably," Raben agreed, "but I think that Thantos has the right of it." The thief turned to Urchin and implored him to listen. "Think about it. If this is the path that the prophet recorded for the Dayquest to take, then it does stand to reason that anyone who is to successfully attain the True Knowledge would travel by this path." *Even if the road has been a miserable trail of dead bodies since the start.* Raben felt that there were no good options, and thus settled with the best logic that had been offered: Thantos'.

"Prophecies. I think we would get there regardless of the path. It's just a matter of making it there, and as you can well see, that has been hard enough without walking into the den of the enemy exactly as it was prescribed by the god of war," Urchin complained. "The god of war! It's probably supposed to be a test! We could just walk around it, but no, we'll make sure and take our lumps on the way, I'm sure." The old man started to walk in the direction of the canyons. "You young fools. Make everything harder. You can't just buy the damsel a sweet cake, and pick her a flower. You always have to kill a dragon before you think you've done it right." The old man stopped after only a few steps, and waited for the thief to accompany him on the way to the canyons that lay ahead.

Black fingers that reached through the green plain, the canyons abruptly started as though some legendary creature of ages passed had raked its massive claws through the fertile grasslands, leaving deep wounds in the rich soil. As the group neared them, they could better see the depth that the canyons reached. The walls were striped with dark brown stone that was occasionally interrupted by lighter shades.

"The rock is ages and ages old," Urchin began as he saw the striped stone. "You can see how the gods layered the rock over and over in order to build it solid. It continues this way deep into Reman until it reaches the boiling core of the world. That is where the lost smith lives, still hammering out layers of our world so that we will always find silver and gold, iron, and diamonds. It is His doing." The old man pointed ahead at the canyons. "The top layer slowly gets pounded down and worn away so that the new layers may come through." Urchin walked in silence for a few moments. "Maybe coming this way was a good idea after all."

They continued their march, advancing towards the deep cracks. Strad offered to range along the edge as they came ever closer, so that the party might find the best way to descend in. The map showed that there was a road that wound through the bottom of the canyons in order to reach a few small towns that lay near the lake to the north, but after walking for a time, the party had seen nothing of the sort and agreed with the Kernishman's idea. Strad happily jogged off ahead of them to the east. *After his collapse, he needs to feel useful since the attack two nights ago. Poor bastard.*

Reaching the edge of the first ravine, the party halted and looked down into it. The canyons stretched from the east to the west. They began as narrow defiles that had worked themselves deep into the ground and inevitably ended in broad fanning valleys where they arrived at the ocean.

"Whatever lake there is probably rides down the canyons and thereby enters the sea," Urchin said as he observed the canyons in greater detail. "They are fantasticly deep."

Though a quarter of the day still remained, the group decided to make camp, and rest while they waited for the Kernishman to search the rim of the canyon for a way down. Having failed to do so for a long time, Raben decided to commune for his spells. It came to him quickly and he immediately entered the world of his host. The host imbued the thief with his spells, and Raben felt like it took a long time. Spell after spell, he practiced and memorized until he felt fatigued. When he finally came out of the trance that accompanied his communion, the sun was nearly setting.

"That took awhile," said Urchin as soon as Raben moved.

"It was different," Raben remarked. He thought through his spells for a moment. "I gained so much more than I normally do. It is strange. I have spells in me that I've never heard of."

"Like what?" Urchin asked. "Can you tell me?"

"Not really," Raben answered. "You'll just have to wait and see. You'll know when I've cast a good one." Urchin looked at him unimpressed by the lame description. "You will know, old man."

"Maybe," he said, "but I've seen a lot, so it had better be impressive if you want me to clap or anything." Raben laughed briefly, but Urchin didn't join in. He remained very serious after his comment, making Raben uncomfortable. *A different man.*

"Has the Kernishman shown up yet?" Raben asked, intentionally changing the subject.

"No," Thantos hissed from behind the thief. "He went around us and is now to the west, but since he had no information of use, he elected to go all the way around us rather than face the possibility that we would blame him for the canyon having no access." The hissing ceased momentarily. "We don't, by chance, have any rope do we?" The priest sounded annoyed. There was an extra edge in his voice.

"Not enough for this," Raben said. "Not by a long way." *I only have two levitation spells.* "He'll find something to get us down there."

"You weren't always the optimist," Thantos commented, his voice slicing through the evening air. "Does your company now demand that you play the part of motivator?" The broken laughter of the priest followed. *The new you is very disturbing, my friend.*

"No," he answered. "I just speak what I feel."

"Really," said Thantos having silently slid up behind Raben. "If you say what you feel, then how come you have yet to tell me that you've lost all respect for me, and that I'm no longer the companion you used to trust with your life, but that you'd rather see me spitted and thrown into that canyon over there." The vampiric priest pointed to the yawning chasm. Raben was set to respond angrily when the priest began laughing. Urchin looked at the vampire worriedly. *Very disturbing. Based on your new humor, I'd hate to see your bad mood.*

"Your sense of humor has changed considerably, Thantos," Raben said as he stood up. Looking to the west he searched the darkening landscape for Strad. Thantos silently closed the distance between the two men, and stood next to him.

"He is on his way back," Thantos murmured, almost inaudibly. "He is coming back after so long. What a surprise it will be." *Some surprise. He left to scout. Is he under attack out there? Leading an enemy to us?*

"What are you saying?" Raben asked, irritated with the priest's antics. "What does that mean?" He faced Thantos directly. "What surprise?" The undead man ignored him, staring intently into the blackness of the night. "What do you mean?"

"It means what I said," snapped the priest. "Just wait and see."

This quest has done so much damage to every person that has walked in it that I cannot imagine somebody of great wisdom scribing this out with the expectation that any one else would want to complete it. I wonder if they foresaw all of this happening to those that went.

Thantos leaned in close to Raben's ear and whispered. "No one knew it would be this way, my friend, but they did warn that evil would first take an interest in the quest. That means that the enemy would be prepared for the questers when they arrived." Raben stood, frozen. A chill prickled across his neck and then fell down through his stomach.

He can read my thoughts. You can read my thoughts? He turned and looked at Thantos, who was looking back. The undead priest nodded. *That is wrong! You know then what I feel for you, and that I have never wanted you out of the party. I envy your freedom.* Thantos nodded again. *Where's that Kernish lout with our route.* Raben couldn't help but look at the priest again. Thantos was smiling after Raben's thought. The thief stomped away.

"It really means," Thantos announced, as he took a step to follow the thief, "that I understand your situation better than you think I do." Urchin perked up, suddenly interested in the conversation. Raben let the priest near him again. "I don't always get exact thoughts, but I do get impressions," Thantos whispered. "I can help you be free." Thantos shot a glance at the old man, who suddenly found his pack more

353

interesting than his two friends. "But be wary of the first person you knew."

The first person I knew. What the hell does that mean? I didn't know anybody until I met you and Urchin. There was nobody else. The Guild hunter?

"He returns," hissed Thantos, pointing not to the west, but to the south.

A chill passed through the thief, and for no reason except for the eerie nature of Thantos' prediction, Raben tore his sword out and held it at the ready. He stood for only a few moments when a fire sprang to life in the blackness of the plain. It was a lantern or a torch. Slowly it moved nearer the party.

"Ho there," came a strong voice. "Are you there?" The voice was familiar. *Hessing? Von Hessing!* Raben sneered at the thought. *After all this time he comes back! I need to be captured so that I can while the days away with a beautiful woman, and then be miraculously transported to the end of the journey.* Suddenly, Raben's frame of mind changed. *I asked for him. They think we need him. It's going to get worse.*

"We're over here, Hessing!" Raben shouted across the plains. "Over here!" The noble followed the voice of the thief and made his way to the camp.

"Well," said Urchin. "I never thought to see you again." The torch lit the huge warrior's face, where a grim look was set. He seemed to have little to be upset about. He looked well rested and well fed. His clothes were mended, and he was clean. Even his boots had a polish on them. The only notable difference in the man was that he wore no armor as he had for the entirety of the quest before now.

"I was captured by our enemy, but since they need us to clear the way for them, they released me back to you that I might fall instead of them," said the noble.

"Just sit down and be quiet," hissed Thantos. "Your capture was a blessing for you. You have sacrificed the least by far, and I don't trust anyone that can return from our enemy untouched by their wily need to warp and crush the human soul." Thantos walked to Hessing and stood only a few knuckles before the huge man when he yanked his hood back, displaying his face.

"Great Gods!" Hessing roared in surprise. He dropped his torch and jumped back, bringing his massive sword out in a fluid motion. The vampiric priest laughed, his mirth sounding like an angry snake.

"Settle warrior, for it is only I, Thantos, servant of Talvo." The priest laughed again.

Raben swept the torch from the ground and carried it over to his pack. In only moments he had a comfortable fire burning. *Talvo has lost one of His priests while on the journey. Was that written?* He snuffed out the torch, and tossed it towards Hessing.

"Thanks," Raben said. "I know where you were, and that's all any of us need to know. Just do your part and don't try to order any of us around. The normal world has lost grasp of us." Hessing nodded his assent, seemingly grateful that the thief had spoken. Thantos sneered as he stormed out of camp, and Hessing simply lay down, making himself ready for bed.

I really don't like him. What has Thantos learned? He never seemed to distrust Hessing so openly before now. Of course, Thantos is a greeching vampire now.

The party had bedded down and fallen asleep by the time Strad returned. Thantos was on watch as he almost always was. Nights ago he had requested to be on the first watch, and had never awakened anyone else. He remained sitting on watch until the sun rose on the following day.

"Is there a way in?" Thantos hissed, waking everyone up.

"Yes," Strad answered. "T'here's a grand road t' west of here. Should make for easy t'ravel." Strad announced his findings with confidence and then bedded down. He was asleep and snoring before any of the rest of the party had been able to fall back asleep.

Everyone is back. Nearly everyone has changed. Hessing has truly escaped it.

"He must be a trap," Thantos stated flatly. "There is no other reason that he would be returned to us. Can't you see?" The priest shot his robed arms out in frustration. His long cowl swirled as he spun angrily. "They gave him back for a reason!" The priest had been fuming since they'd begun marching, but kept it to himself until now.

"I asked them to give that steel covered idiot back to us," Raben said. "They were holding him prisoner to keep me in line, and I told them to kill him because I didn't care, so they gave him back." The thief waved his hands, indicating that he and Thantos needed to talk more quietly.

The vampiric priest had intentionally forced Raben to fall behind the party as they hiked towards the road that Strad had discovered the day before.

"Your enemies are far too crafty, Thief. They need this man to be here," Thantos growled. "They needed to capture him for a reason and they needed to give him back! We should just leave him somewhere, poison him, something. He's the enemy now!" *Greeching blood! Who are you?*

"Can you hear yourself? The man is pompous and far too full of being Lord Von Hessing, but he has defended us enough times in battle. He fell every bit as often as the rest of us. More even," Raben reasoned. *Thantos has changed!*

"You have that right, Thief," hissed Thantos. "I'm no longer the naïve, foolish, blind man that I was. Giving everyone a chance. Now that chance only prolongs the opportunity of the enemy to leave us bleeding with a knife in our back. And he will, Thief. You will pay the price for not ending him now. More than the rest of us. He has no reason to help you."

"Let me think," Raben said. *Bloody gods! The advice of the dead. Kill.* The thief walked ahead of the priest, intentionally putting some distance between the two in the hopes that Thantos couldn't read his thoughts from a distance. *Kill him? What in the blazes is happening here?*

What is going on? Thantos is quickly becoming a cold, cruel, maybe insane undead. Hessing is back, but hasn't said or done anything. Urchin! I should get his opinion. This journey is getting out of control. Getting? Ha! Does it mean anything that Hessing is back? Is she helping me? Or have they planted a trap amidst us? I don't know who to trust anymore. It is back to me. There is only me.

As he walked, Raben could hear Strad describing the road. He, Hessing and Urchin were a short distance ahead of him, while Thantos still lagged behind, preferring solitude to the uncomfortable feeling of the party.

Walking faster, Raben slowly started to catch up with the others. He looked around himself. To the south were the soft green plains and beyond them, Kernish. To the east was a distant sea. To the west was a land he knew nothing about, except what Urchin had told him. *To the north is a lake, a canyon, and the end of us all. How's that for a motivational attitude, priest?*

Raben could see that Strad and those with him had stopped walking. He came upon them a few moments later. "Are we at the road?" the thief asked. Strad nodded and pointed further to the west.

"Just around t' next curve in t' canyon," he said. "T' noble here has suggested t'hat it may be guarded. He asked to wait for ye." The Kernishman pointed at Hessing as if blame needed to be assigned.

Raben indicated that he understood, shooting Hessing a glance. The noble nodded slowly, and then lifted his sword from its scabbard. He inspected it, and then held it at the ready. It alarmed the thief, and for no reason beyond distrust, he did the same.

"I'm still glad that you stole that sword from me, Thief," said Hessing. "It has been nothing but a curse to us all. You have weathered the storm better than I would have." Urchin nodded his approval of the compliment.

"It seems," answered Raben, staring hard at the noble, "that I was built to do exactly that." Hessing nodded, raising his sword in salute. *Did the Guild tell him what I am, or does he still just think I'm an evil thief. The last time he saw me, he accused me of being one of them.* It had been a while since he'd last seen Hessing at the farmhouse. It felt like years, but the venom of the noble's words still lingered.

Raben kept his sword lowered. "Why do you trust me now?" he asked. "The last time you were around, you told me that the vampires must have wanted to not cast their spells on one of their own." *Not to mention the number of times you have threatened to shorten me with your blade.*

"I now know your enemies," he stated. "And if you can survive against them, then I shouldn't be surprised that the vampires couldn't get you. It is not trust I gained for you, Thief, but respect for what you're fighting." Hessing raised his sword again, and Raben, somewhat impressed with the answer, followed suit.

"Let's get to this road," the thief said as he lowered his sword. "Thantos will be along at his own pace, but he'll be right with us if there is trouble. Hessing, you look the most like a normal person anymore. You lead, followed by Strad. Urchin, cover the back with me."

Hessing nodded. *Just like that.* The huge warrior began walking to the west and Strad followed him closely. *That Kernishman is probably thrilled to find anyone that still seems normal. None of us are, Strad. Don't let him tell you otherwise.* Immediately after Hessing was out of earshot, Raben turned to Urchin.

"Thantos has shared more than enough of his thoughts, so I'd like to hear yours," said the thief. "You've always been neutral and able to reason things out. What do you think of Hessing's sudden arrival back into the quest?" *The greeching priest wants to...*

"Kill him," came the hissing voice of Thantos. Urchin and Raben spun in surprise at hearing the priest. *Hells and flame!*

"Damn it, Thantos! I'm trying to have a private discussion with Urchin!" Raben complained. *How'd you sneak up on us, you greeching corpse!*

Thantos' smile was visible. His hood hung just low enough to cover his eyes. "Don't fret, friends. I know each of your thoughts at any rate. Consider that I will keep everyone absolutely honest. And I will. The three of us have given more than the others. We will complete this quest if it turns us into even worse life forms than we already are." Thantos turned to Urchin. "So speak up, old man. What do you think of our noble returning at the final hour?"

"Blazes!" Urchin swore. "I think we need to get rid of him. There is something about him now. He feels wrong to me." The old man shifted uncomfortably and began walking after Strad and Hessing. "This has all been too easy on the noble. If he was captured and they did nothing to him, then it seems like he helped them. That's the only way he could come back unharmed as far as I see it. He needs to go away."

"Go away?" Raben repeated it as a question. "Do you mean that we should abandon him, or would you have the man killed?" Raben caught up with Urchin, and matched him step for step, leaning into the old man, waiting for the answer.

"Whatever we have to do," Urchin responded. "We do what we have to do in order to get to the end of this journey. If we can get rid of him living, we do. But to leave him behind is to leave him for the enemy."

"So you want to kill him?" Raben couldn't believe what he heard. "I can almost accept that answer from him!" Raben shouted, pointing at Thantos. "He's a vampire, or near enough! But you have always seemed the decent one, the accepting one." Raben stopped walking and looked up into the clear sky. *What has happened? I have worked to find a way to stop killing and all of my companions are starved for it.* "You really want to kill him?"

Urchin nodded slowly, and Thantos was silent, but Raben had no doubt that Thantos would kill the noble. The priest had been hard on Hessing since the first moment that he had come back.

"Give him some time, and if he does anything suspicious we'll deal with him then," Raben said. "Can you live with that?" Both of his companions nodded this time. Thantos still wore his grin, enjoying the situation. Unable to bear the priest's joy, Raben continued after the Kernishman. Thantos and Urchin followed.

By the time they caught up with Hessing and Strad, the two men looked impatient and irritated. Raben and Urchin had fallen further behind than they expected to, and required some time to catch back up.

"The road starts on the next switchback about fifty paces," Hessing said, as the three companions finally arrived. "We should get started. The daylight is wasted if we don't make good time. The road doesn't look to be guarded at all."

"Fine," Urchin said. "You lead."

The huge warrior immediately complied with the request, still holding his sword before him as though he expected to be in combat at any given moment. He moved cautiously, but with great speed, forcing the party to move with him or fall behind.

The road was cut into the canyon's side at a fairly steep angle. Each of the members of the party had to lean against the wall, holding on to any number of natural handholds in order to keep from sliding down the road, or falling. Hessing and Raben were forced to put their blades away so that they could descend into the canyons safely. The walls grew over them as they worked their way down into the canyon, cutting off the light. The air cooled significantly as the group moved deeper and deeper away from the sun. Strad complained that the walls were suffocating him, as they rose ever higher with each step. The first leg of the road was the steepest and took the party several hundred paces lower in elevation. Each of the men were breathing hard from the exertion it had taken to make it down to the first place where they might take a break. The road evened out for a time, giving the party a much needed rest. They sat down and ate some venison, and checked and bandaged their hands, which had been cut and battered on the rocky walls that had risen on either side of them as they descended. Moving a slight distance ahead, Strad came jogging back to tell the others to come and look at what he'd found. Strapping on their packs, the group followed him.

A few hundred steps further on the road, the left wall fell away from the road, leaving a sheer cliff over the side. A short distance beyond that was a turn in the road and the canyon wall that allowed the party to see for leagues into the canyon. The bottom seemed almost impossibly far away, and at the furthest reach of their vision, a narrow break in the many folding walls of the canyon let through a glimpse of water. Though it was impossible to tell how big it was, or if it was the lake they sought, it gave the group a goal, and a hope that there was a town in the bottom of the winding canyon.

For the rest of the day, they made their way downward. The road never dropped at a rate so steeply as it had in the beginning, but once their hands were sliced and tired, every descent that required their effort and attention was accomplished more and more slowly.

By the time the sun set, they hadn't reached the bottom. *If ever this road takes us to the bottom.* It wound along the wall of the canyon. Though it seemed always to be dropping nearer the canyon's floor, the road stretched continuously around every bend in the wall that any of the tired companions could see.

"It must surely have been simpler t' cut t' road to t' floor, t'hen to keep it running on t'his wall," Strad said once the blue was fading from the sky above.

"I agree," Hessing added. "I think there must be some reasoning behind the way this road is built. Maybe defenses are laid out along this road ahead, or maybe it makes it impossible to enter the canyon unnoticed. It surely must have been simpler for whoever built it to just cut it straight to the canyon floor. Think of the time and effort involved in cutting this road out of the rock here."

"I've never met any who could so perfectly create such as this," Urchin said. The old man had been mumbling to himself for a while, but since the topic had been brought up. "I don't think humans built this road." The group halted as one, and looked to the old man for an explanation. "There was once a race of stocky folk who thrived on stonework."

"Dwarves," said Hessing. "They still do, but they never work on the surface, and never for a human town. They live in caves and tunnels."

"When I traveled in the west, they would contract themselves to the kings and queens there in order to make money," countered Urchin. "But only the very rich could afford them, for their work was superb, like this," he waved at the road, "but so were their prices."

"A wonderful tale," interrupted Thantos, "but are we going to sleep on this superb road, or are we going to continue blindly?" The hissing voice got their attention, and the question woke them up to their situation.

"Why not sleep in the road?" asked Urchin. "We haven't seen anybody around here since we've started out from Kernish." The old man didn't wait for agreement. He pulled his bedroll from his pack and spread it out on the stony road, preparing to sleep.

"Guess that's decided," Hessing said, and mimicked Urchin. After watching for a moment, Strad and then Raben did the same. Thantos sat at the edge of the road with his legs over the side.

"I'll keep watch," he said. "While you all sleep." With that, everyone slowly slipped into a shallow, uncomfortable sleep.

Raben slept only half the night. As the stars made their way half way across the sky, a wind picked up. It howled as it passed through the canyon around him. The thief woke up alarmed, already clutching his weapons. Looking around, he could see almost nothing. His friends lay sleeping around him and Thantos still sat on the edge of the road, but beyond that lay darkness, shapeless stone, and the stars above. Raben got up off of the ground and walked through the cold night air to Thantos.

"Seen anything tonight, my friend?" Raben asked, trying to keep the priest from addressing any of the many terrible topics that they could discuss.

"No," he said softly, just above the wind. "But there is something living down there. Someone still thrives in the bottom of this great canyon. Alone and forgotten about, they make their lives without interference from others."

"Sounds like a good place to stop and live when this is over," Raben said. *What I wouldn't give to live somewhere where others could not bother me.*

"Yes," Thantos agreed. "Do you remember when we planned to live together in some quiet place with that old man over there?" Raben nodded in the dark. "Before I was a vampire, you were a slave, and Urchin was corrupted?" *Corrupted? Urchin is corrupted?* "I thought I could save you from them," Thantos said. "I didn't know what it was you were dealing with, but I thought that my want to save you and the power of Talvo could rescue you from the pain you were in." Thantos sat quietly for just a brief time. "Look what has happened." He laughed his thin hissing laugh.

"Why is that dream so far gone, my friend?" Raben asked, believing that the dream was gone. "Perhaps finishing this trek will get us there, to that dream."

"No," Thantos snapped. "It cannot." Thantos brought one leg up on the road so that he could turn and face Raben. "I will eventually have to start feeding on humans, and one of you will have to kill me. You will eventually have to start killing people and one of us will have to kill you. Urchin has been twisted ever so slightly. I think he gave himself up for power, and that will inevitably result in him doing something for which one of us will have to kill him. Hessing has been infected by the enemy, and also must die. I'll consider this a successful journey if Strad comes out alive, though I cannot tell you if even he deserves to." *So much for having a light conversation.* Thantos laughed again. *We have all changed. We can all change back.*

"I remember," Thantos laughed, "how you used to anger that noble. I thought you were terrible for upsetting him so, and yet his reaction was so comic." The vampire pointed to Hessing, as he continued enjoying the memory. It was strange to hear. It was the same terrible laugh, but now mirth rather than malice fueled it. "He turned so red!" Thantos burst into a fit of laughter. Raben sat stunned, and slowly began laughing. Something kept him from joining in fully. He was simply amazed to see some genuine joy from Thantos. He missed having the actual companionship from his friends. Thantos wheezed and fell on his side, slowly recovering.

"I hope that the end of this journey does reward you, Thantos. It might be worth living as a normal human without the weight of your religion." The priest sat up, his amusement interrupted, and the two sat silently, looking over the edge of the road into the blackness below until the sky began to lighten overhead.

Dawn lightened the sky over them, though no light directly shone on them. It would be almost midday before the sun actually touched the base of the canyon walls. The group started to awaken, each of them grouchy. Their heads ached and their noses ran after sleeping in the cold howling wind all night. Sure that a warm meal would help, Urchin collected wood from anyone that still had any in their packs and began preparing breakfast. Warm meat and hard bread improved the morale somewhat, but reaching the bottom, or finding a town where they might pass the next night in a bed, seemed more influential.

Once they began to move, and the food settled, the group began to feel a little better. They worked the kinks and stiffness out of their arms and legs, which a long night's sleep on a rock slab will provide, and they got their blood going, excited that they would hopefully reach the bottom that day.

They didn't have to hike for very long in order to reach the floor of the canyon. It was only a few hundred paces from where they camped. They could still see other cuts in the canyon walls further in the canyon ahead of them, but those seemingly had nothing to do with the one they now stood on.

"Doesn't that take all," Urchin complained. "If we had walked a few more steps we'd have been able to bed down in this sand, or one of those thick bushes." The old man's head shook as he looked around himself. Much to everyone's irritation, he pointed out at least ten places that would have better suited him as a bed than the hard rock he'd slept on the night before.

He overlooks the fact that we only stopped to listen to him talk about the races that carved that damned road. He was even the one to suggest sleeping there. We should have kept walking. I might have slept a full night. Raben was exhausted from not sleeping most of the night, but actually felt privileged to have seen Thantos laughing genuinely. The thief decided that it was a fair trade, and he too searched the canyon floor, though he didn't point out good spots to sleep.

The canyon had brooks running along the floor of it, which carved snaking paths along the winding bottom as they headed towards the sea. Huge feathery plants grew at the sides of every stream, creating a very limited visibility, but splashing a healthy green throughout the red and brown stony colors of the canyon. Occasionally the party would come across a sandy spot at the end of a sharp curve in any of the streams, which Urchin said was where rocks and other sediments must have washed by during flood seasons.

The sand was very fine and felt smooth, almost fluid to the touch. Raben filled a small pouch and tucked it into his pack. *You never know.* Urchin celebrated the sand by laying down in it and swishing his arms and legs until he left an angelic imprint. Carefully climbing up off of his natural art, he beamed.

"You should try it," the old man said. "You'd be surprised how good it makes the body feel." As he urged the others to repeat his comical display, Strad lay down in his place to give it a try. The Kernishman swung his arms and legs for several moments and then got up shaking his head in consideration.

"T' is different," he said as he brushed sand off of himself.

Thantos scoffed and walked past the diversion while Hessing appeared to be considering the sand. Raben followed Thantos, smiling. *This is the Urchin I know. Disregarding the prudence of continuing the march in a foreign land in order to lay down in a pile of sand.* He caught up to the priest, trying to find out if maybe the undead man had detected something that the rest of the party had not.

"Is there something you are feeling?" Raben asked as he neared the priest. "You seem to be bothered."

"I feel," Thantos said almost whimsically. "There is something in this canyon. A magic perhaps, or a force. It might be natural, except that if it were I would think that the old man would have picked up on it by now." Thantos knelt down and placed a hand on the ground as if he were Urchin. "It is dangerous and familiar somehow."

"Please tell me if it gets any stronger or worse," Raben said. "I want to try and detect it through my magics, if I can." Thantos nodded. The sound of the rest of the group grew louder behind them. "Here come the others."

Lead by Hessing, who had not been talked into lying down in the sand, the group appeared, pushing their way between a few large bushes. Urchin was still making a case for the sand, but the noble shook his head, and kept moving forward. Eventually, a new topic of discussion diverted the old man.

"These," announced Urchin, "are Drowning Luviana bushes. They grow only by streams such as these. Their roots actually grow sideways until they stick out into the current of the water. I believe they are named after a witch named Luviana, who was ambushed and held under the water by a mob of plagued villagers. She was trying to collect the roots of such a bush for a spell she was working on. Though I doubt she had anything to do with the plague that each of them suffered, they held her responsible for the boils and wounds that grew on their bodies."

"They killed her?" Hessing asked.

"Yep."

"Nice name," Thantos said quietly, regarding the plants skeptically. "Even nicer story."

Urchin looked up at the priest. "True story," he said.

For two days the party hiked through the maze on the canyon floor. It was easy to navigate because they had only to follow the path that had been beaten down by regular use. Who used it remained a mystery to all of them. They had seen nothing living larger than a rock squirrel. Urchin said that it was normal for a rodent of that nature to be seen in such an area, though its fur should have changed to gray already.

Each night they camped wherever there was an opening large enough to suit them, which wasn't hard to find. Huge flat spaces broke up the carpeting of brush. Despite being at the bottom of the canyon, rather than still holding up on the side wall as they had the first night, the wind howled fiercely. Almost continuous, it swept overhead, calling out like a troubled voice, making it difficult to sleep. Only Hessing and Strad seemed to nod off normally. Raben usually ended up talking with Thantos at some point in his sleepless night, and together they watched Urchin toss and turn in his relentless battle to rest peacefully.

"I've sat here since the sky turned black, listening to this wind. This is the third night," Thantos said, his voice mixing well with the wind, forcing Raben to focus. "I think we are no closer to the end of the canyon," he said.

"What do you mean?" Raben asked. The thief had barely slept for three nights, and had no patience to figure out the riddle that the priest was preparing. It was hard enough to just hear the man's voice, let alone put together the pieces of some obscure game.

"Pay attention to the wind and tell me what you hear," answered Thantos cryptically.

Raben sat in an irritated tired stupor and listened to the wind. It howled and stopped, and then howled again. The breeze blew Raben's hair around, bringing a quick chill to him, forcing the thief to wrap his blanket tighter around his body. He shrugged. *Nothing.*

"Listen," Thantos said. "And feel."

Raben sat listening. *Greeching corpse! Just tell me!* The wind howled as it passed. It howled again. And exactly as it had done before, it then gusted through him, making him cold for an instant. "It howls and it's freezing," he growled. "What do you want? Every time I listen, it howls, and then..." *It howls again.* Raben's stomach tingled just before the chill crawled up his spine, causing him to tremble in the cold night air. *And then it gusts.* "The howling has nothing to do with the wind," said the thief. Thantos nodded.

"That's what I think," said the priest. "That, and the fact that we could see some kind of lake when we were coming into this damned canyon, and after two full days of hiking we haven't caught so much as a glimpse of it. We should have already been on any lake we could have seen from there."

Raben hadn't really heard Thantos' further reasoning. He was now thinking only about the wind. It howled almost at random. It truly had nothing to do with the gusts of wind that he felt. He shivered, thinking about what it meant. *It isn't wolves, they sound different. This is...unnatural.* He looked over at Strad and Hessing. *How can they sleep in this? Should we tell them?*

Thantos was shaking his head. "Tell them and they will not sleep either," he hissed. "I think the party is about to be culled down to the one who will complete the prophecy, my friend. I think that we are hearing the incessant cries of the long dead whose only purpose is to now protect the pure people that live on that lake."

Raben's trembling escalated to shaking. *I don't even want to know why you think that, my friend.* "I need to take a walk," he said. The priest nodded as the thief climbed to his feet and began to aimlessly wander. He stopped at his pack and grabbed an extra sword, some venison, and the map. The sword he really didn't want, the venison he brought because he was hungry, or had been moments before, and the map because he thought that he couldn't die if it would lose the map for the chosen one. Raben walked away from the party, keeping a very specific bearing in case he lost his nerve and needed to return in a hurry. *What am I doing out here?* He looked up at the sky, half expecting to see ghosts and spirits passing by, howling their tortured story. *Forcing it. I am forcing it.* Unable to wait and see if the priest was right, Raben decided to face the howling wind on his own. *If I am going to die, better alone than with all of my friends.* He walked with no destination in mind, trying not to hear the wind as it droned on overhead. It was unrelenting. It howled over and over, slowly reducing Raben's courage. *I should go back. This is yet another foolish idea. Go back.* He spun to go back, and stopped. He forced himself to take a step forward, and then froze. *Am I in control? Why am I out here?* He looked up into the black sky, and saw that a silver crescent moon was overhead. *The nights will be lit again soon. Go back!* He took another step, but then he heard a voice.

"A pity if you go now," she said. He was excited that she was here. He turned to find her, but when he spun and saw the being, his face grew pale. *Blazes!* It was not the elf whom he had expected. *The voice. So alike.* "You're staying," she said. "Good." *Staying?* Raben was stunned, unable to decide what to do.

"Who are you?" he stammered. *I can't die, or it's over. Need to live.*

"I help decide," she said. "I help decide if evil is crossing to the north." The creature walked up to the stunned thief.

She was tall, three and a half, maybe four reaches in height. *Taller than Hessing.* She towered over Raben. He couldn't make out how she actually looked, but her eyes glowed with a yellow intensity. They were solid orbs of golden fire. They reminded him of the vampires, except that her eyes were fueled by energy, maybe magic, while the eyes of the vampires were just a predatory reflection of light, like a dog's.

"At dusk tomorrow, the spirits will come down and judge each of you," she told him. "And if you do not enter the north for a righteous reason, then you will be struck down or banished." She looked down at him. "The power of the gods met the might of the white mages on the plains above you now, and the result was these canyons where the souls of many were lost forever. We judge who may continue their present journey, for we are the Meriss."

"Meriss?" Raben had trouble saying the name. "I have heard of you."

Her mouth parted, letting a similar light to her eyes shine out, and she smiled. "You must keep the judgement to yourself as well as you can. There is no escape from it." She leaned down and kissed Raben lightly on the forehead. He felt the heat from her mouth as it pressed to his skin. When she was bent in close to him, he could see by the light she created that she was a lithe, slender creature. Her skin was a light blue so far as he could tell. *Blue.* He'd seen the exact color before. *The regal tower in Liveport. That was a temple to Meriss.* He wanted to get a better view of her, but she was gone moments later. The feel of her kiss was lasting. It warmed him. He walked easily back to the camp where his companions still lay sleeping, or trying to.

"What has changed?" Thantos asked the moment Raben arrived back at camp. "Tell me what happened. I can sense it." *I cannot tell you my friend. It is coming, though. You were right.*

"I have been told to sleep," Raben said. *Tomorrow we are culled.* Thantos had already turned away from the thief by the time he had looked up to make sure the message made it. *Pray that you survive to see tomorrow night, my friend.*

Raben lay on his bedroll for a short while trying to figure out what a righteous reason was, but soon found that he had no energy for it. He had to make up for three nights of missed sleep. He looked over to the warrior and the Kernishman, watched them sleep. *Maybe she has visited Hessing and Strad already.* Sleep came easily to him.

Raben woke up in the warmth of the sun. *Half the day must have passed.* Having climbed up into the sky high enough to send its beams down to the deep-set floor of the canyon, the sun was nearly at its apex. Raben sat up, and as he did so, Hessing, Urchin, and Strad did the same. They shook their heads in turn trying to clear the fog of a long sleep.

"So," came the familiar hiss of Thantos, "you finally join the dead in the world of the living. I have been sitting here all night and most of the day waiting for you to awaken." The priest walked amongst the bleary-eyed group, and stood amidst them as he spoke. "I couldn't even shake you awake from your sleep. I thought the white mage may have caught up with us for some reason."

"Or the vampires again," Raben croaked as he began climbing to his feet.

"No," Thantos countered. "I would know if they were near. At any rate, should we travel on?" The priest asked the question while staring at Raben. His hood was pulled down over his face, protecting him from the sun, but the thief knew what the question really entailed. *Do we tell them about Meriss, or do we walk around for another day knowing full well that we won't gain a step in our journey until tomorrow.*

"It wasn't that blazing white mage either," Urchin said. "After sitting in his prison, or whatever that was, I know the feel of his magics as well. Whatever held us in our sleep must be new, and quite powerful to ensnare all of us." The old man began digging his hands into the floor of the canyon, and murmuring in a familiar way as he searched for any cause that might have been behind the unnatural sleep. *Nothing feels wrong.*

Raben felt quite comfortable, and as he looked around at the faces of the others in the group he felt certain that none of the party felt as if anything were amiss, or unbalanced. It was as if the long sleep was as common and correct as breathing. *I feel good.*

Hessing stood up and stretched in a number of athletic ways, isolating each major group of muscles on his bulky frame and slowly putting his sleepy body through a number of intense and deliberate motions.

Strad sat on the ground as if struck by a thousand thoughts. He would move his head, cocking it at an odd angle, and sit, lost in thought. After several moments, he would simply change the angle and the direction that his unfocused eyes were pointed, and resume his silent pondering.

"The decision of travel seems to have been made for us," Thantos observed. The undead priest slowly turned in a circle, looking at each of his companions. "Not one of you is actually motivated to go anywhere. I wish I were not immune to the effects you feel. It looks peaceful." Thantos finished his survey of the group as he spun back to face the thief. *Yes, peaceful.*

Urchin barked an incomprehensible noise, and Raben turned his head slowly to watch the old man. His robes covered in dust, Urchin was laying face down on the ground moving his arms and legs purposefully as though he were trying to swim through the sand and stone of the canyon floor. *He doesn't seem as happy as the warriors.* Thantos turned to look at Urchin and the others. Hessing was definitely content with his excessive physical preparations, and Strad may have been viewing heaven itself from the calm expression on his face. Urchin though, seemed to be struggling somewhat as he lay on the ground slowly flailing his arms and legs. *Strange. What am I doing?* It occurred to Raben that he was standing still, amused with the happenings of his companions. He did nothing himself, but watch. *Well, Thantos my friend, what can we do now but wait and see what becomes of the Dayquest?* The priest looked back to Raben and his hood moved in slow swoops as the vampire shook his head in confusion.

Thantos walked over to a canyon wall where a shadow fed off of a jutting rock, creating a dark oasis on the sunny floor. He sat in the cool shade and became as motionless and silent as a statue.

I need to do something. Raben's thoughts felt slower as he tried to organize them. They seemed to have to travel too far rather than pouring into his mind at the panicked rate that they usually did. *I wonder what did this? The Meriss? Are they trapping us here until the judgment? Is this it?* The thief let out a long sigh. *A righteous cause.* Raben fell suddenly backwards into a sitting position, landing hard on his tail bone. Leaning forward gradually, he reached back and rubbed the injury. *That was strange.* The thief sat massaging his sore spot for several moments. *Thantos is the only one of us that is aware at all.* He pushed hard on his tail bone. *Damn that hurts! Don't need more of those.* Raben crawled over to the priest and wedged himself between the vampire and the canyon wall. *Are you going to survive the night, my friend? I hope so.* Feeling the cool air that filled the shade, Raben smiled happily, laid down, and fell back to sleep.

Slowly Raben opened his eyes. He remembered the last time he'd been awake as if it were a dream. It seemed a hundred years ago that he was watching the group through his tired, hazy eyes. He looked up at the sky and knew instantly that it wasn't a dream. That he had been awake before and had slept through the entire day. He felt the hard rocky wall of the canyon pressing into his back, and could see the dying light of the sun as it slowly climbed up the high walls of the canyon. It would be dark soon. *Dusk will come and judgment will come with it.* The thief tried to remember what everyone had been doing, tried to recall the foggy memory of the last time he'd been awake. Thantos had been unaffected. Hessing and Strad seemed fine, but Urchin had seemed troubled. *It was real. What was it? Was that the judgment?*

He rolled away from the wall and struggled to get to his feet. The thief's entire body was stiff from sleeping on the hard earthen floor. Once he was on his feet, Raben could see the rest of the party. Urchin, Strad, and Hessing sat around a small fire. None of them even looked up at him as he gained his feet. Urchin looked pale and exhausted, as though he'd spent the time that Raben had slept doing hard labor. Hessing and Strad looked fine, though the Kernishman wore a troubled look. Thantos stood a short distance away from the rest of them.

The priest was more heavily cowled than normal, having thrown an extra cloak on over those he had already been wearing. His sinewy frame was draped with material that swayed methodically as he swayed from foot to foot. *He looks nervous. A nervous vampire. Poor bastard.* Raben watched Thantos for some time. The vampiric priest was rocking back and forth waving his arms as though he was involved in an intense conversation. He then suddenly began pacing a few steps at a time, zigzagging back and forth on the edge of the fire light. Thantos began to look more and more like an undead as the sun faded from the sky, leaving the canyon to grow ever darker. His murky cloaks made him look like a wraith in the impinging darkness. No face, no hands, no sound. Only rags that waved from his form as he moved. The sight bothered Raben. *I remember when you were the shining example of goodness my friend. A priest that defended any in need. Now you must justify to yourself how you will live if you give in to the need of eating the blood of those you would have once fought for.* A chill passed through Raben as he watched. *And I must kill the innocent if I'm to ever join you in the final moments of this quest. If we survive the night.* Raben began to walk to the fire when a gust of wind reminded him that the night air would only grow colder. *If we survive the night...* Raben could feel the strange pressure of the oncoming night. It was tangible, the danger that hung in the night, veiling the party. *The judgment is still coming.*

"An ill feeling in the night," Urchin said, as he looked up to the thief. "Something is dreadfully amiss." The old man scooted over and allowed Raben to sit near the fire. "We all awoke earlier to find ourselves locked in a state of ineptitude. I couldn't feel the earth at all, and felt as though I would die. I struggled to reach into the ground but could not concentrate, or organize my thinking." Urchin looked to Raben. "What of you?"

"I don't know," answered the thief. "I guess…," he said as he sat down and reached his hands toward the flame. "I guess I was too, but I didn't try to use any ability at all that I know of. I was stunned. I just watched everyone else. I saw Hessing doing some practices and Strad looked to be lost in great thought. Thantos did very little, though I did talk to him."

"I awoke in a memory of the distant past," Hessing interrupted. "I was aboard my first ship, the Wave Mastiff, and I was preparing to train my men in some battle drills." Hessing looked over at Urchin who sat across the fire from him. The noble locked his eyes in place as though something fascinating were just up and behind the old man. "It was incredible. I could even smell the salty, bitter air of the Green Sea that surrounds the Hatcher islands. I was there. It was real." Hessing looked at Urchin and then swung his intense gaze to Raben. "It was no dream." He fell silent. *You used to be a proud man. One that lived life, and enjoyed the things you did. You have lost something after all.*

Strad looked to each of the members of the party as though he were going to impart a great and wondrous tale of his own, but said nothing. The Kernishman sat silently, as though the power of speech had been rend from him by the day as it passed. He gave each of the party another meaningful gaze, one that implored them to guess at his thoughts, but still said nothing. He only bowed his head and folded his arms across his chest.

"Needless to say," Thantos interrupted them with his hissing voice, "an ill magic fell upon you all and we must wait the night and travel tomorrow." Urchin's head shot up as he heard this. He looked to Thantos and then Raben, his eyes stretching open as he did.

"Folly!" he shouted. "We mustn't stay here any longer than we are forced," the old man added. He looked back and forth between the priest and thief. "Can you not feel it?" Raben looked to the ground. Urchin looked to Strad and Hessing, but they regarded the old man with no more interest than they would a stone. "This place is our undoing. The priest and I, we are going to perish. I can feel it." Urchin turned back to Thantos. "Your life, my friend, is imperiled. You need to reach with your senses," implored the old man. "Feel your demise!"

"I have." The undead priest's voice was no more than a sharp whisper. "I have felt what you describe, old man." Thantos walked up to Urchin and stood just before him. "Use your senses." Raben could barely hear the words. "You will see that there is no escape. We chose to allow ourselves to become what we have become, and that is the reason we will fall." The vampire took Urchin's chin into his hands. He lifted the old man's head up until his eyes were looking at the priest's eye, visible only through a narrow slit under his draping cowl. "Look into your future with courage, my friend. It is all we have left."

Hells! That was the greeching judgment, just not the sentencing. They examined us and tonight they will come and destroy us. Gods! He looked from Urchin to Thantos. *Don't leave me with Hessing!*

Tears built in Urchin's eyes as Thantos let go of the old man's chin and walked into the darkness that was quickly forming in the deep canyon. Urchin began to sob as the power of Thantos' words struck home. He struggled to breathe with each resurgence of sadness and fear that welled up in him. Raben stared at the ground, listening to the old man, trying to keep his own tears at bay, and wishing that there was something that he could do in order to ease the old man's pain, or protect him from what must be coming. Suddenly, Urchin became silent. The sobbing froze in his throat with his breath as he heard the howling of the Meriss.

It began as a low whistle and climbed through the night air until it was echoing through the canyon like a lost banshee. Urchin sat motionless, waiting. Raben could still see Thantos standing just outside of the light of the fire, his face now exposed catching the orange light of the fire, his predatory eye flaring yellow. The howling increased to an almost constant deafening sound. It relented for only short spans before it regained its force, sending chills through all of the members of the party. No wind traveled with the sounds of the night. The air was still, lending an even more unnatural quality to the howling.

Hessing stood as the calling spirits grew ever louder, and braced himself against a wall as though the sound might force him from his feet. He drew his swords and leaned against the wall expecting something to attack him from the darkness of the night. Raben watched him, and couldn't help but think of the night in the farmhouse when the vampires had attacked the group, magically putting Hessing to sleep. *Except that he doesn't look as though he's about to face an opponent he can't handle this time.*

Hessing had had no better idea on how to defeat the vampires than anyone else that night, and it had shown. Tonight he looked confident with his swords at the ready, and a resolved look etched onto his weathered face. *Good luck to you Von Hessing.*

Strad did absolutely nothing. The Kernishman had not spoken a word in days, and remained completely passive amidst the crashing sounds of the howling Meriss. He neither readied himself for battle, nor reacted in fear. The Kernishman simply looked around himself in awe and waited to see the outcome of all of the excitement that was building. He had an almost childlike innocence in his eyes which instilled Raben with the feeling that the man had nothing to fear. *He was safe from the first moment he decided to protect the priest. What could be more righteous than giving of yourself to aid someone less fortunate. What have I given?* The thief's breath came short. *What have I given? Hells!* Terror struck him with the notion that the righteousness of his cause might be based on such a simple notion. *What have I given?*

A great voice rose through the noise. Words could be heard in the powerful notes though the language it used was foreign. Stones trembled where they sat. Dirt and rock fell from the walls of the canyon as it shook from the force of the sound. Raben lurched forward onto his hands and knees in anxiety and dread as the unnatural voice began. He felt sweat cover his skin before chills began to crawl on him like hundreds of spiders. His breathing was still labored. He tried to raise himself up onto his knees, but the shrill power of the voice grew stronger and he thought the joints of his arms and legs might give out. He turned his head enough to see that Hessing still stood. Raben shook his head in disbelief. *Man's an ox.* He tried to focus on the ground and tune out everything else around him, including the Meriss. It worked until the screaming began.

He didn't know where it was coming from, but Raben found it impossible to do anything but hear the strident cry that cut the night air, drowning out everything including the Meriss. So forcefully was the shriek being ripped from the lungs of whomever it was that Raben couldn't begin to pick which of his companions was being so tortured.

As he listened to the terrorized call of one of his friends, Raben's elbows gave out and his head and shoulders fell heavily onto the ground. He just lay there with his eyes closed, hearing the painful scream. It seemed to last too long, as though it transcended the need for air and came straight from the soul of someone newly damned. *Thantos! Thantos! Gods No!* Where he lay crumpled on the ground beneath the weight of horror, Raben forced his eyes to open, and there he watched one of his friends embattle the judgment of the Meriss.

Urchin's arms were weaving around his body in a rhythmic defense as his mouth spat out words of magic and command. He looked nothing like the man that Raben knew. He was neither fearful, nor defenseless, from what the thief could see. Without touching the ground at all, the old man seemed to be holding his attackers at bay with gouts of flame and barriers of bluish magic that repelled the ghostly beings as they incessantly attempted to grapple the man where he stood.

The Meriss were spirits. They had bodies that resembled humans though they consisted only of a smoky white vapor. Their heads were faceless, yet when he looked into the missing faces of the things, Raben could feel their emotions more strongly than he could handle.

While the screaming continued from its tormented source, feeling the anger of the spirits forced Raben to shut his eyes hard. Only the need to see if Urchin could survive the night opened the thief's eyes again. His body wracked by the sadness and helplessness, he could only wait to see if he or any of his companions would continue the journey. *Avoid looking at them.* Raben cautiously forced his eyes open and watched Urchin.

The old man moved so skillfully that Raben had trouble believing that he was not dreaming. Urchin continuously brought up defense after defense, weaving shields before the Meriss which would dissolve their white misty bodies on contact, and surrounding himself with spherical lattices of blue magic that the spirits would have to pick apart one strand at a time, being destroyed by intense white sheets of conjured magical fire all the while. The old man had learned somewhere how to wield the forces of magic like no one that Raben had ever witnessed before, and tens upon tens of the Meriss were disintegrated trying to reach him.

They stretched their hazy limbs towards him in a desperate attempt to make contact, but the aged man was deathly fast, creating a defense that would cut through the hazy form of the spirits, sending them instantly from existence.

Raben was forced to look down and focus again on the ground as the wretched shrieking doubled in strength. *Death is a mercy from this life.* The screaming hit a terrible pitch and ceased momentarily, only to resume at the torturous pace it had been before. The thief looked up to see how Urchin fared. The old man held strong, his incessant slew of defenses holding back the groping spirits. *They are closer.* They had worked nearer to the old man.

Even as Raben watched, he could tell that the ghosts would eventually make it to Urchin. The spells were starting to come slower while the number of spirits was increasing. *They are probably done with everyone else.* Urchin still articulated the incantations in the face of his decline. He was graceful to a fault. So ingenious was he with his magic against the Meriss that he never imagined they could reach him until he let them.

He had a number of lattice defenses up around himself and the spirits were quickly tearing them apart. Raben could see that each time a lattice fell, a number of the hazy forms would lay on the ground and slowly edge toward the old man, no more than a few knuckles from the ground. Raben tried to yell, but his voice was gone. He wanted to move, but his body was weak, unable. Urchin was casting, his mouth ever moving, though Raben could only hear the screams of the suffering. The old man placed a number of new shields before him, but Raben could see that they would be of no use. Four of the spirits were now inside of the defenses after having slowly drifted along the ground and Urchin had no idea. They slowly formed into their normal humanoid shapes and stood behind the casting wizard. A white hot sheet of power erupted from Urchin, vanquishing eight of the spirits before him. Just after the flash of magical energy, the Meriss struck. Raben was trapped, horrified as he watched his companion.

One of the smoky forms reached into the back of Urchin and the old man's head shot straight back as if he'd been stabbed in the back. His mouth shot open, and Raben could easily imagine the scream that ensued. Another of the ghosts floated over him and reached into each of the old man's eyes, pushing them into his skull and releasing waves of white energy into the sunken sockets. The remaining spirits began to circle the old man, creating a mist around him that slowly constricted towards his paralyzed body, stealing the pallor from his skin as it wrapped around him. Urchin looked a pale blue. Suddenly the four spirits pulled their hazy limbs from his body and he fell, but as he did so, his skin, which looked frozen, shattered from his body. Raben struggled to cover his face, but was too horrified to do anything but watch. The old man slumped into the ground, but not as a bloody spectacle. He was a different form. *What the Hells?* It looked nothing like Urchin anymore. Raben looked, and tried his best to raise his head in order to see exactly what was happening. *It's not Urchin. By the Gods!* Raben began to feel dizzy as he watched the battle progress. The spirits began to dismember the fallen man. They tore the arms and legs cleanly from his body, and held them in the air where they shrunk to only bones. The skin and tissue that once wound around the ivory skeleton merely shriveled away in the grasp of the Meriss. The terror that Raben felt agreed with the continued cries of agony that now regained his attention. *What is this?* One of the spirits fell into the torso of Urchin's collapsed body while another tore his head from it and held it aloft. The Meriss held it at just such an angle that Raben could finally see his friend's lifeless face. *Gods!* It didn't look like Urchin. It wasn't Urchin. *Kelc!*

Greeching Hells! Greeching Hells! The head that was held by the Meriss looked like the severed head of the white mage. *Urchin! Where in the greeching blazes?*

Raben looked down to the ground, where he began to try and think through the part of the journey that included the white mage. The screaming was breaking his concentration. He focused on it. *Who is it?* He tried to take deep breath, but his lungs were exhausted, and unable to draw air. A final burst of pain cut through the air, and then silence. The howling of the Meriss had gone, the calls of combat and pain had ceased for the most part, and the screaming that had so incapacitated Raben had seemingly ended. The thief looked up, but there was only darkness. He could still hear something, but it was far away, and sounded minor. *Nothing.*

"My...friend," came the broken whisper of Thantos. His voice was tight, as though he were still locked in battle. "Control your pain. Call out no more. You have survived. Quit your anguished cry. You have survived." His friend's voice strained as he finished speaking, fading from a whisper until it slipped out of Raben's hearing. *It was me.* Raben collapsed. *I made it.* The thief could still hear the tortured scream that had filled his ears and mind during the battle. *It was me.*

Raben lay in the dark for the rest of the night. He could hear the limited and infrequent movement of his remaining companions though he didn't know which of them survived. *Thantos, my friend, we have left one of us behind, I think. Urchin. Damn it! How did this happen? Was it illusion? Were we walking all this way with the white mage, or was he in you like my masters are in me. Did you die, or do you yet live, imprisoned?* Raben tried to stand, but the effort was fruitless. His body was fatigued to the point of immobility. The attack had so agitated his emotions that he was unable to close his eyes. Sleep was impossible. He lay on his stomach with his face pressed into the earthy floor of the canyon, thinking, until the sun lit the sky. *We need to find out if Urchin lives. He deserves to live. Thantos made it.* The thief took a moment to let the relief he felt calm him. Thantos had made it. *You are still righteous, my friend, even if you are a vampire.* Raben opened his eyes, but could see nothing of use. The little light that the sun did provide was meaningless to the limited field of vision he had. He struggled to just roll his head over in order to evaluate the survivors of the quest, but found that even that simple request of his body seemed impossible. As the warmth of the day began to massage his tired body, Raben slowly slipped into a long sleep.

Raben was no more aware that he'd awakened than he was when he'd first fallen asleep. His eyes were open, but there was nothing to see. After a few moments of recollection, he surmised that it must be the next night, and that he had slept through the entire day. He could hear nothing. He listened intently with the hope that he would overhear a conversation going on between his companions, but the canyon was completely silent. The thief began sitting up, but stopped suddenly and then resumed far more cautiously. The noise of his body moving, and the sound of the rock and dirt as it shifted under him when he moved seemed too loud in the calm that surrounded him. *If anything is keeping a watch, I might as well wave a flag.* Once he was sitting up, he felt the cloudiness of mind that irregular sleep inflicted. His mind was dull, and his head felt heavy while his limbs were sluggish as he required them to move. He brought his feet under him so that he could rock up onto them and stand soundlessly. His knees and ankles popped with the effort, but otherwise he succeeded. Standing up, Raben could see no more, but he felt better, more in charge of his situation, whatever that may be. He looked about himself, not sure what he should expect. *Anyone could be here. I could be in the Guild's world. I could be dead for the final time. I might still be in the canyon, and have actually just slept. Where is my pack?* The thief tried to remember where his equipment would have been from two days ago. He'd given it to Urchin the last time the old man had prepared a meal for the party. *Urchin! I can't believe he is gone. He and Thantos. They deserve to see the end of this. Urchin always kept such a good outlook. He laughed, even as we were thrashed over and over again. Talvo couldn't save the priest. I suppose worshipping the ground will get you no further.*

He looked up at the sky, but there was nothing but blackness. He was about to guess at the direction he should try and go when the muted sound of a chirper played through the night. Raben swept his blade from its sheath and held it before himself, ready to defend himself blindly, before he recognized the noise. He took a deep breath of relief. He was not only not being attacked, but he felt more certain that he was still in the canyon rather than dead. *I doubt there are chirpers in the afterlife.* He stepped in the direction that he guessed his pack would be. He had very little bearing regarding direction. He remembered that the canyon wall should be to his right. That was where Hessing stood when the Meriss attacked. The camp fire would then be on his left. Somewhere in front of him and to the right, Urchin had fallen. *Or the white mage. Not now. Need light.* So his pack should have remained near the fire. He turned squarely to his left and began slowly shuffling towards what he suspected was the camp. Raben dragged his feet so that he wouldn't trip, and so he would notice anything that was lying on the ground. He fumbled through the darkness for sometime before he happened across a pack.

Crouching in the total darkness, he began to rummage the bag. He quickly encountered a large book. *Thantos or Urchin.* He pulled it out and tossed it to the ground. Below it was extra clothing. This too, he removed and dropped. Digging further, he began to find cups and small pots. He let his fingers wiggle through the smaller items, sifting them by touch until he found what he wanted. *Hand lantern.* He clutched the valuable item to his side as he began his check of the exterior pockets of the pack. After only a few moments he found flint and steel. He sat where he was working and began to strike up the lantern.

"T'hantos." The name came softly through the air, Strad's voice incapable of greater volume. "T'hantos, is that you?" It seemed strange to Raben that Strad should be the first voice he heard. The thief hadn't heard a single thing from the Kernishman in days.

"No," Raben answered. "I haven't found the priest yet. I'm trying to get some light." He struck the flint and steel together a few times. Sparks flew and another wave of relief flooded through Raben. He felt for just a moment that he would be unable to produce light, as though it were a continued sentence from the spirits that attacked yesterday. But the sparks leapt from the flint and steel with each aimed strike until he finally saw an orange ember catch in the base of the lantern. Hastily dropping both the flint wedge and steel file, Raben blew softly on the ember, fostering it to grow larger. Soon, when the spark had grown in size and strength, he shut the lantern door which also exposed the ember of fire to the oil doused wick. In only moments a flame sprung to life, giving the thief his first view of the battle ground on which he'd collapsed and cowered only one night before.

His eyes quickly adjusted to the weak light of the lantern. Five backpacks lay at his feet in a semicircle, as they had two nights ago. Strad lay only a few paces away. He was on his back and his chest moved only slightly as he labored to breathe. Raben stepped over the packs and knelt next to the Kernishman. Clasping his hands, the thief looked him over. There were no wounds that Raben could see, but Strad was obviously having trouble both breathing and moving, or else he'd have at least made his way back to the bedrolls, which were within arms reach if he'd just stretched to find out.

"Strad," Raben urged the man while shaking him. "Strad, can you talk still? Help me. What's wrong? What can I do for you?" *You were safe. I was sure of it. What could have happened to him?* Raben shook him again, but Strad needed to collect his breath in order to answer, and after several deep breaths, he did.

"Find T'hantos," exhaled the fallen Kernishman. "He is near death, and needs help. He can, in turn, help me." Strad's eyes shot open. "Please! He needs to eat." Raben suddenly stopped gently shaking the Kernishman, and

391

wrapped his hands in the man's coat and pulled hard. Anger flooded the thief. *He needs to eat?*

"What!" he barked. "Say that again. What is going on here?" The Kernishman remained limp in Raben's grasp, and said nothing. *He needs to eat. Eat what? Why does he know? He led us to Thantos and then was part of the party. We never really questioned his purpose. He said that he went where Thantos went. Damn it!* "Talk fool!" Raben shook Strad again. "I must know." Silence. Raben dropped him, grabbed the lantern and jumped to his feet. *Where are you, priest? We need to talk about your friend here.*

Despite his want to locate Thantos, he couldn't. He didn't have any idea where the priest had even been during the battle. It was Hessing that he first encountered, having a fair idea where the man would be. The noble was sitting against the wall where he'd stood to fight the Meriss, and looked in good condition. A dark spot marred the ground just in front of him as though he'd been awake and had a fire. After inspecting the charred ground, Raben concluded that that must have been exactly what occurred. He reached a hand to the unconscious noble, and Hessing came to life.

One of the warrior's large calloused hands rose up and gripped Raben's wrist, dragging it downward, while his other hand shot out to hold a dagger under the thief's chin.

"Any movement and you're dead, rogue," Hessing snarled. Raben looked at the noble, shocked at the reaction. He remained calm, waiting for Hessing to recognize him and come to his senses. "Where did you bring me to now?" asked the warrior, pressing the edge of his blade into Raben's neck. The thief tensed, feeling the knife slowly cut him. *Come on you greeching fool!*

"I'm no spirit," Raben said. "Get your dagger back!" The thief's voice had risen with the fear that Hessing would kill him in his deluded state. *I can't die. I have to see the end of this. Come on fool. Wake up!* "It's me, Hessing. Thief!"

Hessing blinked several times and then his whole demeanor changed. His eyes became unfocused and then cleared. He focused them on Raben and sneered. After a few moments he began to chuckle from behind his twisted face.

"I'm not dead yet," he said. "I'm fine. Go find that priest. The ghosts were having some fight with him," he stated as he withdrew his dagger. "He'll need any help we can give, if he yet lives. They fought with him long after everyone else. Even after you stopped screeching." The noble released Raben's wrist and then sheathed his dagger in his belt. Hessing then surged to his feet as though he had just risen from a peaceful night's sleep. Raben looked up at the huge warrior, astonished. Hessing misread the expression. "Oh, sorry about your neck. You took me by surprise. I'd been dreaming that someone would come along and kill us while we slept." The noble stepped past Raben, and then looked back to him after a few steps. "Are you going to help me find Thantos?"

Raben nodded and slowly regained his feet. He reached up to his neck and felt the slim cut and sticky blood. It was minor, but stung when he touched it. *Fool! Next time I have a greeching bad dream I'm going to go ahead and slice you up.* When he satisfied his need to aggravate the knife wound, Raben followed Hessing who was bounding across the canyon floor. *Greeching fool! You don't even have a lantern.* Opening up the one he held to its brightest setting, Raben moved as quickly as he could.

"They were shredding each other in this area the last time I saw them," Hessing told the thief, gesturing at an area of the canyon a few hundred paces from camp. "It was an odd battle from what I could see. It lasted for a very long time. I was knocked out before it was over, like you.

The ghosts attacked by touching, and so did Thantos. It looked like whoever was more focused, or had more will power won each engagement." The noble stepped into the middle of a bush and let his weight drive his booted foot downward, cracking branches out of his way so that he could step through. "At first that priest was annihilating as many of those things as Urchin was, but after a time, they overwhelmed him just as they did the old man."

"You saw!" Raben blurted. "You watched as Urchin fell?" Hessing nodded. "Did you see at the end when they tore him apart and ripped his skin from his body?" Again Hessing nodded, eyeing Raben distastefully. "I'm not trying to be a ghoul. Did you see the face on the skull when they lifted it?" Hessing shook his head, his face slowly twisting with sadness and pain as he thought back to the battle.

"No, it wasn't facing me," he spat. That was right. Hessing would have been almost directly behind Urchin. Tears formed in the massive warrior's eyes, though he turned away from the thief to hide them. "You needn't ever bring this up to me again. I have had enough trouble knowing that I couldn't reach the old fool before he died without you describing the event in detail. So discuss it with the priest if you want. He might enjoy these terrible details."

"Sorry," Raben said lamely. *It wasn't him, Hessing. It wasn't Urchin.* Raben didn't feel comfortable telling the noble what he suspected. The words of his friends echoed in the back of his mind. *The enemy sent him for a purpose.* "What did the things do to you?" asked the thief. *Anything? Or did you breeze through yet another terrible part of this journey?*

"They entered me, saw that I was pure, and then seized me, forcing me to look at the unrighteous band that I was traveling with," answered Hessing as he forced another bush to give under his weight. "I'll tell you no more. I was judged and permitted to continue so that I may find the True Knowledge and return to my people with it."

Hearing this, Raben fell silent, and Hessing seemed to mind not at all. The two slowly carved a path through the thick underbrush of the canyon floor, searching for the missing priest.

"Here he is!" Hessing called out through the night. "Thief! I've found him! Come quickly!" Raben spun to the sound of the noble and quickly covered the thirty paces between the two of them. As he neared Hessing, the warrior dropped from view, as though he'd jumped into a pit, and as the thief came upon him, he saw that that was exactly what he'd done.

Hessing stood at the bottom of a pit, or a crater. The sides were freshly turned and formed an inverted cone in the ground. Thantos lay at the bottom with the noble standing over him. The priest's clothes were burned and did little to cover him. He had no hair on his entire body and his finger and toe nails were burnt black. Raben could smell the grotesque odor of burnt skin. The priest no longer looked healthy and strong. His frame was once again skeletal and fragile looking, and his eye stood out from its socket as it had when Raben first saw him in Kernish. *They have fed on you, my friend.* The thief watched as Hessing checked Thantos' breathing.

"He is very warm, but appears to be dead." Hessing looked up to Raben for some idea on what they should do. "Take him to the fire?" he asked.

"Strad seems to think that Thantos needs to eat," Raben said. Hessing looked at him, letting the words sink in. "I think that Strad has been feeding him," he added. "Let's get them together and see what happens." *Get them together and see what happens. What am I doing?* His own words shocked him.

"You want me to carry him," Hessing said, as he pointed at Thantos, "over to Strad, so that he can feed the priest blood!" The enormous noble shook his head as his voice gained in volume. "Are you mad? We are not going to sacrifice the most innocent member of this party to save a priest that turned into a vampire. What greater mockery of Talvo could we perform than to do this?" Hessing flexed his hands as he stood in the hole glaring up at Raben. "Thantos must simply be left to die if that is the will of the spirits. We were supposed to be judged. Meriss told me this Herself. If he dies in this hole by morning, then he was not supposed to be allowed to continue." Hessing looked up to see if the thief had anything he'd like to add to the noble's decision, but Raben was in no mood to debate with the arrogance of Von Hessing. *Damn you Lord Von Hessing! I suppose you're the noble again and we have regained our status as unimportant.* He shook his head while Hessing climbed out of the hole and made his way back to camp. *Entered you and saw that you were pure and then forced you to look at the unrighteous band that you traveled with.* The thief remained. *I'll bet you watched me too.* He stood at the top of the crater, unsure of his course. He knew that Hessing wasn't altogether wrong about the situation. Raben felt much the same, but seeing the priest lying in the dirt at the bottom of the pit brought out a need to help his friend.

Sitting down on the edge of the crater, he slid down the side of the hole to Thantos. He didn't trust his sluggish legs to handle the short slope. He reached out and felt the priest's skin. *Blazing Hells.* Hessing had understated. Thantos' skin was hot enough to the touch to be uncomfortable. Raben pulled away. *What do you need, my friend? Have you been feeding on Strad, or do you have some abilities he's never talked about? Wake up, damn it! Tell me.*

Blood. Raben heard the response. Thantos hadn't spoken, but the thief was sure he'd heard him speak. He stared hard at the priest, waiting for him to speak. *I was watching him. He said nothing. His mouth never moved and his chest never drew air. Hells! Blood. What is this?* Raben felt as if he were still being judged. *What if I am? I'm so selfish. I left Strad unconscious because I care more for Thantos, and Thantos is a vampire. I forgive him for wanting blood because he is my friend. I want to finish this quest, damn it! I have been the unwilling pawn of fate, and simply wish to be free of this mess. What can I do?* Raben looked up into the sky. It was still black. *Blood. Say it again. Tell me again. I need to be sure it was you. Say it again.* Nothing. *Hells! Hells! Hells!* Raben brought a sickle from its sheath and inspected it in the lantern light. A corona of red light reflected off of the curved blade. *This is madness. My madness. I'm out of my mind.* The thief turned the blade over so that its sharp edge faced downward and held it over his forearm. *Blood. Why blood, Thantos? Why did this man have to be tortured to the point that he would elect to become a vampire? Damn!* Raben lowered the sickle until its cold sharp metallic edge was touching his skin. He shook with apprehension. A constant chill stretched from the contact point between his arm and the weapon. It tingled through his body causing him to breathe erratically and tremble. His hand shook so badly that he thought he might accidentally cut himself. *Blood. Thantos needs blood.* Raben used the words. *Thantos needs blood.* He focused on them and tried to derive a confidence from some inner strength that existed only to push people through crises; the confidence that exploded from the souls of men as they gave themselves up in order to save the weak. *Damn it.* Fear welled up inside of Raben. He clutched the sickle tighter. *Thantos needs blood. He can survive. He needs blood. I can save him.* The thief lifted the sickle slightly off of his arm and prepared himself. *Thantos needs blood.* He lowered the sickle to his arm. It touched his skin, its icy, razor edge causing a chill to prickle across his flesh where the blade would soon bite into him. *I must. He needs it.* He flexed his hand, slowly oscillating the blade in the yellow lantern light, ready to do it, but as soon he started, he froze, and then hurled it from the pit. *Damn you, Thantos. Damn!* Tears began to form. *You asked me to kill you when you needed blood! Do you remember that? Now you need me to feed you blood, or drag you to Strad so that he can feed you. How can I? We talked about this! You know I can't! It's wrong! Thantos! You are all that I have left.* He sucked in a breath, trying to compose himself, humiliated that he broke down. *Need to help.* He began to shake again as he thought about the few ways he could help.

"I can't. My friend, I tried." Raben sobbed, wrapping his face up in his arms. He turned away from the priest as though Thantos lay in the pit staring at him, hating him for not being able to give his blood to save the priest's life. "I tried." *This is a place no man should ever have to know. The Dayquest! The entire journey has been made in the darkness of our souls.* Just thinking of the journey made Raben want to kill. It had been an exercise in desperation and pain since the very beginning. His life had been included for a purpose he may never learn. It infuriated him. The group had been stripped of man after man until only a few remained, and excepting Hessing, they had all been tormented until they no longer even resembled the men who had left Liveport. *Now Urchin is gone. Either held or killed by Kelc, or taken by the Meriss. Greeching Hells!* Raben looked back over at Thantos and watched the lifeless priest. *Friend, what has become of us?* Thantos looked peaceful. *Maybe Hessing is right. Maybe you're not supposed to continue. How much could he enjoy life as a vampire?* He heard Thantos in his mind. Heard him speak of how healthy he felt. How much better he felt now that he wasn't living for a god, but for himself. How he knew his direction was his and how free he felt. *By the gods! He was happy.*

Before another thought could prevail, Raben tore a dagger from one of his arm sheaths and held it over his forearm where he'd had the sickle. *Whatever god is watching. Whichever one of you gives a fiery damn. Help us all.* He had no clue to whom he prayed, but Raben certainly wished that a greater force would assist him. He dragged the blade across his arm. It left a dark line as it cut a razor-thin gash in the thief's arm. It didn't hurt at first. It felt strange, almost unreal. Raben could feel the blade pulling across his arm, catching on and then slicing through his skin, and then it felt cold. It was as if he'd thrust his arm into a snowdrift and left it for a moment. Then the pain crashed into him, the searing fiery hurt that left no doubt as to the exact size and depth of the wound. The thief held his arm out to his side, clenching his teeth as he silently dealt with the fury of the injury. After only a few moments it lessened, shock being as great a force as the pain of the cut. Almost mechanically, Raben lowered his arm to Thantos' mouth. He was forced to lie down on his side in order to get the flowing wound to the priest's mouth. He could feel the warm blood running down his arm, and felt the exact point that the blood was streaming from his wounded limb into Thantos' mouth. It itched as it exited his veins. He reached out and massaged the arm, squeezing it ever harder, forcing more blood to gush from the wound. Raben lay there letting his lifeblood flow into the priest for a short while before he began to wonder how long he should do this before giving up. *How long before it kills me? How much blood does it take?* Thantos wasn't responding at all. The thief sat up, clutching the wound with his other hand. Blood still poured from the wound, through his fingers. He snapped his lantern up.

Thrusting it close to the priest's face, Raben could see that the undead man's mouth was almost full of the red fluid. Quickly setting the lantern down beside him, Raben tried not to vomit. He gagged as soon as he saw Thantos, his mouth brimming with blood, and now tried to keep from letting it get the best of him. His stomach heaved while the thief tried to catch his breath, hurriedly gulping air. After a few moments the nausea subsided. Raben lifted his arm and held it over his head. With his free hand, he tore a strip of shredded cloth from what remained of Thantos' robe. Using this, he tied off his arm, restricting the flow of blood. He'd be able to bandage it better at camp.

Trying to keep his arm elevated as he did so, Raben snatched the lantern up from the ground and attempted to climb out of the crater. It proved harder than he expected. His legs were a little shaky, but not using his arms was even more frustrating. The thief was forced to dig out a shelf where he set the lantern. He then pulled himself from the hole, and reached down to the lantern, lifting it from the crater. *I have done all that I could, my friend. I hope to see you again. Awaken. I believe that Hessing has every intention of leaving you here tomorrow.* Raben directed his thoughts, focusing on each word as he would if he were speaking them aloud, hoping that the priest could still somehow read his thoughts. Without Thantos, Raben would have to face Hessing alone. *No. You must come with us, my friend. You must!*

The thief turned from his fallen friend, and weaved his way back to camp, following the obvious trail of crushed and broken bushes that Hessing left behind. After making his way out of the densest portion of the shrubberies, Raben could see that the noble had managed to get a fire going. It looked very inviting. Wiping his forehead, Raben realized that all of the drama and effort in the crater had caused him to sweat considerably. As the night air slowly dried him, shivers shot through his body. Queasiness ebbed through him, slowing his gait, forcing the thief to concentrate on just taking each step. *That fire is exactly what I want.* He hobbled into camp, and Hessing nodded at him, and then looked back to what he was working on.

The noble was sharpening and cleaning all of the weapons he could find. Some of them weren't even his. A few of the daggers lying around the noble were Raben's, and the sword he was working on at the moment was Strad's. Hessing was putting every effort into getting the polished steel emblem of Kernish that stood out on the sword's hilt to shine as it must have when it was new. *One of those twisted trees from the forest with a full moon behind it. What a bunch of fools. Don't they know that that forest is evil?* Raben collapsed next to his pack, across the fire from Hessing, and began to dig through his pack. He pulled out a number of rags and a few healing herbs that had been included. The thief closed his lamp, killing its flame, and set it behind him. He then began wrapping his arm in the bandages after rubbing the herbs into them. *Wait!* He looked up from what he was doing and looked at Hessing, then the sword. *What the blazes?*

Raben scrambled to his feet and walked clumsily around the fire, and stood in front of Hessing, inspecting the hilt of Strad's sword.

"Look at that symbol," Raben said, his voice beginning to slur. "Where have I seen that symbol?" The noble waved Raben out of the firelight and then inspected the sword. He shook his head slowly.

"It is the crest of some family in Kernish," Hessing responded. "Where were you?" The noble nodded in the direction that he'd left Thantos. His eyes slowly swept down Raben, slowing at the new bandages on his arm. "What were you doing?"

"Seeing if the priest had anything valuable on him in case we are forced to leave him," Raben answered. "That symbol." He pointed at it as he thought. *Where have I seen that symbol? I know I have.* "You're sure we haven't seen that in some temple or...Hells, you weren't at the white wizard's."

"Thank Talvo, I wasn't," Hessing said. "It's unimportant, Thief." The noble looked behind him at Strad who still lay there unmoving. "So was there anything on the priest? He looked pretty naked to me. Not many hiding spots." Hessing resumed polishing the weapon.

"No." *To the Hells with you, Hessing!* Raben began walking back to his spot when it struck him. "The messenger," he announced, turning back to the warrior. "The messenger of Thannon had that crest emblazoned on his breastplate." A wave of shock pulsed through the thief where he stood. He immediately sat down, realizing what he'd just said. *That is the same symbol the messenger had. Strad shares the same symbol the messenger had. Thantos and Strad are linked, and Strad has the same symbol as the undead servant of Gul Thannon. Blazes!* Hessing shared this assessment of the weapon. After a few moments of thought, he tossed the weapon away from himself as though it were a long dead rat.

"What does that make him?" Hessing asked, looking back at Strad. "Is he a spy of the dark god? What do you know of him?" The noble looked over at Raben, waiting for the thief to fill him in. He seemed more alarmed than Raben felt. His eyes were looming. *I guess Thannon did knock you around a bit.* "Well?"

"Nothing. I realized earlier that we knew nothing about him," the thief answered. "He joined us in Kernish, and swore that he would follow Thantos. We were attacked in the plains by vampires and he fell to the ground, paralyzed by fear. Since that point he'd been volunteering to scout and help Urchin make meals. After the attack of the spirits, he told me that we needed to find Thantos, and that the priest would need to eat. After that, he fell silent, and has remained as you see him." Raben looked over to the Kernishman, making sure that he was still there.

After having dealt with the lich, the thief felt very uneasy about the presence of any creature who shared the same crest. Thannon had played a number of parts in the destruction of the Dayquest. The messenger and his army of zombies had killed the knights of Liveport. The vampires had wanted Raben to lead them only because they felt that he was invisible to the searching eye of Gul Thannon. After the first meeting with the vampires, Hessing had left the house to be captured by the Guild. Because of the slaughter of Nestor's Ferry, and through the advice of one of those vampires, the party sought out the white mage. During his captivity at the wizard's hands, Thantos was broken to the point that he denounced Talvo and was forced to turn into a vampire. Urchin was somehow corrupted and possessed by the white wizard. He's dead because of it. *Is Thannon directing this? Is He who is in control of me? This only gets worse.* Now Strad was somehow affiliated with the dark god. *How did that bastard survive the Meriss? He should have died.*

"We need to do something," Hessing observed lamely. "Maybe we should tie him up, or kill him in his sleep." Raben shook his head. *You too? I want him dead too, but in due course. Everyone on this quest solves every problem with mindless slaughter. So have the gods thus far.* "Yes," Hessing stated, watching the thief's reaction, "that would be dishonorable. We'll tie him up and then question him when he comes to." *And then kill him.* The noble rose from where he sat and walked to his nearby pack. Digging in it for only a moment he produced a rope. He then walked over to Strad and began tying him up. Arms, legs, both knotted together behind his back, the Kernishman wasn't going to be able to move one bit when he awoke. "There," Hessing said as he finished. "That skeleton messenger dealt me grievous wounds on several occasions. I know I may look a little over eager to punish Strad, but Thannon deserves no mercy by our hands. None!" Hessing's voice grew powerful as he said it.

"No argument from me," Raben agreed. "I fought it too. It just makes me suspicious. I was able to defeat the messenger in a way that it could never overcome, so now we have Strad. What could he do?" he asked, looking at the Kernishman's sword, where it lay on the ground. "Be an assassin? Against this party?" Raben shook his head again. "Not likely. What is his role?"

"I have no idea, Thief, but he won't get the chance to do it." Hessing sounded resolute. "I find that there are several among us that deserve little trust, though some of you hide it better than he did." Hessing watched Raben intently, waiting for the thief's reaction. Rather than humoring the noble with a response, Raben leaned back and let himself fall asleep.

My friend. Raben could hear the words in his sleep. *Wake up, my friend.* The thief rolled over and tried to get comfortable. He'd spent the remainder of the night trying to sleep. Hessing said that he would keep the watch until dawn, so Raben did his best to get much needed rest. Memories of Thantos, however, kept running through his mind, causing him to have terrible dreams in which he is damned for abandoning his only friends. *Wake up! You need to come with me.* Words that he had thought to Thantos. His thoughts seemed to be alive in his skull, arriving at the forefront of his consciousness without invitation. *Raben!*

He sat up, shaking violently. *Raben! My name was called. Raben, look over here!* The thief tried to calm himself. He raised his eyes and searched the area. He looked past the fire and could see Hessing. The noble was looking right at him, but looked away as soon as the thief noticed him. *Damn it, Raben! Look behind you.* He did, and there, blending into the canyon wall, almost invisible, was Thantos. The thief took measured breaths as his body succumbed to the need to be calm. *You survived! Come over here! My friend! Now! What can I do? No time! Come over here!* Raben clutched his head as thoughts, both his and Thantos' tumbled through his mind.

"Are you alright?" Hessing asked. "There is nothing nearby, if that's what you are worried about, and Strad is still firmly bound. I have checked several times." *Hessing!*

406

Sit there and be silent! Silence! No thoughts crashed into him for a few moments.

"I'm fine, I think," Raben answered. "I just need to walk a bit." Hessing arched an eyebrow as he looked at the thief. "Really, I'm fine." Raben pulled his sword from its sheath and held it away from his body where he let it drop from his grip. The blade immediately floated in the air next to him. "I'll be safe, even if I'm not personally up to the battle." Hessing shrugged his approval while Raben picked up an extra robe and walked from the fire light into the unlit obscurity of the canyon brush. As soon as he was sure he was covered from Hessing's vision, the thief began to walk in a semi circle, making his way into the logical path that Thantos would take. Once he was as close to the camp as he dared get, Raben sat down on the ground and waited. Even in the dark, he could see his hovering sword. It had a dim light of its own. It looked like a blade that had the slightest hint of fire in it from the forge. It was a deep cherry red. Seeing it this way, Raben feared touching it, afraid that it might actually have the heat that it appeared to have.

"My friend," the quiet hiss almost forced a yell from the thief as he concentrated on his sword. "My friend, I need help," Thantos said. "Come further away from the camp so that we can have light." *Light! Damn. I should have brought a lantern.* "Don't worry," the vampiric priest answered Raben's thought. "We'll be alright."

Thantos staggered away from the thief, leading him through the darkness. Raben only knew where the undead man was because the priest would let out a low hiss as he forced his broken body to place one foot in front of the other. Raben progressed slowly as he followed the vampiric priest through the darkness. *Really need a lantern.*

Only a moment after he'd thought it, a bright blue light erupted around the two men. *Hells! Too bright.* Raben covered his eyes with one hand and yanked out a sickle with his other. *Light! This is Talvo's light!*

"Yes," Thantos hissed, his bulging eye looking at Raben. "Talvo has allowed me one chance to save this trek, but I find it highly unlikely. The Meriss removed Gabriel from me, and in doing so, took any health that I had gained from him. I am still a vampire, and yet, still gain my spells. I will continue to gain them so long as I don't feed on the unwilling." Thantos lowered himself onto a large rock with a sigh. Seeing the battered and naked priest, Raben offered his extra robe. Thantos took it with an appreciative nod, and pulled the black robe on, tightening it around his slender frame. "In order to save the Dayquest, I am to allow only the prophesied one entry to the final temple of Talvo. The Well of Offering. It is there that the chosen one will offer himself to Talvo. It is strange. I know this is my mission from Him, yet I am not sure I want it. I think we all deserve to walk through the final archway and know the True Knowledge." Thantos held his bald head with both of his bony hands. "You, me, Urchin. How could I decide that we weren't allowed to walk the final part of this journey, while someone like Hessing could." *Urchin is gone.* Thantos looked up as soon as the thought came. "Gone!" he hissed. Raben nodded. "Last night?" Another nod. "Damn it! I knew he'd been corrupted by something. I knew it. He could feel it," Thantos hissed loudly. "Do you remember? He told us that he and I were going to die." *He'd been possessed by the white wizard.* Thantos sucked his breath in slowly, using the inhalation only as a moment to think. "We'll have to revisit that wizard one day." *If he survived last night.* Thantos nodded. "Do you still feel compelled to find him when the journey is done?" *Yes.* "He lives yet." *Could the old man have survived then?* "Not likely. Not after what I went through."

"Enough about all of that," Raben interrupted. "Tell me about Strad." Thantos looked at the thief curiously. "The sword he carries has the same symbol on it that the messenger of Thannon had on his armor." *Where did you get him, and why in all the Hells are you bonded to a member of Thannon's following?*

"I didn't know that," Thantos answered. "After I collapsed on the Shao plains, I awoke in Kernish, and Strad was there. He and Gabriel. Gabriel told me that he was a healer of sorts and that he could aid me. Strad came near me and offered a hand. I took it, and instantly I could feel that Gabriel was trying to merge some of his energy with mine. As he began, I feared death. I knew that I wouldn't survive, so I bent my will, which must have been more than they expected, to consuming Gabriel. Once they had begun, I decided that I must be the controlling force. So I trapped him in me, rather than being controlled by him. I know that you understand the reasons I did it. Somehow I became linked to Strad, and our healths are interrelated. If one of us is ill, we both feel it. If one of us is injured, we both know it. If one of us is trapped in thought," Thantos emphasized, "we are both." *That's why the Kernishman had said nothing for days on end.* Thantos nodded. "That's the reason he came with us, and that's all I really know about him."

"That calms me a little," Raben said. "Now tell me what help I can offer." *Did the blood actually help?* The priest nodded. *Gah! You should see yourself when you have it in your mouth.* A shiver climbed the thief's back.

"It saved my life, my friend. It did," Thantos said. "I need you to keep Hessing from killing Strad. I don't think I can survive his death right now. I know that both of you have been thinking about killing the man, but he needs to live. Our health is one." *Hells! He works for Thannon. He is the enemy, Thantos. What possible reasoning can I use to keep that honor-bound noble from killing an agent of evil?*

"I would suggest this rationale," Thantos offered. "If the two of you know that Strad is the agent of evil, and that Thannon will send no other agent until Strad dies, then at least you are controlling what form your enemy can take." The vampiric priest raised his hands as if he'd just performed a miracle.

"We don't know any of that, though," countered Raben.

"True," Thantos hissed, "but Hessing doesn't either." He stood up and walked over to Raben, grunting each time he had to force his slightly charred peg leg forward. "My friend, you have to understand, that I still distrust Hessing, and now I have even more reason to dislike Strad. We should use them to keep an eye on each other. Strad will do nothing that might cause me displeasure or pain. He feels it if it happens to me." *So he won't attack me or you?* Thantos indicated that he would not.

"Does he care for Hessing?" Raben asked purely for sake of knowing.

"Eh," Thantos began, as he reached out and leaned on the thief for support. "He doesn't really care one way or the other. He does think that Hessing is the safest of us all, protected. I can't disagree with that idea after all of the things that have happened to the rest of us in the course of this journey." *But I couldn't say he likes him either.* The thought slowly materialized. *He was a laborer and a sell sword. Not a real supporter of pompous rich knights.*

The thief nodded. "Are you going to come back to camp, or are you going to lay out here in the dust all night?" Raben asked as he looked at his friend. His missing eye looked terrible, his good eye was eerie to look upon nearly falling from his skull, his body was wasting away, and until moments ago he'd been without proper clothing. "Come back to the camp, my friend. Be warm for a while."

"Hessing won't react badly?" Thantos asked. "Attack me or anything like that?"

"I don't think so," Raben answered, sheathing his floating sword. "He left your destiny in fate's hands. He said that you'd be up and around by dawn if you were supposed to continue on the journey. You are. He'll be satisfied." Keeping Thantos close to him, the thief supported him as they began walking back to camp.

"Do you think Urchin is dead?" Thantos asked.

"I can't decide," Raben said. "I want him to be alive, but there were times as we came through the canyons that only could have been Urchin. You can see it in his eyes sometimes. That mirth and youth that should never have been in a man as old as he was." The thief thought about the old man and all of the childish things that he'd done. He'd stood in the rain naked, flailed in the dirt just to make a shape, kept everyone on their toes with his dry humor. "I want him to be alive, but I think he's gone."

"If so, I hope he has a great big pile of dirt to lie on," offered Thantos. *He'll be taken care of. He was a good friend.* "He was. I think Talvo put him in my life just to show me that there is such power in nature. I had heard tales of such cults, but always doubted that they were capable of doing any good."

"It seems that he was, at least," Raben agreed. The two men walked for a short while, weaving through the maze of bushes and canyon walls. "There's our camp fire." The thief urged Thantos forward as the flicker of the flames started to become visible through the brush, beckoning the two men. Pushing forward, they crashed through the thick undergrowth to the outside perimeter of the camp.

"Need help?" Hessing offered as soon as he could see them. He had a sword in each hand, as was his way. He had been ducked down behind some thick brush, but the moment he identified who was making all of the noise he heard, he stood up while sheathing his weapons.

"Only if you want to carry Thantos over to his bedroll," Raben said, only half joking. Without a word, Hessing walked forward and swept the nearly weightless priest from his feet and carried him to camp. Raben followed. Hessing gently laid Thantos on the noble's bedroll and covered him, head to toe, in a thick blanket.

"How did you know he was out there?" Hessing asked.

"A dream," Raben answered. "When I woke up, it was because of a dream, and so I walked out there, and he was up and around, but barely so. I helped him back to camp." The thief looked away from the noble as he answered.

"Strange," Hessing said. "This whole trek grows stranger by the moment. Strad has not moved or made a noise." The noble looked from Raben to Thantos and back. The priest was on his back, covered by the blanket, and unable to see the noble and the thief where they stood. "I had expected the Kernishman to change before now." Hessing nodded at Thantos. *The two are connected. What did you think would happen? What did I think would happen?* Raben shrugged. The noble worked his jaw as he thought through the situation. *Is he afraid? Angry?*

"We'll just have to keep an eye on him," Raben answered out loud as he walked over to Strad's unconscious form. "Can you check on him, Thantos? Whenever you feel like you can make it over here?" The priest raised his head from the ground and turned to look at Raben through the thick cover. "We should try and make the most of this situation." The thief could tell that Thantos was nodding weakly.

"What do you think you are doing, Thief?" Hessing was angry. His voiced was booming. "You can't feed a man to Thantos right under my nose." The noble stomped over to where the Kernishman lay. "He may be evil,"

Hessing thundered as he gestured to Strad, "but that does not mean that we toss him to a vampire. What does that make us?" The noble pointed an accusatory finger at Raben. "What if he is the unwilling servant of a force he doesn't understand?" *What?* The shock that he felt showed through onto the thief's face. Hessing stared at him for a moment, and then stalked away, shaking his head while he fumed.

What if he is the unwilling servant of a force he doesn't understand? Raben let the question slide through his mind, trying to get a grip on exactly what it meant that Hessing had asked it. *He knows something more than he has let on. I have been the servant of a force that I don't understand. Has Thantos? Yes. His god is a mystery to him, or was. Urchin? No. Hessing? Who do you serve Lord Von Hessing? Yourself? I think not. There must be someone out there, something. Why would you trek so faithfully? Duty? Are you that good?*

"No," Thantos said, his voice a light gasp of air. "He too serves someone. His might be the worst situation of us all." The priest's head fell back to the ground. *Maybe. But I doubt it, my friend.* Raben moved next to Thantos and reached down to him. He pulled the blanket back and touched the vampiric man's forehead. The priest's eye opened displaying glazed slivers of yellow and then closed again.

"Do you sleep?" Raben asked. *Yes. I must.* He felt the answer in his mind. He shook his head. It felt wrong to have another's thoughts come through to him like that. The thief pulled the blanket back over Thantos and stood up, looking around himself. Strad lay unconscious. Hessing had walked away only moments earlier, but as Raben slowly inspected his surroundings, he saw that the noble had left camp altogether. *What the greeching Hells! If you disappear again, Hessing, I will kill you! Damn it all!* The thief knew that he was in no condition to fight, yet expected that he would have to once again rely on only himself should trouble arise. *Maybe he does have more to worry about than we do. Maybe.*

Raben sat in front of the fire, watching the dancing flames as they stretched upwards. The warmth felt good on his skin. He moved nearer, keeping his legs just far enough from the fire that they didn't feel like they were burning, but close enough that his robes became full of the fire's intense warmth. Every small noise caused the thief to look around searchingly. He felt exposed and vulnerable. Reaching for his sword, he took it from the air, where it had faithfully bobbed the whole time, and held it out to his side.

"As much a blessing as it has been my curse," the thief said as he released it again. Dutifully, the blade rose over Raben, keeping a magical watch over him as he obsessed over the ever changing pattern of flames before him. *Unwilling servant. The noble has a problem that he has not shared with the rest of us. Strad's troubles become clearer with each moment. How he arrived there? Who knows? Thantos, I understand. My own troubles remain mysterious at best. I need to talk to her. I need to find a way to die. Someone innocent that I can kill. How do you define innocent?* The thief's eyes wandered over to Strad. *That would only hurt Thantos.* His vision swept back to the fire. *Urchin. Why the hell aren't you here? Why did you have to go when you did? I need your help, old man.* The sound of bushes being crushed caused the thief to leap to his feet, rotating until his back was to the fire. His sword bobbed listlessly by his side. *Hessing!* It sounded big enough and clumsy enough to be the warrior, but as the thief rose to his feet, it stopped. Raben quickly brought two sickles out, their reddish blades glinting menacingly in the firelight.

Raben sprinted to the nearby canyon wall. As he did so, the crashing sound resumed. *Chasing!* The thief smashed himself against the wall, keeping it at his back. His eyes searched the leaping shadows and erratic shafts of firelight for the source of the sound, but as he stopped, it too stopped. *Damn.* Slowly, the sound came to him again, but this time it sounded as though the creature was moving more slowly. It crushed through the bushes to Raben's right as it made its way in his direction. The sound grew louder as it neared. Watching the brush shake at the limit of the firelight, Raben crouched and prepared himself for a short ferocious attack. He wouldn't last very long in combat. His body ached from the mistreatment he'd been subjected to in the last few days. He was sluggish and in desperate need of sleep. The bushes just before the thief began to crack and split. He held his sickles at the ready, hoping that his magical blade would be able to defeat whatever was coming.

Tensing his muscles, preparing to spring, Raben gasped when he saw his enemy. It was a messenger of Thannon. A lich stood before him, its lavender eyes blazing in the night. Its bare teeth shone in a wicked smile that stole the confidence from the thief. Climbing from the midst of a large bush, the skeleton stood before the crouched man and pointed one of its segmented fingers at him.

"The map," it said, its hollow voice carrying through the air with unnatural strength. "We must have the map." The lich stepped forward, and anger preceded him. Raben could feel the hatred of the skeleton as he had before. "We must have the map." The thief raised his weapons, preparing to defend himself with what little ability remained in him. He looked quickly to his floating sword, but the magical blade sat by his side, subdued.

Raben nearly became dizzy with remembrance. He quickly cast a spell of protection on himself, the same spell that had rendered the lich unable to touch him on the Shao plains. After uttering the spell, the thief stood up, feeling more confident.

"I have no such map, and if you do not flee I will be forced to destroy you." He sounded weak after the force of the lich's voice, but felt that his words were full of danger for the messenger. "Leave now. You cannot harm me in any way." Both man and lich turned their heads as the sound of another figure crashing through the underbrush broke into their conversation. Moments later, Hessing broke through the bushes and into the light. He held a sword in each hand and walked angrily at the lich.

"Haven't had enough, fool?" The voice of the lich thundered as it turned to face Hessing, disregarding Raben completely. The thief immediately grasped his floating sword and attacked the skeletal messenger. Swinging furiously, he hacked at the lich's legs.

"I said now, fool!" Hessing's voice shook Raben into wakefulness. The thief immediately sprung to life in the firelight, looking for the messenger of Thannon, but only the night and Hessing were there to greet him.

"Calm down, man," Hessing said. "It was another dream. You must have nodded off sitting by the fire. I just got back. I had to get away from this mess for a while, and when I tried to wake you up, you wouldn't. I only yelled to make sure you weren't dying or bespelled." The noble ushered the thief to a bedroll. "Sleep, Thief. It is a short while before dawn, and we must move then. You'll be worthless if you aren't at all rested. I'll keep watch, and sleep tomorrow."

Raben nodded, not remembering the point when he must have fallen asleep. *It seemed so real. What is real? Is this?* He looked around. *It could be illusion.* He lay down on the bedroll, watching Hessing as he did. The big man looked calm. Raben saw that Hessing sat exactly where the thief did when he watched the fire. *Sleep.* He did.

Coughing brought Raben to Thantos. The priest sat up suddenly after sleeping halfway through the day. He was hacking and gasping as he tore the blanket from his head. Shielding his eyes, the vampiric man crawled towards the canyon wall where the direct sunlight could not touch him. He stopped several times as his body heaved in an attempt to vomit, but there was nothing inside of the undead man to bring up.

Raben walked with him, trying to hold the blanket over Thantos in order to shield him from the sun. The thief had been awake for some time, and convinced Hessing that they would move out when at least three of the party awakened. The warrior grunted and left, saying that he was going to range the path they would be taking. Since then, Raben watched the two sleeping men while the sun rose into the sky. Only when the light of the rising sun crept down the walls, onto the canyon floor where it could hit Thantos directly, did either man stir. Thantos fled the sun and only stopped his convulsive fit once he was sitting in the shade cast by the outcropping of rock that he'd sat under two nights ago, before the Meriss attacked. He held himself tightly, burying his head between his knees.

"Are you going to be alright, my friend?" Raben asked, unsure of what he should be doing. "Is there something I can do?" Thantos said nothing, but pointed away past Raben. The thief was hurt that he was being sent away from

417

his friend until he looked to where the priest was pointing. Strad lay in the sun, struggling against the many knotted ropes that Hessing had bound him with. *Help him and help me.* The thought appeared in Raben's mind, jolting him into activity. He ran over to Strad and knelt next to the man.

"Calm yourself," he told the Kernishman. "You have many things to explain before we untie you." Strad continued his attempt to stretch and break the ropes, but Hessing had once been a sailor, and a good one. His knots were solid. "You can't escape. And if you do, I'll be forced to kill Thantos." Strad stopped, and stared at Raben, his dark eyes showing the anger and fear that filled the man. "Yes, we know much, now that we have all been judged. Not the least noticeable thing was your sword." Quickly moving to where the sword lay, Raben lifted the weapon into the sunlight. "This symbol. Do you know what it is?" Strad shook his head. "Really? You've been carrying it the entire time we've known you." The Kernishman continued shaking his head. *Shame, anger, or confusion.* "Are you going to say anything?" Strad shook his head more violently this time, tears beginning to shimmer in his eyes.

The Kernishman's mouth opened and then closed. He opened it again, and a hollow moan came out. Then a number of jumbled and awkward sounds poured from him before he gave up and looked up at Raben with panic in his eyes. The thief could sense that something was terribly wrong. Looking over to Thantos, the thief's feeling was confirmed. The priest was staring hard at the two men, intent on every sound and movement. *His mouth.* Raben shook off the thought as he looked back to Strad, where he lay terrified.

"Open your mouth," he ordered. Strad shook violently at the request, tears pouring down his face. *Poor bastard. What has he gotten himself into? Maybe I'm not in the worst trouble after all.* Raben tapped the hilt of his sword as he leaned over his prisoner. The Kernishman opened his mouth, and Raben leaned in to inspect it, seeing if there was something wrong. Using a dagger to reflect sunlight into Strad's mouth, the thief fell away almost immediately. While his mouth seemed fine, Strad's tongue had been shredded. *Cut out?* Raben collapsed when Thantos' question hit him. It wasn't missing. *His tongue is shredded into strips of flesh. It fills his mouth like worms.* Raben's stomach heaved inside of him. He tried to regulate his breathing. *He cannot speak. I'm surprised he can breathe.* The thief's stomach lurched again, bringing up his breakfast. He vomited until there was nothing left, and then lay on the ground, struggling to calm his body. *What in the Hells could do such a thing? Is that the price for opposing our masters? Great gods! The cruelties I have seen while walking on Your quest.*

Raben couldn't name the reasons that this injury bothered him so. Was it the effect of it? Being cut off from the ease of communication with all other people? Was it the way it left you, almost addled when others regarded you? The absolute malice that had to drive such an attack, and the time and mind set that the attacker had to have? *That is evil. Torturous, cruel, worse than death. Evil. In all the Hells, what could do such a thing?*

Raben couldn't even look at Strad without feeling his nausea coming back. He wanted to cut the man free, yet felt that there was something now completely wrong around him. Cutting Strad free had a strong probability of creating more difficulties rather than simplifying them. *Get a hold of the situation. Where is that fool of a noble? He has probably left the lot of us behind. He would just want to kill the Kernishman anyway.*

The thief climbed back to his feet, forcing himself to not look at the Kernishman where he lay. He walked back in Thantos' direction, stopping at his pack, where he picked up a water skin. Turning back towards Strad, Raben tossed the skin to the bound man. The Kernishman rolled onto his side, but was unable pick up the bottle. Sympathy overwhelmed him and the thief walked over and cut Strad's arms free. With his arms free, the Kernishman took the water skin with both hands and guzzled the contents. Raben backed away from him, making sure that there were no weapons close by, and then sat down with Thantos in the shade.

"That wound, my friend. I've never seen anything that required so much hatred and disregard for life." Talking about it made him feel ill. He began taking deep breaths. "Can you feel it? Can you speak?" *Say something!*

"Yes, I feel it, and yes I can speak," Thantos hissed. "The wound is new. Strad got it last night. He woke up, and his eyes were covered. They flayed his tongue, and then knocked him unconscious. He doesn't know who did it."

"Last night," Raben said in disbelief. "Hessing was on guard all night. There was no time for anyone to do anything like that. Wouldn't it have awakened you if that was going on, anyway?" the thief asked.

"Our enemies are not simple creatures, my friend," Thantos answered. "They may have carried him far to exact this punishment on him. It may have been the discovery of the symbol on his sword that brought the punishment. Look at the Meriss. Think of the power they had. What if your enemies are like them?" The priest's voice fell quiet as he finished. "The wound made me ill, as well. I could feel it."

"It wasn't the sun then?" asked Raben. "That made you wake up gagging?" Thantos shook his head. *What if my enemies are like them? Boiling gods! What can we even do against that, if our enemies are like the Meriss?*

"This link was never so strong before, but it was suddenly becoming aware of Strad's condition that made me sick. He is terribly unhealthy," Thantos said. "I never felt his fear during an attack, or felt his thoughts as he ranged the plains above. I think the Meriss treated him harshly. It seems that any impurities of his soul were ripped away as well, and that may well have been more than he could handle." Thantos looked at Raben knowingly. *He might lose his mind.* "And his discovery was obviously far more than his master could handle."

"I fell asleep," Raben blurted out. "I let it happen. I was on watch and fell asleep. I even dreamt of a damned messenger of Thannon. I sat right there and let them come and torture him. Greeching Hells!" *Damn it all. How can we survive?*

"We must survive," Thantos hissed forcefully. "We must. And you will be the one to make sure of it."

Nothing was said for some time. Raben stood up and walked over to Strad. The Kernishman had been weeping since he'd finished the water. The thief pitied him, and cut him free. Needing time away from everyone else, he then walked a good distance away where he could practice with his weapons. Taking his robes off, the thief stood in the sun, feeling the warmth. *We have been cold for so much of this quest.* He stretched his arms out slowly, and then began his dance. He purposefully went through the motions of attack and defense, allowing his body to work the patterns almost automatically. *Where is Hessing? How greeching long did he think we would sleep?* He swept his sword horizontally at shoulder height. *He'd better not turn up missing again.* His sickle spun from his hand, cutting several limbs from a nearby bush. *We must survive. Pure magic.* Another sickle leapt into the thief's hand while his sword arced through the air over his head. He then let go of the enchanted blade, and it began bobbing next to him. *All magic can be altered or reversed.* Raben tore another curved blade from its sheath, and crisscrossed his sickles like shears in front of himself before he threw them both through a dense shrub. Branches dropped from the bush as he came to a rest. *She has to kill me as I exit the final temple of Talvo, or was it when I was entering? More practice.* He whipped two daggers from their wrist sheaths and thrust them into a bush before he parried and rolled away from an imagined attack. *My friends are dead or dying. What can we do?* He stopped his practice and looked around. It was a beautiful day. *The only thing wrong with this day is us. Even Strad is now mangled. Only Hessing remains. He truly must be the chosen for the Dayquest. Where in the blazes is he?*

Am I supposed to finish this damned quest? Would I live long if I tried to walk away from it now? Or would they jump into my head and control me, forcing me to pursue this journey. I am pure magic. I am directed magic. Magic can be reversed. My direction can be reversed. I can be reversed. By dying right now. What happens to me if I die without killing someone else? Am I truly dead? Or am I back with whoever created me? What does it matter if she were to kill me at the temple if I had several lives stored up? I need to see her, talk to her. She must be magic. I need to die to talk to her. We need people. We need to leave here.

Raben watched as Strad made it to his feet and fumbled his way over to Thantos. The Kernishman collapsed next to the priest. Thantos seemed less than alarmed. *He is harmless as long as Thantos is alive. Servant to a force he doesn't understand. Hessing knew something. He feared. He tied that man up so tight that no one could untie him. What was he afraid of? Should I be afraid?* Thantos leaned over Strad. Raben winced as he watched, turning away from the two men. *That is a priest of Talvo. What a twisted man! I am no better. I fed the damned idiot when he lay dying in the hole. Greech! We need to go. Where is the noble? Fool. Even Urchin wanted to leave him behind.*

Raben spun on his heel and marched back over to the camp. He pulled his last clean robe from his pack. It was brand new and had no holes. He would have to wear the clothes that he'd purchased to look like a noble if this robe was destroyed. Thantos had apparently already finished what he was doing by the time Raben cleaned up and put his robe on. The priest looked far stronger and more alert, and surprisingly, so did Strad. *That's wrong.*

"No," Thantos answered aloud. "Our strengths are combined. As is our blood." The priest climbed to his feet, and then helped Strad to his. "So, leaving without Hessing?"

"Not really," Raben answered unconvincingly. "We ought to run into him as we go. He's ahead of us, and should be returning by now." The thief began putting all of his equipment back into his pack in an ordered manner. "Besides, the man is like the plague. No matter how far we ran or tried to escape him, he'd catch up with us and make us miserable anyway."

"He is too lucky," Thantos said, echoing something that Raben felt on several occasions. "It's as though he is protected by something very powerful, though I refuse to say whether it is good or evil."

"Whichever it is, he is going to reach the end of this journey," Raben said. "He is supposed to make it, and we are not. Before he died, Urchin once told me that I would die on this journey. He told me that anyone who wasn't supposed to go on the trek would end up dead. I think the man had information beyond his abilities."

"Perhaps," hissed Thantos. "Does that mean you're turning back when you have the chance?" Raben looked to the priest, looking for the sarcasm, but Thantos appeared to be serious.

"I've thought about it, but it seems that I have been chosen to walk this road wherever it leads," the thief said. "I might as well find out how far it goes. You never know. Maybe the people who built it did a poor job."

"Optimism," Thantos observed with a wry smile. "Has lying always been easy for you, my friend?" The vampire pulled one of the packs onto his back. "You have noticed, of course, that the noble took his pack with him when he went, correct?"

"Yeah, he said he might need the ropes and food and other things," Raben said. "And it wouldn't bother me if he decided to try and make it on his own. Either way, this is all beyond our control for now. Whatever the fool decided, we should follow. Based on the past weeks, he'd be dead in a few days if he went alone."

"Well then," said Thantos, his voice cold, "let's hope he went alone."

Raben focused on the clicking sound as he walked. Travel was easy. Someone had taken great pain to build the road through the canyon, and the farther they marched, the more maintained the road was. Each of its flat paving stones had been meticulously interlocked and then packed with some type of filler that made the road incredibly smooth to walk on. Were it not for the worn condition of the travelers, they would have made the best time yet on their journey.

The thief spent the whole night stepping methodically to the sound of Thantos walking. Each time the vampiric priest brought his peg leg down onto the hard paving stones, a loud click snapped through the night air. It was the cadence of the slowest member of the party, and it was the rhythm to which Raben marched. The sound was a constant reminder that his friend was nearby. The thief had never before felt so grateful to have someone near. Urchin had been the person he'd most readily turned to, and somewhere in the background of nearly every situation, Thantos had been there. Now, however, Urchin was gone, probably dead, and Thantos had very nearly died as well. Hearing him walking only a few paces ahead was the only comfort Raben had.

It was seemingly true for Strad as well. They had let him walk with Thantos since dusk. Walking through the night, Raben worried that the man might try to attack or escape, but Thantos reminded the thief that an attack was out of the question because of the link between the Kernishman and the priest. As far as escape, Thantos could feel that as well. Strad displayed no want to pursue either idea, but walked with the vampiric priest, staring at the ground and all but dragging a hooded lantern along side of himself. *Good thing he isn't armed anymore.* Raben held the emblazoned sword up, angling it until the dim light from Strad's lantern reflected across the symbol of Thannon. *How did that man ever end up in the grips of Gul Thannon? How did any of us end up where we are? And where is the noble?*

Raben wondered often about the location of Hessing since he'd left camp early in the day. It was now the middle of the night and they'd neither heard nor seen any sign of him. That was less than surprising considering the road they walked on. It was so well built, and clear of bushes and obstructions, that no sign of Hessing's passing could ever be found unless he intentionally marked it, and he hadn't. The strange part was that the noble was simply going to travel ahead to scout out the trail, and that seemed to hardly indicate being gone as long as he had been. In fact, now that Raben was himself walking along the easy road, it seemed that only one of two things could have resulted from Hessing's scouting mission. Either he had been taken by the enemy, or the noble had decided to carry on the quest without the others, feeling that he was the single prophesied member of the Dayquest. *The man walks and breathes to do his duty, but would he simply abandon us in order to perform the quest? Would he abandon the helpless? Helpless. A vampire, an agent of Thannon, and a thief.* Raben scowled at the realization. *Abandon. Cut away the impurities. If he left us, it is not because he was bound by duty, but because we are the wretched dangers that the whole quest is designed to fight.*

"Go easy, my friend," Thantos hissed through the night. "We have borne the noble to his destination, if we are even near." *If we are even near. The end. How will Hessing even know? Map!* Raben fell instantly to one knee and unslung his pack, dropping it on the ground before him.

"Strad, get over here," the thief commanded. "Bring the light. Open it up so that I can see." The Kernishman did so, and as he opened the shutters around the flames, Thantos' hungry eye gathered the light.

Raben barely noticed while he began to ransack his own backpack. He dug through the clothing and equipment rummaging past it in order to get to the bottom where he kept the map case. He threw his blanket onto the stony road and continued digging past it. *Damn it! We have been betrayed, my friend! Is betrayal part of the damned quest, part of the greeching prophecy? Is that how it ends? Nothing. No map, no map case.* Raben began taking every piece of equipment from the pack and letting it fall to the ground, hoping that he'd simply missed the map in his speed, but that was not the case. Kneeling before the other two men, he glared angrily into the empty backpack, hating the missing map case. Hating himself for not being more alert, and most of all, hating Von Hessing, who had obviously planned the whole thing out. *You will die on my blade, Hessing. It will be your head that I take back to Liveport. Damn it!*

"We will still make it, my friend," Thantos said. "Put your things away and let us continue on the trek that only we deserve to finish." The priest leaned over and picked up a small metal box that Raben had dropped. "Here," he hissed. The thief took the box and then began placing his equipment back into his pack. Thantos began folding robes and the heavy blanket that Raben had thrown onto the road. Strad stood frozen, holding his lantern while the other two men worked.

"How can we finish this quest if we don't have the map anymore?" Raben asked, unwilling to think the problem through. "We aren't going to accidentally make it to the end of this journey, my friend. We will need to have some direction before all of this is over, and Hessing took the only known copy of the map." *How can we ever hope to beat him? He's healthy, luckier than a rich man, and he has the only map.*

"Quit your whining and remember where we are," Thantos hissed. "The purest and most honorable followers of Talvo lived in the north. Many of their souls fell into these canyons while they defended the north against the armies and magics of the white wizards. If anyone has information on the whereabouts of the one temple of Talvo that we need," said the vampire, "it will be those that we now march to find." Thantos handed Raben the last of his things to place in the open pack and motioned for the thief to hurry up.

"And these pure folk are simply going to leap to our aid?" Raben asked. "Have you looked at us lately? We are the enemy. Hessing is right. We look like we should be walking with the dark one's messenger." *Hells!* He shot a glance to Strad. *We are walking with the greeching dark lord's messenger.*

"Nonsense!" Thantos barked. "I am still a priest of Talvo. You are in a clean robe. Strad needs to be cleaned and clothed and we are three travelers in need that they must help."

"Must help?" Raben snapped. "Why must they help us? Because you are a priest? You're a vampire, my friend." The thief sucked in a deep breath. "I know who you are, but they are only going to see the most suspicious looking priest of their order that has ever come through this canyon. So why won't they question, and why must they help?"

"Because," sighed Thantos. "We did make it through this canyon." The undead priest spun on his peg leg and began walking away from the thief. "They'll already know we're coming, and they'll already know that we must have faced the god-given guardian in the canyon. They must help, or at least not hinder. It may even be their decision to make, but I think they will help."

Raben shook his head as Thantos walked away, sending clicks off through the night. Strad began to follow, taking the light with him. After a moment, the thief climbed up off of the stone road, and began to trail the other two.

The situation was maddening to him. He felt that he'd fought through so many obstacles to make it to the end of the quest, that once they were finally arriving at some serious progress, losing the map was a death blow. It was only after the initial shock of Hessing's action wore off that Raben realized how the future of the journey might feel to the others that walked with him. *I apologize, my friend. There is no way that this can be easy for you. An undead priest of Talvo walking into the purest of your order.*

Raben marched mechanically through the night contemplating the difficulties that Thantos might face when he is confronted by what can only amount to the most righteous and strictest members of the priesthood of Talvo. *What do you tell them? Will they know he is a vampire? How can he explain his reasoning? Will they ever accept him, or care for what he is trying to do, or will they scorn him openly? Perhaps fear or even capture him. Would I, were I not part of this ridiculous quest?*

He thought about it as he walked, but he found that every time he tried to rationalize the terrible state of Thantos and the rest of the party, the reasons always amounted to fears and desires and personal failings. *They will only understand if they have been beset by evil themselves. If they have not, we will only look like an evil to defend themselves against.*

"My friend," came Thantos' voice. "There is a building ahead." The vampiric hiss broke up Raben's thoughts, but he felt that that was probably for the better. He'd been driving himself into a deeper and deeper depression as he tried to work out the explanation that the party could give to a truly pure following of Talvo. He was unable to come up with any explanation that might assuage the fears that any sensible person would have after seeing the beleaguered party. *If they won't entertain the truth, we have nothing.* "The building," Thantos persisted, patiently waiting until Raben finished his thoughts.

"Why don't I look into it while you two stay back," Raben said. *Yes.* The thief blinked away the answer, the priest's thought arriving like a shadow in his mind. "Just speak, Thantos. Those thoughts will one day drive me insane." He turned from the priest to the Kernishman. "And shutter that lantern." Strad did.

As soon as it was dark, Raben pulled his weapon from its sheath and held it in both hands before him. He began trotting up the road toward the structure. He only knew it was there from the dim outline of reddish light that formed a square framework around each of the large shuttered windows that adorned the front of the three story building. If the thief had any fears about what lay inside, they were quickly allayed by the sounds and smells that reached him as he began approaching it.

Laughter and talk poured from the warmly lit inside. A fire obviously warmed all of those lucky enough to inhabit the place. The smell of oven baked bread and roasted meat reached through the air pulling him ever closer. He could see that a porch had been built onto the front of the building, and several chairs sat on it. Children looked to be sitting in them, rocking slowly as the night wore on around them. *Little late for kids. Nearly dawn.* Raben slid closer and closer to the massive structure, trying to remain wary should anyone suddenly emerge from the festivity that noisily carried on inside.

"Yer a graceful fellow, but ye don't know nothing about dwarves if yer going to try and sneak past us in the night," announced a deep gravelly voice. Raben immediately searched around himself. The only people near him were the kids on the porch. Otherwise, he thought he was alone. "Up here, ye fool of a human. On the porch. Yer hopeless, it's true."

Raben kept looking into the darkness, but this time it was quite obvious that the voice had come from up on the porch. Knowing that he was caught, the thief began making his way to the wooden platform.

"What's yer name, human?" asked the voice. It sounded like an old man, but the force of it was hale, as though it was coming from a man of middle age. "Yer name," it demanded. "Was a simple enough question. Even fer ye." Laughter came from a number of places scattered across the porch.

"I am called Raben," said the thief. He fought the want to give a false name, but it seemed that he was in the one place where lying could really get him into trouble.

"Well," said the deep voice. "I am called Andragin."

"And Mule head," added another voice. Laughter.

"And Minesister," added another.

"Let's not forget," came yet another voice. "Dullaxe." Laughter boomed from the porch, pouring past Raben in a comforting and strange current that let him feel at ease. He lowered his weapon.

"Pardon me, but I have never known your kind. I thought you all to be children," Raben said. "What are you?" *Dwarves. The noble had said something of them when we had first walked onto the road in the canyon.*

"We are the oldest race in Reman, human. We are the stone cutting dwarves that taught yer kind how to house themselves, build roads and sewers, and make weapons and armor, but in yer haste, ye've all managed to forget."

"That's wonderful!" Raben exclaimed. *This is incredible.* "Are you followers of Talvo?" he asked. *We made it! After traveling through all of that mess, and being cut apart and nearly killed. We made it.*

Soft laughter rippled across the porch and then a soft blue light followed it. *The light of Talvo.* "Yes, we are followers of Talvo. Yet another thing that we taught to yer kind that was lost over the years. We have defended the cause of Talvo for centuries upon centuries, against evil and ambition, and defend it still we do," Andragin said, his deep voice booming with pride.

As the light grew, Raben could see the speaker. He looked like an old man. His beard was full, long and grey. He had eyebrows that stood out over his eyes, and looked so bushy that they should impair his ability to see. The dwarf's shoulders were broad, even wider than Hessing's, and his arms were massive and thick with muscles. The dwarven man stood only two reaches high and wore a chain mail shirt that reached down to his knees. From beneath it came robust legs that looked almost misshapen from the muscle that filled them out.

"So," Andragin challenged, "how do we look?" The dwarf leapt up to his feet, leaving his chair behind. He held a double bladed axe that was almost a reach wide from blade to blade. He had a black steel cap on his head and his mail jingled quietly as he moved. With his first step, his heavy boots sounded out on the wooden porch. "We are the warriors of Talvo. We are the army that is called when no other can defend what is right and good. We are a family of folk so old that we have seen the making of this world, and will live to see it break apart one day. Why are you here?" The dwarf stumped across the porch and now stood on the stairs, eyeing the thief with huge dark eyes that glittered brightly under the bushy brows that stuck out over them. He jabbed a thumb at Raben as he waited for an answer.

"You look stronger and happier than any people I have ever seen," Raben answered truthfully. "I have come from a human city many leagues to the south in search of a destination I know nothing about, but want to attain more than anything in my life. I am a member of the Dayquest." With the word, everything went silent. Slowly, murmuring began on the porch behind the dwarf. No sooner had it begun, than it stopped.

"Are ye?" asked Andragin. "Well then, ye have seen troubles uncounted, haven't ye?" The dwarf nodded after his own question. He jumped down the stairs, landing heavily on the grassy lawn below, and then walked straight at the thief. "Ye were preceded by a warrior, but he hadn't the key to the journey. He said it was stolen. He said that the sword of the quest was taken from him before the quest even began. He asked that we kill whoever had it that it might be restored to the glory of Talvo." The dwarf held his axe out in front of himself. It looked huge. The shaft was as tall as he was. Raben stepped back, suddenly getting the impression that the dwarf was preparing for an attack.

"I seek no quarrel. I have been part of this quest only to find the truth about myself, and to aid my friends," Raben pleaded, his voice giving out somewhat as the dwarf neared. *He's going to attack. Damn you, Hessing!*

"Raise yer weapon, human," Andragin ordered. His axe leapt into action, cleaving through the air. Raben was faster, and metal rang out as he blocked the dwarf's swing. The thief kicked at the dwarf, but his foot was deflected by the long handle of the axe. The dwarf charged forward, ramming a huge shoulder into the unbalanced thief, sending him rolling. Raben leapt up and waited. The dwarf was already charging with his axe over his head. The thief let him swing, jumping back out of the range of the blade. As it hacked past his chest, Raben trapped the weapon to the ground with his sword and punched the dwarf in the jaw.

Pain sped up the thief's arm as he connected with the bony jaw of the dwarf. Andragin only grinned and bashed his helmet into Raben's throat. Falling back, the thief lifted his sword. He gasped for breath as the dwarf charged forward yet again.

"We don't get tired, human," yelled Andragin as he hurled his body at his opponent. Spinning and ducking, the thief used the momentum of the battle-crazed dwarf to throw him to the ground. Raben leapt in the air over Andragin and pointed his sword downward, putting his entire weight behind the leaping thrust, but the dwarf rolled to the side, leaving only the broad blade of his mighty axe under Raben. The thief landed, straddling the double edged blade, and Andragin swept upward with the axe. Raben tumbled sideways, and narrowly escaped being cloven in two. He let go of his sword, tearing two sickles from their sheaths. Backing away from Andragin, Raben prepared to dice the insane dwarf when he charged again, but he stood several paces away. He raised his huge axe above himself and then, using his entire body, he hurled the massive axe at Raben. Without his sword, the thief used the two sickles to try and deflect the heavy weapon.

Both of the small curved blades were swept from his hands as the axe whipped by. Raben immediately brought daggers out in their place. The dwarf began to charge forward, but the thief's now floating sword poised itself between him and the oncoming dwarven warrior.

"Ye have the key to the quest," Andragin said, his voice showing no sign of weariness. "And it fights for ye." The dwarf held out his right hand, and his axe suddenly appeared in it. A heavy and sudden stillness filled the air. The dwarven warrior watched the blade quiver as it reached in his direction, pushing the magical boundaries of its nature. Suddenly, the weapon fell back, bobbing lazily at Raben's right side.

"Enter our home and let us talk about yer journey," Andragin said, unexpectedly. "Are you alone, or is there a small army of humans hiding in the canyons back there?"

"There are two more of us," Raben said between breaths. *Greeching dwarf. Attack and then just expect me to make pleasant.* "They are hiding, because we had no idea what manner of creature lived here, and after the canyon, we needed caution." *Blazing insane! I would have preferred a hug or if you had just said hello.*

"Go find yer companions, and then feel at home with us," Andragin said as he walked up to Raben. He extended his left hand. "Well fought, human. Ye'd have lost, but I'd have bled for it." *We might have to see about that.* Raben began turning away from the dwarf.

Just then, a number of the dwarves on the porch called out as they armed themselves for combat. Raben spun, claiming his sword from the air, ready to face the threat. A dark figure was sitting on the top step of the porch. It was Thantos. The thief lowered his weapon. Andragin charged past. Raben reached out to stop him, and to say something.

"Wait!" Thantos hissed. "I have come to assist you." The shattered man sprang to his feet and lifted his arms skyward. His pale body was radiating a dim blue light from the power of Talvo. Thantos chanted a spell as he slowly wove his hands through the air. His thready, yet unwavering, voice gathered strength as a number of dwarves closed in on him.

Just as Andragin arrived in front of the vampiric priest, another dwarf loomed behind him. Each of them reached for the stranger, preparing to rip him from the porch, but stopped as they did. A great pillar of white light erupted from him, shedding itself unbearably onto the porch and across the yard. Each of the dwarves turned away from it, raising their arms to shield their eyes, as did Raben. *Greeching Hells!* Only a moment after it began, darkness reclaimed the night. Even the bluish light of Talvo was now gone.

"I offered the true light of Talvo," Thantos said, his voice cutting through the silence. "None of you could look upon it. None of us are so whole and at one with our devotion to Him that we may accept the sight of His power without shying away." A sphere of blue light lit the yard again. It came from the priest's left hand. He held it high over his head. "I am no different. I have broken the body I was given. I have forsaken the vows that I took to enter His service. I am far from the symbol of the pure warrior that Talvo and the priesthood have asked me to be, yet still I fight for Him, and still I fight the darkness, though I might easily be mistaken as a part of it." He paused. "I am not!" The ground trembled with the force of Thantos' voice. "I serve Talvo by the sacrifice of my body, my mind, and my soul, as do my companions. Put us to no further trial, and doubt us not!" Again the ground vibrated with the resonance of the priest's voice. "Or you contend with His power." The blue light vanished and darkness fell again.

"By the strong arm I hammer with," swore one of the dwarves, "I will trust His power."

"Talvo has blessed us," said another.

"Priest," came Andragin's voice. "Fear none of us. Your display was more proof than we could ask for that you are a servant of Talvo. We will aid you as we can, but I fear we may have grievously harmed you." The door to the large building opened up, letting the warm yellow light from the fire inside spill out. "Let us go in and I will explain."

All of the stout dwarves on the porch stood motionless, allowing Thantos the right to enter first. Each of them bowed, or touched their forehead as he passed, according him great respect. The priest entered the warm inn, and sat close to the fire. He still had not recovered from the attack of the Meriss despite having drunk the blood of both Raben and Strad. *I doubt they serve your vintage here, my friend.*

Raben entered with the dwarves and made his way to the table where Thantos was seated. It was a huge stone block that had been smoothed on top. The benches were made likewise. In fact, the entire interior of the inn was carved of stone. The bar and each of the stools and benches were stone that had been cut and shaped until it suited the skilled eye of a dwarven craftsmen. The walls too, were made of stone. Raben couldn't even see a seam. The thief couldn't imagine where one could find a single piece of rock large enough to carve an entire building. *These dwarves must have carried an entire damned mountain to build this place.*

"I am weak from the casting," Thantos said as soon as Raben sat down. "If they need explanations and answers, then you give them." The priest bowed his head, staring at the polished grey top of the table. "I will send you thoughts if you do not know what it is they seek."

"Fine," Raben answered. "Is there anything that I can get you in order to improve your health? Water, food?" Thantos looked up at him, and while both knew the answer, neither of them so much as even thought it. Asking the dwarves for a cup of blood might ruin things. *You told them you were different, but we shouldn't strain our welcome.*

Thantos nodded. He looked terrible. His hair had all been burned off during the attack of the Meriss. His eye patch was charred, as was his peg leg. His skin was pale with a few bruised blotches on it, making him look diseased, or long dead. Were it not for his constant movement, he would easily look like a cadaver. And the only clothes he had to wear were the black robes that Raben had given him. Both of them were robed in black. *We do look evil, my friend.*

"So," Andragin interrupted Raben's thoughts. "Where was it that ye came from?"

The burly dwarf sat down at the same table as Raben and Thantos along with another of his kind. Andragin's skin was a deep tan color, from being outside almost constantly. The other dwarf was more careworn and a little paler. *He works inside.* The second dwarf's hair and beard were brown, and he seemed less muscular, but his green eyes were sharp and seemed to be taking in every detail, spending a lot of time sorting through the thousands of small oddities presented by Thantos. *That one's the danger here, not Andragin.* Each time the second dwarf looked at Raben, he felt as though he was being examined. The dwarf's eyes had an invasive feel to them. It seemed to the thief that he could hide nothing so long as he was looking at him.

"I am Raben," the thief said as he reached across the table to the brown haired dwarf.

"Tavner," answered the dwarf. He left the thief's hand hanging as his eyes began boring into Raben. "I'll be the warden of this clan. The head priest, as you humans might say. The archpriest." Tavner's green eyes quickly took Raben in, and then resumed there intense scrutiny of Thantos.

"Forgive me," Andragin said, having missed his chance to lead the introductions. "I never meant to be rude." Raben nodded his acceptance of the dwarf's apology. "Back to business. Where was it that you said you came from, in the beginning of this quest?"

"We come from a city called Liveport. Many leagues to the south." Raben thought for a moment. "I can't rightly tell you when we even began this journey, so difficult as it has been."

"Just the two of you?" Andragin asked.

"No," Raben said, cutting his word short. "There were nearly a dozen and a half of us when we began, but many fell to evil quickly, being cut down only two days into the journey. Another dear friend fell in the canyons after being corrupted by a white mage." Tavner scowled as Raben mentioned the white mage.

"White mage?" he asked, his voice full of accusation. "You've had dealings with a white mage?" The dwarven priest's bushy eyebrows crowded into his eyes as he deepened his scowl. *Hells! Are you going to help me with this, priest, or are you going to sit back and laugh as I single handedly land us in a prison or worse?*

"We had no choice," Raben answered. "We were captured and held for what we guess was six or seven days. We are unsure. He let us go, but only after he had bound himself to one of our friends. It was that bond that cost him his life in the canyon." The thief took a deep breath. "At any rate, there are two more of us, or were. One, a huge warrior who came ahead of us yesterday, and a man from Kernish, who remains outside," Raben finished. *Afraid. Strad is terrified. Where is he?* His eyes closed as the thief received the thought. "He is terribly afraid of you all."

"He should be," Tavner said. "We are the guardians of the north. Any fear you have, you bring with you. If he is afraid then he is hiding something. What are you hiding?" Tavner looked at Raben as he asked the question, but his eyes immediately slid to Thantos who sat motionless, his head tilted forward as though his sight was riveted to the table top.

"We hide our pasts and the troubles we have encountered to get here," hissed Thantos. "I am not aware of every wart and pock on your ancient body, but were I curious I would ask rather than insinuating that it was being hidden from me. And if you have more questions of me even after I have demonstrated myself and Talvo's will, then look to me, rather than to him. He fought his way through your trial, and I felt that I had demonstrated my faith well enough. Why do you still doubt? Can you not look upon a servant of Talvo and know him? Must you fear even those who can pass through the canyons? Surely you know what is out there." Thantos raised his head and leveled his good eye at Tavner. The two locked their eyes on one another and poured the heat of their dispute into them. An almost tangible battle was being fought across the table. Raben and Andragin looked to one another and shared their confusion. They then watched the two priests silently duel, as did every other person in the inn. It lasted for some time.

Neither man moved, and Raben thought the contest unfair. Thantos was undead. He had eternity to sit there, and from what the thief knew of vampires, they never had to close their eyes or even blink. Both priests were steadfast as the lengthy contest wore on. It seemed as though the two were digging through each other's soul and causing pain as they did so, and whoever fell away first would lose. Raben's money was on Thantos, but Tavner was displaying an incredible stubbornness that was unlike anything a human could normally match. The dwarf sat unmoving.

Even his breathing was shallow and almost undetectable. *Must be part of the priesthood. Just look away and start talking. Dwarven disagreements must take years to settle.* As the contest continued and the pressure built up in the room, Raben began to feel that something unspoken was riding on this duel. Everyone watching became as intent as the two priests. *What does this mean? Seems more than pride, or does pride mean that much to these folk?*

"You," growled Tavner without allowing his eyes to shift at all, "are not pure."

"Neither do I claim to be," Thantos answered, his voice a slight whisper. "And I know that you see the decay in me, but look harder, dwarf. There is no answer to it. Talvo has granted me my life, even if it must be lived in pain." Thantos leaned forward, letting a little air hiss through his teeth as he did. His eye didn't waver at all. "You would die if you were asked to bear my pain for one day. Only with His help have I lived to make it to your home." The priests seemingly bore into one another even further. "Do you see the truth, or must I do more for you?" Thantos asked, waiting for the dwarf to respond.

"I see it," Tavner responded, "but I want it to make better sense. I suppose that it is not my place to force such an explanation." The dwarven priest leaned back in his chair, still keeping his green eyes locked on Thantos.

Andragin stood suddenly, forcing everyone to turn their eyes onto him, including the priests.

"Enough of this!" he barked. "Let us make our visitors feel welcome. Heavier issues can be dealt with tomorrow when everyone feels better rested. Tempers are short this eve and we need to rest," he said. "All of us."

Raben woke up at about midday. The sound of hammers woke him. He'd slept in a room at the inn since the earliest light of the morning. He and Thantos had been given a room together. The thief had been so exhausted that he'd accepted the room, walked up to it, and fallen asleep without even a second thought as to where Strad was.

Thantos still lay in his bed. The priest looked dead. His chest didn't move, he made no noise, and his skin was pasty white.

Walking to the window, Raben pushed a curtain aside and looked upon the town of dwarves. *RedAxe.* That was what one of the dwarves had called it. It was beautiful. All of the buildings were cut from stone, and seemed to be meticulously crafted until they could have born no more decoration. Regardless of color, be it red, gray, or white, the buildings were engraved with reliefs and runes. Each structure had carved borders and etched, decorated pillars. The buildings were a beautiful myriad of color and art that reached from just below the window of the inn to the shore of a clear blue lake that looked refreshing even from the long distance that Raben admired it.

He could see the masts of ships that sat on the water, but buildings blocked his ability to see the boats themselves. More wondrous than the beautiful lake and buildings, however, were the people. Dwarves. Thousands of them. Red hair, brown hair, blonde, light skin, dark. All of them stocky and two reaches or so in height. They amazed the thief. They looked so healthy and each of them productive. He couldn't see anyone not pitching in and doing his or her part as he looked at them from behind his curtain. He watched three dwarves gathered at an armory, the source of the hammering that woke him, bent over whatever they'd been working on, arguing over the exact way to strike the metal. *Such detail and pride in their work.* Raben smiled. He liked the dwarves. *I should ask them about my sickles. Seems no one else knows anything about the red metal they are forged from. Not that I've asked.*

The thief cleaned himself in cool water that had been left in a wooden basin in the room, and pulled on his robe. *Sleep well, my friend.* Eager to learn about RedAxe, Raben slipped out of the room, leaving the priest behind, and made his way out amongst the dwarves. The fastidiously cobbled streets made for a comfortable walk through the warm air that settled on the dwarven town. *Just like the road through the canyon. How long it must take to build. Years upon years. Just for a road.*

Every dwarf that he passed greeted him warmly, and then turned a wary eye to him as he continued by. The thief could feel the searching gaze of each of the stocky people as he strolled through their town. *They seldom see humans.* They were a driven people. Raben couldn't find a single dwarf that was loafing in the middle of the day. *How remarkable! Humans have indeed forgotten, if these are the founders of our ways.* Certain that he could find someone begging or wasting the day away, Raben inspected the town with a critical eye, working to find the hidden blemish of the dwarves of Redaxe, but there was simply nothing. More still, all of them seemed entirely content. None of them lacked for any necessity and each of them filled a vital service for the rest of their kind. The dwarves here had

443

developed the most efficient running town that the thief had ever seen.

Strange! A notion dawned on Raben. None of the dwarves seemed any more important than the others. Taking interest, he observed several of the dwarves, particularly those that looked rich. Even the well dressed and obviously richer dwarves were accorded no titles, or special regard. They had first names just as any other did, and were happily called by them.

"Ye must be the human that is chasing yer friend," said a doughty dwarf, interrupting the thief's quiet investigation of Redaxe. Covered in animal pelts, the dwarf stood a little shorter than Andragin, and seemed to be bent with age. His balding head and thick waist-length beard assisted Raben in deciding that this was the oldest member of the dwarven race that he'd encountered so far. "Are ye?"

"Yes," said the thief, a little startled that one of the strangers had addressed him so openly. "My name is Raben." *They must fear allowing a stranger to go unwatched through their city.* He smiled, deciding that an escort for him was probably a good idea.

"Moragin," announced the dwarf as he adjusted a wolf fur, settling it over his shoulder. "I have been looking for ye for some time, ye move very quickly. It's a wonder ye see anything that ye want to, as quickly as ye go from place to place." Moragin pointed back towards the part of the town that Raben had just come from. "Have ye even looked behind ye?"

The thief turned, following the stubby finger of the dwarf, and then stopped, astounded. Behind him, where the group had spent so many days, stood cliffs. The canyon had wound along their bottom, having been carved by water, but now that he was out of them, it hadn't dawned on him that they would look so formidable. Rising from the ground just beyond the first buildings of Redaxe, a reddish brown wall of rock stretched up into the sky, closing the town off from every direction except the lake that lay almost directly behind Raben. The thief stared at the immense cliffs in awe. They rose so high into the air, he couldn't believe that he had ever stood atop them.

"Quite a sight isn't it?" laughed Moragin. "No one ever looks back. They are so dead set on getting to the lake that they seldom realize that the most incredible thing to look at lay right where they just came from."

"Do many people come through here?" asked Raben, still wrestling with the immensity of the cliffs. He could see white birds gliding on the prevailing wind that shattered itself against the cliffs, but even as he watched, they rose ever higher, becoming little more than specks that his eyes couldn't focus on.

"Not so much these days, but in the olden times, thousands of folks used to trek to the temple in order to offer prayers and ask for miracles," stated the old dwarf as he thought deeply about a time he'd lived through. "That was a long time ago."

"Does everyone face the test in that canyon?" asked the thief. He lowered his eyes to the bottom of the cliff, remembering the Meriss and the fear he'd felt. He dropped his vision to the ground. *Urchin, my friend. You would have loved arguing with these folk.*

"What test?" Moragin asked. "I know of no one having any troubles in that canyon. I suppose we'll have to send some militia through there and make sure no bandits have taken up in there." The dwarf looked to the red cliffs, eyeing them suspiciously, and turned to Raben as the thief spoke.

"Whatever bandits there were, we killed," Raben said. *How can you not know about the Meriss?* "Have you walked through the canyons lately?"

"Hmm, yes," Moragin answered. "I spend a good portion of my days in that canyon. I spied ye and yer friends

445

days out. I must say, it took you a while to make it here, but if ye were attacked then I suppose it makes some sense." The old dwarf turned and looked out over the lake. Raben joined him. From their vantage point, they could see the ships that lined the peers, bobbing on the water. They were broad and low, their sides only extending a few reaches over the smooth surface of the lake.

"So," Raben said, turning to the balding dwarf. "Why was it that you were looking for me to begin with?" The thief slowly stepped forward, allowing Moragin to join him as he walked towards the docks on the lake.

"I am to answer any questions ye have about the terrain ahead, and show ye about Redaxe," Moragin said as he stumped along side of the thief. "I suppose Tavner didn't want ye to get yerself in trouble should ye have hot blood in yer veins."

"Well, I hadn't planned on doing anything dangerous, but by the looks of you, I think I now have the proper escort to show me just how to work myself into a good hard fix," Raben said. Moragin stopped immediately and looked hard into the thief's eyes. After a moment, a smile crept across the human's face, and Moragin smirked, and then laughed. His laugh was welcome. It boomed from him, and echoed off of the stone buildings that surrounded the two.

"Well then," he said. "Ye are going to get into some trouble, but it'll be me that'll be flattening yer head with the blade of my axe." The dwarf chuckled as he resumed walking. "Damned humans! Ye always have to push the limits of everything, don't ye? That humor of yers could get ye into a battle amongst dwarves. Yer lucky I've had time with yer kind."

"That's probably why you were sent to find me," Raben joked. "I've always needed looking after." The thief looked to Moragin for only a moment, and saw the aged dwarf smiling. He then turned to look at the lake and the many ships that were moored at the docks that stretched along the shore. They were all built similarly, and they each had a silver emblem of Talvo worked on the side of them. *An axe. Of course.* After seeing all of the dwarves, most of them armed with the double edged axes, Talvo's symbol was starting to make far more sense. Nearing the shore, the two turned and walked along it for a time.

"What's that place there?" Raben asked as he looked at a massive and beautiful structure. It looked like a castle for all the towers and defensive stonework that had been built into it.

"That," Moragin emphasized, "is the only cathedral to Talvo to ever be built by the dwarves. It is meant to be a stronghold that could resist any army of evil." The old dwarf looked at it and silently spoke a prayer. "We have never had to use it as such."

"Is that where people would offer their prayers?" Raben asked. "Is that the first temple of Talvo?" *That easy? I can't believe we've made it at all, and for it to be so easy all of the sudden.*

"No, they would come in tremendous pilgrimages and cross the lake. A few days to the north of the north shore lies the First Temple. It is there that they would take their hope and troubles, but now it is hard to get to. If ye wish to see something fantastic, go to our church and see the gauntlets of Kaylor. He was the only warrior to survive the white mage battle that created those canyons ye walked through, and many think that Talvo saved him. His armor had been stripped from his body and he had been wracked by the magics used by the mages. He crawled back to Redaxe holding only his sword and wearing his gauntlets. He laid both the weapon and the gauntlets on the steps to our temple. They are fantastically worked. I believe that a god made them. Talvo." Moragin mouthed another silent prayer, focusing on the cathedral.

447

"What became of the sword?" Raben asked. He reached down to his, suspecting the answer. "I would think that all of you liked to wield axes from what I've seen since I arrived."

"We do," Moragin barked as he brought two single-bladed hand axes from under his furs. He held them before the human, displaying them with pride "The sword he wielded was magical by all accounts." The ancient dwarf tapped Raben's hilt with one of his axes, narrowly missing the thief's hand. "Yer wearing the blade. It is the key to the quest. The Dayquest must have it in order to enter the temple and seek the True Knowledge." Moragin moved his axes deftly before throwing them one after another. They both smacked into a docking post side by side, burying their sharp blades deep into the hard wood. Before the dwarf had even recovered from the throw, Raben hurled four daggers after the axes. They impacted the wooden post tip-first, and planted themselves on each side of the axes.

"Ye can fight," Moragin said, a bit crestfallen that his display had been so quickly upstaged. "Good. I'd hate to get into a scrape with someone who couldn't hold his own." The dwarf walked up to the post and yanked his axes free. He immediately checked their edges and then plucked the thief's daggers free. He tossed the knives to Raben, who caught them and sheathed them without inspection. Moragin raised an eyebrow. "I hope we don't get into too many fixes though. Yer blades will get so dull ye won't be able to break the skin."

"We'll see," laughed the human. "Shall we head back? I'm sure my friend is awake by now, and he'll be interested in hearing any information you have on where we're going." Moragin nodded, and the two set out back across the town. They headed straight at the ominous cliffs that rose behind it. Raben couldn't help but be impressed as he looked upon them again. They climbed so far over Redaxe that as they neared the inn he was staying at, it almost seemed to him that the red walls were leaning out over him. It was exhilarating and scary.

He and Moragin entered the inn and passed through the tavern, which was the bottom floor. A number of dwarves already gathered there after working through a hard day. Bounding up the stairs, Raben saw that the door to his room was ajar. He yanked his sword free and burst through the door, kicking it hard before him. Thantos looked at him with a smirk etched onto his pale face. Tavner, who sat with him, reacted differently.

"Burning dogs!" he yelled. "What kind of courtesy is that? Do ye always explode into a room like a yearling, without some respect for the folks that might be inside?" The grouchy dwarf knit his brows and was now fuming as he dumped all of the heat he was feeling into his scowl.

"Forgive me," the thief stammered while he fought back laughter. He'd shocked the proud dwarf, and now tried not to bask in the humorous anger that grew from Tavner's surprise. Thantos sat, unmoving, a slight smile playing across his face. "I have seen much trouble until arriving in Redaxe, and was only being cautious," said the thief.

"Fine," Tavner barked. "We'll be down in a moment. Let yer elders speak without yer noise and confusion."

Raben nodded curtly and backed out of the room. As he pulled the door closed, a heavy hand clapped him on the shoulder. *Blood and Hells, he's prickly. I wonder if anyone can put up with him.*

"I knew ye couldn't make it through the whole day without scuffing someone's boots," Moragin said, a toothy grin showing under his moustache. The two went back downstairs and sat down to a meal.

They ordered roast and potatoes because Andragin swore that it was the best thing to have. They then had four mugs of ale brought to them.

"Ye can't drink just one in this tavern," the balding dwarf said. "It's a rule that if ye come here to drink then ye must have at least two ales. If ye don't then ye might get into a serious talk and make sense. Work is for the day, and now ye should be relaxing." The old dwarf nodded at his own advice and brought out a long curved pipe which he lit, sucking the flame through it with great pulls. Once he had it lit, he took long puffs on it and held them until his eyes watered. He would then blow great clouds of smoke out before him, and watch them float through the thick air to the ceiling. He offered the pipe to Raben, but the thief declined.

Dinner arrived a short time later and both of them dived in, eating like starved people. They were nearly finished when Tavner and Thantos walked up to the table. Each of them nodded at the eating men, and gained a like greeting.

As they sat down, Andragin pushed his plate away.

"Yer late," he said. "Dinner's over." Tavner waved the comment away and ordered roast for himself along with an ale and a spare. Thantos order a glass of wine and was brought two.

"So," Raben said between bites. "You said you knew about the road north. Tell me."

"There's a tribe of monsters that live north," Moragin said, drawing the table in closer as he leaned forward. "They are Mogrin and they call themselves the tribe of Stonehole. They have caused trouble to all who've approached the temple for the last two generations."

"Mogrin?" Raben asked. He'd now finished his dinner and pushed his plate away. Moments later a serving maid reached past him and picked it and several empty cups from the table. She looked to Tavner and Thantos, but both priests had only just sat down and were barely starting.

"Yes, Mogrin," answered Moragin, spitting the word out as if it tasted bad. "They stand maybe half a reach taller than a dwarf and have ruddy skin. Their heads are full of sharp teeth and covered with shaggy heads of greasy hair. Anything but brains. They fight with stone weapons, and aren't very skilled. It's there numbers and their ferocity that make them dangerous. Though they can speak, they have little more instinct than a dog. They love to chase, and will do so indefinitely, hunting, killing, and loving it."

"They make for a fine weapons training," said Andragin, his strong voice booming through the tavern as he walked up to the table. The bulky dwarf motioned for Moragin to slide to the side, and pushed a stool into the vacancy. He ordered two ales and plopped down on the stool. "Tell on, Bounty," he said. Raben looked at Andragin curiously. "The name?" The thief nodded. "We call him Bounty because he makes his living tracking down Mogrin that are causing trouble. He gets a bounty for each left ear he brings in."

"Anyway," Moragin interrupted, waving Andragin's explanation away. "They are numerous, and anyone who goes north needs to know what they are doing, or they are sure to get killed. Spitted and cooked for a Mogrin feast." The table fell silent. The sounds of knives grinding on plates and the thunking of mugs onto the stone tables filled the room for a time. It seemed as though the entire room was focused on the conversation going on at the one table.

"So how are we expected to finish this quest if there is an army of hungry Mogrins waiting for us?" Raben asked, looking from Andragin to Moragin. Bounty shook his head.

"It's Mogrin, for one or for many," Moragin corrected, shaking his head. "And if ye wanted to make it, ye'd take someone who knew what to do with ye." The old dwarf nodded at Andragin, who responded exactly the same way, nodding back at Bounty.

"These oafs are offering their service because they have nothing better to do with their lives than throw them away on humans," Tavner declared, offering Raben the obvious as though he were too daft to understand. "Do ye want their help or not?" the grouchy dwarf said, his temper growing shorter with each moment.

"Yes!" Raben almost shouted. He breathed in deeply as he looked to Andragin and Moragin. Each of the dwarves was smiling as though they were sharing a private joke. "I would. We would very much appreciate your assistance."

"Good," Tavner said. "I'll have to come along too." Thantos turned his head slightly when he heard, and Raben less subtly shot an annoyed look at the irritating dwarven priest. "None of my warriors may travel on such an important quest without a protector priest from our clan along." Raben looked back to the two dwarven warriors. *You knew what he'd say. You knew what he was going to do.* Moragin nodded at Raben and smiled innocently, as though he could hear the thief's thoughts. *I'll get you,* Raben thought as he looked at the two smiling dwarves. *I'll have my chance to catch you when you're off your guard. Maybe fill your helms with dung, and then charge into battle.* The thought made Raben smile, and the two dwarves clasped his arms, mistaking the smile for understanding of another kind.

"So," hissed Thantos, causing the smiles to vanish. "Last night you said that you may have harmed our journey somehow. You sent us to bed before you were able to explain." The undead priest's eye homed in on Andragin, for he had been the one to say that the dwarves may have grievously harmed Raben and Thantos.

"Well," Andragin began, obviously uncomfortable under the gaze of the vampiric priest. "I may have spoken overly hastily. It seems our decision is less important than we thought." Andragin shifted in his chair, looking to Tavner for direction, but the dwarven priest sat expressionless. "We thought that the human warrior yesterday was the questor for the prophecy, and we aided him to the north shore, and that cannot be correct. You," he said looking intently at Raben, "have the key. The sword." Andragin cleared his throat. "At any rate. I thought that we had either helped the wrong man go forward, or left him on his way to the temple without the key, thus dooming him."

"You thought," contested Thantos evenly. "What has convinced you that you have not done those things?" The undead human stood up, and leaned across the table. *Blazes, friend! I haven't seen you like this since the Shao.* "Why do you now think that our hero isn't north of us, standing in a chaotic mess of Mogrin, dying alone because he doesn't have the key?" The room was totally silent. No one was eating, or even moving, as Thantos bore down on Andragin. *What are you doing? Has something happened?*

"Why would he have left you?" Andragin asked the question to answer Thantos. "Why would he leave his help behind him? He must have known the road would get darker as he neared the temple. That the opposition would grow more formidable. He chose badly, and if he dies, then fate has worked it so. He couldn't have been the chosen." Thantos began to open his mouth, but it was Raben who spoke, trying to quote a priest he'd once known.

"Many of us want to think that a prophecy is destined to occur, fated to pass, but it must be labored after," he said. "If you sit and watch, it will pass by, but those who care the most for it, will affect it." *I understand. They no longer truly care. And they must.* Thantos nodded to seemingly no one.

"What?" Andragin asked, anger and confusion simultaneously woven into his voice. "We care the most for it. We have worked for centuries on His bidding and there are none in all of Reman that so stoutly endure and care for the workings of Talvo as we do."

"I have seen," Tavner broke in, "a different side of us." The dwarven priest rose from his seat and took a few steps away from the table. Thantos quietly sat back down. "The force that presently cares the most about this quest is not us, warrior. Unfortunately, it is the side of evil. We expect that the power of Talvo will prevail, and we criticize the humans and the elves as they lose sight of the high standards that we taught to them, but it is we who have failed. Evil has been beating down our doors for centuries and we have done nothing. We sat, isolated up here in our god-given paradise, resting on the laurels of our sacrifice though even the pages it is recorded on fade and blow away, unwilling to make the long journeys to human lands, or elven, though it is we who have the longest years to do so. We have done nothing to concentrate the wills of Talvo's followers on insisting that this journey be a success, and now it has fallen to almost irreparable folly. Perhaps it has failed, and we must bear a large portion of the blame if we are to claim a high place in the church of Talvo. We must therefore do our part to make it a success. I have spoken with this priest for some time." Tavner pointed to Thantos. "He has asked for my help, and I will give it. So will Andragin, and Bounty, Moragin." The dwarf turned to Thantos. "You have suffered and have been given a difficult lot, but if you say that the human warrior is the chosen, then I find it difficult to argue."

Human warrior! Raben looked to Thantos. The undead had focused his eye on the thief as though he were waiting for the thief to react. *Hessing?* Thantos nodded. *Is the chosen?* Another nod. *How can he be? I'm going to die.* The thief focused on his breathing as his chest closed in. Words that Urchin had spoken to him long ago lodged themselves in his mind. *You are not part of this quest, and those who have no part will be killed. Death. He'd said he only came on this journey to find out how all of us would die. I need to live. I need to figure this all out. I need to get out of here. How can I make sure that I will live through this? Kill! Greech! I can't kill anyone innocent. Particularly not here, in Redaxe.*

Tavner had been speaking and addressing the rest of the room, explaining the strategy behind sending a small group as to not alert the Mogrin of their presence when they left the next day, but Raben heard little of it. His soul was suffocating on his own thoughts and fears. Thantos stared at him in alarm. Never before had the thief been so terrified, worried, and anxious. Only now, as it truly hit home that they were near the end of the journey, and Raben was not the chosen member of the prophecy, did the idea that he might die strike him in full force. *I'll have served no function. Even if I did get Hessing to the greeching temple, I'll have only been a slave to a cause other than what I expected.*

Raben scrambled to his feet, initiating a shocked silence in the room. "Pardon me," he blurted as he made for the door. "I need air." Tavner scowled as the thief left. Raben had to escape the confines of the tavern and get his thinking straight. *What in all the blazes can I do? I need to find a way to make it, and there's no one to kill. Damn it! I should have struck when I could. I could have killed a few beggars. Reman would never miss them. I need the life. I must have something to feed this damned sword.*

"Now you know," came the familiar hiss, sending Raben into a defensive tumble. He regained his feet, sword in hand. "I have that same hunger for other living things," Thantos said from the darkness that surrounded the inn. He was barely visible in the dim light that streamed from inside the building. "I have the insatiable need to prolong myself and yet, there is no way to do so."

"My friend, it never seemed possible that Hessing could really be the reason we all came so far. It had to be you or me, or even that fool of an old man," Raben said as he sheathed his sword. "It just seems wrong."

"Does it?" asked Thantos. "He is the purest. The Meriss barely touched him. The rest of us were attacked outright and some of us killed. I should have died, my friend, were it not for you. And how did you save me?" The undead priest hissed. "You fed me your blood."

Damn it! I should have seen it. He can't even finish without this damned sword. I stole it. He should have it. I was sent by someone to steal this sword, and then ordered to further disrupt the Dayquest. So after all this time. I am the evil still.

"Not the evil," Thantos said, interrupting the incessant stream of thoughts. "Perhaps maneuvered by evil. It is up to you whether or not you are evil."

"You once decided to bear a vampire next to your soul in order to carry on, my friend." Raben stood just a pace before Thantos. "Would you do it again to ensure that you finished this journey now that you're here?" *You used to defend the innocent, and curse the walking dead. You have joined them. You yearn to drink blood with all the casual want that I might wish for an ale.*

Thantos turned away from the question and paced away from the thief. He looked up into the dark sky. Raben could only guess what the undead priest saw there. The thief could see nothing, but Thantos stared for some time.

"I think," Thantos began and then paused. "I think that I would do something terrible to continue, but I would kill no one if I could help it." The priest turned back to Raben. "I understand you, my friend. I know what you need, and feel the compulsion to figure out who has been leading you through this mess, and find out exactly who you are, but I can't tell you that I would slaughter a few dwarves in order to keep myself alive." Thantos lowered his vision to the ground. "I cannot say that. I have taken no lives in my present state, Raben. None."

"Hessing can't succeed without the sword," Raben said. "Yet he is two days ahead of us, and the dwarves say that the temple is only three days north of the north shore." *How can he live, and what in all the Hells can he be doing?*

"Yes," Thantos replied. "We will have to make great time. Strad will help."

"Yeah," Raben said, looking to Thantos. "Where in the blazes is that fool?"

"He has gone ahead to give Hessing more to think about, and perhaps save the metal covered fool from himself so that he might actually complete this quest," Thantos said. "I sent him last night rather than bring him amongst the dwarves. He won't hurt Hessing because of our bond. I couldn't guarantee as much with the dwarves."

Raben nodded, only half understanding. "I need to decide what I'm going to do."

"Whatever you decide, my friend. Know this." Thantos lifted a hand, holding it out to the perplexed thief. "I will understand." Raben looked to the undead priest. *Understand. You haven't decided so terrible a thing yet. Why forgive me?* "There are others that will judge you." The words had no more traveled to Raben's ears than Thantos was gone.

Others will judge me. Go ahead, kill some folk, I won't mind, but the dwarves, the humans, history, and all the gods will hate you. Some choice. There is no choice. Raben began walking through the city, barely noticing how it looked with its hundreds of street lanterns and its bright torches that burned near the docks. *If I die, and it is only to have led that greeching noble to where I wanted to go... Damn it! Have I had any choice but to do this? I could say no, but I have this damned sword.* He ripped the blade from its sheath and hurled it up the street, but it flew no more than a few paces and then bobbed readily by his side. He snapped it out of the air, and dropped it straight down.

457

It clattered on the stone street, but he could no more walk away from it than he could his own soul. He struggled to take the step, to leave the blade, but before he knew it, he'd sheathed it again, and continued thinking. *They have to have the sword. That is why I was made to steal it. I need to be there, because I am delivering the next great evil, which lives in my soul like a damned flea on a dog, yet I can't not go because I bear the key. Hells! How could this be allowed to happen?*

Raben didn't remember the walk, but he stood on the dock staring out into the shapeless dark of the lake. *How can I do this? Where can I find someone to help me. Help me?* Raben sneered at how he'd worded it. *Where can I find someone to kill in order to keep my undeserving soul alive?* The thief turned away from the lake and looked over the dwarven town. A thousand lights in a thousand windows twinkled through the night. The beauty of it annoyed him. He searched through his options, shocked at how few they were. *I swear to you, Thantos, I will try and do as few terrible things as I can.* It was simple. He'd have to kill someone innocent. *I need to make it to the temple, help Hessing. And then she will come. I need to have lives to face her. She'll cut me down, and then I can come back and flee this whole mess. No! I need...maybe...that.* Having made up his mind, Raben began making his way through Redaxe.

He let his toes scrape along the stone, searching for any imperfection that might allow him to gain a little room to reach the final half reach to the window. He couldn't seem to locate one, however. The dwarves had such a skill with stonecraft that they left not so much as a crack in any of the walls they built. *I suppose they'd try extra hard on these walls.* He dropped back to the roof of the stable.

He'd noticed the window from the street and thought it was the perfect opportunity. It had a locked grate across it, but that wouldn't be a problem if he could just get to it. The thief had been shocked to find out that his magic wouldn't work. He'd cast the spell twice, and created no result whatsoever, so once again he was restricted to more conventional techniques than he would otherwise prefer.

He climbed onto the roof of a horse stable and made his way beneath the window. A dwarf had been sitting just inside of it, keeping watch, but a well aimed throw landed the butt of a dagger square on the watchmen's head, knocking him unconscious. But now it was the window and not the watchman that was giving Raben trouble. He stood on the stable trying to figure out how to get to the grate just over him. He had very little of his equipment. Most of it lay in the inn. *I can pick the lock and move the grate. The window. Why are my spells failing? Damned dwarves. I suppose with your history of mages, I would find a way to negate magic as well.*

He stood, staring at the window. He knew he needed to act quickly. The watchman wouldn't lay there unconscious for too long. Resolved on a desperate measure, Raben drew his sword from its sheath. *All I need is a little rope.* He shook his head in irritation, and then backed away from the wall. Holding his sword out in front of him, he drew it back like a battering ram and then charged the wall. When he was close to it, he thrust it forward with all his might. His arms jarred when it struck and the force of the impact tore the hilt from his hands. He ducked away from the sharp noise it caused, but after a few moments of silence, the only important thing was that the blade stuck there. It stood out of the wall, a few knuckles of steel buried in the seamless rock.

Raben waited a few more moments, and still no one appeared to have noticed. He leapt up on the flat of the blade, keeping his foot jammed up against the wall in order to lessen the stress on the weapon, and reduce the chances of it falling, and looked into the grate.

Wasting no time, Raben brought out several picks and began working the heavy tumblers in the enormous lock. It was immaculately crafted but lasted mere moments against the determination and skill of the thief. As soon as it fell open, the thief slid the grate open. It swung out just like a shutter. He reached into the window and pulled himself up. As he dragged himself through the window, his sword began to try and join him. A scraping sound pierced the night as the sword released itself from the stone wall in order to float up to Raben. It scraped all the way up, dragging its tip along the stone wall until it bobbed through the window and floated by his side. Terrified, the thief immediately reached out of the window and pulled the grate closed with a clang. He then replaced the lock. *Damn it! Greeching sword. I could have just shouted for help.*

He looked down at the dwarf that lay unconscious at his feet. Nudging the sleeping guard with his foot, Raben rolled him back and forth for a few moments. He then bent down and placed his hand on the guard's neck to see if he still lived. He did. Pulling a tube from his belt pouch, the thief poured a fine powder into his palm and then sifted it lightly into the dwarf's mouth and spoke a word of magic. The guard choked momentarily and then resumed sleeping, only this time it was a deep sleep. He took full breaths as though he were in his own bed.

Once he was satisfied with the guard, Raben searched for and found his dagger. He sheathed it and made his way to the door. Stopping behind it, he pressed an ear up against it, trying to hear if anyone lay in wait behind it. *Nothing.* He eased it open, keeping one hand free, and letting his sword float at his side. Outside was a hallway that went both right and left. Based on the layout of the building, Raben was fairly certain that he wanted to go right. He jogged along the hallway, making no noise. Each door he passed was closed, and there was very little light. The thief wasn't sure that was such a good thing. He usually celebrated dim lighting, but since the dwarves could see in the night, it might be a disadvantage.

At the end of the hallway was the great hall, as Raben had guessed. It was well lit. Numerous large candelabra burned in the center of it, and a number of single torches were sconced on the walls. Between the two candelabra, a golden chest sat. *There it is. Far too easy.*

His reasoning seemed to make more sense to him when he considered his other options. *No priest of Talvo would kill innocent people to further his own prowess in battle. This sword would not have been the aid to such a moral man as it has been to me, yet that dwarf survived the most horrible battle in the history of Reman. He alone survived. If it wasn't the sword.* Raben looked at the golden chest. *It must have been the gauntlets.* It felt better to him to steal than to kill, but he wasn't so sure the dwarves would share his thinking when they found out. *But hopefully we will be on our way before anyone figures this out.* The magical poison he gave to the watchman would remove the whole instance from the dwarf's memory and keep him asleep for some time, and since the lock was still in place, he would have to figure that he'd fallen asleep and banged his head on the window sill. *I should have taken that poison one day after I started this quest.* He'd borne it the whole time. *They'll never know how I made it here.*

As far as what would be in the golden chest after he removed the pieces of armor, Raben hoped to figure out how to avoid that by the time he was leaving with the gauntlets. *It wouldn't do for the whole town to go crazy after discovering that their treasure was missing before we left.* He hoped that they wouldn't be visiting the holy relics before the quest continued the next day, but after seeing how dutiful and productive everyone was, he wouldn't be surprised if the whole town visited the cathedral before going off to work.

Staying in the shadows, Raben slid into the great hall. His eyes crept over every part of the room, searching for any movement, other people, traps, anything. He took cautious short steps, forcing himself to abuse time in order to remain invisible to possible onlookers. Creeping along the walls was fairly simple. There were various flames lighting the room, and one was always brighter than another, casting a shadow against the wall that an experienced thief could use. The real trick, as Raben saw it, was the chest itself.

It sat in the center of the room, which was the worst location. It made the thief feel naked to attempt to steal something in the open like that. Furthermore, it sat between the two brightest sources of light in the entire hall. There would be no shadow to hide in. *How do I do that?* He crouched in a good shadow that was maybe ten paces from the golden chest, pondering the problem at hand. If he just walked up there, then anyone in the room could see. *I could end up in the middle of a war in only a moment.* He shook his head, unhappy with that approach. *What the greeching Hells am I going to do? Everything will draw attention.* Deciding that he needed to see the chest from the side with the lock, Raben skulked from shadow to shadow until he had gone all the way around the room, and was sitting in a shadow exactly opposite of the position he'd been in. He scrutinized the chest. As he'd expected, a golden lock was built into the frame work of the chest. *Harder to work. Almost impossible to unlock.* He stared hard at the chest. *Even harder to lock.*

Deciding on his course, Raben wrapped the picks he guessed he would need in the satin vest he'd purchased in Liveport. He then tossed them to the chest where they landed softly. Taking off his robe, the thief crouched in his small clothes near the wall. He drew his sword and let it float next to him. Just after letting it go, he darted from his shadow, running full on at the candelabra. He swung his robe, using it to fan all of the candles out. Quickly he leapt to the other candelabra and doused all but a few of the candles there. In the dim light that remained, he tumbled down in front of the chest and began to work the lock. *Blazes.* It wasn't locked. Pulling himself away from the chest in case it was trapped, he lifted the top, but nothing adverse happened. He looked inside, and saw the gauntlets.

They were magnificent. Hammers and axes crisscrossed each other all the way around them, and they glittered, their polished golden surfaces reflecting even the few candles that remained burning in the dim hall. Reaching in, Raben grasped them and immediately pushed his hands through, in order to quickly transport them. They seemed a perfect fit.

In fact, he began to wonder if he could even remove them if he had to.

He lowered the lid to the chest and looked around. Nothing. *These people are too trusting.* The thief looked down at his wrists, looked at the golden armor he just put on. *I suppose it has been a long time since the dwarves have had to distrust anyone.* Raben calmly stood up and pulled his robe on and sheathed his sword. He then moved to the candelabra that still held a few burning candles and plucked one of them from the holder. Using it, he relit each of the candles there, and then did the same on the other. *I hope you all understand that I did this only to keep from killing. I did.* The thief stood near the center of the great hall and admired it. Clean stone stretched without a single break across the floor and then up the walls and across the ceiling. Not a single thing decorated the room. Nothing was needed. *Perfect.* It was a testimony to the dwarves and the precision and skill that they made a part of their daily life.

Expecting that any guard that might have seen him would have reacted by now, Raben walked across the room to the immense front doors which he had seen only from the outside. He lifted the thin stone bar that held them shut and pulled the door open slightly. Though the bar was heavy, he managed to balance it on the saw that he carried, and once he'd stepped out side, he pulled the bar to the door and lowered it into place.

Standing outside of the cathedral, wearing the gauntlets, Raben truly began to feel the fear that he should have suffered inside. *What have I done? I took the only relic these people love. They're going to know. I can't go back. That Tavner will be able to look me in the eye and see what I've done.* He looked at the door behind him. *I could give them back.* He walked to the door, and felt a chill climb through him. *I can't give it back. I'm not allowed.*

He pulled his saw back out of his belt and began pushing it through the door resolved on putting the gauntlets back in the chest, and within moments he found himself walking away from the cathedral against his will. *Damn it. Greeching hells. Burning Dogs is right. I'm being led like a damned dog. This is why I must finish this quest. You don't view me as a piece of your journey because I'm not. I'm the enemy.*

"Ho there," said a dwarf with a scratchy voice. He sat on one of the piers as it reached out into the blackness of the lake. "Ye shouldn't walk around at night grumbling to yerself like that. Ye look drunk."

"Not drunk," Raben snapped. "Beset with my duty." He looked at the dwarf. *What am I going to do? I'm a fool. They'd be better off if I were dead and gone. Gone.* "Tell me, sir dwarf, are you a sailor?"

"Yep," responded the dwarf. He climbed to his feet. He was slender for a dwarf and had less of a beard. His skin was tanned darkly from spending long days exposed to the sun. He had dark hair and darker eyes. He appeared quite young for a dwarf. "I own that little dooz there. Just docked in and am feeling the earth under my feet." Raben tried to really examine this dwarf. His voice was less hearty than any other dwarf so far.

"I am a member of…"

"The quest," he said, finishing Raben's statement. "I've heard. So what can I do for you?" *He might help. He knows about the Dayquest. Good.*

"I was wondering if you could land me on the north shore in the dark?" the thief asked. "Are you that good? Is anyone?" Raben walked up to the dwarf. "Could you take me across the lake and land me there? It would be for the good of all people." *Say that you will, my friend. Tell me that you can help, and if I live, I will pay you all that I can.*

465

Rather than inquiring any further, the dwarf began walking to his ship. A few steps up the pier, he turned to the thief and waved to him, gesturing him to get aboard. *Is this a trap?* Raben pulled his sword out again and followed the scrawny dwarf.

When he walked up the plank to get on the ship, Raben was stunned. Ten dwarves, all of them thin and lean from being seamen, sat on benches, ready to row. The dwarf that Raben had first seen was already standing in the back of the ship, holding a huge wheel that he employed to steer the ship.

"Pull up the plank," he said. "My crew is prepared to go. Kura!" barked the captain, and the crew pushed forward on the oars simultaneously. The boat lurched backwards. Raben scrambled to pull the wooden plank aboard before it fell in the murky water below. The captain repeated the strange word, keeping a cadence. He then called out another foreign word and only one side rowed. After a few times, he changed the command and the other side joined in, but now they were pulling the oars rather than pushing on them, and Raben could feel that the ship was moving forward. Once the rowing became almost mechanical, the captain stepped down from the wheel and walked over to Raben.

"I am Greev, and I will see you safely landed on the other side of the lake," said the dwarf as he walked to the side of the ship and peered out into the darkness. Raben watched him, still waiting for something to give. *This has been too strange to be normal.*

"Why are you helping me so easily?" the thief asked. "You've not asked a single question." *Maybe you're that religious. Maybe you're a sot.*

"I landed your friend two days ago," answered the dwarf as he faced the water. "He came to me just as you did, and asked for the exact same thing, though not as politely as you did. He more or less ordered me to take him across, but I felt it was what I had to do. It was my part in the world. If that is all I must do in the greater workings of things, then why question?" The dark-skinned dwarf turned and faced Raben. "One of you is meant to go there, and the other would likely have killed me had I refused my service. So I take both of you." The dwarf pointed to a hatch in the deck. "Come with me below deck. The journey is long, but we can have a warm drink and a good talk."

Raben held his sword the entire time he spoke to Greev. Nearly everything about the dwarf was strange. Most of it obvious, once Raben saw him in direct light. His skin wasn't tanned, but gray. And his eyes were pure black. The beard that grew from his face fell in thin dirty wisps rather than the full proud flowing beards that all the dwarves at the inn had had. While strange, these things didn't bother Raben as much as the way the dwarf moved. His arms were not only scrawny when compared to every other dwarf that Raben had seen, but they moved differently. He was nimble. The other dwarves were methodical and robust. The fact that this dwarf was quick and graceful bothered the thief. It made him dangerous somehow. It made him not a dwarf.

"Are there no people of your race that look differently?" asked Greev when he saw how Raben regarded him. "I have seen humans with dark skin, but I did not scoff and treat them as less. I am a dwarf, and still have my honor," he said.

"Forgive me, but I've only come to know dwarves at all in the last couple of days, and you are the first of your sort that I've seen," Raben explained. "I gaped the same way when I came across the other dwarves." He gestured behind himself with his sword, imagining that that was the direction that Redaxe lay. "I held the sword for the whole time when dealing with them as well." *Something about you*… Greev seemed to have the upper hand, though Raben couldn't explain why.

"I see," answered Greev as he pulled a bottle from a foot locker at the side of the cabin. "Sit down and calm yerself," ordered the dark dwarf. "I can't drink with someone as paranoid as you. Sit down and at least pretend to be comfortable. It'll help me be at ease and pass the time more quickly."

Raben lowered himself onto a bench that ran all the way around the room. Greev rummaged through some crates that had been pushed under the bench before standing up holding two mugs and the bottle. He sat down to Raben's left and set the mugs down, pulled the stopper from the bottle, and poured some of the liquid into each. Picking one up, he handed it to Raben. "This'll keep ye warm through the journey." The thief shook his head. He had a poor history where alcohol was concerned. "Fine, suit yerself. Yer friend wouldn't drink it either." The dark dwarf chuckled. "In fact, he felt so threatened by the gesture that he spilled the stuff. He was far more tense than you are. Waste of good whiskey. The journey must have been far easier for you." *Ha! Far easier on me? It could have been no easier than it was on that fool.* After thinking about Hessing turning the dark dwarf down, and watching Greev drink from his mug, Raben picked up the mug and smelled the contents. It was strong, but pleasing. He took a sip.

"Thank you," the thief said, raising his sword in a salute as he drank. The drink warmed his stomach, in much the same way flaming pitch might. It sat, burning in his stomach while the thief tried to decide if the sensation was normal.

"My pleasure," Greev answered, watching the thief squirm on the bench. "Tis normal for it to burn. That's how it keeps ye warm." He chuckled again. "That is a fine weapon ye have there. Looks like a sword right from the

469

history of my people." The dwarf leaned down to inspect Raben's blade. "Valuable it is. I hope ye honor it the way it should be honored. The greatest hero ever known in Redaxe carried that blade for years. Only survivor of the White Mage battles that made the towering cliffs and canyons beyond the town."

"You're a learned fellow," Raben stated. "Most human sailors know not a thing about the past. They live only for each journey they take, and that's it." The thief looked at the dwarf, trying to figure why he couldn't trust him. "When they reach shore they drink and cause problems." *Hells!*

"I have help so far as the weapon is concerned," Greev said. "Yer friend told me ye had it. He said ye stole it, and would probably leave me with nothing if I ever saw ye, but I don't think I have anything that would be worth yer time." The dark dwarf leaned back, letting his head rest on the wall. "Besides, ye seem less strange than he did, even though ye look more dark and mysterious."

"He told you I had it?" The dark dwarf nodded. "What else did he tell you?" *Did he tell you that I am the evil? That I have killed the innocent. Did he tell you that I am Gannon's agent, sent to destroy the known world? How good to have so much information precede me. That's why you look at me that way. Why you bother me. Damn it all!*

"A lot I guess. He said that you traveled with a vampire priest that needed to be killed. He said that you and the priest were traveling for selfish reasons and not for the glory of Talvo. He griped a lot about how low the standards of men had fallen," Greev stated, his voice getting even scratchier as he drank. He cleared his throat and resumed. "He told me about all these battles and crazy things that happened to your group as you traveled here. He was so antsy that he talked almost the whole time." The dark dwarf topped off his mug and held out the bottle. Raben had drunk very little, but held out his mug none the less. *This is the only time I may ever learn real information about Hessing.*

"Please, Greev, continue with your tale," Raben insisted. "I don't feel like telling mine yet, and am glad to hear about my friend. What else did he tell you?" *About him, hopefully.*

"Too much. Some of it quite terrible." The dark dwarf shook his head in remembrance, and then took a sip of the whiskey. "He told me about a battle where an army of vampires destroyed an entire town, but you and your friends tried to stop them. He said you and that sword lost your mind and killed everyone that neared you. He told me that you were so far gone that you slaughtered two children who were trying to hide behind you, terrified of the vampires. Is that true?" Greev looked at the ceiling as he asked. His hands tapped nervously on the mug he held.

Raben scowled and clutched his sword tighter. "Don't trust everything you hear." Greev looked away from the ceiling, and after watching the thief's mood darken, he stood up.

"I think I'll go above deck and check on the crew," he said as he walked out the door. "Make sure we're going the right way." He didn't even look back as he left. He just stepped out and pulled the door tightly shut behind him.

Damn it! Why did Hessing have to tell him about that? He must know how terrible I feel about that day. That's the same day Urchin died. He knows it bothers me. He knows... nothing. He wasn't there. How in the greeching blazes did he know? Fear pierced Raben. He sat frozen on the bench. His sword crashed to the floor, and the mug dangled from his open hand. *How could Hessing have known? Can he see my thoughts? What does he know? Did the Guild tell him? Did they tell him everything? Would they? Why would they? They wouldn't. They wouldn't unless he was part of the Guild. This whole mess started in his house.*

471

Why there? Because the sword was there. Or he's Guild. Thantos thinks he's the one. He couldn't be the one and be Guild. The Meriss didn't do anything to him. Damn!

Raben threw his mug across the cabin, sending its contents flying. The whiskey splashed onto the wall, leaving a dark wet mark through the dust that coated it. *Nothing is as it seems. I am the only person who wants to be simply me, and the last to get it.* He recovered his blade from the floor.

Raben jumped to his feet and walked back to the deck. A blast of cold wind met him when he opened the hatch, causing him to wince. He could hear the dwarves calling out the cadence as they continued rowing. He tried to wrap his robe around himself to fend off the cold, but the wind swept up his legs and through the thick material. The dwarves sat in the freezing air with little more than sleeveless shirts and trousers. They were accustomed to the cold air that rose from the lake.

"Hey," Raben called out to Greev. "Come here!" The thief waved at the dwarf. The dark dwarf maintained a cool expression, but walked over to him tentatively. "Tell me something. Did my friend tell you about when we found my priest friend Thantos, when he first turned into a vampire?" Raben asked. Greev nodded. "Help me out, I forgot. What was the name of the city we were in?" The wind washed past Raben's ears as he waited for the dwarf to answer. Raben leaned in with one ear, making certain that he could hear the answer. Then the dark dwarf looked up to the thief.

"He said it was Kerney, I think," Greev answered. Raben nodded.

"That's right. Close enough anyway. Thank you." Turning away, the thief fumed as he crossed the deck. Greev followed. Raben marched to the front of the ship and stared into the wind, letting it tear at him. *He knows everything.*

Damn it! He knows every single thing. He wasn't even there. That bastard has all of it. How? Why? Why does he deserve to hold that power over the rest of us? We haven't gotten to know a damned blazing thing about him. Hells! It surprising when someone even knows his name, but he knows every terrible crime we've committed.

"You know what really gets me about yer friend?" Greev asked from behind Raben. "He told me to have my crew ready because you'd come by tonight. He even knew what ye'd say and everything. He told me to tell ye these things. He said I'd know it was ye from the reactions ye gave me." Raben spun to face the dwarf, ready to kill, his face flushed with heat. *He told you I would be here?*

"He said that, did he?" Raben yelled. "He's a pompous ass!" *Hells and blood. We will meet, and you will die, Von Hessing!*

Greev laughed, unaffected by the thief's outburst. "I suppose he might be, but he's right. He even told me that this would anger you. He ordered me to remain unarmed, because ye might need someone to attack, but ye'd never harm me if I was unarmed."

"Like I said before," Raben growled, lifting his sword, "don't trust everything you hear." The dark dwarf backed away from the enraged thief, calmly retreating to his station at the wheel. Raben turned back to the wind. It felt good. It froze him, but something about it ate away at his anger and let him gain perspective on the situation he was in. Hessing knew everything somehow, and had arranged for Raben's escape from Redaxe.

He needs the sword to gain entrance to the temple. Thantos says he's the one. He knows that I can't give him the sword. Raben opened his eyes wide and tried futilely to see through the darkness ahead. Tears formed and the wind pushed them back from the corners of his eyes. *If I die while in possession of the sword, my soul will enter it and serve it eternally. Who told me that? Hessing. He knew about the sword. He told me I couldn't throw it away. If he killed me, could he then pick it up?* Raben blinked as more tears formed. The streaks they formed left a freezing trail behind. *You're going with me. You're bait. Hessing called me bait. The sword shall draw the foemen. I've carried this sword just so he wouldn't have to fight. And he knows everything. He must know more about me. Why else trust that I could make it this far? He must know who made me. Damn! I hate him. He's going to attack me. I have to die. Does he know I have no life in the sword? Did he leave knowing what I would do? Knowing that he could attack me one on one and kill me?* Raben crouched down behind the rail of the ship. *I'm playing right into his hands. I should have come across with Thantos.*

Leaping to his feet, Raben almost ran to Greev. The dark dwarf lifted his hands defensively. "No," the thief said. "I'm not angry. Can we turn back?" He spit the words out, one on top of the other.

"Turn back?" Greev marveled. "Yer friend said ye wouldn't want to. Ye want to go back now? We're half way there." The dark dwarf narrowed his eyes, trying to understand. "We can I suppose, if that is what ye really want to do."

"I," Raben said. *Need to go back. Take us back.* "Guess not." *No! Greech! Take us back.* The thief listened to his own voice as though it were another person. "Continue on, it'll be alright. Pardon me." Greev nodded slowly, waiting to see if the human had more to say. Raben turned, defeated, and walked slowly below deck, where he slumped on a bench and waited.

Raben took a few moments to realize where he was. He could hear knocking on the cabin door, but he'd slept for such a short time, and the night before had been such an eventful blur that he required some thought to figure out exactly where he was. The knocking on the door escalated. The thief could hear the impatience as the wood shuddered under the constant pounding. Once he remembered exactly where he was, he rolled off of the bench. His arms and legs were stiff and his neck ached from the abnormal position he adopted in sleeping on the wooden surface. *I wonder if it's daylight yet.*

He didn't remember falling asleep, but that didn't surprise him very much. So much had happened, and his situation developed in such a dangerous direction that he was certain he must have passed out as soon as he closed his eyes. *Liquor didn't help much either.* The pounding continued as he unbolted the door. He'd wanted to feel a little security after discovering that Hessing knew so much about his situation that he locked himself in upon arriving last night. He'd left his sword bobbing over him protectively, but now the sword was sheathed at his side. As the bolt slid from the latch, Raben palmed a dagger in his right hand. When he was set, he pulled the door open.

Greev stood on the other side, a scowl etched deeply on his exhausted face. He looked at Raben with obvious irritation. After a few moments, the dark dwarf spun on his

475

heel, and without saying a single word, stalked away from his human passenger.

Raben decided that he earned any discourtesy that he received from the dwarf, and accepted the dwarf's action as an invitation to follow, rude though it may have been. *What can I expect? I held a dagger just to greet him. Fair trade for a nasty look.* Raben massaged his neck as he made his way up the stairs.

He felt better when he saw that there was sunlight on the deck. As he emerged from the hatch, he could see the dwarven crew excitedly racing around on deck, preparing hoists and straightening and directing numerous ropes. A couple of the sinewy dwarves were laboring to heave an anchor over the side of the boat. Raben sprinted over to them, and leant his strength to the effort, immediately heaving the weighty piece of curved iron overboard. The dwarves said no word of thanks, they only nodded curtly before they sprang to their next task. Every bit of the industriousness that had impressed Raben about the dwarves in Redaxe was apparent in these dwarves now that they were working. None of them did anything but give their fullest effort. *Cornerstone of being dwarven, I guess.*

Raben looked across the deck to where Greev was. The captain of the ship was directing three other dwarves who were preparing a rowboat. It was presently hoisted just slightly off the deck by two ropes, but as the dwarves took turns cranking a winch, it rose steadily. After several long shifts at the winch by the three dwarves, the boat was several reaches from the deck and they were able to spin the angled support that held the rowboat, thus pushing it out over the water.

Suddenly curious, the thief then crossed the deck and looked through the growing light of the morning at the shore that he'd sailed through the night to see. It looked cold and dangerous. Pine trees sat in sparse bluffs, overwhelming the landscape in some areas while leaving open stretches of barren land in others. *They look like the perfect place to be chased by wolves.* The ground was brown and unadorned by undergrowth. The only breaks in the dull earthy floor of the scattered wood were the occasional pieces of granite that jutted through the dirt like a craggy mountain that had suffered long enough in the confines of the ground. The rock that emerged from the soil was tremendous in some places, bigger than some of the buildings in Redaxe. *I suppose it wasn't that hard to find the stone to build the place.* Raben looked the next step of his journey over with a critical eye, wondering about only one thing. *When will Hessing appear?*

"We're ready to launch when ye are," Greev rasped. Exhaustion had taken his voice and worn it to a wretched sound. "Come along quickly. My crew hasn't slept for an entire day." The dark dwarf stumped back across the deck of the ship and stood near a rope ladder which extended the short distance down to the rowboat.

Are you watching me right now? The thief's eyes scanned the shoreline, looking for any sign that Hessing might be there. *You'll come at night won't you? Chosen or not, you have a devious mind. You think I'm a criminal and you intend to outthink me.* Raben smirked at the thought as he crossed the deck. *Perhaps this can be less torment for me, and a little more for you.* The thief had no idea what lay in his immediate future, but he did know that he could not turn back. Besides that, he only needed to know that he would fight the direction that he was being pushed until he died. That seemed to be enough. *The further I go, the more aware I am that I am being manipulated. Perhaps before this is over, I will get to do something I really want to do.* A wicked grin spread across Raben's face as he stood next to Greev. The dwarf shied away from looking at the human and climbed quickly into the small boat. Raben followed, gracefully sliding down the taut ropes to the rowboat.

"Let's go," he said, his eyes never giving up their vigilant search of the coast. "Do you think he's nearby, Greev, or do you think he'll wait for me at the temple?" Raben looked intently at the dwarf, the touch of madness that he felt obvious. *He'll hit me in the trees. He knows how much I hate them. He never had the pleasure of walking through the Narwood, but he'll know that I hate them.*

"Were it me, I would take cover in the trees and wait for any help to arrive," Greev said, taking great caution in his words. "I wouldn't want to stand too far out in the open lest the Mogrin see me. That happens, and the whole journey takes a quick step to the blazes. The Mogrin are relentless, they are. Chase ye to the Hells and back." Greev looked away from the thief as he spoke, unwilling to meet eyes with him. *Then they'll chase me to wherever I'm going. The Hells.* Raben grinned again, his malice filling him.

"I suppose you're right," he answered. "There are surely dangers afoot that one wouldn't want to hazard unnecessarily. After all, there is only life and caution. You can't do too much in order to remain safe and healthy." The thief chuckled. A panic that needed to escape him was emerging as both droll and morbid. The dark dwarf had no wish to explore its depth.

"Yes," he agreed. "There cannot be enough ways to stay safe. And if ye do then ye might miss out on all the world has to show ye. Once ye done that, what good is having ever lived? Ye have to have a good life to report by the end."

"That's what it should be," Raben agreed whimsically. "A good life by the end. Real pity so many people get there and wonder what they've been doing all these years." Again the thief laughed. None of the dwarves joined him. Startled by its presence in his hand, Raben sheathed his sword. He had no clue when he'd brought it out. *No wonder they're all worried about me.*

Hysterical energies washed through the thief as the little boat edged closer and closer to the shore. His stomach clenched tightly, and his hands clenched and unclenched as he waited. His jaw was clamped tight and his teeth ground while his mind worked, trying to decide when the noble would attack. *Perhaps I've missed something vital and it's not an attack that he intends, but a joint effort without Thantos. I know he can't stand Thantos, but has he enough hatred for me that he would kill me out here?* Raben tried to knit his fingers together and found that he had daggers. He was gripping them maniacally, trembling with nervousness as the boat drew within fifty paces of the beach. *What is this? I need to get control. I'll end up killing myself if I can't get any better control.* Suddenly it dawned on him. He was feeling the same type of shock and inability to cope that he felt when Thantos sent thoughts to him. *I'm being controlled right now. You!* Raben looked straight into the sky. *You want me to do something right now. What is it? Kill these dwarves?* Raben grinned at the sky like a psychotic. *Whatever it is that you want of me. It will not happen. I won't let it.*

Suddenly there was splashing around the boat. *We're here. Let's do this quickly, Hessing. You've had two days to prepare for me. What the blazing Hells?* His hand outstretched, Raben stared horrified. His sword extended from his hand, unknown to him, straight away from his body and through Greev's head. It had sliced each side of the dwarf's mouth and punctured the back of his throat, just making it out of the back of the dwarf's head at the base of his skull. Even as Raben first saw the terrible wound, the dark dwarf fell to the bottom of the wooden rowboat, dragging the tip of the thief's blade with him. The human's arm sunk with the dead captain, unable to resist his weight.

The dwarves hadn't jumped ship to help land the boat, they had been fleeing the thief. *How in the greeching Hells?* Raben bent to the fallen dwarf and felt his neck. Greev was dead, his spine cut cleanly by the blow. Nausea swept through the thief. His stomach, which had been so tense, bound itself even tighter, causing Raben pain as it forced him to wretch.

He heaved over the side of the small vessel, unable to look at the corpse inside. As he grew more and more ill, the boat struck ground. Raben looked into the water he'd been soiling and saw the rocky floor of the lake only a pace or two beneath the surface. Reflected in the rippling water, he could see his magical sword bouncing in the air just above his head. It was painted with blood. The thief watched it drip slowly, rhythmically. *Serve a real purpose!* Raben willed the blade to turn over and thrust itself through him, ending his miserable existence. *Why serve me? You're supposed to be the most honorable weapon in the service of Talvo!*

Tears fell from Raben's eyes as he pushed himself up from the side of the boat. Tears of sadness and frustration. Tears of anger. He hurled himself over the side and landed almost chest deep in freezing water. He struggled to breathe normally as the water's temperature shocked his senses. It served to calm him. He forgot his nausea, and focused on making it to shore before he became paralyzed by the frigid water. For the second time in a day, the harsh conditions of nature served to ease the thief.

Walking on the rocky lake bottom proved more difficult than Raben would have guessed. Several times, his footing slipped causing him to fall under the water, immersing his head. Each time it happened he became more and more aware of the terribly low temperature of the water. He couldn't remember when he'd been so cold. He trudged onward, forcing himself to the shore. Once he finally managed to climb from the water, he peeled his soaked robe from his body and threw it into the low branches of a nearby pine tree to dry. He then dug through the few belt pouches that he had, hoping that he might have a flint with him, but he was not so lucky. Running amongst the trees in nothing but his smallclothes, Raben began collecting any branches that he could find, which were surprisingly numerous. *Not many people come here. Mogrin don't build fires. Damn it's cold.* He kept himself moving at the fastest speed he could muster, his boots slogging all the while. He couldn't feel his toes at all.

As soon as he had a pile of branches suitable for a bonfire, the thief raised his hands in the air and began weaving them through intricate somatics while pronouncing the arcane language of magic. Feeling that he was already being watched, Raben decided that he could only serve himself by appearing dangerous and powerful, so he over performed the spell. At the conclusion of his casting, fire erupted from his hands, snaking forward to any location he desired. Just as it had in the map room in the temple of Talvo, the fire leapt forward to consume anything in its path. Raben ran it across the pile of wood twice and the fire was roaring. He then turned the tracts of fire out onto the water, letting the flames burn themselves out on the lapping water of the lake. After a few moments passed, the spell ended, and the thief lowered his arms.

Between the sun and his roaring fire, the cold northern air didn't keep the thief cold for very long. He dried his robe with the blaze and put them on over the silk pants and shirt he'd carried since Liveport. Raben had kept the clothes rolled in one of his pouches should he need a disguise in a pinch, and because he didn't want them damaged by being thrown in with the rest of his equipment. Now that freezing became the most local threat, he decided that preserving the fine garments was less than important. Once he had them on, he was warmer than he imagined. After only a few practice swings with his sword, he was so warm that he had to let his robe hang open.

Satisfied with the way that his clothes felt, Raben started to survey his surroundings. He was amazed and a little intimidated by the size of the stone monoliths that tore out of the ground amidst all of the trees. They seemed violent. Probably a result of the White Mage wars. They drew his eye, forcing his respect as both a natural marvel and the perfect place to hide an ambush. *Anything could be behind those things. Come and get me, Hessing.* Raben began to walk along the shore with no particular destination in mind. He knew that the temple was to the north, but had no better directions than that. Something had to give, and the thief remained alert.

After walking for some time, Raben looked back over the terrain he'd covered. *Nothing but the boat. Damned dwarf. Damn you, whoever you are.* Though his hand had acted without even so much as his awareness, Raben felt the guilt of Greev's death. The dwarf had done nothing but help him, and for being near enough to do that, he'd paid with his life. *One day, the right people will pay with their lives. Damned dwarf.* He suddenly found himself thinking about Reese, the small boy he'd cut down in Kelc's tower. Emotion started to climb into the thief's mind, but he tore his sword from its sheath and held it out in a practice stance, driving his wrongdoings out of his mind, driving the recent memory of Greev's death away. He worked the pattern of combat only long enough to recover. Once his mind was clear and set on the problems he was about to face, he put the sword away and continued walking.

The trees seemed eerie. They grouped so densely in places and yet covered very little of the ground overall. *Urchin could explain this. Fool old man spent half his days rolling around in the dirt.* Keeping his eyes trained on each tree he passed, Raben continued walking up the beach.

A short while later, he figured out why so few people had troubled themselves to explain the exact location of the temple. Beginning ahead of him further up the shore, a beaten path began across one of the yawning glades between two particularly dense pine clusters. As he approached it, Raben began searching for tracks, bending to the ground and inspecting it, looking for one set of boot prints in particular. He'd spent so many days watching the noble pace around their campsites that he'd know the look of Hessing's print the moment he saw it. Besides the etched name of the cobbler, which was illegible, or in another language, each boot had a strange cut just before the heel that was more like a shoe for how narrow it was. An odd mark for a boot, and one that would be simple to track if the thief were lucky enough to spot it.

And when I do find you, my dear noble, we're going to have a little chat. Maybe I'll lose control and my sword will wind up in your throat. The thief lifted his eyes and made sure that nothing was coming upon him unaware while he focused his attention on the ground. *Thantos could probably feel the damned noble were he here. Hell, I ought to be able to hear the thundering idiot before he would be able to sneak up on me.* Finding no tracks at all, Raben rose back to his feet and began making his way to the path. He wanted to arrive there under some kind of cover, but the trees bothered him more than the idea of being out in the open, so he elected to intentionally keep the two thick copses equidistant from him rather than favoring one in order to cover his approach.

By the time he made his way to the path, he had fully convinced himself that the trees were somehow sinister, or full of sinister things. *Just like the last forest I was in. Damned trees always closing in on you.* Raben reached for his sword as though it might make the trees think twice before attacking, and then decided that he relied too heavily on his blade, and left it sheathed. *I have spells. Use them. Hessing might be the better swordsman, but he can't dodge lightning. The sword has only been trouble anyway.*

The thief crouched down to the ground and inspected the path for tracks, and was immediately rewarded. The noble's prints were obvious in the fine silt on the path. They came right up from the lake. *That dwarf dropped him off right at the damned path, and then made me walk a greeching league.* The tracks continued onward, heading north amidst the trees and the gargantuan granite forms. *You went, or at least want me to think you went.* Raben began following the tracks, making sure to keep his eyes open and his awareness up just in case the tracks were a trap. He didn't think that Hessing would weave such a subtle design for a trap, but the Hessing he knew didn't know every thought that passed through his head either.

As he began walking under the eaves of some of the pine trees, Raben decided that his sword did need to be in hand. He felt as though he were being watched by the trees. He tried, on numerous occasions, to turn suddenly and catch some hidden creature off guard, but each time he spun, there were only the trees. *Perhaps I'm losing my mind. I went crazy in the last forest I had to pass through. The Guild hunter said it was poison, but maybe it was just me.* Anxiety began to build in Raben's chest as he continued. It was too quiet and nothing acted evil though everything felt evil. His breathing became labored, and sweat beaded on his forehead.

The path then left the trees behind for a while, letting Raben regain his composure. Instead, the only things that intruded on the nearly straight path were the enormous chunks of granite that stood like monuments on the soft earth. They appeared to have just been set on the ground by gods, or have burrowed up from the earth like huge gray beetles. He liked them. They were a tactical nightmare, but they were impressive to behold. In better times, Raben would have loved to try and climb one of the gigantic things and look out over the lake. As it was, he regarded them as a danger, and paid particular attention to them, making sure that he wasn't overlooking some hidden niche or hollow that might conceal an enemy.

He walked by one of the mighty boulders, and then faced another. Raben spent a great deal of time navigating his way around the second for fear of an attack coming from the first. Many times he suddenly turned to reevaluate the first piece of granite, while slowly creeping around the second. The path gave the stones a wide berth, but unlike his strategy with the trees, the thief left the path and walked snugly against the rock. He only backed off of them as he first approached, in order to make sure that no one and nothing was atop their lofty caps. *It would be way too high for something to aim a shot or leap on you at any rate.* The stones were taller than any he'd ever seen. Some of them were fifty to sixty paces tall. *Huge.* Keeping his back to whichever piece of granite was on the inside curve of the path, Raben made his way through four more of them.

Then the path became absolutely straight, and after checking the ground, Raben knew that Hessing had passed this point. Taking his time to verify that the noble had indeed made his way along the path, the thief began following the dirt track across an expanse of bland terrain. No trees, no stones, just short brown grass. It was the most barren terrain Raben had traveled in since he'd begun the journey.

By the time he walked out of the large and desolate glade and back into the gloom of more pine trees, the light began to fade from the sky. Being so intent on following tracks and keeping on or near the path, Raben hadn't even noticed that clouds rolled in and blocked the sun out of the sky, but the value of the natural light rose quickly as he found himself in the dimness of dusk surrounded by the trees he had recently grown to hate.

It's the Narwood all over again. Greeching trees are alive. The green needles that adorned the pines that surrounded Raben faded from a deep green, which the thief felt housed his watchers, to an ominous gray which limited his vision and caused him to slow down in order to inspect each new tree with painstaking effort. They then deepened to a stifling black. He felt helpless. Memories of the Narwood sat like emperors in his mind, ruling over his every thought, spreading fear throughout the man. The thief was defenseless against the enveloping night. He thought the forest was overwhelming when he could see the looming rocks and suffocating trees, but the pressure of their presence only grew with his inability to watch them.

He had thought to try and feel his way along the path, trusting his instincts to keep him moving in the right direction, but soon after dark he found himself hunkered down in a ball, sitting in the inescapable blackness. He knew his sword was bobbing somewhere over his head, but needed further assurance that weapons were at the ready. He clutched a dagger in each hand, letting the razor sharp blades slightly graze his forearms as he crossed them. He let his eyes close, though sleep was not an option. He simply hated the idea that his eyes were open and he could see absolutely nothing. *They are there. All of them. Even that fool of a noble is probably sitting out in the trees, watching me here. I hate trees.*

487

Though he wasn't pushing his way through the same hostile environment and having fits of madness that had been so inspired in him in the Narwood, Raben waited just the same. *If it's not the trees, it's the Mogrin, and Hessing. He needs to just show himself. Attack me, or try and capture me, or whatever it is that he wants. Just sitting in this damned forest is insane.* He rose to his feet and stood in the impenetrable night. Turning around slowly, he unfolded his arms and held his daggers at the ready. *Come on, damn it. Attack!* His anxiety began to rise again as he waited for the attack he anticipated. *Why is it so greeching quiet? Shouldn't there be some kind of forest squirrel, or a damned rat, or something.* He focused entirely on listening for anything. *Nothing! Nothing!* He spun again, intentionally letting his feet land heavily on the dirt floor of the wood, happy to hear any sound. As he did so, he leaned into the silence, ready to pounce on any familiar sound, be it Hessing's battle cry or the high pitched song of a single chirper, but only a continuous silence answered.

How do I end up in places like this? Where is Hessing? I shouldn't have left Thantos back in Redaxe. He'd be perfect right now. Who better to have by your side in the greeching dark than a vampire? Raben slowly raised his right hand and felt for his sword. It hung in the air exactly where he expected it to be. He tapped on it with his dagger, listening to the metallic clink of the weapons, directing all of his attention to it. He pushed on the floating weapon with his dagger, curious if it would resist, but it gave easily before his thrust.

Reminded of the last time he was in a night as dark as this, he stared hard at where the sword levitated, and as he did so, he became immediately aware of the deep heated look to the magical blade. It was such a dark hue of red that it could only be described as a weapon that had just been fired in a forge. Just as it had the last time he'd noticed,

Raben became alarmed that it might actually be able to burn him. He jerked his hand away from it, but inspected it further. He tried to lean in as close as he could, almost touching his nose to it. With the limitations on his sight he found the sword not only welcome, but fascinating. It claimed his full attention at once. He let his eyes slowly climb from the hilt to the tip, over and over, never tiring of his repetitive inspection of the blade. The coloration and lethal shape of the weapon kept his eyes fixed on it. *I wield you,* he thought. *I call on you for death and you leap to my assistance, over eager.* As soon as the thought passed through his mind, Raben froze. A sudden chill burst through him, causing the hair on his arms and neck to prickle. *Was that me?* He looked at the sword with a renewed scrutiny. *Or was that you?* He looked up into the sky, wanting an answer to his question. *I wield you, or do you wield me? Which is it?* Raben forgot all of his fear and anxiety and now grinned wickedly into the night. *I call on you for death and you leap to my assistance? Me? It's the blade that kills. It's my hand that wields it.* He let go of his dagger and ripped the blade from the air. *Are you talking to me, Hessing? Are you wielding me in your little game? Or has someone new climbed into my head?* He chuckled at the absurdity. *Come on in. There's plenty of room. Bring all of your friends. I have something for all of you.* Leaping forward into the darkness he whipped the blade about his body, cutting the air with an almost unnoticeable red blur. His wicked grin returned as he completed the arcing swing, listening to the weapon cutting through the air. *Something for everyone.* He thrust the weapon forward, imagining that he was striking whoever was directing him, whoever had control. *The Guild. They seem to have everything to do with this. Who are they? The only member I get to meet is the hunter woman.*

He lowered his blade as he thought about the woman. He'd wanted to kill before just so he could talk to her again, and try to get her to help him. *She is trapped just as I am. No different.* The elven woman had become so angry when Raben insisted that the two of them were alike that she sent him away. *I know why she felt angry, but am not so skilled as to order the entire realm away. Order my life away.* He thought of her. The way she looked, the shape of her eyes and the smell of her perfume. He hated that perfume, yet wished he could smell it again. He remembered the way she treated him the last time they spoke. She'd been kinder, and freed him from the bindings that held him nearly every time they met before. And she listened to him. *I got to her. I know it. I could see it in her. She was hoping that I had a solution for her. A way of stealing her from there and bringing her with me.*

Raben's eyes blinked in the darkness as he tried to picture the exact look she'd given him when he told her that there had to be a way to become free of their master. He told her that they were alike and that escape has to be possible. *She had looked...excited. She wanted me to know a way to escape. She told me that they had to capture me once before. Maybe she already thought that I knew a way to break free. Maybe she expects me to. I wish she would have told me more about the last time I did this, if that was the case. About the me that escaped and had to be tracked down and forced back into service.*

In the pitch black night, Raben turned his sword until he held the tip of its magical blade at his own chest. His right arm was fully extended out before him and could barely grip the hilt from the odd angle. *What would it do? Would I be innocent?* He laughed, not even capable of viewing himself as innocent. *I killed Greev, though. I have a life. I could talk to her and figure out a little more. Gain some helpful information and maybe bring her out somehow.* He took a deep breath, feeling the point of the weapon press into his skin. *What if it doesn't work? It could be the last time. Would I be peaceful, or would it all start over again, on some other nightmare journey.* He dropped the point of the sword from his chest. *They'd never let me do it. They'd stop me, or make me kill some other person before I was dead forever.* The thief sheathed the sword, not wanting to feel it in his hand, nor have it protect him. *I need to be rid of this thing. I wonder if Hessing just wants the blade for himself. If so, he can have it. He can take the sword and do whatever he wants with it so long as I get to walk away. But that will never happen.*

Interrupting his thoughts, the slightest bit of light broke through the branches above and caught Raben's attention. Before he could even blink, he'd swept his sword from its sheath, preparing for battle. Only a moment later, he calmed himself and was straining his eyes to see the slender crescent of the moon that splashed its weak light on the world below. The thick pines were strangling the moon's efforts to bathe the land in gray light, but after the complete darkness that Raben had been trapped in for half the night, he felt blessed that there was any source of light that he could see by.

He began moving forward at once, using the occasional patches of light to guide him along the path. The majority of breaks in the branches overhead occurred because of the beaten down roadway that used the broadest passage between the numerous trees. Walking from one patch of moonlight to the next allowed the thief to make progress through the trees. He was moving slowly, unable to make good time as he tracked the road only by the rogue bits of light, but speed was a distant secondary concern to Raben's need to move. He even managed to disregard the paranoia that had consumed him earlier, content to have something

491

other than his own thoughts and the unyielding darkness to work with.

The magical blade preceded each step. The thief held the weapon in a state of constant readiness. His eyes darted from place to place, but he could see nothing beyond the marks of gray moonlight that struck the ground. The rest of the terrain that surrounded him remained veiled in the night. Though he felt that anything could be hidden in the obscure surroundings, he refused to let himself become too obsessed with that fact. He needed to find a place where he might be able to rest before he was forced to deal with Hessing, and he hoped that he would be able to find it soon.

No such luck. For the remainder of the night, the thief made sporadic progress in the woods. Several times he became unsure if he was still on the crude pathway, feeling that he could have wandered off of it at any time were it to veer in any odd direction. Forced to continue blindly forward, he was only able to put himself at ease when he found another stretch of the path with several splotches of light lined out on the ground. Likewise, he lost his ability to gauge the course he needed to follow each time a cloud passed in front of the moon. Everything plunged back into the complete blackness, leaving the thief stranded for as long as it took for the cloud to pass. He never knew how long it might be, unaware if it were a wisp of a cloud or the beginning of a thunderstorm. With no other options, he just waited in the darkness, clutching his sword and hoping that the light would resume, which it eventually did.

After a seemingly unending trek through the pines at night, the sky began to lighten with the oncoming sun. It was then that Raben found an opening in the woods that might allow him to rest. He inspected it thoroughly, walking from side to side and then moving all the way around the perimeter of it. Only a few hundred paces across, it was a strange glen. It was almost perfectly round, and the only thing that interrupted the stubby brown grass that covered the ground were two granite boulders. They stood about three reaches high and were mirror images of each other, standing only two paces apart in the center of the circular field. The stone itself was plain, no writing, no marks, and no chips. Though the rocks didn't look polished, they certainly appeared to have been worked by someone. They, like the suddenly barren ground they stood on, appeared unnatural.

After circling the rocks several more times, Raben found nothing more odd about them than their location. He held his sword out and set it floating alertly by his side and then lowered himself down between the stones. Doing little more than murmuring, the thief cast a spell, which caused the ground to bow further into the earth below him. Soon he had a depression between the stones that would make him all but invisible to any searcher that didn't take the effort of actually approaching the massive rock twins. Knowing that the midday sun would awaken him, the exhausted thief lay down and tried to fall asleep. For a while, he couldn't escape his thoughts. He tried to figure out how far behind him Thantos and the dwarves would be if they followed the thief the morning after he'd left. He worried about Hessing and wondered exactly when he would encounter the noble, how the noble would react, and if he would survive the meeting. Most of all, Raben weighed the value of the one life that the sword had accrued for him when he'd involuntarily killed Greev versus being able to have another chance to talk to the elven Guild hunter. *Greev. Damn your luck for being part of this mess. I suffer along side of every one of the innocents that die. I have to bear that pain. I am only able to do what they want me to do. It's not my choosing.* He tried to justify the dark dwarf's death by thinking that he had no control over himself, but in the end, he could only picture the sword slicing the dwarf's mouth open, the blade extending from the hideous wound back to his own hand. *Someone will pay.* He closed his eyes, too tired to grieve. *I just hope it isn't me.*

What the? Icy rain shocked Raben into wakefulness. It belted him as he lay on the ground, soaking him at an alarming rate. He sprung to his feet, and evaluated the situation in only a moment. He was still between the stones in the glade. He counted that as a good start. He'd suspected that he might end up in a cook pot as he fell asleep. He searched for his sword only to find it sheathed at his hip. He yanked it free and began jogging towards the trees that ringed the circular field. He headed for the pathway, ready to cover what he felt would be the final distance between himself and the temple where all of this had to ultimately finish. *At least this will all be over. One way or another.* He did his best to keep his robe wrapped around him as he ran to the pines, hoping to keep the silk underneath dry.

As he entered the woods again, the rain lessened, unable to make its way through the same denseness that had blocked out the moon on the night before. *The moon will be brighter tonight.* The thief looked at the sky from beneath the pine canopy. *Greeching rain.* He quickly took his robe off and shook it in the hopes that most of the water would roll off, but after inspecting it he found that it was quite drenched. His silks, however, were almost completely dry. Deciding that he'd be warmer without the wet robe, he doubled it over and tucked it through one of the straps that held three of his dagger sheaths to his body. The robe hung off of his back, bouncing off of his thighs when he moved. Deciding that any kind of warmth would serve him, he enchanted his blade as he had at Nestor's Ferry. The sword burst into fire, licking the magical steel with sorcerer's flame. As Raben walked, the fire dripped from the edges of the blade as though it were liquid. He held it before him, almost hoping that something would attack. He willed Hessing to appear. He'd slept, felt as good as he was likely to feel, and had nothing to lose. The only problem he had that didn't require the noble to resolve was hunger.

Raben hadn't had any food or drink since the boat trip across the lake, and that was only whiskey. He'd not eaten since the inn before he'd stolen the gauntlets. His stomach felt as though it were folding over itself in order to satisfy its need to consume something. While his right hand held the flaming sword out before him, his left hand was busy kneading his stomach, trying to ease the hollow pain of hunger. Raben was considering the edibility of pine cones when he heard a high pitched blast threw the air.

It sounded like a hunter's horn, but was higher pitched and inconsistent. It sounded crude, as it cracked the silence of the woods, as though the horn were poorly built or the blower out of practice. Either way, Raben decided that he wanted nothing to do with its owner. He began to move with more caution, but only moments later a sharp blast answered the first. He sucked in his breath as his hair prickled. *Greech!* The note came from just ahead of him and a little to the left. He listened to its echo fading through the thick pines. *Hells!* Raben thought it was less than a hundred paces away. Backpedaling towards the grassy dale that he'd just slept in, he rammed his sword into the ground, extinguishing the flame that now served as much as a beacon as it would a weapon. Once he removed the blade from the earthy ground he kept walking backwards up the road, facing the direction from which the horn blast had come.

After a few hundred steps, he decided to leave the path and he walked amidst the tightly packed trees for a short distance. Once he felt that he was a safe distance from the path, he leapt up into the lower branches of the largest pine that stood near at hand. Its robust limbs were covered with dark gray and brown knobs that made it easy for the thief to grip, but once he was sitting amidst the deformed branches he found that his hands had stripes of sticky sap on them. He rubbed his hands together quickly in order to burn the sap off, but it served only to make the natural adhesive dirty. Short for time, he ignored the problem and clutched his sword, waiting in the tree branches for the owner of the horn to either pass by or move farther off. *How ironic,* Raben mused. *Here I am hiding in these trees. All this time I feared that I would die from the monsters in these pines and now it's me that is sitting in them, waiting to rain death onto whoever walks below.* He shook his head. Though the situation had become reverse of what he might have expected, his opinion of the woods remained the same. He folded his left hand over itself, working on the sap on the palm of his hands with his fingers. *I hate trees.*

A stick cracked not far from where he perched. Someone was walking below. *A lot of them.* Raben tensed and nearly fell from his branch. He reached out and steadied himself against the trunk of the tree with his left hand. His sword he held against the branch that his right hand rested on, hoping to keep the blade from sight. Another sound. This time it sounded like something scraping on the ground, or perhaps on the trees. *Chain mail maybe.* He heard the sound again. *No, it's intentional. They are intentionally scraping on the trees. Or they are truly loud and clumsy.* He strained to hear each noise, eager to identify the sound of his adversary. He heard it again. It sounded as though they were pulling a steel spike across each tree that they passed. *Maybe it's both. Dwarves?* He moved a little further out on his branch,

497

leaving the trunk a pace and a half behind him. The sound grew louder as the creatures obviously drew nearer. The scraping began to come from both in front of him and to his right. They were passing by on the roadway. He looked to where he had exited the road. Several trees stood between where he was and where he'd actually left the path, but if someone were going to track his footprints, he'd see them far in advance.

"You're a tricky devil to find," said a man behind Raben. The thief didn't recognize the voice and therefore whirled blade first to meet the speaker, but there was no one. He struggled to recover as his swing missed, nearly knocking him from the branch. He searched the limbs and then the ground as he tried to steady himself. *Blazes! What was that?* "Come on down, and have a chat," said the same voice from under him. *Where the greech is he?* Sweat beaded on his forehead as he looked for the invisible speaker. "Over here, Raben. Come along to the temple, before I get angry." Raben scooted along the branch until he could put his back firmly against the trunk of the tree. *The temple! Who? The temple?* He held his sword out and let go. It immediately leapt up beside him. *Hessing?* After a few moments of adjusting himself to where he felt secure on the branch, the thief prepared to cast a spell if the need should arise. *Hells!*

Ready to weave his magics, Raben looked up and saw the warped humanoid creatures that could only be the Mogrin. They were bent to the ground, following the obvious trail that he'd left when he'd walked off of the pathway. *Burning voice! Now I have an army of these things to deal with. Greech! All I want to do is get to this temple and kill Hessing. Can't I have a single thing go right?* The thief leaned over and looked around the base of the trunk, examining the terrain around the tree, trying to see if there was a sensible escape route. Thick pine trunks sprung from the ground depriving the earthen forest floor of light, and therefore undergrowth. It would be easy travel, but the Mogrin were reputed to love the chase. Looking back to the apish things, Raben could see them slowly moving along his trail about two hundred paces away. There were too many of them. They snaked back through the trees. He couldn't get an accurate count, but it looked like more than twenty. *Just blazing perfect! Perfect! Who in all the Hells was the voice?* Unsure of his course, Raben dropped from his tree branch and began skulking from tree to tree in a semicircle around the Mogrin, heading back in the general direction of the path, farther north. The last time the voice spoke it came from that direction. *I'll either escape or meet whoever brought these monsters to me. One way or the other I'll get to a battle that I'll be happy to fight.* As if in agreement, the floating sword surged just ahead of the thief.

He slowed, paying attention to the weapon. It pushed ahead of him, struggling to move forward. Raben looked through the pines ahead, but saw nothing. The blade continued its emphatic surge. *Who's here? What is this? The voice? The temple?* Raben looked at every tree and then let his gaze climb up into the branches, trying to see through to the thick needle-covered limbs. *How many times has this sword not reacted when I thought something was there, and now that I can see nothing, it's greeching pulling me.*

He jumped as the sound of the Mogrin grew closer. *Escape. Need to go.* Trying to ignore the sword and focusing on stealth, the thief began weaving through the old knobby pines, cautiously passing from one to the next, constantly keeping several of the towering trees between himself and the creatures following. As he moved, he made no sound, stepping only on dirt or rock. He scrutinized the ground as he took each step, making sure that there was not a twig or a pine cone, or anything that might make a sound were it to come under his weight. The Mogrin, however, did not share this philosophy.

Crashing through the woods, they seemed intent on making noise. *Maybe they intend to startle their prey from a hiding place.* The monsters were loud, even as they fell behind the thief. They hacked at the trees with some type of blade. Raben could hear them doing it. It sounded like they were grinding their weapons into the bark of the old trees as they slowly passed. *It must be to drive their enemies before them.*

Keeping an eye on his sword, which still yearned to leap forward, Raben moved away from the Mogrin with considerable ease. The raucous they caused fell more and more behind him as he passed through the silent forest. He found that moving in the silk clothes was far easier than the robes he always wore. The cloth slid along his skin as he stretched and spun in order to move without noise, not to mention the fact that they were far lighter, thus making it easier to move at any rate. He clutched his sickles as he made his way towards the road, a little anxious about the sword. It seemed an enemy was staying just ahead of him, because even as he turned to the road, making his way more easterly, the sword slowly turned and still pushed on exactly ahead of the thief. *Hessing knew my every thought. Didn't sound like him. Maybe one of his though. An enemy.* A feeling passed through the thief. *Not an enemy. The voice. The temple.* Something impressed a notion upon the thief's mind. *It is the voice of the temple. It is calling me. The temple wants me to arrive. I have the key. The chosen. I am the chosen. The temple wants me, and I have the key.* The enchanted sword jerked forward roughly. Raben heeded the blade, creeping forward.

As the pathway came into view, he slowed down and redoubled his efforts to be quiet. He held his sickles at the ready and the magical blade still reached out before him, pointing right to the road. Pouring his attention on the road, the thief felt his muscles slowly grow tight as his eyes beheld nothing. *Maybe it's pointing at the temple. It's supposed to be the key to the quest. The temple is calling me. It makes sense.* Raben stepped forward and froze mid-step. He lowered himself to the ground, watching what he first suspected was a trick on his eyes. *Dust. Footsteps.*

As he watched the beaten path that he'd been following for two days, he could see slight puffs of dust rise from it in a way that would only be caused by someone walking. *No one is there!* He stared in awe as he witnessed dust slowly rise from each step of the invisible creature. It appeared to leave no discernible footprints, but even from the short distance that Raben was from the trail, it was possible that he just couldn't see them. The steps, however, were definite. He watched as the being moved along the path, just where he would have walked. It slowly moved north, exactly as Raben needed to. *It knows where I'm going.* The hair on his neck prickled as a chill dropped through his stomach. *Greech! This can't be. I won't be led to my own death because everyone else on Reman knows what I'm doing.* He took a slow breath. *Maybe it is some guardian of the temple. No!* The thought rocked Raben, nearly forcing him to collapse onto the ground. It had nothing to do with the temple. *It is telling me, helping me.* The thief grinned just before he charged.

Moving faster than the creature could react, Raben dropped his sickles. Before the curved blades touched the ground, the thief had whipped four of his many daggers at the invisible being. He aimed his first at knee height and the following three each climbed the creature's position in the expectation that it would be the size of a human. While the throw for the knee skittered across the trail, the next one sunk into the beings thigh. After that, the third buried itself at the stomach level and the fourth was chest high.

Bursting from his hiding place, Raben held two more daggers. He was content to let the sword fight its own battle. He charged at the invisible thing, ready to attack. As he closed he could see a dark fluid coming from it. *Blood! It's blue. Not human! Greech!* He raised his daggers, wishing he had his sickles, which lay on the forest floor. Dark blood streamed from the creature, flying away from it as though it were spinning. Raben tumbled out onto the path, only a few paces from where the creature stood. His sword leapt ahead of him, rising over his head, and striking. A wound opened up a full reach over the thief's head. *Oh Hells!*

Just after the sword struck, a huge bludgeon pounded Raben's torso, sending him flying. His body hurtled back amongst the trees, crashing through smaller branches and being pounded by the large ones. He fell to the ground ten paces from the path. He gasped for air between fits of coughing. Blood spattered the ground as he coughed. He reached instinctively to his mouth, and wiped it, bringing strings of blood and spit.

He climbed to his feet, and ignored the pain that pulsed through his chest and back. Staggering back out onto the road, the thief could see his sword still slicing into the being. He could now hear a deep wheezing coming from the creature. A metallic ringing sound cut through the air loudly as the sword suddenly fell to the ground, followed by a deep concussion that was more easily felt than heard. Dust blew away from the sword in all directions. *What?* Raben looked at the weapon. *It can't.* He stayed back, far beyond the massive creature's reach. *It can't move.* Raben guessed at the creature's tactic. *Stand on my sword.* He snarled and then raised his hands as he began pronouncing a spell. His hands danced through the air. As he spoke the arcane words, the sword leapt up from the ground.

Suddenly the gaping wounds of the invisible being rushed up to the casting thief. A mighty grip clutched Raben by the shoulders. He couldn't breathe as the creature began crushing him. His spell was immediately lost. The magical blade was driving itself into the thing over and over, raining blue gore down onto both Raben and the creature. The thief choked as his breath ran out. His arms immobile, he could only hang in the being's grip, his legs kicking uselessly.

Suddenly one of the meaty hands that held him let go. Raben still hung, suspended by his left arm. He watched, nearly unconscious as his sword was once again battered to the ground. He then felt himself rise and fall as the monster leapt onto the sword, trapping it to the ground. Pointing into the creature, Raben spoke the shortest of his spells. Several small darts of fire flew from his fingers and sunk into the thing. He heard it grunt, but seemingly it ignored the minor wounds. Regaining a little of his awareness, the thief reached into one of his belt pouches and grabbed his thieving tools. Bringing out his saw, he held it firmly against the being's arm and began dragging the serrated edge across it. He fell to the ground almost immediately. As he hit the earthen floor, his sword leapt back into the air once again. Feeling the danger, Raben rolled to his side until it happened. The monster landed. It just missed the thief. Dust blew over him as he lay on his back, looking up into the gory beast, bathed in its own blood. He could see the massive arms and torso of the creature. *Four paces tall!*

Barking the words, and aiming his hand, Raben spat a spell out in a desperate last action. Thunder tore through the pine wood as the electrical charge erupted from the fallen man. Lightning sizzled through the air, vaporizing tree branches that it struck on its way up into the air. *I missed. It's done.* For one short span, the thief closed his eyes, knowing that the enormous being was about to crush him, but it didn't come. He lay there for a moment, and then opened his eyes. Just above him, the magical sword bobbed, ready for combat. *It's gone!* It wasn't.

The blood basted creature lay on its back in the road, its chest still slowly rising and falling. The thief scrambled up, backing away from it, fearful that the thing wasn't completely done. *Get it!* His mind screamed the command at the sword, which hung in the air, not even leaning in the direction of the beaten monster. *Kill it!*

Raben wanted to scream, but his chest radiated pain with each breath. As though he'd swallowed fire, his heart and stomach flared with pain as he moved. He fell to one knee, wishing the mammoth thing would just die. *Stop breathing. Give up and die.* The idea of having to deliver the final blow, or blows, to the gargantuan monster sat poorly with Raben. With the Mogrin on their way, and the quest so nearly finished, the thief wanted to deal with as little as possible, and feeling as mangled as he did, he certainly didn't want to spend the time to hack this huge beast into enough pieces to meet with his usual need for being thorough. *No time anyway. The Mogrin had to hear all of that. Thunder. They might be here in moments.*

With that, the thief struggled to his feet and made his way off of the road to the east. After only a hundred paces or so, he turned north and mirrored the path, keeping it in his sight as he continued on the trek. His chest grew numb, but Raben was sure that it would haunt him with intense pain should he need to fight, and that is exactly what he expected the end of the journey to be.

Battle! He was sure of it. Between the clash of weapons and armor, and the screams of monsters and the distant bellows of men, there could be no doubt. *Thantos. Thantos and the dwarves.* The thought was almost as disconcerting as journeying alone had been. Raben had stolen the gauntlets just before leaving, and never really wanted to face the dwarves again. That was why he'd left. Now it sounded like they'd nearly caught up with him. *Damn it! I wanted to finish this journey without them. It's mine to finish. Thantos will just try and keep me from going into the temple. It's his charge. He probably pushed the stubborn dwarves to march through the night. Damned meddling priest.*

Resolved on making it to the temple ahead of the dwarves, Raben quickened his step. The sword hung passively in the air. *At least I don't have another invisible giant to fight. I wonder if that thing created the voice. Doesn't seem right. The voice is the temple. Helping me. I must make it to the temple, or Thantos will get the wrong person into the temple.* Keeping his thoughts and fears at bay, the thief focused on making good time. The sound of the battle faded behind him until it either ended or fell back enough that he simply couldn't hear it any more. In the silence of the woods, Raben felt comfortable for the first time that he was hidden by the trees. He was certain that he couldn't sustain a battle for very long, and was glad that he had a natural maze to hide himself in. *It's no wonder so many like this feeling. Shrouded from the world. Untouched by the gods.*

Raben passed through the forest for the rest of the day with little trouble. In fact, if he'd had a little medicine for his chest, and a meal, he'd have considered it a fair day after the battle. He made great time, never hearing any other battle in the pine woods, encountering no more Mogrin. Walking amidst the trees, exactly parallel to the road, he covered several leagues, and just as the sun began to fade from the sky, he neared the edge of a clearing. It was enormous. He lowered himself to the ground with a grunt, and crawled up to the edge of the open ground, keeping himself hidden behind a wide tree trunk. Peering around it, he surveyed all that was there.

Blazes! He saw the temple. It stood hundreds of paces away, its aged stone pitted by weather and neglect. Massive gray blocks stacked on top of each other lifted the temple fifteen or twenty paces into the air, creating a formidable keep. Once-majestic columns stood in front of the structure, the roof that the pillars had once held aloft over training warriors reduced to rubble at their bases. The double bladed symbol of Talvo was evident on the front face of the temple, but had faded from its glorious brilliance to a tarnished dark gray. *There it is. All the suffering, all the pain, all the loss. There it is. Hells! Where is the voice to help me with all of this damned mess?*

As his eyes dropped from the temple, which seemed to be elevated above the landscape in its ancient majesty, the thief could see the host that eagerly guarded it. Hundreds of Mogrin camped in the opening. They huddled together, like animals. Sleeping on each other with little regard for one another. They snarled at each other and several fights broke out within moments of watching the disgusting things.

Their pale faces were pinched as though they'd eaten something sour, and their hair was greasy and black. They had noses like a dog's, which stood out of their faces in front of their beady orange eyes. Beneath their snouts, they had a mouth full of sharp little teeth. As he watched, Raben noted that they all walked with their shoulders hunched. *I thought they were following my trail. They just move like that. How can they be effective fighters?* He witnessed the answer a few moments later. As another fight broke out, the creatures' ferocity became obvious. They would leap several paces into the air and land on each other, employing sharp black claws and sinewy pale limbs, which they would use to wrap around one another, rendering their pray completely immobile, so that they could sink their pointy teeth in. *Easily beaten if there weren't a thousand of them.* Looking out over the field of them, Raben couldn't imagine any tactic except sneaking through them. *I'll probably never come out of that temple, so I'll not need to worry about coming back.*

He looked at the host of creatures and tried to imagine passing amongst them undetected, and couldn't. *They probably can smell like a dog. They'd know I was there before I was even there.* Thinking of how he must smell, covered in the invisible thing's blood, and several days of travel, the thief wrinkled his nose, discounting the plan and wishing for a bath. *There has to be something.* He examined their campsite for some time before something caught his eye.

Blazing Hells! Raben almost laughed as he saw him. Hessing sat near the center of the host, but he was not part of their force. The noble was chained to a massive iron spike which had been pounded into the ground. Dejected, beaten, and humiliated, the large warrior sat, his head down, motionless amidst the growling, feuding, stupid Mogrin. *And I've been waiting for you to pounce on me,*

Lord Von Hessing, and here you are captured by the enemy. An impulse to save the noble rose in Raben, and he fought it back. *Unnecessary risk. Besides, he's the chosen, he'll make it. Thantos will make certain of it. He has to. Unless I have completed the quest before they arrive at that notion.* Raben lay behind the tree thinking. *Thantos has to make sure of it. He will come. With the dwarves.*

The thief backed away from the trunk by the clearing, going deeper into the woods where he could consider his options. *I need to get in there. Thantos has to save that fool, and will, somehow. He's a vampire. He'll devastate these weak creatures. That's the only time I'll have. Tonight.* Expecting that Thantos and the dwarves were just behind him, Raben planned out his approach should he be correct in assuming that they would attack the host before him.

He would wait for Thantos and the dwarves to initiate an attack, or at least wait for the Mogrin to become excited. Raben expected Thantos to erupt amidst them with the priest's new flare for melodramatic appearances. Once the monsters were focused on the vampiric priest, he would make his way to the temple from one of its sides rather than walking right along the path. *That's probably what Hessing did.* Raben smiled. *He probably walked right out of the woods thinking a sunbeam would sweep him up to the temple. Poor bastard. Not quite a sunbeam. You should have waited and taken us along, you proud fool.*

Resolved on his plan, the thief began making his way around the clearing. He needed to be on the east or west side of it, and the temple, in order to have a chance of his plan working. He used extreme caution as he made his way, expecting that some of the Mogrin had to leave the camp at one time or another for food and the like. In fact, the thief hoped he'd come across one of the monsters in the hope they would have a rabbit, or anything else to eat. His stomach was beyond rumbling, and beyond pain. Raben simply knew that he needed to eat. He wasn't sure what kept him going, because he knew it wasn't food. *The end. I need to make it to the end. True Knowledge.* He rolled his eyes. *Maybe I'll become a priest and Thantos and I can scare people witless. He'd better understand why I left. He better know. It was his advice that kept me from killing.*

The sound of Mogrin woke Raben up to his surroundings. He stood amidst the pines, but a few of the monsters neared the edge of the clearing and obviously intended to enter the woods. Startled, the thief leapt up into the lower branches of a nearby pine. When he did, several twigs snapped. The Mogrin grunted excitedly as they closed. *Blazes!* Raben could hear them snuffling the air as he'd expected, but as they neared, and caught his scent, they stopped. He could see one of them through the branches, standing near the tree, slowly cocking its hideous head as it tried to interpret the smell. It looked somewhere between vicious and alarmed. The thief stared at the creature, sensing every shift in the monster's temper. It started out as the hunter, but soon became curious. Confusion set in, and moments later, it became afraid. The thief was happy with that until he understood the reaction it would bring.

He dropped from the tree as it began, but he was too late. All three Mogrin had run back out of the woods into the clearing yelping and snarling in alarm. *Hells! Hells! Hells!* The battered thief did his best to run from the scene, heading north, still hoping to execute his plan, but expecting to become the object of the Mogrin's hunting prowess momentarily. He felt his body slowing as he ran. His chest burned as he moved, sending shocks of pain up into his throat, limiting the air he could breathe. He had only run a few hundred steps when he began coughing and gasping for his next breath. *Hells! I'm dead. I've lost to a man who is staked to the damned ground. Greech you, Hessing!* Raben fell to his knees, trying to get air into his body. He hugged himself, trying to keep whatever warmth he had, afraid that death was coming. Air whistled as it entered and exited his lungs. He could feel his throat constricting on the air. His chest burned. *Something is wrong. That invisible thing killed me. It crushed my chest. It killed me.* He lay down on his back, and worked to slow his breathing. Doing so, he got a little more air, and managed to push the panic back. *Come on. Calm down. Calm down.* He held himself tightly, hoping that the Mogrin would have a long discussion about what was in the woods before rushing to meet it, but he knew how they would react. Some big brutish Mogrin would tell the whole host that he was mighty and could fight whatever had scared the weaker ones. He would burst into the woods ready to kill me. *If I'm like this, he will. Come on. Calm.* His breathing began to regulate itself and Raben sat up. He could hear the yelling and snarling of the creatures. *They're coming.* He used a tree to push himself to his feet, and then began hobbling to the north.

He'd not gone far when he heard another surge of yelling. Turning westerly, the thief struggled to get a view of the clearing. After a few moments he could see them. *Boiling Hells!* Nearly the whole host had moved to where Raben scared the Mogrin from the woods, which was only a few hundred paces to the south. Now, however, they were all rushing back across the clearing because they were being attacked. *Damn it! I rescued that idiot. No!* Thantos and the dwarves used the opening to sortie after Hessing. Since the entirety of the Mogrin host had rushed to the woods to see what had scared their comrades, Hessing was basically alone with his iron spike. Now Thantos and the dwarves were with him. *This is my chance and I can't even move.*

Raben watched, dejected, as Hessing was freed. The dwarves, there were six of them, formed a broad semicircle around Thantos and Hessing and fought with incredible ferocity. Though hundreds of Mogrin stood around the few dwarves, after twenty or thirty of their kind littered the ground, the rest were hesitant to attack. They snarled and yipped, but stood away from the party as they broke the chain that bound the noble. Any Mogrin that foolishly stepped near the dwarves was quickly deprived of his life. Soon, the noble was standing, his head held high as he surveyed the hundred paces or so that remained between himself and the front doors of the temple. Despite having been a prisoner just moments before, the man now rose with supreme confidence, looking as though he were a legendary hero who could not be stopped on his way to his destiny. *He is the chosen. Hells! Thantos, my friend, you are about to send the wrong man into that temple, and he will never admit it. Or...Hells! Look at him!*

The thought crushed Raben. Somewhere deep inside, he'd been nursing the idea that maybe everyone else had been wrong and he actually was supposed to complete this journey. But now that he was watching Hessing, who looked every bit the part of the successful hero that would save the world, the thief was certain that the man would do exactly that. Each of the dwarves bowed to the noble in turn, offering great respect and reverence to the man they'd just rescued. *I'm bait. I was bait. I pulled the enemy out of the way just long enough for him to be rescued and delivered to the temple. I was bait. I was a ruse, a feint. My life served as a distraction so that he could make it.* Sadness welled up in Raben. He wanted to weep in the hopes that it would let the terrible error he'd made go away. *I am not the one. Thantos will fight me if I try to enter the temple. He won't let me go. The only person I have left in the world to call friend will kill me if I try to find out what I am.* Laughter came with the tears. *I'm a joke not only here but in the Heavens. I have served nothing but to stand in the path of the storm, and now this fool gets the reward. He will be sung about for years to come, and my name will never be heard again.* He turned his gaze to the temple and anger once again flared inside. *It's mine. I have earned it. There must be a way to at least see the inside before I die. There must be a way. Even the voice called to me.*

Looking back to Hessing and the dwarves, Raben singled out Thantos. While dwarves were bowing to the noble, their long beards sweeping the ground, the priest stood off to the side like a black statue. He didn't move at all, yet the thief felt as though nothing escaped the priest's undead eye. He seemed surreal and powerful even from the great distance away that Raben was.

Even the Mogrin seemed to sense the power of Thantos. They were slowly making their way out of the clearing, but none of them walked anywhere in his direction. Nearly all of them went exactly opposite his location. Though none of them broke for it and ran, they were all slowly backpedaling away from the ceremony occurring before the temple. All of them afraid to interrupt the dwarves as they bowed before Hessing, the Mogrin were left only with escape. Many of them began to walk rapidly away from the rescuers, stopping every few steps to look back and make sure that they were safe. Tens of them were heading right at Raben where he hid in the pine wood.

That's my luck. Tears still ran down his face as he sat watching the ceremony. *It's not over yet. I am going to get into that place and gain the True Knowledge. It is the least that I deserve. They can chase me and try to kill me if they want. They were going to anyway.* Raben backed into the forest where he found a particularly large tree. Climbing up amidst the strong branches at its midsection, he found a spot where he could still see the dwarves, Hessing, and Thantos. He watched them to find out what they were going to do next. *Let them try getting into the temple and then I can find my way in after all the excitement dies down.* He nodded to himself as he pulled his blade from its sheath. *They'll have no luck without this thing, anyway.* He held his sword up where he could inspect it.

The dwarves made a camp right near the iron stake and seemed reluctant to approach the temple. Hessing appeared to be debating with them or giving commands. Regardless of which, when he was done he sat down with them. *Just get on with it.* Thantos stood where he had before, his vampiric gaze covering the clearing. *Just go in.* The thought of sitting in the tree until Hessing felt properly prepared to enter the temple sounded horrible to Raben, but he had little else he could do. *Damned noble needs to have everything his way. Make sure to bathe and prepare your hair, Hessing. Maybe you should send away for a new wardrobe so that the painting of you on the steps of the temple will have you looking extra dashing. This is going to take too long.*

Putting his sword away, Raben decided to make the best of the time he would be perched in the thick pine. Calming himself as well as he could, he reached inside of himself and began to concentrate, attempting to commune for the many spells he'd cast of late. His body shot reminders of the many internal wounds that he'd suffered against the invisible creature, his chest blazing inside of him. It was difficult to concentrate. He slowed his breathing and held a hand to his chest, rubbing it, distracting himself from the pain. He tried again. He felt himself going. His thoughts became clean and directed. He felt his host though sensed some resistance as though something were interfering with him, or his ability to use magic. He felt spells beginning to etch themselves in his mind, and he could feel his hands weaving the intricate patterns of the spells. He let himself sink into it, but before long, he was abruptly awakened from his communion. *What is this?* He focused on his magic. *Missing.* He had far fewer spells than he was used to. He could feel the diminished magic that he had. He knew he was far weaker than he'd ever been where magic was concerned. Worse than the first night he could remember, in Hessing's manor. He had fewer spells and they would produce lesser results than they had before. He stared at his hands. *I need magic. It is what is going to set me apart from him. He has a blade, and can probably outfight me.*

He lowered his hands and tried again to focus on communing with his host spirit, but it didn't take long for the result to be obvious. *Blazing, boiling, greeching Hells!* The thief wanted to yell and throw things, but couldn't. He wanted to kill Hessing. *Even if it does mean that the world won't get the True Knowledge. Damn him! He doesn't deserve to get to have it. He did nothing except play the defeated damsel in distress this whole journey. I did all the work. Thantos gave up nearly everything. Urchin died!* Tears fell from the tree as he thought of his friends. More came as he pictured Thantos fighting him at the doors of the temple.

This is what becomes of those that struggle on a quest for the gods. They go unthanked. They are used. Even Hessing, though he will be congratulated by nearly everyone in Reman. He is simply being used. He didn't train to be the hero. He told me once that he didn't even want to go on this quest, but now he is at its end. A success. He is a fool, and I am a greater one.

Raben adjusted how he was sitting on the knobby gray branch, trying to make himself comfortable. He stuffed his robe underneath him in order to lessen the annoying processes that rose up off of the limb. Once he was as comfortable as he was likely to get, he watched the company in the clearing through the dense coat of needles that hid him from view.

It was a sinking feeling. The priest pointed right to him, and no sooner had he done so, than three of the dwarves began walking to him. He'd sat in the tree for a long time watching the group. They'd cooked a meal, and rested. They'd practiced with their weapons, including Hessing. Raben fumed as they did so. Any of the dwarves that fought the noble would give him tremendous contest and then let him win. Even from the distance Raben watched, he could see the dwarves opening up their otherwise impenetrable defenses to allow the man to strike them for the winning blow. *The hero must be placated in the name of Talvo. What would the war god think if His priests let each other strike in order to conserve one another's manhood. They'd be struck dead in moments.* But they weren't, and the thief watched each staged bout.

After that, and more rest, the group finally opted to approach the temple. They made their way up with Hessing at the head of the dwarves, who walked in a military column, followed by Thantos who approached the church almost as though he had no interest. He seemed to be otherwise occupied when compared to the absolute focus that both Hessing and the dwarves had.

Upon reaching the fallen roof of the training grounds, which had stood in front of the temple, Hessing stopped and led the party in a prayer. Raben could tell by the increased reverence with which the group followed his every gesture and then all saluted each other simultaneously. *Just go in.* Raben could picture the hard working warriors who might have once trained amidst the stone columns if they encountered these followers. *They'd split you down the middle like a log. They fought against something dark, and won. They lived their lives hard in order to fight hard, and here the dwarves, who have admitted to living a better, easier going life, are being led by a man that hasn't faced a real hardship in his life. Thantos should be the one going in. Even I would speak a prayer were he to lead it.*

After the prayer, they made their way through the debris of the training area, and up to the temple stairs. Again, Hessing stopped them. They discussed a number of things, and then ascended the stairs, or more correctly, Hessing ascended the stairs. He left everyone else at the bottom, Thantos included. Upon reaching the door, he placed his hand on the stone handle, and then waved to the group at the base of the temple stairs. Moments later he pulled on the door, and it resisted. He tugged it harder, but it wouldn't budge. With both hands he gave it a massive pull, but again, it didn't open one knuckle.

Thantos then walked smoothly up the stairs behind him and moved to the door. The two talked, Hessing obviously disliking Thantos, what the priest was saying, or both. It was only a moment after that, that the priest had done it. Pointed right to Raben. In the midst of the tree, the priest had picked him out and shown these warriors of Talvo right where he sat. The thief was stunned.

The three dwarves closed in on him as he sat and watched, unable to believe either that they knew where he was, or that Thantos had divulged his hiding place. Something about the priest made it not too difficult to believe when Raben considered how his vampiric friend would have known he was there. *Greeching Priest. What do I do with these greeching dwarves?* Watching the dwarves, Raben realized that a battle wouldn't favor him. He'd watched them fight the Mogrin and knew that these were probably the best fighters in all of Redaxe. He didn't want to kill anyone, but knew that his demise would probably be worse were he caught than if he were able to remain free.

Keeping clear of the dwarves, however, seemed a greater chore than he'd first thought. As they approached, each of the dwarven warriors tugged a couple of hand axes from their belts. Raben had seen a dwarf throw such an ax, and didn't like his chances should he end up exchanging daggers for axes with the heavily armored dwarves. *If I could breathe, I could outrun them without effort.* But he knew his chest wouldn't allow that, and thus negated that option as well. *I could fly away.* He had a spell that would allow him to glide through the air, but he had no idea where he would glide to. He needed to get into the temple just as badly as they did. *Were it just escaping...* He tried to locate the magical incantation should he need it. *Hells!* It wasn't there. He thought hard, but it was gone, along with many other spells. *Damned Talvo and his protections against magic. Same as in Redaxe.*

He lost sight of the dwarves as they made their way under his vision. They were now under his tree more or less. *They know exactly where I am. Curse that priest. He's a walking corpse. Told them right where I am. And I can't even leave.*

"Thief," called one of the dwarves. *That could be Moragin.* "Thief, we need to parlay." *Parlay. They are using the words of war. They think I am their enemy.* He leaned to a side and tried to see down through the branches. *What am I, if not their enemy?* "Raben! It is Moragin. Talk to me before these dullards chop down this tree!"

"For what reason do you need to," Raben paused, considering the word, "parlay?" *You came here to attack me, dwarf. Speak up.*

"As ye no doubt know," said Moragin, his gravelly voice thinning as it passed through the branches of the dense tree, "we have approached the temple." Raben could hear limbs cracking as the dwarves walked beneath the tree. *Probably building a fire.* "We can't get in. That sword yer wearing is the key. In every way. It opens the door. There is a keyhole shaped just like it." The last words were strained as the dwarf tired of yelling. "Come down! We won't hurt ye. We won't even bind ye. Just come down and talk to us." Looking to the nearest tree, Raben judged the distance. As he thought about trying the jump, he heard an ax whack into the trunk of the one he was in. The pine vibrated from the force of the blow. Another landed. Then another. He could hear Moragin yelling at the other two dwarves, who'd obviously decided to chop it down.

Raben sprang to his feet and, with no hesitation, ran up the branch he'd been sitting on. Near the end he leapt out from his tree into the thinner branches of the tree next to it. Crashing through small branches, he finally arrived at the one he'd aimed for, some distance below the one he'd leapt from. As it passed, he reached out his hands and caught it, letting his weight swing under it. He felt the rough bark tearing his hands, but let his momentum carry him. As he swung past the branch, his speed slowed, and he was able to aim for the next, which he dropped to. Upon landing on the new limb, he steadied himself and listened for the dwarves response, while his chest flared. *Hells!* He squatted on the branch, forcing himself to remain calm. *Breathe. Calm.* He listened to the dwarves, who were still hacking at the tree, hoping that he wouldn't have to move again soon. *Did they miss all that noise?*

The dwarves were hacking away at the first tree, and hadn't heard a thing. Moragin was pacing behind them, fuming. Raben could see the dwarf as he grumbled to himself, gesturing angrily at the two other armored dwarves that were now halfway through the trunk of the tree. Wood chips flew as they excitedly let their axes gnaw at the tree. Despite all that he was going through, Raben couldn't help but smile as he watched Moragin. *He cares about all of this. He wants it done right.*

Looking down to the ground, the thief judged that he was only seven or eight paces up. He stepped from branch to branch, slowly descending from the tree, and was soon standing on the ground, on the opposite side of the tree trunk from Moragin and the tree he'd started in. His chest pain receded as the moments passed.

"Almost," said one of the other dwarves, his voice teeming with enthusiasm. "He'll be coming down soon enough." *Well, here's you chance, dwarf. Friend or foe?* Raben watched the grumbling dwarf pace in his heavy plate mail, and when the dwarf had turned away from the others and was walking almost directly at the thief, he stepped from behind his tree. He did so easily to keep Moragin from calling out in alarm, and as soon as the dwarf saw him, Raben waved him over, trying to keep Moragin from alerting the other two, who were fully focused on felling the tree that they thought he was in.

Without a noise, the dwarf walked over to him. He passed right by, leading the thief farther away from the others. Only after they'd gone far enough that they couldn't see the tree or the warriors hacking at it did Moragin speak.

"Look friend, they need yer sword, and they mean to have it. The noble, he cares not a lick for ye, and told us to kill ye, but the other one, Thantos, he said that if we tried to battle ye, we'd all end up dead." Moragin looked at Raben, his eyes serious, measuring the man before him. "Didn't explain if it was because ye'd kill us or he would neither. Can't tell with him most of the time."

"So what?" Raben asked, confused and elated by Thantos defending him. "I walk up to the door and open it, and Hessing walks in, and then I leave?" The thief thought about the idea. It sounded remarkably foolish, yet if they were ready to agree to it, then why not? It let him walk away, and more still, he'd have a chance to enter the temple after Hessing did and gain what he wanted from the quest.

"I guess so," Moragin said. "No one really said how it would be, but I'll swear that that's how it'll work if ye come back with me." A grin spread on the bald dwarf's head. "Don't make me crack yer brain and drag ye back either. Us dwarves are hard to fight with."

"Make those two lumberjacks over there agree to it, and I'll go with you," Raben said. "Otherwise I can't." The thief walked away from Moragin after presenting the dwarf with the ultimatum. *At least then it would be even odds if a battle breaks out between me and Hessing.*

Moragin wasted little time. He marched to the dwarves who were busily rocking the tree, using its weight to break the last of the trunk. Raben heard a quick heated discussion and then heard the all three of the dwarves coming back to where he waited. It was hard not to. Between the ringing of their weapons and armor and the absolute lack of grace and stealth in their walk, they sounded like ten men. Moragin led them. They marched up to Raben and lined up before him.

"I swear by Talvo's name that ye will not be harmed by any member of the questing party for participating in the opening of the door," Moragin said. The other two repeated it. "And furthermore, if ye do nothing that endangers the outcome of the quest then yer safety will be guaranteed, by our weapons and blood back to Redaxe, and beyond in

Talvo's sight." Again the other two repeated the oath word for word.

"Good," Raben said. "Remember this." He turned, looking back to Thantos, Hessing, and the other three dwarves. "Let's go." The dwarves leapt into action. One of the dwarves walked in front of the group, leading them out of the woods, and another fell back to protect their rear. Moragin walked next to Raben, reaching a hand to him. The dwarf began chanting as he clutched a silver chain in his thick fingers.

"Dul artat shand Nosuth," he murmured. A blue light grew in his hand and then slowly passed into the thief's shoulder. Alarmed, Raben almost pulled away, but didn't. He trusted Moragin, and let him finish. Moments after the dwarf completed casting, the thief was glad he had. The pain in his chest diminished, and the pain in his back vanished altogether. He suddenly felt as though he could walk, and more importantly, run a distance without trouble. *Now Hessing, let's have that final battle.* Without the wound eating him from the inside, Raben felt ready deal with the noble.

"Thank you, Bounty. I guess I am just another one of your charges now, huh?" Raben looked to the dwarf, and saw that Moragin had a grim look. "What?"

"I fear what the warrior is going to say," the dwarf said. "Worse still, what he'll do." They walked for a little while, exiting the trees and starting across the clearing. The temple loomed ahead of them. "He seems different from anyone I would have imagined fulfilling the quest. All of ye are a little different from what we might have expected, but he seems to believe in little that he is questing for." Bounty looked to Raben. "Why are ye on the quest?"

"I want to find out who I am," Answered the thief. "I need to know where I came from, and what I was put here to do." He stopped, hoping that the response would satiate the dwarf. *If I tell you everything, you'll cut me down right here.* "I know what you mean, though. I have thought that Thantos was the one to complete the journey, not Hessing." Moragin nodded.

Welcome back. Unready for the thought, Raben nearly dropped to his knees when it hit. *Damned vampire! Stop that!* Looking up, he could see the low hanging hood of Thantos. The vampiric priest stood a hundred paces ahead on the stairs of the temple.

"Are ye alright?" Moragin asked. The thief nodded and began walking faster. Hessing stood at the top of the stairs, waiting for the dwarves, and for Raben. He looked like he always did, except that his armor was new. It had an axe emblazoned on the breastplate. *Dwarven. I'll bet he's louder than ever in that.* The thief held his head up and marched right to the base of the stairs.

"Old Bounty scores another one," Andragin called. "The old fool never fails, though he probably had to pay the man to walk out here with him." The hearty laugh of the dwarf followed. When Raben saw him sitting on a boulder near the stairs, the dwarf waved at him, grinning broadly. "Have a nice trip? Couldn't wait for the rest of us?" Andragin laughed again. *Can they know about the gauntlets? No one seems upset with me except Hessing.* The thief looked right to Thantos. *No.* The answer. They had no idea that he was wearing their only artifact of Talvo like jewelry. They had no reason to be upset with him except that he appeared to have foolishly begun the quest without them. Hessing waited impatiently atop the stairs.

"I see you managed to make it," Hessing said. "I'm glad." His voice sounded less than sincere. "And you have the sword as well. Give it to me." *What? He knows I can't.*

"I told him that he needed only to open the door with the weapon and then he would be free of responsibility, able to keep the sword," Moragin said. Thantos nodded, agreeing with the decision. "He is to open the door to let you enter, Lord Hessing."

"What," Tavner growled. "That sword has to enter the temple. It goes with the chosen to the well of True Knowledge. It protects him from harm. He," the dwarven priest stuck his thumb at Raben, "he can't keep it."

"I can't give it up," said the thief. "Even though I would gladly give it up. I can't. It is magically bound to me, and I to it. To take it away you'd have to kill me." Raben looked to Thantos. "I have to go in with the blade. You can send Thantos in with me to make sure I do nothing that would hinder Hessing from gaining the True Knowledge."

"No!" Hessing yelled out. "He is not going into that temple. Just take the sword from him and bind him until I've returned." Tavner nodded, but no one else did. Thantos took one step down the stairs and everyone fell silent, Hessing included.

"Open the door," he hissed, "and let the chosen in. My studies have not proven that he should need the sword. I agree that the thief can't enter with him, but I do not believe that Hessing will need the sword to obtain the True Knowledge." The undead priest turned and looked back up the stairs to the noble. "Can you agree to that?"

Obviously not. Hessing's face was bright red, full of angry things that he wanted to say, but didn't. Looking down at Thantos, the noble began to take deep breaths, and then slowly nodded, unwilling to fight with him.

"But the prophecy says that the blade will take him to the gate," Tavner argued. "The chosen needs to have the weapon in order to make it." The dwarf was near bursting with anger himself.

"In Talvo's sight, His word can only become truth in the way that He sets it before us," Thantos hissed as he spun to look down at the dwarven priest who stood at the base of the stairs. "We will receive a sign if I am wrong. We will wait until tomorrow to enter. It grows dark, and the Mogrin will come back."

Behind the priest, Hessing raised a hand in order to protest waiting until the next day, but no one looked to him. The dwarves jumped into action as soon as Thantos spoke, and Tavner climbed the stairs to speak privately to the human priest. Raben found himself suddenly alone. *This is strange.* He almost laughed at the relief of how many allies he had here. He looked to Hessing, but the noble was walking back to the temple doors muttering to himself. *Something has been happening to that man since he came back to us. The Guild must have done something to him. Something.*

"Good to see ye, fool of a human," Andragin barked as he pounded his meaty fist on Raben's back. "What in the fire and forge were ye thinking when ye came here by yerself?"

"I didn't want anyone else to have to suffer in order to get that lummox into the temple," Raben answered. "I thought there would be more trouble after hearing you and your friends describe the Mogrin and the evils that prowled the north shore." *I need to get into the temple. Need to know.*

"That's our job," Andragin answered. "Me and Bounty joined into this the moment we saw yer sorry hide." The dwarven warrior laughed. "Never guessed we'd have to pull ye from a tree. I heard those fools were chopping the tree down and ye were standing right behind them." He laughed again. "Wait til I tell their fathers. They'll shave their beards in shame." Andragin walked away, chuckling to himself.

I must get in. What? Get in. I have to go. I killed for no reason. Raben barely kept from falling to the ground. He sat where he was and let the thoughts roll through his mind.

The temple is mine. I traveled too far not to enter. I need to go in. Suddenly they stopped. *Were those mine? Thantos? The sword? The voice from the woods? The voice of the temple? That voice invited me to come to the temple. It wants me here. I need to talk to Thantos.* Raben walked to where camp was, and began settling in. Thoughts continued to hit him. *It is mine. I must go in.*

It was in the middle of the night when the two of them were finally able to talk. It was a standard operation for the two of them. Ever since Kernish, they had spoken in the middle of the night. Being a vampire, Thantos stayed up through the night; he seldom slept at all. Raben, however, tried to sleep through the night, but whenever the undead priest was around, he always woke up in the darkness, and with nothing else to do, he'd had long conversations with the undead priest. It seemed strange to him, and when he found himself doing the exact same thing this night, he said as much.

"That," Thantos hissed, "is because I shoot thoughts at you until you wake up. It is the only time that we can speak without input from nearly everyone else." Thantos smiled, his violet lips parting to show the sharp unnatural teeth that only a vampire had. "Seems like everyone has a little more to say than I want hear these days." *Everyone.*

"You have some things to tell me, my friend," Raben said, becoming serious in an instant. "As the argument was being waged regarding Hessing taking the sword from me today I was nearly killed by all of the thoughts that crashed into me. Were they yours or are there other undead that I have linked with nearby?"

"There are other undead nearby. I have wondered what their purpose was." *The twelve vampires or what's left.* Thantos looked into the blackness of the night. There had been a fire burning in the center of the camp, but after taking over the watch from the dwarves, who'd insisted on doing their part of the duties, Thantos had let the fire burn low. It was almost out. "They are near," he hissed. "They fear us."

"My friend, you've been with too many people that revere you lately," the thief said. "I can tell." The priest looked at him, his confusion obvious. "Answer my question. You can't just shrug my request off like you do all of theirs." The vampiric priest smiled.

"Some of them are mine," he said. "I have a plan. My thinking, your risk." *That will wait until later.* "Did you find and kill Strad?" Thantos asked, taking Raben by surprise.

"No," the thief shot back. "I haven't seen the Kernishman since before we entered Redaxe. You told me he was trailing Hessing. Going to slow him down, or something like that."

"He was," hissed the priest, letting the sound slowly escape between his pointed teeth. "I have lost my link with him. That worries me, especially with the undead around here, but it also helps me. I don't think I can be hurt if something hurts him." Thantos turned around where he stood, looking over the party that he had led here. *Good people. All of them. They really are going to help humans again.*

Raben rolled up one of his sleeves, letting the gauntlet beneath catch a little of the dying firelight. "What are these good for? I assumed that they would somehow protect me, but I really haven't any idea what they are for," Raben admitted. "I just didn't want to kill anyone in order to feel safe."

"No one seems to know what they do, my friend." Thantos walked to the thief and touched the gauntlet. "I checked every book in Redaxe, looking for the abilities of

527

these things, but it was recorded no where. I think they are good, so don't lose them, but I couldn't tell you anything more than that." *Didn't want to kill anyone. Did it work? No. Who? Greev. Who?*

"A dark dwarf that helped me cross the lake," Raben said, breaking the chain of thoughts before he went insane. "I didn't like him, but would never have harmed him. He was helping me when they took over. I had no choice. His death was as much a shock to me as anyone else. I just turned around and there he was. I hate them." *I need to find a way to get back at them Thantos. Whoever they are.*

"My friend, I will help in any way I can, which is why I have decided on a course of action." *You are going into the temple.* "We will wake up Hessing and tell him that he needs to enter now because an attack is imminent, which it is. This might be true, after all." *The Mogrin will be back, and the vampires will attack then as well, with a messenger of Thannon.* "He'll go in and you'll follow to be the sword that takes him to the well, as the dwarves call it. Then," Thantos hissed, "you'll have the chance to see what your purpose is, and Hessing can get the True Knowledge. Protect him, my friend, even if you hate him. He's going to save the world, but I want you to have the chance to save yourself."

"Still working on my soul, Thantos." Raben locked hands with the priest. *Thank you, my friend. You are the only one I trust, and have followed me through a lot. Thank you.* "When do we start this?"

"When I know all of the attackers are prepared," Thantos answered. "I won't lie." Thantos smiled, knowing that he was interpreting his value system a little loosely. *We have gone through too much to get here that we not see the temple and walk through this gate. Both of us.*

"We?" Raben asked. "Are we all going to be there, my friend? Will the party that left Liveport all end up at the end of this? You told me that it was your job to keep everyone but the chosen out of that temple." *What has happened since then?*

"I realized that there is no single perfect person or place," Thantos said in little more than a whisper. "Even Redaxe had become lackadaisical. They were still resting on the laurels of a war they won three hundred years ago. Evil was seeping in, and taking over the world, corrupting everyone around them, and they wanted no part in fixing it. They were happier knowing that their world was right, and letting the rest of Reman fall into ruin. It is not one person that will save this world, but many, so the right people to give the True Knowledge to is the many who will cater to its need as it is spread across the land. You, my friend. Myself. Urchin. Hessing. We deserve to know."

"Urchin," Raben sighed. "He would have loved to see all of this mess. I'm sure he'd have a lot to say just like everyone else. He always did." *I think he lives.* "What!"

"I think he still lives," Thantos repeated the thought out loud. "If I'm right then he is still trapped with the white wizard." The undead priest spun suddenly, peering into the darkness. "We'll save him if we get out of here alive. If he does live. I think he does."

"Wait," Raben said, his voice rising. Moragin sat up, ax in hand and looked to the two men. They waved him back to sleep and the dwarf happily complied. "Explain now. How can he be alive, and what has you so convinced that he is? This had better be some pretty good evidence, priest, or I'll bury you in the ground, not that you'd mind." Raben stared into the vampiric priest's yellow eyes as he listened to his friend's reasoning.

"Look," Thantos hissed. "What happened to me when the Meriss attacked? *I was left for dead and Gabriel was ripped from me.* "But I was left alive," the priest added.

"Do you think Urchin was corrupt himself, or do you think the white wizard did it?"

"The wizard." *Of course. Urchin was a pure piece of nature. He did nothing but try to foster laughter and...*

"Yes," Thantos agreed. "Then if I was left the way I was, then Urchin should have been left the same way, but he wasn't. He wasn't because he wasn't with us since the white wizard. He'd been in the wizard's tower the whole time. When the Meriss removed that mage from him, there was nothing left, so he vanished. Remember when Urchin described how he created a sanctuary that the wizard couldn't enter?"

"Yeah, he said that none of the creatures of the wizard's power were able to walk on the ground that he had protected himself with," Raben said, becoming excited by the priest's logic. "He could still be sitting there, waiting for us. We need to get him."

"He's lasted this long. He'll manage another short while," Thantos hissed. "And he may not be there." *The attack is coming my friend. Prepare yourself.*

Raben walked away from the priest. *Thank you, my friend.* The thief couldn't tell if the thought was his or Thantos'.

Arriving at his bedroll, Raben began sheathing all of the daggers he had. He had far too few, and no sickles. *Damn it! In the pack.* The thief spun to see Thantos pointing to a backpack. It was the thief's, the one he'd left in Redaxe. Pouncing on the pack, he found his remaining two sickles, but no more daggers. He sheathed the curved blades, happy to have them again. *Can't believe I left my weapons in the woods.* He shook his head as he thought about it. Thantos was doing some type of preparation of his own, but he did nothing to wake up the others yet. *Wake them?* Raben needed to know if he was supposed to being taking care of that. Both of them looked at the sleeping dwarves, and then Hessing. *Not yet.*

Drawing the magical blade, Raben set it floating next to him, and then lifted his pack so that he could take a few things. A small hand lantern and a flint made it into his belt pouches along with some food and water. The thief decided that he wasn't going to take his robe or his pack. He wanted to be able to move as freely as possible. He had no idea what he was walking into, and didn't feel that this was the time to take any chances. Nothing else in his pack looked necessary, so he dropped the bag to the ground and began stretching his arms and legs.

"My friend," Thantos hissed. "Let's begin." The undead priest walked towards Hessing and gestured for Raben to follow. He did. *Wake him up and explain our situation. Quickly.*

"Hessing!" The thief said, shaking the noble. "Hessing, wake up!" The warrior's eyes shot open and his hand fell immediately on his sword. "Come on," Raben said. "Thantos says an attack is coming and he wants you in the temple safely before it begins. Quickly."

Hessing jumped to his feet, and began to jog to the temple door. Thantos fell in with the noble, keeping up with him stride for stride. Raben jogged after them a few moments later.

"I have made a decision," Thantos hissed as they ran, "and I won't hear opposition. There is too much at stake, and a massive attack coming." Thantos ran alongside of the noble for a little while longer. "The thief is going in with you to act as the sword. If you say a single word, I will kill him, take the sword and hurl it into the sea," warned the priest, his voice a lethal hiss.

Hessing said nothing, which was how he agreed with the things that he didn't like. He just ran to the temple doors, leaping up the stairs with a long sword in each hand.

How eager to accept my presence that easily. The three arrived, and at that moment, the battle came.

Cobblestones erupted into the air as Raben bounded up the stairs. Dust blocked his view of the temple. He instinctively tumbled to the side, feeling that he was in trouble. Bits of stone pelted him as he regained his feet. He could hear the high-pitched screams of the vampires that had attacked them twice before, and the bellow of Hessing as he attacked or defended himself, but the thief could see nothing through the thick dust that had accompanied the initial explosions.

After a moment, he surged forward through the dust, trusting that his sword, which floated by his side, would defend him. After only a few steps, the blade came to life and began darting after an opponent. Armed with his sickles, Raben joined in. He burrowed into the back of a vampire. It was clawing at Hessing, having little luck getting through the warriors blessed armor. Coming from behind, the thief raked his sickles across the vampire, doing little more than annoying the undead. He then raised his blades, trying to catch the creature's neck between them, that he might shear the thing's head from its shoulders. As he did so, another vampire clutched Raben from behind, and threw the thief to his back. As soon as he landed, the vampire pounced on him. The beast quickly pinned his hands to the ground and lowered its head to his neck. He screamed as it bit into him, but it stopped a moment later as the magical sword began carving into its back. Blood sprayed from the vampire's

533

mouth. It fell from Raben in order to combat the sword and the thief wasted no time. Wrapping his sickles around its neck, he yanked each as hard as he could, tearing into its neck from each side. It screeched in pain, it's painful call ending in a strained gurgle. It spun to face Raben, but the enchanted blade burst through the vampire's chest, dropping the undead to the ground. *Gods!* Raben finally figured out why the vampires looked familiar. *Sir Arris.* The thief leapt up and headed for the creature that had been attacking Hessing, but it was gone. *Arris.* Raben spun back, and looked at the fallen vampire for only a moment. *Sir Arris! The twelve knights were vampires! Hells!* He quickly scanned the battle field for other vampires. Finding one dead on the ground at the bottom of the stairs, he tried to assign it to the group of knights. He couldn't remember the name of the man, but it was one of them. *Gods! They've all been turned!* He remembered when Thantos had come from the temple near Liveport. *They were eating each other. What did he say? Damn! Vampires! I knew that bastard moved too well.*

"Come on!" Hessing yelled, interrupting the thief's concentration. "Open the damned door." Thantos stood with the noble, ready to defend the man. As Raben approached, he saw his friend fling the noble to the side of the door. The vampiric priest then sprang straight up, just before a massive pillar of stone struck the rock doors of the temple, crashing into the temple with a thunderous boom, which sent huge chunks of stone spilling across the ground. Hessing jumped to his feet, a little shaken after the massive chunk of rock nearly pounded him into oblivion. Thantos landed exactly where he'd leapt from, and waited for the attacker. *What?* The thief spun to see what was coming. *The messenger! Hells!* Raben rushed to the noble, sheathing his sickles and tearing his blade from the air so that he could open the door. He lowered the weapon to slide it into the key whole, but a bone hand shot past his shoulder and clutched the blade turning it from the keyhole. A second hand clamped onto his shoulder for a moment, beginning to wrench him backwards. Suddenly the force relented.

Thantos clutched the messenger's bone arm and peeled the lich's grip from the thief's shoulder.

"Aren't you interesting," came the hollow voice of the skeleton. "Yes." Pulling Raben's sword straight back into him, the lich drove the pommel into the thief's stomach, knocking him to the ground. Then the lich leapt on Thantos.

Raben lifted his sword as he gasped for breath, and slammed the blade into the keyhole. Hessing was dicing Mogrin, and paid no attention to what was happening near the temple doors. Raben tried to pull the door open, but a huge piece of the pillars still lay there, blocking the door's path. He bent over the stone and tried to move it, but it weighed far more than he could lift. Resolved on getting through the door, he lay on the ground and wedged himself between the door and the cut stone, using his legs to push the massive column out of the way. He put all of his strength into his attempt and the thing didn't move at all. Trying again, he got it to slide a little, but still fell far short of the distance he would need to open the doors. He was about to try again when he saw Mogrin heading at him. There were four. Springing to his feet, he tore his sickles from their sheaths and waited.

The first Mogrin sprung into the air, as he'd seen them do when they battled each other. He stepped forward, and raked his sickles into the flying creature's gut, and then ducked as it flew past. Swiping his sickles sideways, he cut the next one's face and chest before it was even able to defend itself. The third one reached past the second and took Raben's left arm and sunk its teeth into it. While it was so close, the thief used his right hand and rammed the pointed tip of his sickle into the hideous beast's eye. It crumpled to the ground. The thief spun to the next attack too late. The last healthy Mogrin crashed into him, taking him to the ground. It sat atop the fallen human and wailed on him with its clawed fists. Several blows smashed into Raben's face and the rest bruised his already hurting stomach. He flailed his sickles into the creature, but the sheer fury with which it bludgeoned him thwarted any strong counter by the thief. After a few moments, he just went limp, and as the monster felt it, it leaned its face down to smell its kill. A wounded Mogrin joined him. It had slashes on its face and chest. They leaned in until Raben could feel their hot breath on his skin.

He brought one sickle right up into the throat of the Mogrin that had been beating him so badly, and his other sickle he swept along the stone floor, catching the other doggish monster in the ankle, cutting through the back of its foot. The first fell dead on top of the thief, and the second began hopping on its other foot, yelping in pain. Raben pushed the dead monster off of him, and unleashed his fury on the remaining Mogrin. It fell a few moments later, bleeding from several deeps gashes. The thief spun away from the dead monsters and looked to the door. He rubbed his sleeves across his face, wiping blood from his mouth and nose. *Temple. Go!*

Thantos was still locked in a melee with the lich. The priest had a malicious smile. Hessing was battling numerous Mogrin from atop a pile of the creatures that he'd already slain. The noble bled from several wounds on his face and arms. Raben ran back to the door where his sword was lodged. Falling back on the ground so that he could try and push the pillar out of the way, Raben wedged himself back between the stone and the wall. He yelled out as he pushed and the enormous piece of rock slid until his legs were straight. He rolled to the side and stood up, yanking on the door. It came open. The thief's eyes went wide, and he tugged on his sword. It too came free. Looking at the chaotic battle behind him, Raben wished them well, and stepped into the first temple of Talvo. *Survive this, my friend. We have a great deal to enjoy if we can escape this. Go!*

Once inside, the thief closed the door behind him. He stood in the entry hall, exhilarated to have finally made it, worried that the Guild hunter would appear and attack him, curious if he'd just locked Hessing out, but most of all, ready to end the whole mess. *Let's get this done.*

Raben stared into the dark temple, suddenly realizing that there was no light. It felt odd. Scary yet safe. *Maybe I shouldn't be here.* He dug into his pouches, feeling for the lantern that he'd packed only a short while before. The door suddenly shook as something pounded on it. *Hessing!* The thief took a quick step forward, and as he did so light flooded the chamber he stood in. Two enormous iron chandeliers hung from the ceiling, each of them filled with hundreds of candles, which were now lit. Along each of the long walls, which extended a hundred paces away from Raben on each side and then turned and continued three hundred paces forward, were set sconces with burning torches. There wasn't a single shadow in the entire hall. Everything was washed in orange light.

The thief took a tentative second step towards the center of the room, watching the floor as he did. It was fantastic. Thousands upon thousands of small stone tiles had been cut and worked together to form a scintillating design on the floor. The workmanship was perfect. Not a single tile was missing and none of them were so much as a hair off of the others. They were flawless. *The dwarves deserve to see this. If nothing else, just this floor will wake them up to higher standards.* Despite all of the other things he could, or should, be doing, Raben took a few more moments to really appreciate the artisanship of the floor he was walking on.

The door shook in its jamb as something vast impacted it. The sound and vibration woke the thief up to the fact that he very well might be dealing with a short time limitation. He began crossing the great hall, his eyes unable to avoid looking at all of the incredible work on the walls. Just like the floor, the brick work in the walls was impeccable. Though the bricks were obviously larger than the floor tiles, they had been arranged to tell stories, colored to form words and pictures. *Great gods!* Raben tried to read as much of it as he could, but most of it was in a language he didn't know, but he arrived at one word that was unmistakable. *Rhokar.*

At the end of a long trail of words that the thief couldn't make out, the word was written in a flowing hand. *Rhokar.* The mosaic that had been arranged around the word was the temple Raben stood in, but rather than a clearing surrounded by ancient pines, the temple sat on the brink of the Hells. Fire surrounded it, and all of the priests were standing in a ring around the mighty stone church defending it from hoards of walking dead and red skinned demons with ebony horns growing from their heads. Inspecting the mosaic more closely, Raben could even find the symbol of Gul Thannon. The withered tree with a full moon behind it was on a banner that had been painted in the background of the scene. It was being held aloft by a skeleton. *Burning Hells! That is what is happening right now, outside!* The thief fell away from the mosaic. *Hells! I can't just turn away from them, but Hessing will stop me from using the well. Maybe Thantos can make him let me go.* Confused, the thief sprinted back to the door, and grasped the handle. He stood, his hand on the iron of the handle for several moments. A feeling grew in him, urging him to run into the bowels of the temple, forgetting his friends, and to use the well to get the True Knowledge for him and him alone. *No! Damn it!* He knew if he didn't act soon, whoever was sending the thought to him would win out.

Raben threw the door open and once it stood wide, he dropped a dagger to the floor, trying to wedge it beneath the door to hold it open. The door had been so well constructed that even while kicking his dagger under it, only the tip of the knife would fit underneath. There was enough to hold the door open, however, and the thief then rushed out the door to keep the mosaic of Rhokar from becoming the grisly end of his companions. Thantos was to the right side of the door. He looked indomitable as he used his vampiric claws against a shambling army of zombies. Hessing and the dwarves had joined together and were in a triangular formation at the base of the steps where they were slowly hacking their way through an unending army of Mogrin. All of them had wounds and their armor was battered until some of the pieces were hanging by single rivets or leather bands, exposing the flesh underneath.

They can retreat into the temple. Raben ran to the top of the stairs where he would cast a spell which would serve not only to get his companions attention but kill enough of the Mogrin in the front to give them a space with which they could climb the stairs and fall back to the temple. *Let the spell remain. I need only one.* He slid to a stop on the blood slicked stone and immediately began casting. His hands purposefully flew through the necessary design, and his words came forcefully as he prepared to maximize the little magic that he had left. As he pronounced the final word, he began choking.

The tip of a slender blade slid out of his chest. It stretched his silk shirt up before his eyes and then sliced through, reflecting light from the temple on its bloody blade. The thief reached out and ran his fingers along the steel as the pain of the wound began to reach him. He felt his heart pulse against the weapon, trying to push blood through him, but the fluid only washed out over him covering his legs in a hot wet coat of crimson. It steamed as it pulsed from him. After only a few pulses, his heart then began to quiver in his chest, no longer forcing his lifeblood to gush.

Raben collapsed to one knee, and spun as he fell. He didn't even notice as the sword was ripped back out of his body. Looking up from where he lay, he saw his attacker. She smiled at him as she cleaned her blade. Not a malicious smile, but a warm smile. The elf crouched down next to him.

"I told you I would have to kill you once you were done in the temple. Too bad you weren't able to figure a way out of this." She spoke as though she meant it, though her words seemed not to bear the weight of the situation. She touched his face. "For both of us." Tears welled up in her eyes. "Know that I had no choice. You know. You've done it." She said more to Raben as he passed into death, but he heard no more.

She was there. He opened his eyes and the Guild hunter stood over him, staring at him, the amazement she felt obvious in every part of her expression. She looked as though she were caught between shock and hope. Her hands were constantly moving as she waited to see if Raben was going to speak. She worked her jaw, looking as though she were about to say something, but repeatedly stopped herself.

The thief tried to sit up, but his whole body seemed to resist. *Pain? Here? I've never felt bad here. What is this?* He looked up at the elf, hoping she'd say or do something. She did.

"What in all the Hells are you doing here?" she asked, heat filling her voice. "You can't be here. You can't!" She shook her head as she spoke, not understanding the situation. "You went into the temple with one life in the sword. They told me. You had to die in order to get the True Knowledge, and then when you came out, I killed you, and trapped you in my sword. It's just like yours. You kill them, and they're trapped!" She shouted. "They can't just get back out and appear here." She held her blade up. "You can't be here."

He forced himself into a sitting position. He wasn't bound at all. "Thrilled to see you too," he sneered. "I would think you'd be a little happier to know that I found a way out of this mess." He pushed himself to his feet. "You

541

shouldn't have underestimated me." *Can't be here. Had to die to get the True Knowledge. They finally made a mistake.* He smiled menacingly.

"I had no choice, you know that," she said, almost pleading. "I wasn't striking you under my control. They had control. That's why I apologized. You've killed without being in control. How many souls are trapped in that sword of yours? More than mine." She threw her sword off to the side. "Damned thing is empty. They will finish me soon."

Raben looked around at his surroundings for the first time. They were in an unspectacular stone room. It had one door which was closed and a bed with a wool blanket on it. There was nothing else.

"Would you even want to escape all of this?" Raben asked. *Greeching woman! Probably content to serve them.* "Do you want to leave here, or are you content to be their assassin. Do their dirty work because one day maybe you'll be the head killer. Ha!" he shouted. "They all just use you and walk away when you need something. That's how life is. You're absolutely right they'll kill you soon."

"I want to leave. I have to leave. If you're alive then I have failed and they will kill me or worse," she said, her argument angering Raben.

"You failed. That's all you're worried about. Not," he accused, "that you were sent to kill me, or that you've killed so many innocent people in the past, but that you failed." He scowled at her. "You want me to save you. Why would I bother? There have been times when all I wanted to do was to come back here and talk with you. Rescue you. I was a fool."

"No!" Tears fell from her eyes. "I have hoped that you would come back. I have wanted to escape here with you. I thought that you were the only one that could get away from them, since you have before." She fell to her knees. "You have to believe me. I have never before let myself think that it could be done, but since the last time we spoke, I have thought of nothing other than getting out of here, but when I appeared behind you at the temple, I had no control. My hand struck without my control. My blade struck, and you were dead. They told me you were gone forever, trapped in my blade until they needed you again."

"Who are they?" Raben was still unsure about her, but he did know exactly what it felt like to be helpless while killing people. "Who are our masters?"

"I don't know any more than you do," she said. "I hear voices and they tell me what I need to know, and sometimes I just wake up knowing what I have to do. I never see anything, or talk to anyone face to face."

"Living here all this time, you've never seen anything that would even hint at who is doing all of this?" he asked, looking at her with doubt in his eyes. "You've been trained to do exactly that. You're a Guild hunter. It's what you do."

"Really, there is no one except the voice. I don't talk to anyone except the others that work for them, like you." She flattened her hands out on the floor. "I have never spoken to any of them as much as I have you. They don't have multiple lives to live, so when they die, they're gone forever. You've come back enough times for me to actually learn a little about you. I do want to escape, and I do want to go with you. You're the only person I know, and for some reason, I trust you." *Trust. How can I trust anyone that has so much to do with this place? What is most valuable to them? Their lives and their ambitions. How can she prove to me that she trusts me?*

"This sword of yours functions just like mine?" Raben asked. She nodded her head, never looking up from the floor. "They told you that I had to die to get the True Knowledge?" She sniffled as she nodded. "And you trust

543

me?" She looked up to the thief as she continued nodding. "What controls how I get back to the normal world from here?" he asked.

"You return to where I want you, or as soon as I give up control over you, you go back to where you were," she murmured. "They usually tell me where I have to put you, and I do it to avoid punishment."

"And Hessing. What did you do to him?" he asked. She looked to the floor.

"He's worse off than we are," she spat. "He was identified by a number of factions as the person they felt was the chosen one a long time ago, and they began entering him then. There are three or four forces fighting inside of that man. They can leave him and enter him as they wish. Since he lived in Liveport, he's been under attack. The nobles that surrounded him were Thannon's. Others have shown interest though I don't know who they are. Who knows what will happen if that man makes it to the well. The Hells may become reality."

"Hessing? He has this happening to him?" *There have been times when he reacted as though he were a totally different man. Many times. Yes. Does that mean he is not the chosen? Does Thantos know this, and that is why he wants more of us to know the True Knowledge. It must be. That corpse of a priest knows more than he told.* "You are sure you want to leave them?" he asked. She nodded emphatically. "Fine." He snapped her sword from the ground and walked up next to her. "Stay where you are."

Raben slid her sword slowly from its sheath and looked the long gleaming blade over. In the light of the room, he couldn't see the reddish glow that it had. He ran his fingers along the sword remembering how it felt when he'd had the blade lodged in his body. How it had looked, streaming his own blood as it burst from his chest.

"What are you going to do?" she asked from the floor. "How are we going to be free?"

"I can free you," he said. "You told me how. I had an idea, but now I know that I can free you and live through the temple in order to bring you back."

"Back?" she said, her voice quaking. "From where."

"Your sword."

As he said it, he brought the razor sharp blade down with all his strength. The sword whipped through the air, hissing as it fell. He barely felt resistance as it bit into the elf's neck, nor when it sheared through her delicate bones. A fine mist of blood sprayed into the air as he did it. He could smell the iron. He didn't even look down. He couldn't. Her head hit the stone floor and rolled a short distance, and then her decapitated torso slumped against his legs, oozing hot blood. *Forgive me. You are free of them. Forgive me. I'll bring you back out of the sword. I will. It is your life that will let me live through the temple. We will be free together.* He backed away from her body slowly, letting it slide down his legs until it rested on the floor. Tears began to stream down his cheeks. *Forgive me. Please.* He looked at her sword, with a hand-tall smear of blood across the middle of the blade. It was slender and nearly weightless. Its balance was perfect. He cleaned it off, tucked it through his belt, and waited to return to the temple, hoping it would happen soon.

The battle continued. Screams of pain and conquest filled the air as he awoke. The dwarves were nearly on top of him, having retreated up the steps as they fought the innumerable Mogrin. Pain rolled through Raben's body as he tried to move. Need fueled him. He climbed to all fours and began crawling out of the middle of the melee.

"By Talvo's ax!" a gruff voice called. "Humans are made of tougher stuff than stone!" Strong hands grabbed the thief under his arms and he was dragged out of the battle and dropped in front of the temple. Rolling over, Raben watched Andragin rush back to the battle, his ax spinning in his hands as though it weighed nothing. *Four.* There were only four dwarves and Hessing. *Moragin!* The balding dwarf was no where to be seen. *Burning Hells!*

"To the temple," Raben yelled, his voice stripped from his recent death. "Get into the temple. Quickly!" The thief grabbed onto the nearby door jamb and pulled himself to his feet, still wanting to precede Hessing to the well. Once up, he stumbled in the door.

"My friend," Thantos said, his voice robust as it once was long ago. He was still pasty white, but he stood upright and looked strong. "Beware! This place now belongs to Talvo only. The gods won't hear you." The priest let his eyes bore into the thief.

"They never could," Raben said. *Be careful. I will come. I will be there.*

The thief began walking back through the mighty hall. He intentionally paid no attention to the walls as he walked, afraid that he might become mesmerized by the story there, perhaps alter his present thinking. *Hessing has many factions inside of him. What do I do with that? Should I stop him? Could I? How can I make sure that I am free by the end of this? Will the True Knowledge give me that? I was already able to resist their wants to abandon my friends just by being here. I wasn't supposed to come out until after I had gotten the True Knowledge, and I'm certain that I wasn't supposed to ever go back and see her.* His stomach balled up as he thought about the Guild hunter. *I will free you. I will. There must be a way.*

Passing through the great hall, Raben arrived at two large doors. Each of them had the silver ax of Talvo etched into them. They gave away before his touch as though driven by his will rather than his hands. Silently they swung open and a broad walkway stretched out before him, with long wooden benches filling the room to either side. *The actual church.* Raben could imagine hundreds of dwarves filing into the long benches and sitting through a sermon from one of the oldest and grumpiest dwarves in the clan. He smiled weakly. *Three hundred years old and being lectured by your elders.*

The walls were carved with statues reaching right out of the stone. Each wall was a single massive piece of white stone, and the statues were carved of the exact same stone, one piece with the wall. They were immaculate. They could have been living dwarves from the detail that shaped their faces and each little link of their chain mail armor. The ceiling was also worked with clouds and birds and a brilliant crystal sun that now glowed with candlelight. Catching the orange light from the front hall, the crystal was able to illuminate and shower the church with a comforting glow. *The dwarves that prayed here must have been overflowing with hope and faith. The glory of Talvo. Let the humans see this.*

He stepped into the chamber, and looked at the pews where thousands of dwarves must have sat in prayer. No dwarves sat there now, yet they were not empty. Small figures were hunched in the front three rows. Small, delicate, they looked like children. Bringing his sword out, Raben walked towards them, needing to pass where they were in order to get to one of the doors on either side of the hall of worship. He moved as quickly as his body would go, the pain still restricting his ability.

Once he could see them, he slowed. Children, women, and a few men sat in the benches. They seemed to be in prayer, leaning forward, clutching each other's hands, murmuring soothing words. It was calming. *How did they get here?* He looked around. *Trap! Not here.*

"Hello there, how did you get here?" Raben asked a small child who was staring at the floor as he prayed. "Excuse me, forgive my intrusion, but how did you get here?"

The little boy looked up at the thief. One of his eyes was missing. A long slash wound stretched a pink scar across his face, reaching from his chin up to his forehead above the missing eye. *Greech! Reese. Hells!* The boy smiled cheerily up at the astounded thief. "You brought us here, sir." *Flaming gods! What is this?*

"What?" he said, his stomach suddenly tightening. "What?"

"You brought us here," repeated the boy. "We are here because of you." *Because of me. They are here because of me. What does that mean? I killed them! I'm in the Hells!*

"You killed them," said a man's voice. *The voice.* It was the same voice that had spoken to him in the woods. The voice of the temple. "These are the innocent that you have trapped in your blade. You killed them. They are the reason you made it this far. They accept it, knowing that you killed them sparingly in order to carry on the work of Talvo. They are here should you wish to thank them for their service, and so that they can have their last service before they join Talvo." Raben spun, looking for the speaker, but once again he could see no one. The voice filled his thoughts. *They know I killed them sparingly. I didn't kill them. They did. Greech! I was carrying on the work of Talvo. I was carrying on the work of evil.* The thief looked at the hunched forms in the pews. They all prayed. One of the figures that sat alone in the second pew looked up and waved. It was Greev. His mouth had the scars from where the enchanted blade had sliced into him, taking his life. *Screeching Hells! I need to leave. Gods!*

"Carry on," Greev said with a smile. "Finish the work that you have started. It is important. More than us, more than you, more than anything. Go." *Go. These are the people I killed and they are urging me forward, excited that I am here.* Raben wanted to cry, but no tears were left. He wanted to scream, but didn't want to startle these people or this church. *I have been damned. I am the sword. The sword must bear all of the burden. Hessing is the hero, and I have been damned. He'd better take the True Knowledge and save this whole land. These people deserve it. I don't.* As his eyes swept over the praying people, Raben didn't recognize anyone but Greev. They looked up from their prayers as one, their eyes filled with admiration, their faces scarred by wounds, by the pain of their deaths. He looked at every one. *They were unaware of what was going on, and died in my path, in the path of anger. My path. The path of evil.* Unable to bear the weight of their adoring looks, the thief let his eyes slide down to the church's tiled floor.

"Do not despair for them," said the voice of the temple. "They do not wish it." *They do not wish it? Did they wish to die in the first place? Did I wish for this? Did Talvo ask each of them if they'd like to take part in this glorious quest before I went insane and began dicing them up?* His head snapped up, his eyes filled with rage, but all that he could see was the anguish in the look he received from a woman seated on one of the benches. She had only one arm, and her chest had a crossing wound which had torn from her breast up through her shoulder, leaving a gaping tear where the sword had exited her body. *Save me. Save them. Whoever is in charge of this terrible mess needs to fall in the path of this blade, just so they can see these people.* He looked from the woman to Reese, the child who had spoken to him earlier, and the boy expressed sheer joy in being singled out by Raben once again. He smiled, causing the pink scar that stretched across his face to strain to a dark red color. *Help me.*

Raben could take no more. He walked from the pews and headed to the door to the right side of the room. He threw the door open and stalked through it. *This journey has been little more than a mindless slaughter.* As he left the church, he heard his name being called through the temple. *Hells! This can't get worse.* It was Hessing. *Need to go faster. Must beat him there.* Raben entered a long hall. It was the first part of the temple he'd seen that wasn't a work of art. It was still perfect, but there were no statues and no artwork, and the floor was blank stone as well as the walls. *Why did they have to die? Move on. Get away.*

With nothing to admire, and the pain of his death ebbing away, the thief made his way quickly up the hall. At the end, were several doors. He began throwing them open, abandoning his usual caution. *Where is it? He cannot get there ahead of me. Bait! To the Hells with him!* He flung open door after door exposing room after room. One seemed to be personal quarters, the next a prayer chamber. After that were several closets where ritualistic tools were; hammers, axes, sickles. *What?* He reached into the closet and brought out a sickle. It gleamed red in the torch light that expanded into every room he entered. *My sickles! They came from here. They are the same. What in the Hells does that mean?* He tore his own weapon from its sheath. They were identical. Inspecting them both, he saw on the new one something that was not on his. An inscription. It was written in the language of magic and seemed fairly simple. Murmuring a spell that might help, the thief looked at it and found that he could now read it.

"This symbol of Thannon is blessed in Talvo's sight. The dark is diminished by the light, and this symbol will never bring such dark as the light of Talvo cannot overcome it." *What? This is used to symbolize Thannon. I have been carrying these weapons since I woke up. I am working for Thannon? I am not evil. I will not give up. Thantos has not. He would know if I were bringing Thannon into the temple.* Unsheathing his other sickle, Raben threw the curved weapons into the closet along with the new one. *I have been damned. No wonder every one of the vampires and liches we fought thought I was one of their kind. I was holding a symbol of their god. Burning Hells! I have represented every evil I want nothing to do with.*

Raben backed away from the closet. He stared at it for a few moments before he began throwing more doors open. Empty rooms and personal chambers lay behind every door. Finally, as he heard Hessing calling him from the church area, he found a stairwell. It went up. The thief began leaping up the stairs three at a time, trying to put some distance between himself and the noble. *I wonder if he faced any dead in the church. I wonder if he bears any guilt from this quest.* Raben sneered as he thought about the man, comparing the noble's journey to his own. *Or has it been that easy to ride our shoulders here and then enter the temple?* Something had detained Hessing. *He's not catching up. They'd better not have brought the battle in here. If they damage a single piece of this place, I'll personally give them each a gut full of steel.*

As he bounded up the steps, the thief began arriving at doors. He pushed each of them open, and based on nothing more than how the level felt to him, he decided whether or not he would explore it. The first he passed by. *This well is going to be out of the way. They couldn't have needed it to be readily available. They knew the True Knowledge back then.* The second level felt the same way. It was going to be personal quarters and storage. The third level above seemed less used. Dust was thick on the floor, and no light greeted him when he threw the door open.

Lighting his own lantern, Raben entered. *The stairs continue up. I should go up.* He started to leave, but then decided to explore. Moving quickly through the level, he found personal rooms, and a number of small chambers that were little larger than a closet where people must have gone to pray by themselves. A large pillow lay on the floor of each chamber. *Depressing. Pray downstairs.* It was unimaginable to the thief that someone would forgo the use of the glorious chambers downstairs in order to sit in the blank cubicles that he was discovering.

He burst into another room. It was full of books. *I wish I had a year to spend here before I had to face this.* He looked at the tomes, all of them hundreds of years old. They called to him. It felt as though his answers were there. Just the idea of books appealed to the meticulous and curious nature of the thief. Knowledge was always an advantage, and based on how the trek had gone for him, he felt he could use any advantage he could get.

"Thief!" Hessing bellowed. *He's in the stairwell.* "Thief! Where are you?" Raben backed out of the library and closed the door. He ran back through the level and made his way back to the stairs. As he entered the first room of the level, he saw Hessing in the doorway.

"There you are," Hessing said, irritated. The noble was covered in blood and had scratch marks on his face. His armor had been destroyed. Plates were missing and blood was caked on his clothes beneath. "What are you doing? We need to go up to the top of the temple. That is where the well is." The noble backed out of the door. Raben approached it cautiously.

"Is the battle over?" he asked. Hessing shook his head.

"No," he said. "They still fight below. Three dwarves hold the door along with Thantos. They will last quite a while. Those dwarves are the toughest warriors I've ever seen." Raben nodded in agreement.

"Many things about them are surprising," Raben said. "They will be great help with all that will need to get done." The thief walked through the door, looking straight at Hessing. "How are you feeling?" he asked. "You look like something is wrong." Nothing looked wrong beyond the many wounds that the noble had, which would normally be enough for any person, but Raben was trying to maneuver the noble into telling him about what was really going on.

"Besides watching some of the most valiant people in this world get relentlessly pounded until they fell in battle, and having my body used as a scratching post by the evil that infects this part of Reman, facing perhaps the greatest challenge any person has faced in hundreds of years and being absolutely boiling tired, I suppose," Hessing said with a shrug, "that I could use a warm meal." He couldn't help it, Raben laughed. The noble hadn't been the slightest bit unhinged for a long time. He'd been nothing but Von Hessing, and here, in the midst of the most trying part of the whole trek he found a way to abandon his seriousness in order to lessen the stress. The thief stifled his laughter.

"I did mean besides that." Raben looked to the noble, conveying the seriousness of the question. "It seems as though something is wrong on the inside. I feel like you have been fighting a battle that you have told the rest of us nothing about."

"This one is mine to bear, Thief," Hessing stated. "You've done enough in getting us all here that you don't need to handle this fight as well. I can take care of it. We all have something that is ours and ours alone to bear." Hessing began walking up the stairs ahead of the thief, and then turned suddenly back to Raben. "The benches in the church were empty when I passed through."

What? Raben looked up to the noble, trying to figure out how the huge man meant what he'd said, but Hessing was already continuing up the stairs. *He knows. Why does everyone know what I'm thinking and doing all the time?*

"Wait! How in the boiling fires did you know about that? You have been telling people things that you shouldn't know at all," Raben said. "Greev told me that it was you that described the battle at Nestor's Ferry." Hessing kept walking, showing no interest in answering the thief. "Was it the Guild? Did you make a deal with them?" The noble stopped, freezing on the steps as though he'd been suddenly paralyzed. He said nothing. He just stood there with the thief a few steps behind him, the accusation hanging in the air. A long moment passed, and Raben lowered his voice to a growl. "That's what I thought." *That's how he escaped them. He agreed to do something for them. Urchin and Thantos wanted to kill you out on the plains. We should have. We would be far better off. How many schemes has he worked on? How many deals? We should have diced you out there the very moment you showed back up. Greeching fool.* "They'll get you too, Lord Hessing. They won't let you be. Are you already finding this out, or is this something you're just going to have to prepare for? Or does this reach even further back? Did you deal with Thannon to get me to carry this cursed sword all the way here for you?"

"Mind your tongue before I cut it from your mouth, Thief," snarled the noble. "I am caught in no web of service like you are. I am free. They were unable to bend me to service. I would never play the dog's part like a rogue for hire. They offered a proposition that only served my ends so I accepted. My gain was being informed on your every immoral act and plan. I know every poor bastard that you have mindlessly gutted since this began, and I know how this journey will end for you, and when it happens I will end the possibility for its continuance." Hessing began to slowly climb the steps, but Raben's words stopped him again.

"Were you allowed to keep her sword? Did you have to kill her?" Raben asked. "You ought to know something about the future of your plans and the deal that you made." Looking up to where the noble stood unmoving on the steps, the thief knew he was close to the mark. *You agreed to kill her after she killed me, didn't you. Then you would store the sword, or give it to them. What does that do for them? Why?* The noble didn't respond in any way. He simply stared up the stairwell, frozen where he stood. *Yes, you are caught, your lordship. Have you nothing to say for yourself.* "I expected a more proper response from the chosen member of the quest, Lord Von Hessing. I hope you think of all of the ways that you helped tarnish the image of Talvo while His followers carry you around on their shoulders." Raben gripped his sword, preparing for the noble's response, but when it came it took him totally by surprise.

The large warrior ran up the stairs, leaving Raben behind. After the noble rumbled up the stairs for a good distance, the thief followed, reluctant to run as fast as he might, for fear that the warrior had somehow prepared a trap for him. *Not what I expected. I thought I'd be the one getting chased. Traitor! You'll never get to that parade in one piece.* The thief climbed the stairs, trying to maintain a cautious pursuit of the warrior. *What are you gaining by running from me, Hessing? Where are you going?* The thief passed by a door that he could tell was locked. A quick inspection showed that the door had been locked for a very long time. *Not in there. How can you think to escape me by getting the True Knowledge? Is that your plan?* Raben continued ascending the staircase. *When will you attack? If I were you, what would I use to attack?* The thief slowed down even further, his concern for Hessing's tactics growing as he climbed the long stairwell. He knew that the warrior was intelligent where combat was concerned and he didn't want to walk into something foolishly. It was this caution that had gotten him out of so many other situations.

"Hessing," he yelled up the corridor. "Talk to me. You need me in order to finish this damned quest!" His words resounded off of the stone walls. "Whether you know it or not," he yelled up the stairs. "Neither of us can get the knowledge without the other." It was a lie so far as Raben knew, but he had to get the noble to make some noise in order to ensure that he wouldn't be taken by surprise. "I'm a step ahead of them all, Hessing!"

"You," said the noble from a distance up the staircase, "are destined to die on this journey. I have seen it." Raben slowly climbed the stairs, making sure he was silent with each step. "You die, Thief. Why do I need you?" *Why does he need me? Why do you need me? You need me.* The thief racked his brain trying to come up with a good reason that the noble needed him. "Why...do...I...need...you?" Hessing yelled, making sure that the thief heard every word.

"The well requires the presence of the sword and its wielder in order to function," Raben lied as he stared at the blade, wishing that he'd rammed it through the noble when he'd had the chance. "You need the weapon there, and you need me alive to protect you as you are blessed by Talvo. On the third floor of this building is a book, the original version of the Dayquest prophecy was in it." The thief sucked in a deep breath. *Come on.* "It says that a ruthless man would become master of the sword that he might keep all enemies from the valiant as he saw the light of Talvo, or something like that. I am the ruthless man," Raben yelled.

After shouting the manufactured information up to Hessing, the thief continued up the stairs. Step after step, he silently climbed the stairwell, waiting for the response. He walked for quite a while, arriving at the top of the case without any response from the noble. The door at the top of the stairs was closed. Raben kneeled before the door and looked into the keyhole. The door was locked by a mechanical lock. *How'd he get through? Does the bastard have a key?* Raben prodded the lock with a long narrow pick, gently testing the tumblers inside in order to judge how quickly he could get through it if he disregarded the need to be quiet. He waited for a while outside of the door, and still no response came from Hessing. *Alright, Lord Hessing, I'll come in after you.*

Taking a deep breath, the thief prepared to attack the lock with speed as his main objective rather than silence. *I've broken every thieving code in Reman on this journey. Time for the end.* Inserting two tools into the lock, Raben jostled them until he was sure the first turn would drop a tumbler, then he'd have to get one more as quickly as he could. After a few moments to calm him and prepare for what was to come, he dropped the first tumbler. It clicked like a marble hitting the floor. Instantly he worked the picks into the next tumbler. *Faster than I thought.* He tried to drop the tumbler, but it wouldn't move. *Key's in.* Wasting no time, Raben rammed an awl into the lock and pounded the end of it with the butt of a dagger. He heard the heavy key bounce onto the floor behind the door. Yanking the awl out, he returned his picks to the lock and dropped the second tumbler. Standing before the door, he dropped his picks and ripped his sword from its sheath. He grabbed the door, and just then something crushed into the side of his head.

He tumbled down the stairs, struggling to keep his sword from getting under him. While crashing down the stairs, he saw Hessing drop from the ceiling and charge through the now open door. *Damn!* His head ringing from being kicked, the thief raised himself up off of the stairs. He had a number of scrapes and would have a number of bruises, but was otherwise untouched by the tumble. *How in the blazes did I let that happen?* Raben leapt up the stairs. Just outside of the door he stopped, not wanting to walk into the noble's sword. Looking up at the ceiling, Raben saw that there was a crawl hole with a ladder in it. *Probably goes to the roof. I should have seen that. Burning Hells!*

He stepped in the door with his sword held up in front of him, ready to parry the horizontal swing that people usually used when they leapt from around a corner. The room was circular and had three other doorways in it. One exactly opposite the one he'd just walked through and two that were evenly spaced out to his left and right. No doors blocked them, so there would be very few ways to conceal anything on the other side.

"Hessing," called the thief. "She's already dead. Her sword is gone. I have too many lives. You can't beat me." The thief moved to the center of the room, maximizing his ability to see into the other rooms. All of them were filled with the light of torches that lit as soon as the door was opened. No shadows were visible through any of the doorways. *This place is strange.* Though he hadn't realized at first, Raben now thought it peculiar that there was nothing in the room at all, including furniture. He dragged his foot on the floor. *Not even dust.* The other chambers of the level looked to be the same way. "You'll have to kill me six times to defeat me, Hessing. You might as well come out here and talk to me, because you can't get through the gate unless I'm there anyway."

"If you come in here, Thief, I'll take your head clean off of your shoulders," answered the noble, his voice coming from the center doorway. "This has all been for nothing. It isn't here." Raben walked to the left and then all the way to the right of the chamber he was in, trying to see what was through the center doorway, where Hessing's voice was coming from. "The well isn't in here."

"Why in the Hells did you run from me?" asked the thief. "What are you running from? You are the chosen of the prophecy. What do you think I'm going to do? Tell everyone that you accepted a bargain before the quest even began. That you allowed me to lead you to the end. That the forces of evil, bargained with you, the champion of Talvo, and that you chose the coward's path to glory!" *Bastard!*

"Silence!" Hessing thundered. "They told me what you are for. I know that you were sent to kill all of the questors, Thief, and you have been quite effective thus far," the noble said, regaining control of himself. "But I will not be the grand finale of your murdering spree. No! I will finish the quest, as soon as I figure out where in the blazes the well has gone off to."

As the noble's voice died down in the chamber, Raben could hear another person coming up the stairs. Whoever it was, was fairly light on their feet. *Definitely not a dwarf.* Not wanting to be out in the open, the thief ran into the doorway to the left. Once inside he realized that the three doorways entered into the same chamber. He saw Hessing crouched just to the side of the center doorway. Past Hessing, however, was a beautiful window. Raben couldn't see what it portrayed, but the stained glass that had been painstakingly framed in the window was certainly a depiction of something. *It must be beautiful when the light hits it. If the noble takes longer figuring out what we're doing, we might get to see that.*

Someone entered the level. Raben could hear the soft footsteps. Just realizing for the first time that the thief had entered the chamber with him, Hessing scowled. Before the noble was able to speak, the thief gestured at the main chamber. Listening, the noble climbed into a battle ready stance. Raben held one of his daggers down to the corner of the doorway and slid it slowly out until he could see the chamber. *Greeching Hells.* It was Strad. The Kernishman stood in a tattered robe, clutching a sword close to his body. His eyes looked as though he'd not slept in days. He stood in the room as though he knew they were there, but was baffled at not seeing his victims.

Strad slowly approached Hessing's doorway. The Kernishman had developed a limp. His left foot dragged a little as he moved. He made his way up beside the doorway. The shattered man stood just exactly on the other side of the wall from the noble. After a moment, Strad backed away from the wall, and looked right at it as though he could see through it. He then lowered his sword and pointed it at Hessing through the thick stone wall. A chill passed through Raben's body. *What the blazes?* Suddenly, the Kernishman rammed the sword into the wall. It screeched as it slid into the stone. Sparks flew from the steel and dropped to the floor. Suddenly Hessing leapt away from the wall, his arm cut by Strad's blade. *Boiling Hells!*

The noble roared in pain and charged through the doorway. Raben stood and prepared to join the battle, but no sooner had he stood than Strad caught Hessing's sword in his bare hand, letting the blade cut deep into his flesh. The Kernishman then wrenched the weapon from the noble's grip, letting the blade dig into his palms, and held it backwards. His other hand shot into Hessing with such force that the noble flew out the door, crashing into the stairwell outside.

"You," Strad said, his flayed tongue making him sound as crazed as he looked, "would have been better served were you not disloyal." The Kernishman made his way to the doorway, still clutching the noble's sword by the blade. "Come here," Strad barked, as he threw Hessing's unconscious body back into the room. *What the blazing Hells!* The Kernishman walked to where the noble lay and in a single stroke, buried the noble's sword in the floor, pinning Hessing's leg to the stone. Looking at his handy work, Strad began to chuckle. "No one told you that you could leave our service," he said to the unconscious man. *Thantos! If there was ever a time that you needed to show up and take care of something. It is now.* Raben sat terrified behind the doorway. He had no way of fighting the creature after watching it dispose of Hessing so easily. Strad hobbled through the main chamber over to the doorway opposite Raben's. Passing through it, he walked right to the stained glass window.

"So," he said, suppressing laughter. "The well of Talvo passes to you, my lord. You'll be back on Reman soon enough. Let the priest deliver you to the land." *The priest? Thantos?* Strad balled up his hands and smashed them into the glass. It exploded, cutting the Kernishman's flesh. He only laughed, and hammered on the glass again, making sure every piece of the beautiful window fell away. Sliced and bloody, Strad kicked the last bit of glass out of the mighty framework, exposing what lay behind it. *The well!*

Rather than the outside air, a corridor lay behind the window. It looked to be fairly short, and beyond it, a well lit room. From where he stood, at the farthest point from where the window had been, Raben could see the massive hole in the center of the chamber behind the window. *The well. The True Knowledge. Blazing greech! All this way and there it is. Guarded by him.*

Strad spun away from the window, and walked back into the main chamber as though he couldn't even see Raben, or didn't care that the thief was there. In the main portion of the room, the Kernishman checked Hessing. He was still unconscious. Strad smacked the blade that trapped the warriors leg, forcing it to lean to a side, and then walked out the door, chuckling.

About to run to the noble, the thief stopped. No sooner had the Kernishman walked out the door than he came flying back in. He charged straight at Raben, his mouth hanging wide open, laughter bursting from him. The thief tumbled straight back, putting distance between himself and the doorway. Strad continued through it and bore down on Raben, his arms flailing wildly. The thief, without other options, ran. He fled back through the center doorway and out into the stairwell. Doing his best not to fall, he began leaping down the stairs. Strad followed.

All the way down the stairs and back through the long hallway to the church Raben fled with the crazed Kernishman behind him. He could hear the madman bellowing and laughing maniacally as he chased the thief. Once they were in the church, they came across Thantos. He was sitting in one of the benches, praying.

"My friend! Thantos! Help!" The thief flew to his friend's side, but the vampiric priest only continued praying. "Thantos." The priest looked up. Strad screamed out, sending nonsensical madness through the air of the quiet hall of worship. Raben pointed up the hall, and Thantos looked.

"I cannot," hissed the vampire. "We are still bound after all, and I cannot tell which of us is stronger. Even as I feel his evil, I would be killing myself were I able to defeat him. They took him, and tortured him for failure, and then placed him here, now, broken and insane." *Jump up and fight.* The priest was far too calm for Raben's liking.

"Well can you slow him down?" the thief asked. Thantos nodded and stood. Just then Strad entered the church, his mad laughter destroying the calm environment completely. The priest immediately sprung into the Kernishman's path and they locked arms. Raben looked into the main hall. Moragin held the door, and still monsters attacked. *Hells! If Strad gets in there this whole quest will be a complete greeching failure.* The thief watched as the Kernishman fought with Thantos. It was an odd fight. Both unnatural men struggled to overpower the other without hurting them, thus saving themselves from injury. It was like watching brothers fight. They truly wanted to harm each other, but their bond kept them from doing so.

At one point, Thantos had the Kernishman spun to where his back was facing Raben. The thief leapt into the fray. He brought his sword down on Strad from behind, but both he and Thantos suddenly dodged out of the way. *They are linked. What can we do?*

Oh hells! I'm killing Thantos. Yes! The thought crashed into him. *How do I beat him if doing so kills you?* No answer. *Damn it.* The Kernishman suddenly flew from Thantos, the priest having thrown the possessed man. He waved Raben to him.

"Kill me!" screeched the priest. "Do it!" The thief froze where he stood. "Use any sword but yours. Kill me," hissed the vampire. *Kill me. No! Do it! It is why I am here. No! I'll kill him. No! Me! I can survive a mortal wound. He can't. Do it! Kill me!*

Strad crashed into Thantos breaking through several of the wooden benches. *Greech. I can't. You must! Do it! I may live! Do it. I am different from him! I may survive! Do it!* Thantos had both his arms and legs wrapped around Strad. The Kernishman was bashing his head into the priest's face. A moment later, the two unnatural combatants rolled over. As they did so, Raben moved in closer. *My friend, I'm sorry.* Only a pace behind Thantos, he brought two daggers from their sheaths and rammed them into his vampiric friend's back where his heart would be. Strad screamed louder than Thantos as the blades pierced the priest, but he did not stop wrestling. He reached past the priest, trying to catch the thief by the arms. Raben wrenched the blades from his friend's back and rammed them home again. They both screeched. Thantos slid from on top of the Kernishman, and Strad lay motionless. Raben moved to his friend.

The priest wasn't breathing. His eye stared up at the ceiling. He was dead. *No! It can't happen this way. You said you could survive, you lying fool. Damn you!* Tearing his sword from its sheath, the thief hacked the fallen Kernishman's arm off. *Help me.* Nausea washed over Raben as he tried to rescue his friend. He stood over Thantos, dangling the freshly butchered arm over his mouth, letting the still warm blood flood into the priest's mouth. *Drink it, damn it!* When Thantos' mouth was overflowing, he hurled the arm away, his rising gorge making him heave. He breathed deeply as he watched his friend, but the image of the priest with a mouthful of blood overwhelmed him.

He ran from the room to the hall, where he threw up. Sweat poured from him. He began to shake as he tried to calm himself. *This whole nightmare ends when we get the True Knowledge. When we have that then the battle must end and my friend will live. Or we have failed. Hessing must not fail.* Raben spat as he began to run to the stairs. He felt as though he might still vomit, but time was now the enemy. He needed to save Thantos. He ran at full speed, and then began climbing the stairs, flying up them as if they were no obstacle whatsoever. He passed by the first three levels and erupted through the doorway on the top floor. Hessing still lay pinned to the floor.

The thief slid down onto the floor next to him and prepared to free him from the sword that held his leg, but as he neared the noble he saw that something was horribly wrong. *No! No! This can't be.* Hessing wasn't breathing. He lay in a pool of his own blood. *No!* Raben slapped the warrior, but he didn't react. He punched him in the stomach. "Damn it! We have failed. There is no one!" From where he sat on the ground he could see the passage to the well. Raben tore the blade from Hessing's leg, but it meant nothing. Hessing too had died. *We cannot fail.*

Thantos is dead. Hessing is dead. Most all of the dwarves are dead. Urchin is dead or captured. I am all there is left. Rather than fear and sadness, a strange joy bubbled up in the thief. *I am all there is left. I am the chosen.* He climbed to his feet, and left Hessing, walking through the pool of the noble's blood. He passed through the middle doorway, leaving a trail of bloody footprints behind him.

Raben stood at the entry to the room with the well for a short while and then began walking in. As soon as he stepped through the window, he felt as though he were about to fulfill his destiny. *I have survived to do this thing. I have redeemed myself, Thantos. I will make you proud with the effort I will put forth.* The thief walked up to the edge of the hole. Looking into it, he could see that there were lit rings in it that divided it into three sections. *It falls through each of the levels of the temple. It looks to be leagues deep beyond the bottom level. It must fall to the fires. The temple called me. It invited me.*

"You have come to claim the right?" asked the voice that had first spoken to him in the forest. *It knows me.*

"Yes," he stated. "I am in need for a friend, and for all people. I have come to claim the True Knowledge that I might take it to everyone else in Reman." *I am the chosen.*

"Step forward and let your faith show you the knowledge," ordered the voice. *Gods guide me,* Raben thought. *It knows me. It invited me to come here. There is no one else. I am the chosen.* He stepped into the well.

"Thief!" bellowed a hoarse voice, but it was too late.

Hessing. He's alive! Raben panicked as he fell. *He was dead. How?*

"You are not the chosen," a booming voice echoed through his mind. *Not the chosen! Hessing! I have to find out who. Who am I?* The air whipped by, ripping through his clothes as he fell tumbling into the darkness of the well. *He lived. How? Help me!*

"You are a messenger from Arsonin," it said. *Arsonin! What? Why? I need to live. I have a life. Messenger! How?* Voices from Raben's past began to echo through his thoughts while the voice of the well continued to boom through the air. *You brought us here. We are here because of you.* He could see the injured boy in the temple's church, the slash wound on his face. *You brought us here.*

"You have brought the god of ambition to the beginning of the new war. You are corrupted." *New war? What's that? Corrupted!* He heard the voice from the church. *These are all of the innocent that gave their lives. The church. She wasn't there. I killed her, but she wasn't there. She wasn't sitting in the damned church.*

He plummeted past the first ring of light. *I'm going to die. She wasn't in the church. I don't have a life. I'm going to die and return to...who? Arsonin? I can't. I don't deserve death. Especially this death. I've done too much.*

"You are a magical soul. A weapon of the gods, made by war, magic, and murder," thundered the voice. *You are pure magic.* He sped past the second ring of light. *Magic. All magic can be altered. I was going to save her. I trapped her in her sword. She was magic. Her soul was free. I just had to alter the sword somehow. Magic can be altered. Magic!*

"Gul asama!" he screamed the levitation spell, but he sped on. *Beware,* Thantos had said, *the gods won't hear you.* Raben knew that his host spirit couldn't answer the spell. He was going to die. *You have no part in this quest and those that have no part are going to die. I've come to see how everyone dies. Urchin, why? Why didn't you tell me?* The third ring of light blurred past as he fell towards the bottom of the well. *Greech! Talvo help me. Why didn't I listen?* He sped on. *I have no life. I am going to die. Damned sword.* He tore the enchanted blade from its sheath as he fell and ran one hand across the thinner sword he had tucked through his belt. *She's in there. Not innocent. No life. Hessing is the chosen. She's in there. All magic can be altered. I am pure magic. She's free from them. In the sword. Trapped to serve it.*

"You have completed the task you were assigned," the voice resounded. "Arsonin has challenged." *Challenged? The new war? I'm going to die. Alone. She's in there. In the sword. Die.*

Raben could see the floor as he hurtled towards it. He held out his arms, steadying himself as he plummeted, and flattened himself out in the air. He clutched the sword as the wind swept through him. He was suddenly freezing. *If you die, you'll be trapped in the sword to serve its magic for eternity.* He was falling face down, watching the floor coming. Tears streamed from his face. *In the sword. For eternity.* He held the enchanted blade out under him, carefully positioning it point-first into his chest. *All magic can be altered. I have no life. Our deaths will come without explanation. I have lived to serve evil, and then die? No!*

"No!" The sword pierced Raben's chest.
His body crumpled as it smashed into the stone floor.

The Story Continues!
LOOK FOR
<u>PILGRIMMAGE OF THE DEAD</u>
Book 2 of The Unlife Legend
SEQUEL TO
<u>NO GODS OF CONSCIENCE</u>

About The Author

Intrigued by language since his childhood, Jason Bilicic gained a degree in order to teach. He eventually created the Pelican Bay Company to assist future novelists. Bilicic has authored a number of short stories and critical articles which were then published in a variety of magazines and short story collaboratives. Moved by the work of Tolkien, Elizabeth Moon, and George R.R. Martin, Bilicic aspired to create his own fantasy series. No Gods of Conscience is the first novel in that series.

Jason Bilicic has held a number of teaching and instructional positions while writing his first novel. He loves the outdoors and is a long time fan of Role Playing Games.

Bilicic presently lives with his wife in the mountains of Northern Arizona.

ISBN 0-9761227-1-5

9 780976 122715   51199